Sailor Man

Leo Simpson

Sailor Man

The Porcupine's Quill

CANADIAN CATALOGUING IN PUBLICATION DATA

Simpson, Leo, 1934-
    Sailor man

ISBN 0-88984-171-3

I. Title.

PS8587.I55S35 1996   C813'.54   C96-930665-2
PR9199.3.S56S35 1996

Published by The Porcupine's Quill, Inc., 68 Main Street, Erin, Ontario
NOB ITO, with financial assistance from The Canada Council and the
Ontario Arts Council. The support of the Department of Canadian Heri-
tage through the Book and Periodical Industry Development programme
and the Periodical Distribution Assistance Programme is also gratefully
acknowledged.

This is a work of fiction. Any resemblance of characters to persons, living or
dead, is purely co-incidental.

Represented in Canada by the Literary Press Group. Trade orders are available from General Distribution Services.

Readied for the press by John Metcalf. Copy edited by Doris Cowan.

Cover is after an original wood engraving by Wesley W. Bates. Typeset in
Ehrhardt, printed on Zephyr Antique Laid, sewn into signatues and bound
at The Porcupine's Quill.

For Julie, the beautiful Bear, with all my love.

Contents

Chapter 1

A Sailor's Kisses

THE WORLD HE LIVED IN seemed to Jack to consist of people who had sprung from a particular place and tribe. Everybody he knew had a background. Sometimes this was most of the personality.

When Jack worked for Technoptrax he had two assistants, one named Ian Peveril, a Maritimer with a seaman's walk. Scotch stock, Glace Bay coalfields money in the family, and everybody went to Dalhousie University. Ian made the journey home to Cape Breton regularly and always returned refreshed. He was a tribesman, he had a place to remember and to go to.

It wasn't a simple matter of family and security and familiar habits either. The other assistant of Jack's at Technoptrax was George Wienewski, aged forty and bibulous by habit. George had to claw and scrabble his way, an inch a year, up to the same modest niche at Technoptrax that Ian Peveril strolled into after Dalhousie. Well, in those days a name like Ian Peveril pretty much made its own way past one like Wienewski.

George's tribe's place was a street of tenement houses in Toronto near the old Riverdale zoo, a foul diseased, rat-infested warren, Bleecker Street. A street worse than a death-camp, the way George Wienewski told the story of his childhood and hard origins with drink taken.

Jack was in a north Yonge bar with George one night drinking rum when a giant German man wearing a mailman's hat and a Blue Jay T-shirt clapped George powerfully on the shoulder, crying: 'Charge! Pleecker Street!'

George responded with equal delight: 'Mule! Where the fog've you been?'

Mule brought over two more people, also from Bleecker Street, a gloomy Italian, Trick, and a small bullet-like man with a walrus moustache, Estonian, called Jumper. Travellers just returned from Eldorado might have been as enthusiastic in their memories of a place. It all came out in rich anecdote and recollection, the magic of the past, the inadequate present life we were now all condemned to. Quite early in the toasting of Bleecker Street Jack felt that he knew every rotten staircase in the tenement as it had been, every alley and rat-breeding garbage can. They were all sacredly haloed. Even the cockroaches in the recall had had individuality and class.

Once George suddenly interrupted a ripe golden memory of Jumper's with urgent input. 'They tore it down, you know,' George Wienewski said. 'They tore down every house on the street in the summer of sixty-four. Every ... single ... *house*. I watched them doing it. Bastards.' The two stared at George with hollow eyes, the three considering this very pith of vandalism.

Then they called for more rum and diet Cokes to ease the loss. And when the bar was closing they shook hands and hugged each other, excluding Jack from their circle with the absentminded courtesy of true elitists. Had Bleecker Street been a college they would have sung the good old song then.

Jack's envy was intense. Here was something he'd never had. In his mind's eye he saw children in Hollywood rags perpetually at play along streets all a-clutter with adventure and companionship. Sleeping at night in the family solidarity of six to a room. The moonlight shone on tenement gutters as beautiful as Alph the sacred river, and the jungle darkness was pierced by the awful wail of police vehicle sirens. Each dawn was made musical by the orchestra of voices of tigers screaming farewells to their mates of the alleys.

Jack's own memories were of faces that looked at him with revulsion or indifference. He'd had no place, no tribe, no magical time that impressed the mind forever, the poor lad. Those seasons of significance in a life that summon up tears and smiles, passions and loyalties, had apparently just slipped off the calendar in Jack's case.

He was reminded of this void in his past from time to time. Once on a summer's evening toward the beginning of the century's eighth decade, he was sitting outside a bar in Montreal with a newspaper and a glass of beer. He was in acceptable health and his work of the time was satisfying. His mind, though by no means at peace – well, there's no such thing as peace of mind, is there, except for short sprints, usually delusional – wasn't uncomfortably troubled. Some angry words came from the table next to his, where two women were having aperitifs. One was about fifty, neatly dressed and businesslike, a professional person. She talked English rapidly, chopping the air with her right hand and holding a cigarette in her left. The other woman, in her thirties, had been listening quietly but was now doing the shouting.

'What nonsense, we were undergraduates, we weren't children,' this younger woman said. 'We weren't naïve in the group, and we did understand politics. How dare you insult my generation!' She was distressed by anger. She seized the cigarette from the older woman and threw it down, critically. Then she grabbed her handbag and left.

Jack found that he couldn't continue reading his paper. The young woman's sensitivity as a member of a generation was unfathomable in his experience. How dare you insult my generation! What a beautiful encompassing loyalty, what security of identification and touchstone of tribe. Of course the source of Jack's dismay, a sense of somehow having been cheated, was that he didn't have a generation. He'd never had one. The time past was empty.

Being twenty-seven years old just then, he could figure out that his generation, as the woman used the word, had started when he was eighteen, continuing perhaps until he was twenty-five. The place and tribe had not occurred so he wasn't aligned in memory with the music, the politics, or any particular clothes or hair-dos or values or thoughts or people of those seven years. The circumstances of Jack's upbringing isolated him too but considering what a terrible lottery birth is these could have been far worse.

He was born in that same city in an apartment over a shoe store, Clement's Foot Fashions, on Ste-Catherine Street. That area isn't and never has been a community. His father converted a stockroom into an apartment. Jack's *place* on Ste-Catherine was a sweep of city-planning concrete built up with multi-level parking garages that voraciously sucked people in every morning and exploded them out in the afternoons. The sharpest sense memory Jack has of infancy is of being in a stroller with diesel fumes in his nostrils watching umbrellas and briefcases flashing by his head. At the present time, in other words, Jack never feels a compulsion to return to this spot in a wistful frame of mind.

Here's something too. While Jack was a child his mother was active in a family planning group. These were Unitarians and other kinds of religious liberals. Looking back on this career of his mother's Jack has no choice but to assume that her interest in missionary birth-control began practically immediately after she bore him. He sees her gazing down at the child in her arms and making the resolve. Her life was devoted to the cause for several years. There were brochures to be got out, issues and cases to debate, amendments to the abortion laws to be fought or supported.

His mother brought Jack to all the meetings. Maybe because it felt embattled, on nominal Catholic territory, this particular group was an uncompromising one, with members who took the logic of their cause to extremes. Some of them were anti-baby rednecks.

So Jack did not attract many smiles and tickles from his mother's friends as a toddler. He was a flag of failure in a sense, and those closest to his mother found it simplest to look through Jack, or over him, or around him. It was a true experience of being invisible for the child.

Now to bring us to matters of retailing, it must be mentioned that Jack's mother had a habit of losing the infant on shopping trips. Well, she was a person of quick interests: her mind would spring to another store, or to an item she wanted to look at in a different department, and it might be an hour later that she tried to remember where she had left her baby. Maybe it wasn't a matter of actually wishing to lose Jack, to answer that query. She misplaced lots of stuff. She sometimes drove to a place and walked or took a bus home, subsequently forgetting where she'd left the car. And there were constant searches for gloves, keys, wallets and suchlike. Still, Jack does remember an infancy in a context of retailing, of merchandise for sale, ages of waiting, bereft in a glittering souk. If you asked him for a dominant memory of early life this would be it, a sense of knowing himself abandoned where there was retail trade. The floor was usually a carpet or a commercial tile, a marble imitation ceramic sometimes. Shoppers and salesfolk like uncaring ghosts drifted past overhead without seeing him while he waited for rescue by the higher authority, now and then bawling in pain.

His mother was Megan McMurray before her marriage and worked as a saleswoman and model for a cosmetics manufacturer. Jack's father, who owned Clement's Foot Fashions, had a difficult and eclectic mind and a disgruntled temperament. He disliked his fellow man as a rule, and he was hostile to most of the institutions of the society. He was also, unluckily, ugly in appearance, thin and chicken-chested, bald and small in stature. His name was Hahka Clemmaknohke in Taleaturovan, or Jack Clements approximately.

When Jack was six his father decided to go into the business of raising greyhounds, having heard from his French business friends that there was money to be made selling racing dogs to sportsmen in France. The

Montreal shoe store was sold and the family moved to a farm in eastern Ontario, in the rocky Shield country northwest of Belleville.

Some kind of schooling had to be obtained for the child Jack out there on the Shield. This was before education was taken over by the central boards and bureaucracies, and the consequent spread of the educational theories that have produced a number of ignorant generations. Even so the system of public education was a prime antipathy of Jack Clemmaknohke's, who arranged a private education for his son by engaging a retired clergyman as a tutor at a low fee. He resented paying the fee, small as it was, parsimony being a vigorous part of his character, and being convinced also that the Christian churches owned secret wealth on a vast and threatening scale.

Horsy Stacpole was an energetic old parson who wore threadbare tweeds and shiny flannel slacks. His hair was long, grey-speckled brown and always looked wild and blown as if he had been caught out in a storm. His manner with everybody was much the same, consisting of unfailing enthusiasm, a loud voice, glowing evocations of the world's wonders, a slide into a sermon occasionally whenever he saw an opportunity, and a habit of overriding interruptions and ignoring questions. He was on earth to pass on messages, not to listen to folk. And he was here to teach everybody.

So one of the local farmers from the school board who came to check on Jack might find himself included in the lesson and asked his opinion on the usage of a French preposition or to supply the latitude and longitude of Bombay. And Jack's father was often roped in by Horsy to give an opinion on questions that came up during the school day, a phrase in Matthew, the identification of a plant or a piece of rock, or even a comment from his experience on human nature. Horsy Stacpole's view of this last subject, human nature, was joyous and narrowly focused by religion while Jack Clemmaknohke's was broad, terse and irascible. They nevertheless endured each other very well.

Jack's mother was another matter, being witless and at the same time feeling that she understood the world better than most people. She did not take to country life. Her neighbours seemed to her dull and practical; there was nobody to talk to and nothing to do. When Horsy Stacpole arrived she fell into the habit of dressing for his approval, playing the role of an urban sophisticate forced into this rural backwater by domestic circumstances.

She was a stocky and shapely woman with red hair, and pale eyes that seemed to be introspective because she was myopic but would not wear glasses. She tried to make a friend of Horsy Stacpole. She needed somebody to complain to about the absence of stimulation in her life.

No doubt many men would have seen a duty to be sympathetic, but of course Horsy Stacpole wasn't a listener. He saw no duty at all, having heard no plea. He did manage to hear an argument, that country life was uninteresting for Mrs Megan Clemmaknohke, to which he responded with substantial discussions of the city-versus-country argument, going back to classical times and favouring the country side overwhelmingly. To supply the only stimulation he could see lacking in Mrs Clemmaknohke's surroundings the parson brought her an ancient wind-up gramophone and a couple of boxfuls of Elgar and Bach 78s, and also several armfuls of old books from the twenties, all memoirs of the Chinese missions.

Horsy Stacpole favoured outdoor lessons for Jack, given a choice by weather, and Jack being of a thin frame like his father was often carried on his teacher's shoulders for long distances over the rough east Ontario terrain: through swamp and bush, up escarpments and down the hillsides that were scattered with giant rocks, the teacher talking and explaining and questioning as they went. It was on one of these outings that Revd Stacpole gave himself the name Horsy. They were the best voyages of Jack's life, of course.

In the next little while Mrs Clemmaknohke became suspicious of Horsy Stacpole's sexual direction. She knew that pressing old records and books on a woman who complained of boredom was unusual behaviour in a man. She noticed that Horsy Stacpole enjoyed her son's company, and could not understand this as a natural affection. Jack's father, who spent all day in the yards and the kennels, wasn't interested in speculation on the matter, and gave it as an opinion that the old scholar was almost certainly queer, like all churchmen, but seemed harmless enough and worked hard and cheap.

Jack remembers the day his mother confronted his teacher with her suspicions. It was a flash event of childhood that remained in his mind, luminously, forever afterward. He was aged ten at the time, listening outside a room that contained two people he loved. He could hear only the distant-thunder rumble of Horsy Stacpole's loud voice and strident questions from his mother. Jack was walking away, crying, when Horsy Stacpole opened the door and said into the room with civility: 'Well, we must talk more about the Greeks, but set your mind at rest as to me. I like the lad and I agree that I'm a very strange bird but I am not a pederast.'

Jack can recall that there was a dictionary in his father's office among the dog-breeding manuals. When he went to check the word pederast after he'd overcome his tears he found his mother already in there and hogging the dictionary, slapping through the P section in a bad temper and with undiminished suspicion.

In Ottawa and at a much later time Jack was assigned the duties of a lover in the Sutton. Like any job it had good and bad days. On the night he was sent to Imogene Wedekind he'd had a busy trivial day. Looking back on it he couldn't see anything that had been accomplished. He was tired but since Imogene didn't live in the Sutton he had no way of postponing his appointment with her.

Imogene Wedekind was more intelligent than most of her office colleagues at Morosoph Educational Supply. They played business politics and office and meetings games which Imogene tried to remain above. But also she enjoyed her work and wanted to advance in it. She corrected the blunders that crossed her desk without making a fuss and smiled a good deal. At meetings she made her sensible suggestions indirectly, not wishing to look pushy. Her colleagues would sometimes catch Imogene's thoughts from their oblique expression and make them theirs. And she took work home, using a shopping bag instead of a briefcase.

This life shortened her illusions. Imogene at twenty-four had a sense of men as large boys, guileful and selfish and immature, an understanding the majority of women don't reach until they're well into their thirties. She had a sense of women as becoming simple and indignant, Pavlovian and robbed of subtlety by the broad axes that were ground daily on their behalf. She seemed to be failing sexually. While men found her attractive, and Imogene mixed with them easily, she hadn't met any man she could be herself with, in or out of bed. She worried from time to time about the effect a life of short illusions was having on her. As she grew in confidence and charm her inner world was becoming pettier.

Her evening with one Barry Dalmadge was typically depressing, even though it hadn't started with unrealistic expectations. She didn't date men from Morosoph usually but Dalmadge worked in a separate division, almost another company. Imogene wondered what Dalmadge's assumption about their relationship could be, since he'd talked a little about his wife at dinner, frankly and even affectionately. It was the first Imogene had heard about a wife.

He steered her into one of the elevators of the Parthenon Tower in the Sutton. The only reason Imogene could give herself for going along with this was that it was early in the evening. There was brown flock wallpaper on the walls of the elevator to match the chocolate carpet.

'You can even rent a horse in the Sutton,' Barry said. He had picked up a brochure from a stand inside the Sutton entranceway. 'We're taking you back now to the golden age of retailing, several years ago.'

'Where would you ride the horse?'

'It doesn't say.'

They walked along a corridor with a carpet so thick that the cut loops turned the heels of Imogene's shoes. He was looking at apartment numbers. It wasn't his own place, so Imogene concluded that she wouldn't be meeting the wife. She wasn't interested enough in Barry Dalmadge to be interested in his wife.

'Living here automatically entitles you to membership of the Sutton Golf Club too.'

'Oh my.'

Barry Dalmadge finally unlocked a door and Imogene Wedekind stared at a gaudy oriental interior: huge tasselled cushions on the floor, a camel-saddle chair, silk rugs on the walls, Wedgwood broadloom and three little lacquer tables each with its own Chinese-lantern lamp.

Like a small upscale Chinese restaurant, Imogene thought, I wonder who owns this awful place. She slipped her shoes off because the carpet had hurt an ankle, smiling, and Dalmadge instantly put a hand around her waist and captured a breast. He held her close while they surveyed the oriental lair. I am laying this at your feet, seemed to be his attitude. Wedekind told herself: his idea of him and me is clear enough now, Imogene. He shows me some tacky furniture that doesn't belong to him and we go to bed together. He'll drop me off at my place on his way home to his wife. When he feels like doing it again he'll give me a buzz.

Barry Dalmadge meanwhile took her into his arms. He appeared to believe that what she would enjoy was rugged handling – having the nape of her neck viced between a finger and thumb, for instance. When Imogene found herself with an attractive man she always seemed to be wearing an old sweater from high school and baggy jeans. Now she was with rough Dalmadge in a cool cotton for evening, practically naked. Back in her throat she shrieked.

She said into his shoulder: 'This is lovely, but I have to go, Barry. What about coffee?'

Then a voice inside said wait, Wedekind. She was being gently held. It was true that one of Dalmadge's hands was using her breast as if checking out grapefruit for ripeness. But the other one, flat on her spine, had respect and authority. Well, maybe I'm throwing people out of my life without giving them a chance, Imogene Wedekind thought. I could be making judgements too fast and turning into a brittle woman.

Dalmadge's other hand was still painfully pronging her neck, though. Imogene considered this for a moment. It seemed that she was being held by one hand and quite separately fondled by two others. She pushed Dalmadge away and took a look around. They were alone in the centre of the oriental room.

Barry Dalmadge complacently went into his we-are-together-in-this-paradise posture, one of his hands groping for the breast he hadn't bruised yet. But still, a daring, yet somehow friendly and gentle hand moved down the ridge of Imogene's spine – almost reluctantly, tiredly. God, she thought, what a godawful evening, this man has three hands. She could see the hand on her breast. She brushed her own hands against the other two, which were on her body without a doubt. Imogene was amazed. She thought of strange births for a moment, and the prosthetics involved. Well, the tailoring, at least. Oh dear, she wondered, will it be embarrassing? Oh the poor guy, she thought.

Dalmadge released her and Imogene Wedekind cast a glance at his back from beneath demurely lowered eyelids. His rear looked okay, somewhat pudgy at the shoulders and heavy around the hips. He brought a bottle of vodka and a couple of tonic splits, with an ice bucket and lemons, on a tray from the kitchen and put it on one of the tables. The front of Barry Dalmadge was normal too. He didn't have three hands.

But while Imogene watched him she thought she saw one of the glasses move and a fine powder floating into it. She wasn't sure of this, however. It was becoming an evening of illusions. The Chinese lantern provided only an uncertain green-red light. She sat on one of the tasselled cushions, noting that the tray had been prepared in advance.

What a ratty way to live, was her thought then, deceit and betrayal. He would probably tell me a lot of lies if I wanted him to. I wonder how much time he spends on this hobby.

'This section of the Sutton is called the Parthenon Tower. It's the apartment section of the complex,' said Barry Dalmadge, who was at peace with himself. He obeyed nature's law, Barry felt, a matter of courage and enterprise. He was conscious of having some trouble getting Imogene's attention – she was good-looking but absentminded. He said, reading the brochure: 'It's created for people who must have a commodious living suite within easy reach of the heart of the national capital. Each of the suites on the Tower's sixteen floors is a masterpiece of individualized custom interior design. They may be purchased or leased ...'

It was the great decade of real estate too, you'll agree: nobody who owned a building could lose money, and fools were borne aloft on the tide and thought of themselves as masters of their ascent and great spinners of fortunes.

'... and twenty-four hour room service. Valet and maid. Parking for Parthenon Tower tenants is underneath. Plenty of extra parking out on the Sutton lots, of course.'

'Well, you're a lucky man, Barry. In your lifestyle.' She understood that he was revving the Sutton, in the way a boy might put a sports car through its growly paces for a girl, vroom vroom, and then the girl falls for the boy because of the Maserati motor company or whichever. Dalmadge seemed to be driving a borrowed car though.

'Yes. This one is their top-of-the-line apartment.' He unfolded all the gates of the brochure and scanned them seriously, looking for more wonders. Dalmadge was thirty-four, plump in the face with a handlebar moustache and pouches under his eyes.

Imogene thought that the oriental apartment might belong to somebody at Morosoph.

'... and all the professional services and offices are in the Tower too. Here we are, shopping. "In the Court you will find banks and boutiques, carpets and cameras, wigs and watchmakers. Relax for an evening of superb cuisine on the Gourmet Mezzanine. The Concourse will supply all your demanding needs, a rare gem from the Jewel Chest or a humble hamburger grilled to perfection over charcoal at Rob's Snackery ..."'

Well, we were in such clover that we could sell garbage, actual beach garbage imported from abroad. One of the items the Concourse could supply, in stock at the Sea-Art boutique, was *a piece of genuine flotsam crafted by nature and brought to you from a faraway romantic lagoon.*

Imogene put her glass down and picked up her handbag, smiling. 'I really have to go now, Barry.'

He nodded once, twice, as if his head had grown heavier on his neck. 'Theatre, tennis, polo. Polo, I guess that's why you'd need to rent a horse. There's some advertising at the end,' Dalmadge said, making a literary point, that up to then he'd been reading descriptive material. "The ultimate in convenience and luxury living, year-round comfort in a unique environment, the world's greatest enclosed complex – the Sutton."

He refolded the brochure with tremendous care and hiked himself closer to Imogene. Then, like a dog playing dead, he toppled sideways and rolled over and lay on his back. He began to snore.

She wondered about a heart attack. However, Barry Dalmadge sleepily snuggled down as she watched him, adjusting the cushion under his head for better cosiness. What a rotten evening, Imogene Wedekind thought, the mistakes I make.

She was looking for the bathroom when one of the lamps went out. There's somebody else in here, Imogene said to herself. From across the room a grumbling voice said: 'Long hours an short rest. The sailor's life, in a jail with the chance of being drownded.' The last lamp went out. The same voice said in her ear: 'Don't ee be frightened now. It's your new man Jack, take im or leave im. Ee won't hurt ee.'

In the perfectly dark room she felt fingers on the zipper that went down the back of her cotton dress. She drew in a breath to scream. The voice said: 'There's a purty. You see? Harmless as peelin a banana, this be. Munchin on a peach.'

He was soft-spoken, with old-fashioned cadences in his accent. Some manner of seafaring man was suggested to Imogene Wedekind. Not a modern sailor but a bygone one, a tar down from the rigging of an old wind ship. They carried knives, she remembered. She flinched slightly.

He said: 'Tell me be off if you've a mind, an I'll obey ee. Be outspoke an sincere, it's t'end of a long day fer me. I'm tireder'n you I bet. Jest a turrible day I had an no end o't in sight either. Buttons to the left, eh.' He had taken away her dress meanwhile without a jostle or a fumble, holding her lightly and peeling the cotton from her body. 'If ee don't need a invisible lover I'll be glad o t'rest. Speak out.'

'Are you a friend of Barry's?'

'Him, there?'

'Yes. Barry Dalmadge.'

'Never saw t'little crod before in me life,' the voice said. It added critically: 'He be a porky little bastard right enough, eh. All galley-hangin an guzzlin, looks like, an no hard sweat in the crod's day. Well, I had to put a little medicine in his drink, won't do im no arm, not a pennyweight a arm. It's a seafrin tradition, the Mickey Finn, fer shanghaiin an suchlike, he'll sleep like a innocent babe.' He was stroking her shoulder and putting light kisses on her face, and Imogene Wedekind was less scared than she thought she should be. The gentling hands made no demands. The need for a decision on her part receded as time went by. He would just hold her through the night it seemed.

Whenever Imogene Wedekind moved to ease her position on the floor he yielded. Once she thought she heard a snore that didn't come from Barry Dalmadge. She said: 'I want to go now.'

Silence.

'Well, what's your name?'

'Eh? Oh. Name. Name's Jack, obedient servant.'

'Could we have the lights on, Jack?'

'No lights. Nothing to see. Invisible.'

'Well, what's your last name? Who are you exactly? Do you live here?'

On the third question he was forthcoming at once, speaking with relaxed candour. 'No, not in these particular lodgins. These be rented by a scratch name o Kiley fer the Morosoph owners. I do ave lodgins mesel on the eighth floor, nothin fancy like this yur though.'

'Well, is it just sex that's on your mind? I'd like to know.'

Kisses were placed on Imogene's eyelids and cushions were folded by Jack underneath her shoulders and thighs. She hadn't the least intention of lying down under somebody she didn't know and couldn't see. I am the world's fool, thought Imogene Wedekind. Kiley was a languages programme vice president in her own department. Her name had come up over a few beers … A sinewy arm swept along Wedekind's flank and down over her ankles. She pushed then against a naked chest, hairy and bony. She pushed first, then she grasped and enfolded the bony one. She opened her mouth to speak an objection but instead allowed the other mouth to come down on hers.

They had rolled off the cushions and seemed to have moved far from their table. Imogene didn't know what part of the room they were in. She didn't have a sense of time passing either. Her awareness of particular moments, though, immediate tastes and feelings, astonished her when she trusted them. She seemed to be yielding to greed, plundering the chocolate cake.

Trusting the man in the dark was an utterly strange experience for Imogene. She was kissing a body she didn't know and crying out in affection for some anonymous person, whereas by nature she was reserved and liked to look before she leaped – well, she was fastidious in fact, and having an excellent body herself usually wanted to see clear physical attractiveness in a man. She was behaving with full awareness too, including a knowledge that she'd be remorseful later for what she was doing now. So the sooner she put a stop to it the better. But every time she shuddered, relaxing feebly on the carpet, the invisible man drew her to him again, waking another unsuspected animal in her belly, one of the little beasts with soft paws. Her own skin felt like silk to Imogene. She went to sleep with her arms flopped by her sides, palms upward. A towel was being used on her body, she thought, drying her mouth and then her thighs and loins. She also felt a tremor of binding at her hips. The hiss of her zipper closing seemed loud.

She felt herself lifted and carried and then laid again on the cushion. She opened her eyes wide in the dark. 'Don't run away. I want to see you.'

She heard a jaw-breaking yawn. He said: 'Ye'll get times an places fr'm the preacher if this yur suits ye. Now it's bedtime fer me. Can ardly keep me cacky ol eyes open a minute longer.'

'Opportunistic bastard,' she said, a little sleepily herself, sitting up and feeling around. Then the dark and silence brought some fear back. Had he said preacher? Preacher, what preacher? There were certainly demented men she'd heard of who spent their days muttering their way through the blacker parts of the Bible. Sometimes they took revenge for God on wanton women. One of the lamps lighted itself. The other lamps switched themselves on one by one. Barry Dalmadge was sleeping on his back again, like a puppy asking to have its tummy scratched. The moustache hairs on Dalmadge's upper lip fluttered as he breathed. She went through the apartment, looking in closets and under the bed. Looking for the hit-and-run bogeyman, she told herself irritably. He doesn't feel like talking, well that's nothing new. He's a man and not a ghost.

'What?' said Dalmadge, coming awake.

And this porky little guy borrowed Kiley's apartment for the evening. I have an image problem at Morosoph. I'm down as the lonely career person. This must be why girls chatter about their boyfriends, to keep their images in good focus. I thought it was just chatter. I'm not myself a chatterer so I've become what, a candy bar. The world is divided into candy bars and consumers of candy bars, or maybe we should be saying chocolate cake.

Time to send this entrepreneur home to his wife.

'Do you know how late it is, Barry?'

Dalmadge nodded. He stared with great concentration at his shoes, trying to remember something.

Chapter 2

The Fat End of the Cornucopia

WELL YE CRODS an scratches, Jack's been these thirty years a down-easter on the flyin clips, yar, once made New York to Callao in eighty days, rounded the Horn in twelve hour, jest slantin her in there across no wind at all. That's the truth. I'se an ol Cape Horner, mateys, with ribaldries to sing an stories to tell. Jack's many's the time sold his hard-weather tackle fer black rum an then rode them long Atlantic swells under Diego Ramirez bones bare t'the wind, riggin froze an the deck a sheet a ice. Down there below fifty south lookin to break west fer the Pacific, change his aches an chillyblains fer a wench fat as butter in Honolulu, yar, an a snug little berth in a Telegraph Hill whorehouse.

Jack was fond of the romance of the sea. He's inclined to talk like a sailor man because a sailor man is what Jack feels himself to be. Where am I bound, he often asks himself naïvely, what manner of oblivion, what dread penal isle, what enchanted harbour. What indeed is the voyage, and will the weather hold. Lest we are all accused of mongering costly metaphors in this plain tale, do kindly make a note that he's given no spell at the helm or watch in the chartroom. He doesn't pace the after-deck, and has never been the master of any vessel he's trodden the planks of. He's a sailor man. His freedom is only to peer in wonderment into the murk, and to drown should the uncertain seas open under him.

He was making his way toward the Concourse. The Sutton in its day had its seasons, more prolifically than nature. Jack could have been placed inside the Sutton – where there are no clues of temperature or of the wheel of stars and the cycle of the sun in the firmament – at any time of the year and by studying the scene for a few moments he'd be able to fix you the date on a calendar, correct to within a week at most.

In the autumn season there were the Shopper Stopper and the Super Shopper Stopper sales and the Fashion and Winterizing sales. The Winterizing was accompanied by giveaways of Old Man Winterbeater savings coupons, which overfilled the litter stations and indeed did drift underfoot like snow. Christmas was celebrated abundantly, too much so said many. The Christmas countdown sales began in October, and coming fast we had the Giant Yuletide and the GSCB, the great Sutton Christmas Bonanza. All the supermarkets combined in the Festival Fare Money Saver, as did the fashion outlets in the Christmas Jubilee. The Open Late took off like a rocket with the arrival of Santa Claus in early November, catching many shoppers who were lagging in the fall season by surprise. Then frosty January arrived and the new year's birth was marked inside the Sutton by blizzards of two-for-ones, ninety-centres, half-price super clearances, and of course the Grand Springerama. After those came intricate bunches of third-off sellouts and selected spring vacation promotions, until the great Sutton Fiesta and the Taking-It-Easy lotteries and coupon contests brought us all into summer. That was how our year went, and we had no reason to believe the world would ever end.

Spring was yielding to summer on the Concourse as Jack took the route through Eaton's from the west mall. The bunting was already up for the Here Comes Summer Fun days. Jack was heading for the Bank of Montreal in the Court. He used a kangaroo hop, a system of evasive two-footed swerves and sidesteps. An invisible man takes quite a buffeting in the souks. Well, you are bumped even when you're visible, so the problem of occupying apparently empty space can be imagined. Threading a way along the Concourse wasn't so bad for Jack because the customers out there on the main stem moved in a tolerably straight line.

The Wake-Up Man was wearing a rosebud in his buttonhole to mark the change of season. His pitch this morning was at the junction of the west mall and the Concourse, considerably back from the stream of traffic. He wore a tasteful Harrotex jacket in the Sutherland tartan with a white silk cravat fastened by a gold pin and wine-coloured doubleknit wool slacks. His comfortable but elegant loafers looked to be Italian and made by hand.

It was the Wake-Up Man's custom to commune with the marketplace public. That public isn't fond of the Wake-Up Man – well, it doesn't like anybody that gets in its way and has no tolerance for metaphysical propagandists. But children liked him, and the Sutton security staff turned a blind eye on the old man. It could be that he had influence with the governors of the complex. He wasn't much trouble. He didn't shout or thrust pamphlets at people, though he would address his remarks to individuals sometimes.

He carried an old-fashioned walking stick of black cherry with a silver knob. He usually rested both hands on the stick, in the manner of the vaudevillians, addressing his public in a firm, raspy voice. The Wake-Up Man was seventy-five, thin of frame, with a lined yellow face and civil eyes.

'Wake up,' said the Wake-Up Man as Jack went by. He spoke sincerely and persuasively. 'You people are not thinking straight. Wake up, please. Most of you aren't thinking at all, that's what's causing the problem we have to deal with here.' He paused as if sensing Jack, who was taking the easy route through the clear space in front of the Wake-Up Man's pitch. Then he resumed his function, leaning courteously toward the shoppers, hands clasped atop the silver knob of his walking stick. 'We need some action,' he told them. 'Just working and playing and sleeping and making money doesn't do it. The problem calls for more poetry than that. We're selling ourselves short here.'

The crowd streamed on by, pretending not to see or hear the Wake-Up Man. Some children loitered around the pitch however and watched him with sombre faces, hopeful that he would do tricks or hand out balloons. Jack just then was nudged off course by a cross-tide, of men mostly, which settled in front of the Stax TV & Stereo window. A salesman had just switched on a fifty-inch Sony.

The customer with the salesman was known to Jack as Cleveland Dan. He lived on the tenth floor of the Parthenon Tower. Dan was forty, though he looked much younger because his body was in good trim and he always dressed young and to the fashion of the moment. He enjoyed life. Now his hands were deep in the pockets of a pair of Eddie Savage chinos while he watched the TV, conversing with the salesman. Cleveland Dan's face was pink, with ginger eyebrows and lashes, and he could show a perfect set of big white teeth when he smiled, as he often did. In the snow months Cleveland Dan could be seen in the early mornings in his running outfit jogging through the Sutton's empty labyrinths.

As it happened Jack knew that Cleveland Dan already owned a Hitachi fifty-inch, a unit that decoded broadcast stereo and provided an ambiance choice. The Sony, however, came with a VHF remote rather than your commonplace infrared. The salesman had handed this control to Cleveland Dan who was holding it with reverent joy. A beautiful pearly palm-sized module inlaid with black touch plates it was. Its green and red diodes glowed like jewels under Cleveland Dan's dazzled eyes.

The crowd had been attracted to the Stax window by a clip of the Expos on the TV screen. They were due to come back again this year, according to the publicity. Jerry Rodriguez of the Pirates was pitching to Andy Wish in a heartbreaker from last season. He hit a single to left off the left-hander and the crowd at the Stax window cheered. Willie Crowner came to bat and hit into a double-play. Then the TV programme went to an interview with Jerry Rodriguez, modestly explaining how he'd pitched Crowner for the double play and sunk the Expos' hopes. The fans at the Stax window would have preferred an explanation from Willie, who shouldn't even have tried to hit the Rodriguez slider, and broke up grumbling. Cleveland Dan thumbed a touch plate as Jack was moving off, pausing on a channel that showed General Schata surrounded by a thicket of microphones in the White House rose garden with the President.

Jack paused at once to watch that. The big screen showed Schata with terrific definition, the man as if present in the Stax window wearing a business suit instead of a uniform for his visits to the Western countries. The hairs on the back of Jack's neck rose like an animal's.

The sailor's roused hatred of General Schata is racial, or maybe tribal. Or it could be a prejudice of species, like a forest creature's whose wrath boils up most surely when he recognizes his own skin and colours on another beast. The inevitable supply of tyrants in the world, according to Jack's opinion, was an important corrective to sentimental hopes for spiritual evolution and every manner of wistful Bergsonism, the hard evidence that no evolution worth noting was going on. But he could manage to live with the tales of slaughter in the news when the bloody-handed men were of an alien race. The epicanthic fold on a Mongolian eye, the high-cheeked glitter of a South American one, or some Middle Eastern eye cold as ice behind sunglasses could with moderate self-deception be thought of as peering in on us from a separate planet. The victims in their villages and torture chambers were within his realization of horror but beyond his world, like the moaning people in a woodcut of a medieval pageant of cruelty.

Schata was too near to Jack. The general lived in the same world Jack lived in, which wasn't so big a place. A stoop-shouldered stalky man with lank brown hair, he could have passed for a university professor except for an excited glitter at the back of his eyes now and then, an indication of enthusiasm, which Jack thought of as fanaticism. The same glitter could be seen behind the eyes of plenty of black leaders too but they lived, usually, in distant parts of faraway countries. Schata spoke and thought in the same kind of English that Jack used. He was taken to be a personal threat by Jack who felt that if he had children of his own at some future date it would be a man like General Schata who sent them to the interrogators.

The President as a politician smiled at General Schata. Since the President was certainly an inherently humane man, however, his smile had tight edges, like a mailman's acknowledgement of a new dog on the block. Cleveland Dan switched the remote on the Sony. George Garvey for the Expos hit a screwball from Enrique Ramone of the Mets out of the infield. Expo fans pressed in at once on Jack, jostling to occupy the empty space he stood in. But a Mets outfielder appeared on the screen to say that catching the Garvey long fly had been routine for a player of his speed and the crowd dispersed again, cursing all baseballers' vanity and salaries. Come the season though, they'd be at their sets, and drinking the beer too, watching the rich kids play. The sailor believes the game to be an allegory of tribal warfare.

Well, he believes all team sport is. Right now he noticed that he was having a sportsman's morning. He spotted a star of the Canadiens, the Golden Great One, who lives in Vanier, as he rejoined the Concourse and turned left through a domain of health and gourmet food vendors, pasta makers and home bakeries. Jean-Guy Pickett was strolling in the throng with a companion who also had the sloped shoulders and muscled build of an ice gladiator. The regular hockey season was winding down.

Other famous people live in the Parthenon Tower. We have the novelist Douglas T. Harder, scourge of liberalism and fuzzy thinking, who writes a column for an Ottawa paper on the side to contain his briefer inspirations. The way a man with a hangover on a Monday morning might view the smelly press of humanity on a crowded subway is how Harder sees his fellows all through the week. In his career he's worked this sensibility, Monday morning grouchiness, into a philosophy that people are buying. Everybody in the world is greedy, vicious and corrupt. Those who seem not to be so are faking it. The masses are spoilt by social welfare and their laziness will bring the civilized world to its knees. Our political leaders have lost the willpower to govern with strength. Mind you there are dark stations in Jack's life where you could get him to endorse all these thoughts and add a few bleak ones of his own. Lately Harder's been writing gritty little pieces defending General Schata.

Harder at home eats sardines with his fingers, and dog food on whole wheat, though he pays thirty-five hundred dollars a month for his Parthenon Tower suite. All his furniture came from the Salvation Army and cost a total of sixty dollars. This is asceticism. The way he lives, as he tells his newspaper readers, is spartan and individual. He gets an exemption from commonplace judgements by being a writer who has a novel on the *New York Times* bestseller list every two or three years. He'd be otherwise just a man who lived like a slob.

The novels contain energetic searches for God and the meaning of life, and they have an appeal for people who like to argue such questions, high school kids and undergraduates, and that broad audience of comfortable folk who always feel that there might be more to life than they're getting: the short-changed majority.

Lots of politicians lived in the Tower, naturally. Eight members of the federal parliament, two privy councillors and a number of senators, at this moment we speak of. There were dozens of high mandarins and hundreds of board chairmen and company presidents famous among their own kind, and franchise chain owners, real estate princes, importers, corporation lawyers, and a large population of indisputably prosperous individuals whose occupations weren't clear to Jack, although he's curious by nature and often spends time in their apartments browsing through their stuff. Publishers lived in the Tower, gallery owners, cultural bureaucrats, and various people connected to the film industry on the financial and distribution sides. Also two other famous writers besides Douglas T. Harder. No poets, however.

We have four TV personalities who are famous, among them Ralph Jim Trasker of the Trasker Television Chapel. One of the others is Burlington Broom who parlayed an appearance of being a sympathetic listener into a big career as an interviewer. Burly's manner of leaning forward so eagerly that he's practically in his subject's face isn't really sympathy though. The truth is that Burly's a hearing-impaired person. When he knows what people are saying he's easily bored. Off the sound stage he wears a big German hearing aid and yawns and looks away and jingles the change in his pocket when people try to talk to him.

Burly's career's been slipping over the last year or so. But there's a combined network telethon in the planning stage for late this summer. Burly's been chosen as main-anchor host. So he has a chance at a comeback.

A new teller occupied Jack's usual wicket at the Bank of Montreal in the

Court. Dorothy Savoy, said the nameplate, customer representative, a husky woman in her early twenties with steel-rimmed glasses and pimples on her cheeks who had a warm smile. She loved her work. Her fingers flew through the documents and money bills like a pianist's.

There was something about banks and sex. Jack couldn't put a finger on it. Unfortunately the tellers he made his withdrawals from didn't last long in the banking business. Dorothy Savoy had had a run of withdrawals and was down to insufficient bills for Jack's needs. He risked a few steps farther in from the door to the wicket of Heather Hanklyn.

A uniformed security man, alert and bored, stood inside the door and Jack noticed one of the Sutton's plain-clothes women cruising the queues. Jack studied the situation from outside the counter and to the left of Heather Hanklyn's line. He couldn't imagine what kind of mistake he might make that would start the alarm bells ringing but he is aware that it can happen at any time in his life. Any day, any minute, cries of consternation, hullabaloo.

The bank has a high ambient noise level. The Court outside is a ghetto of shops where such items as handmade candles, soapstone carved by aboriginal artists and tropical birds in exotic cages could be purchased. It is octagonal in shape as we view it, reverberant, with a splashy floodlit fountain in the centre surrounded by cedarwood seats. The Sutton pipes music into the Court, and promotion messages and news of sales, as it does to all the complex. So inside the bank we have fountain-splash and the Court music and also the bank's own commercial hum and its own easy-listening deck.

Jean-Guy Pickett, the Golden Great One, was in Heather Hanklyn's line with his younger companion. Jack guessed that they'd been at a TV taping because they were still using TV interview speech, sprinkled with words like heck and darn and gosh. Their tongues just hesitated enough on the word they used most regularly to slur it coming from their lips.

'Everybody's too young. What do they know? All the head coaches, they're all fogging young now. He worked two seasons in the Western division, I forget, Kamloops or somewhere. Now he knows all about hockey. He can tell me how to play the darn game.'

Heather Hanklyn was grey-haired and compact, a disciplinarian who brought her stamps down hard on the cheques and issued loud advice and instructions. She had a brilliant, impersonal, stainless steel smile for the customer at the conclusion of each transaction.

'Now I'm supposed to use the wing more. I haven't got the fogging puck because I can't go back to pick the fogger up but I'm supposed to take it along the side. I'm not doing any fogging thing right any more, the TV guys keep asking me do I have any plans to retire. Well, you heard him.'

'It's the Russian style, that tic-tac-toe,' said the younger player tactfully. 'They started it, equal shares for everybody. Now look at them.'

Jack went inside the counter, standing behind Heather Hanklyn's shoulder. A fussy well-dressed lady with bond coupons was the customer, executing her at-the-bank routine. To command the space the lady disposed cheque-book, bankbook, coupons, handbag, glasses, wallet, a pen and a collapsible umbrella on the counter, making everything tidy before she looked at the teller to open negotiations. Heather Hanklyn's observation of the procedure was neither approving nor disapproving, but it was unblinkingly interested.

'Goons, too, hey Jean? Well, at home they're looking for blood, they don't think it's real. It's ketchup like on the other TV shows.'

Said the Golden Great One: 'We always had fogging goons. They sent those guys out on you, fogging crazy men, and they took penalties, and you could win the game. What don't work now is they don't call the penalties. They gotta call the fogging penalties, but what do you expect, referees who aren't shaving yet? It was something I liked when I was a kid, hockey. It was my whole darn world. Now I'm thirty-fogging-one years old. I have eighteen fogging teeth left in my mouth now. Last season I had twenty. A fogging Chicago guy gave me a stick in the face and it nearly brought the house down ...'

A big and breezy golfing kind of man in his fifties with a Florida tan took his place at the wicket. Heather Hanklyn counted out eight hundreds for him in her loud voice. Jack added two extras. When the man fanned the money he was looking at ten big bills.

This is where you get your authentic capitalist style, a matter of ingenuity and nerve. The regular bank customer might hand the extra money back, feeling the glow of integrity certainly but then fighting a sense of loss too, walking to the door. I had that money! Or else the risk was of a court appearance and the explanation 'I don't know what came over me', which most judges have heard before. Either way there's psychic unease down in the roots. At a bank money is the whole game. The golfer with no hesitation whatsoever shot his right cuff back to check his watch and said to Heather Hanklyn, loud enough to turn Dorothy Savoy's head toward them, 'You've counted this, right?' He was pushed for time.

Heather Hanklyn's brilliant smile died into a tight stare and wordlessly she reached for the money again. But he had several witnesses now and slipped the banknotes comfortably into his wallet. He looked at his watch again and with a farewell nod of thanks off he went.

'So we needed a score and I had to work on that. I had to like play a little of the game of hockey, and between me and Jacques we went two ahead. Then when I had time I gave a little crosscheck to the Blackhawks guy. So that brought the house down too, never mind it's their own guy.'

'Well, on that particular play, the crosscheck,' the younger hockey player said, speaking tactfully again to the Golden Great One but perhaps not agreeing with all the criticism of youth in the national sport, 'I know the one you mean, and the guy had broken ribs, didn't he, Jean. Three or four. I heard something about his lung collapsing. He's still in the hospital, isn't he, he's not even in rehab yet. I guess what I'm trying to say is you never won the Lady Byng or anything yourself.'

'What a fogging pisser though, after the times you get up at dawn when you're a kid, all those mornings you spend on the ice. When you're a kid hockey is the world. Like I can't fogging well understand why they still bother to keep the fogging score. It's like the lions and the fogging Christians, first the fogging lions went out and ate the fogging Christians, that was how simple it was. I guess the next thing was a lion putting on a show for the fans. He's jumping around hot-dogging, he tears an arm off a Christian and waves it, a leg, some fogging Christian's head. He's forgotten he's only out there because he's a hungry fogging lion.'

'That'd make great fogging TV.'

'Okay, well, they should fogging put it on TV. Like they could put the hockey on separate for people who want to watch hockey. I don't mind losing a tooth here and there playing hockey but I'm fogging ... I'm *forking* ashamed of myself losing teeth for forking entertainment purposes. I'm worse'n a whore, doing that, at least a whore's doing something natural. Now I'm on the ice and some forker has his head down, I don't even feel like giving him a check any more. I mean darn it. I hit the guy and the crowd goes wild. I'm great. I'm the Golden Great One, just as good as I ever was. Then some gooney who can't see where he's skating he's so full of pills does the same thing and they go wild again. Why should I care about them?'

'Well, it's changed but it's the same game. New people come along, new fans too, but the game's still in there, Jean.'

'Maybe for you, and like your age group, I'm not arguing, but not for me. Most of the time now I don't even know what's the score without checking the board. Somebody hands me the forking puck now, I don't want the forking puck. The last couple of seasons I don't even feel like stepping out on the ice, playing hockey against guys who can't trap a pass. Maybe it's a career in forking sports all right, but it makes me feel ashamed of myself. I feel like a freak in a fogging circus. A forking circus. That's funny you know too, because I always wanted to play hockey. That's about all I ever really wanted to forking do.'

Being then next up for Heather Hanklyn the younger hockey player handed her his cheques for deposit. Whenever Jack does banking business a phenomenon that banks don't care for occurs, a flash of disappearing assets. Money rises in an arc from the drawer and vanishes in midair, the effect of Jack seizing the visible money with his invisible gloved hand and tucking it away inside his green cloak.

He'd helped himself to a few bills in this manner from Heather Hanklyn's drawer without drawing comment when Dorothy Savoy's voice seemed to hang with great clarity on a silent bar of the banking hubbub.

She said: 'Thank you, Mr Apse.'

Jack went still in shock. An obese young bank worker took this moment to move between Jack and Dorothy Savoy, however, and in skirting the fat man Jack was diverted into a cul-de-sac of file cabinets and desks. He vaulted an empty desk but caught his foot in an open lower drawer and went all asprawl on the carpet. When Jack reached Dorothy Savoy there was no sign of Elmo Apse.

He was excited and did not use good sense. He grabbed Dorothy Savoy's arm and shook the woman. He shouted at her. Normally he knows better. 'Was your customer named Elmo Apse?'

Dorothy Savoy stared at the nothingness beside her and then her eyes rolled upward and she collapsed to the floor. Jack stepped over her body to look at her papers. As a rule he isn't this callous. Right away he saw a personal cheque made out to Elmo Apse. He would have taken cash for it. Jack already knew that Elmo Apse didn't have an account at this bank.

Elmo Apse had been standing practically beside Jack on the other side of the counter, showing identification and his current address!

But the security man arrived even as Jack reached for the cheque and to avoid a collision the sailor had to do a tricky backward kangaroo hop over the teller's body. The security man swept all of Dorothy Savoy's papers into her drawer and locked it before bending to attend to her. There were some movements of concern and curiosity among customers and bank employees, but no tumult, and business went right on.

Jack's next move here should have been a patient dawdle in some quiet corner until the teller was brought to. He just needed a glance at the back of Apse's cheque. Instead he rushed from the bank out into the Court, looking to left and right with people caroming off his shoulders, and he shouted: 'Elmo Apse! Elmo Apse! Elmo Apse, you draff spawn, where are you?'

One of the Court's speakers cut the music and a man said in a pleasant voice: 'Shoppers, the Summer Fun giveaway has just started on the Concourse, your chance for valuable prizes. Hundreds of free gifts. The Summer Fun giveaway, shoppers, just under way on the Concourse.'

Shoppers in Jack's vicinity stopped and looked about them, wanting to see who the draff spawn might be. Scanning the crowd, Jack pushed his way angrily through the mill to the Concourse. He shoved and shouldered and body-checked without apology. The people hit by Jack retaliated blindly, striking out at those around them, since we were exceedingly thin of patience in the Sutton despite the splendour of wares for sale and the willing buyers, we were always quickly irritated and easily provoked. A bump by an unknown person was a serious matter in the marketways.

A girl in a blue gown lit by sequins stood on a platform under floods beside the Summer Fun giveaway booth. An elderly benign man of managerial aspect checked ticket counterfoils and handed out the prizes. The announcer at the mike was a grinning youngster in a plaid jacket, and he unfolded a new ticket even as Jack clubbed his way brutally to the front row of onlookers. It was a steam iron from House Hardware. The announcer read out the name of the winner and the model in the blue gown spun the drum again.

The prizes were all on display on a long trestle, stereos and chain-saws, cordless tools and computers, but Jack couldn't see one that would attract Apse. He would write his own ticket. But he didn't have a pen on him. He needed a pen.

Down among the people again the first pen Jack found happened to be a heavy old solid-gold Parker. Its owner felt it go and clapped his hand to his breast pocket in anguish, crying out with pain that the pen had sentimental value, which is always so of old gold. On the list of prizes Jack improved a Timex Sports to a Rolex Oyster Perpetual, writing Apse's name clearly on the ticket and the counterfoil. When the Rolex was announced he twitched the ticket she drew from the model's elegant fingers and gave her Elmo Apse's.

Here there were a few mutters in the audience, a little uprush of concern. The suspicious by nature had noticed an oddity in the draw for the watch, a ticket flying laterally from the girl's fingers and vanishing, and a substitute ticket gyrating out of empty air and into her hand. But Elmo Apse's name was sent into every remote corner of the Sutton, to the last washroom in the Annex, to the concrete frontier of the most distant parking lot.

Now we move with Jack over to the line of folk at the side waiting to collect prizes. Most of the folk are here for filler prizes and, except for a few eager children, the line was orderly and not much impressed by its good fortune. They were receiving little boxes of candy and stationery and cosmetic items from the managerial man, who could have been a Sutton governor for all anybody knew. Jack got up on the platform with him, for a better overview of the terrain.

Then he watched there, like a hunter who has put down bait and now waits for a beast to come out of the dark. Elmo Apse did come presently, with a little smile on his face. Apse felt superior to the Summer Fun promo but he knows what a Rolex is. He had just lit a panatela cigar, thin as a pencil. Jack was smiling too. Ar it do bring joy to me cacky old eyes, the salt clipperman told himself, ee in me clutch at last. It do be a wonder o t'god, a judgement an a deliverance. Come aboard yur, Elmo ye bilge-rat an draff scum, come into me, thought Jack.

Chapter 3

Cuckoo

JACK FOLLOWED Elmo Apse to a bakery where Apse bought a loaf of rye bread, and to a delicatessen where he bought cheese and sausage, ham and black olives. He bought fresh grapes. He bought a bottle of the true Liebfraumilch of Worms, Liebfrauenstift. The liquor-store man had to go to a special-order bin for it.

The sailor understood that Apse was for the moment under somebody's civilizing influence. His regular taste in a white wine would have been a litre of Bright's. They rode together with a few other tenants up to the ninth floor of the Parthenon Tower, a condo level, where Apse let himself into 9011.

Jack went to his own place then and brought up the number on his data file. Nine-oh-one-one belonged to Buz Hoeglin and his wife Albreda. Jack had been searching for Elmo Apse among the apartments of unattached women. The Tower is a deep forest for a hunter on the prowl and hides much strange and shifting life.

Apse was inspecting plants when Jack got back. The Hoeglin condo was a bower of plant life. The green growth and floral spread made the room look like a section of a suburban garden, an inside-outside swap made by the Hoeglins. There was a even a tiny cloud up near the ceiling where the water the plants lived on had been condensed by the air-conditioning. The half of the living room not covered by potted vines and small trees had a white rug on it; the chairs and tables were made of Lucite with chrome fittings. A genial human presence was hard to see in the place. Well, birds didn't chirp in the trees either, a timid rabbit didn't nibble the shrub leaves, but on the cheerful side neither did snakes or other outdoor undesirables slide through the sheepskin undergrowth.

Insect life was forbidden too, though harder to keep out than birds and rabbits. As Apse moved through the foliage he gave it a burst now and then from a can of Raid.

He had time on his hands. When he'd finished with the plants he loosened his tie, yawning, and making his way through a glade, started a bath running.

What Jack needed now was a philosophy for the act he'd been brought to, murder. He also needed the kind of detachment toward death that's sold in aerosol cans. He didn't feel like looking at Elmo Apse's surprise. Apse would certainly be just as surprised as any insect he had just spritzed. Jack thought about the insect, to see if he could arrive at a philosophy for looking at Apse's surprise. Here is after all an anonymous insect that has somehow found itself in insect paradise. Then from the vault of the sky a rushing cloud brings agony and death. Can bewilderment and the need of an explanation be more severely felt?

It wasn't even an important event, as Jack explained death to himself. Only the theatres surrounded death with importance, nurses in lavish supply at the bedside and two or more doctors. Jack had stood by a dying pedestrian on a roadway once while the autos honked and blared because traffic was being blocked. The moment of killing Elmo Apse had occurred to Jack, theatrically, as having drama, a horror-movie scene with Jack's cloak flying open and his mask off to let Apse see the avenger. Jack would have a maniac's two-handed clutch on Apse's windpipe, wolfishly meeting his popping eyes. That would constitute an explanation, knowing why he died, but was it a sufficient one? In the case of the imaginary insect, what improvement would be made upon its situation by a voice from the vault that spoke insect language and accompanied the rush of Raid death with the explanation: 'It is decreed from up here, by creatures of immensely superior sensibility, that nasty little hardskins such as yourself shall not live in this place'?

Apse was expecting somebody for lunch. Jack's guesses at the situation in 9011 went this way, that Elmo Apse was living with Mrs Hoeglin. Buz could be dead. But Apse's luncheon guest might be someone other than Albreda. That happy picnic of wine and bread and grapes is one of hands and mouths that's independent of the clock, a meal that steals time, a spontaneous meal for brand new lovers. In a settled relationship, and he'd been settled in 9011 for some months, the requirements as to food are more and less complicated.

Jack made a tour of the condo apartment with experienced nosiness. Some of Apse's clothes were in the bedroom closet alongside those of a bulkier and shorter man. Buz wasn't dead. He had a small office adjoining the TV room. In the desk Jack found letterhead stationery for the firm Kajel & Hoeglin Electrostatics. He found old calendars of trade exhibitions in places like Frankfurt and Tokyo and Las Vegas. These seemed to place Buz away from Ottawa for half the summer months and most of the winter.

Going through Albreda's bedside drawers Jack came upon caches of Buz's letters home. The traveller had somehow got business performance mixed up with love in his mind. '*They want us to make a production run of the zone limiter!*' Buz Hoeglin revealed to his wife in blunt and sincere roller-ball from a hotel in Denmark. '*My darling that's a wonderful opportunity for us, I have patents of my own in it and we can make it in Korea. I love you and I miss you …*' Jack didn't see anything to explain where Albreda was at the moment.

Elmo Apse, towelling himself, joined Jack in the bedroom. He was an attractive man with his clothes on. Naked he could be seen to be somewhat out of shape, flesh bulging at the shoulders and the thighs and rounding his lower belly. He was 180 centimetres tall and had an impressive face, long and dark Modigliani or quattrocento features with teeth that showed up to the gums. He had a black moustache and the Italian beard that was shaped to a point. His genitals were of average appearance, neither large nor small. Jack wasn't a good judge of these, however. He had no standards of comparison, never having been much of a locker-room man. The maleness was unquestionable. Black hair covered his body, all knobby bone and angles and planes where it wasn't flaccid, yet the way Apse moved had always struck Jack as epicene. It was not an affectation of grace but a performance of ritual. Apse had certain prescribed ways of moving. He had the manner always of a subtly thoughtful priest.

Dressing was a serious matter for the man. He spent time choosing between a white open-neck shirt with gold necklet and a grey turtleneck sweater. Meanwhile Jack was still looking for Albreda. There was a fresh Hull number for a Marge in Apse's writing on a phone pad in the living-room. Jack returned to the bedroom on cat feet to consult Mrs Albreda Hoeglin's personal directory on the telephone table beside her dresser. He found the same number in there after Marge, and a Hull address, an early entry, which Jack took to mean that Marge was an old friend or relative of Albreda's, and not Apse's new girl.

So Mrs Hoeglin was in Hull with Marge. Buz was away on business. Elmo Apse was the cuckoo in the nest among the trees.

While Jack leafed through the directory Apse had been standing at Buz Hoeglin's bachelor chest on the other side of the large Gibbard bed. He was using the vacant stare that folk use to appraise themselves in mirrors. Jack suddenly noticed a shift of Apse's head in Buz's mirror. His eyes had been attracted to the pages of the telephone directory, turning of their own accord.

Apse came around the bed and squinted down at the book as Jack waited tolerantly, knowing Elmo Apse not to be an imaginative man. As Jack understood him, at Apse's level of curiosity about things outside of himself, spread through humanity, we would all still be tilling patches of ground with sharp sticks. Now that the telephone book was inert Apse did not pick it up, nor did he check for an air current in the room that might have moved the pages.

His eye was caught again by his own reflection in Albreda Hoeglin's dresser mirror. He gave himself the thousand-yard stare and began to practise smiles, maybe for his luncheon engagement. There was a tiny smile that barely moved the lips while the eyes remained dark and sincere. A level gaze followed, then an appreciative smile, and an awed smile – something's been said to earn his respect. He did a full-range smile next, with his upper lip peeled back from his big teeth and his mouth wide open and eyes closed in mirth. Jack's problem here was that he was boxed in behind the Hoeglin family bed. He had to wait through the full catalogue of Elmo Apse's smiles and happy faces.

Jack took the elevator down to the second floor, crossing the corridors of the Medical Wing, which are carpeted, to an asphalt-tiled section beyond, the Nailer.

The outside door of the Nailer suggests a place dedicated to healing science, like the other laboratories and small hospitals in the wing. NAILER GERIATRIC CLINIC, it says, and underneath is this information: *Consultations with Dr Gerald A. Nailer by Referral and Appointment.*

In fact the Nailer is only a nursing home of the regular kind. At the door you're met by an atmosphere of loneliness and boredom and routine pain. The Nailer doesn't do research and therapy, the projection of a clinical image notwithstanding. A worry about old people as such was never an advanced concern of medicine in the Sutton. We stayed with the nursing-home idea, to make a dollar for the owner, which placed us somewhat ahead of the primitive tribes that ate their old people or threw them over cliffs but behind those that allowed the old folk a respectable role or function in the body of the community.

Once while he wasn't wearing his green cloak Jack was drinking wine and Etobicoke vodka in the John Peel lounge and struck up an acquaintance with another midday drinker, an orderly who'd just been fired from one of the cancer clinics. The orderly's name was Harris, an intense hard-faced youth, hungry for success, who was knowledgeable about money-management matters. He talked slickly about shelter investments and tax-deferring pension funds. He had been stealing morphine and topping up the vials with sterile water. The police hadn't been called in because the clinic was self-conscious about the cancer patients who'd been getting sterile water as an analgesic for a couple of years.

Harris thought he'd been treated harshly. He couldn't understand the fuss. His attitude went: why fire me for such a small thing, me for this but not him for that? Or them for such-and-such? He protested that he'd given loyalty and faithful service and had always been discreet. After three stirrup cups he was close to feeling that the clinic should have allowed him to steal the drug, as a perk of the job, in return for his loyalty and discretion.

Harris gave Jack an account of how a nursing home came to be in the Medical Wing of the Sutton. Jack in fact had never questioned its presence. There is after all an undertaker in the complex, Mandrake Funeral Services, though on the West Plaza walk and not in the Parthenon Tower Medical Wing.

Dr Nailer originally signed a ten-year lease with the Medical Wing management, a doctors' consortium which leased from the Sutton. He went into practice as an orthopaedic surgeon.

According to the aggrieved orderly Harris, Dr Nailer worked as a surgeon for a year and then his colleagues in the wing called a meeting and put it to him that he was making too many mistakes. He was excising a lot of sound tissue and sawing away whole cords of healthy bone.

Dr Nailer tended to dither with the scalpel, changing his mind while he was cutting here and deciding to work over there, then having second thoughts, or thinking of something he should have done earlier. There was also some confusion between left and right in the doctor's mind. Before an operation he'd been heard reminding himself sometimes *Left hits the ball when my back's towards the wall, right is the might when I get in a fight*, passing this off as a joke to the nurses.

Doctors are overworked though, and on a busy day Dr Nailer wasn't always able to get himself oriented to distinguish his left side from his right. Well, also he thought he knew which was which much of the time, and was making a mistake. The two operating room tables contributed another dimension of ambiguity by being arranged at right angles to each other. Depending on which table the patient occupied, left did not always hit the ball when Dr Nailer's back was toward the wall. It became a fifty-fifty chance, random choice.

Dr Nailer's colleagues complained about amputations – this was like a writer throwing a page away for Dr Nailer, or an artist ripping a sheet off a drawing pad to start afresh – and there were records too of patients who arrived using walking sticks, left on crutches and after two or three weeks' convalescence were in wheelchairs, always embarrassing for an orthopaedic clinic no matter how reasonably the individual circumstances are explained. To the doctors' credit they insisted that Dr Nailer take his orthopaedic clinic elsewhere.

He moved it to midtown Ottawa, to the Medical Arts building on Metcalfe. He did still own the lease in the Medical Wing of the Tower, though, and this had become valuable with the success of the complex in the early eighties. When Dr Nailer decided upon a nursing home his medical colleagues had no hesitation about putting money into the project, because nursing homes are blue chip.

In the course of his conversation with the orderly Jack also learnt something about the buying and selling of illegal drugs. The mistake that's easily made, Harris told Jack, is to assume that a Mountie will look clean-cut. In reality an opposite assumption is safest, a broken-down derelict with a gen-uine death-rattle cough and needle scabs will be the police agent while somebody with blue eyes and a frank manner who can be solidly imagined wearing a red tunic on a horse up on Parliament Hill is likely to be a drug dealer. As it happened, Harris's talk of Ottawa bars and cops and drug dealers proved useful to Jack before the end of that summer.

A man and a woman stood at the reception desk inside the Nailer facing Mrs Aquerra the receptionist. Jack was fond of Mrs Aquerra, who is a small nurse of about forty with wise inquisitive eyes and frizzy black hair. The receptionists at the other clinics tended to be blondes, as if by rule. They were mannered to ice-maidenhood or detached efficiency, to smiling grace or whatever they thought worked best for them. They played vivid roles, but Mrs Aquerra always played herself. Jack assumed she cost less than a blonde from the blond receptionist training school.

Her interest in the patients' relatives who came to her desk was lively, as if they might surprise her. Jack didn't think they ever would. Drop off the aged person, that was the pattern, tell me the aged person will be happy here and that I'm doing the right thing. I'd prefer not to know too many of the small details.

The man had the look of somebody who is up against bureaucratic harassment. He was big and tidy-looking, in a grey suit with a trimmed silver moustache and wings of hair brushed back over his ears. The woman seemed anxious and out of her depth. She wore a smart navy-blue wool dress that was somewhat too tight, as if she didn't wear her good clothes much. Perhaps she didn't often participate in matters outside the house.

'We could take your forms and mail them to you,' the man said. 'But that'd be too easy I suppose.'

'Mr Prentiss Nightingale and Mrs Eugenie Nightingale,' said Mrs Aquerra, writing it down. 'Patient's name is Mrs Agnes Nightingale, relationship mother. Okay, whose mother?'

'She's my mother,' Mr Nightingale said.

'I'm not so much worried about the medical care,' said Mrs Nightingale, 'as the recreation facilities. At Bewdley Manor they have outings, a hairdresser and a physiotherapist and musical events and bingo. They get other medication besides tranquillizers at Bewdley too, so I'm told. Well, I'm sure the medication here is good too – isn't it? They have a VCR and lots of old tapes of Lawrence Welk and George Burns, and so on. They have those big TV floor consoles.'

'Well, we shouldn't even have that little black-and-white in the day room, Mrs Nightingale,' Mrs Aquerra said frankly. 'That isn't part of the Nailer programme. Some kid brought it for his grandmother and didn't pick it up after she ... left us.'

'My husband wants his mother to have every care. But he doesn't have much free time. Do you, Prentiss.'

'I'm not driving halfway to Belleville to Bewdley Manor,' Mr Nightingale said and shot a look at his watch.

'We're not thinking about the money,' Mrs Nightingale explained. However, she looked at her husband.

Mr Nightingale was over at the door reading the posters from the health organizations recommending jogging and hiking and fat-free foods and urging the aged Nailer inmates to beware of smoking, obesity and venereal diseases. He was doing the dance called *the Nailer hover*. With that a door is always centre stage and the feet drift toward it. The face can be taut in the flamenco style, the wrist is bent often in consultation of a watch, the mood is of farewell, there is an eagerness to fly away. It was Mrs Aquerra's policy to discourage the Nailer hover. 'Mrs Nightingale should be settled in nicely now,' said she. 'This way.'

But the dancer toed the ground. 'Look, we'll let her get used to the place. Give me a call if she needs anything and I'll have somebody drop it off.'

'Very well. I'll make a list. Say I give it to you on Tuesday. Our visiting day,' Mrs Aquerra told the Nightingales before either of them could ask why she expected to see them on Tuesday.

'That's typical. Tuesday is the worst possible day.'

'And Wednesday. Thursdays, Fridays. Weekends too, naturally.'

'Not Monday?' said Mr Nightingale, stopping and staring as if this created an instant difficulty of great proportion.

'Not Monday. I'm sorry.'

Mr Nightingale seemed to gain in stature and self-confidence. 'Well, I'll have to get back to you on it,' he said with crisp discontentment while his wife watched him in anxiety and with respect for the disciplines of his calendar, not understood by her it seemed. 'Monday would've been good.'

'In that case let's say Monday.'

Mr Nightingale directed a look of brooding, thoughtful rancour at the non-blond receptionist. He'd always had trouble with pushy, manipulative immigrants. 'What are your visiting hours on Monday, please?'

'Any time during the day.' Mrs Aquerra then added, with an extra glitter in her black eyes: 'Except two to four in the afternoon.'

For a second or so here it looked as if two to four in the afternoon of a Monday would have been perfect for Mr Nightingale. He started to speak in fact but might have seen a trap. Instead of helping Mr Nightingale to arrange his timetable for visiting his mother in the Nailer, Mrs Aquerra seemed to be hindering him. He was uncomfortable and she was causing it. 'Is it wise to let visitors in all the time?' he asked sharply. 'I guess you know your own business but doesn't it disturb the patients, people trudging in and out? At all hours?'

'No, it doesn't, Mr Nightingale. We never have trouble that way.'

'Well, I'll get back to you on it. We'll do our best. We have the problem of a babysitter.'

'Bring the children.'

'Do you allow that? God. Children in here. Well, damn. Children. I'll think it over. I didn't know they allowed children into places like this.'

'That's nice, though, Prentiss. They can still visit their grandma.'

'If we bring the children here they'll see all these old people. I'm surprised it's allowed.'

'Children aren't bothered by old people, Mr Nightingale.'

'We should think about the risk.' Mr Nightingale explained to his wife: 'TV and drugs and now this.' He said to Mrs Aquerra: 'I'll let you know. I have to think of what's best for everybody.'

That's a characteristic of the Nailer dancers, they always say they must think of what's best for everybody, as if putting an aged person in the Nailer sends out ripples of anguish that have equal force for the new patient and for every family member, which isn't usually how it happens.

On the other hand the Nailer does smell of bodily function and decay and a close sense of death hangs in the rooms there always. At the Nailer in the Sutton we've gathered the aged together in one place from far and near, and confronting them as a mass is for many sensitive people like being compelled to think about death. Who wants to hang around an anteroom to the grave? Spread out among the population like other people Nailerians wouldn't present this threat.

Some Nailerians have managed to retain their individuality. It's brutal uphill work. Others are unarguably gone silly, whether from natural senility or from the circumstances of incarceration and boredom and the medication is difficult to say. We do anyway lose one or two minds a week to the hard grind. Snap.

Jack is just like everybody else. He doesn't care for the Nailer's atmosphere, but he's fond of a number of the inmates. He's most fond of Mrs Delgardo's group. He can see himself as an inmate too, and not at some comfortably distant date either.

According to Jack's opinion, aging happens instantaneously. It is how you are whenever you look at yourself. A man, say, goes to bed aged twenty-five, virile and popular and with more hair than he can use, and when he wakes up the next morning he's forty-nine and considerably less virile, tangibly less popular. One of his first morning acts will be to look in the mirror at his bald and shrunken parts. His inside organs will have grown wearier. He'll have to start taking pills for this and that.

Then on the following morning he'll be aged fifty-six, and he'll have more adjustments to make, none easy. On the very next morning after that he'll be aged eighty-three and much, much more decayed and pain-ridden, and without even a good memory of zest and virility as he had it a couple of days ago. Of course he will be very unpopular now too, especially with the people closest to him, formerly his children. They are likely to be bossy and exasperated and talking nursing home, as to somebody who has forgotten the language, with their faces close and a repetition of short simple phrases, sometimes interrogatory but usually admonitory.

This isn't only a fancy theory. Jack has Mrs Delgardo's word that aging happens exactly that way, and that fast. It is the very method and the measurable time. Anybody resting upon a secure age – let's say thirty-seven, and thinking: Well, I'm okay for a while, anyway – is just asleep, dreaming in the night, and will awaken to his true state when morning comes.

Mrs Delgardo's group right now is sitting in the day room waiting for the lunch trays.

Like people in other closed communities, jails or prisoner-of-war camps say, inmates of the Nailer tend to form friendships in groups and it is sometimes hard for an outsider to see why members of a particular group clot together, or why a particular person should be a group's leader. Mrs Delgardo was the undisputed leader of a group that you could call impoverished white-collar.

It included Mr Dolly, a round and tiny man of timid disposition. The stock exchange floors and telex machines had been taken away from Mr Dolly rather than he from them. Their withdrawal collapsed such self-confidence as Mr Dolly might once have had, when he was in his prime. But even then he hadn't been a strong force in the money world, as his presence in the Nailer proves. Stock exchange men who have provided for themselves – and who have been untrusting enough to place the provision beyond the reach of their dear offspring – spend their pasture years in their own homes, enjoying the role of patriarch. They are visited by their loved ones as often as they wish to be, not just on Mondays.

Here is Judge Wainwright too. He had believed while on the bench that politics and the judiciary are separate, and had consequently been without a pension since his retirement. He had had a stroke. A sleek man in the courtroom, Judge Wainwright now has the stricken, gaunt face of a tragic actor. His memories were of lawyers who waited upon his words, and he often forgot that the words themselves had lost all value in the absence of the panelled chambers, the clerk's cry and the gowned obeisances.

The judge still felt sure, somehow, that a distinction between right and wrong is important. This is something that can fade from consciousness at the Nailer, where because of the incapacity of the inmates, good and evil in their more striking forms no longer exist.

The judge's companion in Mrs Delgardo's group was often Mr Smith. During his active life in the world Mr Smith might have practised versions of evil. He might have been a Mafia man. Nobody knows for sure. In nursing homes as in jails some inmates will claim colourful career pedigrees which can't be checked out. But Mr Smith does slyly change his name now and then. He's also answered to the names Mr Challedon and Mr Gavrilov while Jack's been dropping in on Mrs Delgardo's gang.

For what it's worth Mr Smith does have an evil appearance as this is understood by the world, one eye hanging lower than the other in his shrunken pouch of a face. He's lost his false teeth since he arrived at the Nailer, bringing the top half of his features closer to the bottom. The lower eye almost touches his chin when he speaks, which he does indistinctly but always with emphasis.

The group has plenty of time to listen and can figure out what Mr Smith says. But the nursing staff, Nurse Pugg in particular, found it simplest to be cheerful and reassuring when Mr Smith spoke to them. Hanging around the Nailer Jack often heard Nurse Pugg calling out: 'Just fine, Mr Smith! Don't worry! Yes, I'll take care of it, whatever it is! Relax!' While Mr Smith limped at her heels mumbling a specific question, almost always about his teeth.

His search for his teeth is the centre of Mr Smith's life. When he finds the teeth the pain of Mr Smith's old age will disappear. So the magical journey seems more important to Jack than the finding of the teeth as an event. It's a quest. It puts a jewel of a day in the future for Mr Smith where there would otherwise be nothing.

Mrs Delgardo's campaign for better food in the Nailer isn't in the same chivalrous category. At mealtimes she'd like to get something on her tray that she would enjoy eating, and the sooner the better.

Most of the Nailer nurses are part-timers, odd peasants untrained and working for very little money, yet with unusual power over lives. The odd-ness of these nurses' characters in the Nailer, quite a public part of the Sutton Medical Wing, made Jack wonder sometimes what nursing homes would be like elsewhere. With his Gothic imagination he was inclined to picture full Dickensian models, shabby houses in remote places run by renegades who took the low pay because they liked the power. Petty tyrants and satraps, gnarled of soul, saddle-tramps of the nursing-home cheap-power territory, and they were always in familiar surroundings wherever they spread their blankets.

In this company Nurse Pugg was a flower of the profession, enrolled in an advanced nursing programme at a university and working at the Nailer as part of a cooperative study course. But she saw patients who behaved child-ishly, as admittedly many Nailerians do, and so she dealt with them as if they were children. She put on a kindergarten-teacher manner to handle everybody. This can break down character.

In Jack's view a scientific experiment could be conducted with a perfectly healthy and responsible group of subjects, for instance corporation lawyers in their best years. First take away their clothes. Give them bleached cotton robes that fasten with tape at the back, making sure that a lot of the tapes are missing. Then put somebody like Nurse Pugg in charge of their lives.

Nurse Pugg is a jolly girl with big eyes and fluffy eyelashes, bouncing breasts and an indomitably kind personality. Say with the corporation law-yers she just behaves normally. She wheels them into the washroom for bowel movements and writes the results on a chart. The lawyers are plunged at once into a system where their minds, thoughts, character and talents are ignored, but their bowel movements, in all likelihood a previously uncon-sidered part of what they do, are dramatically a matter of intense interest to the outside world, indeed their only interesting function.

Nurse Pugg pats their heads and jokily smacks their bottoms when this is going well. A flow of banter invades all conversations, burying them. 'You naughty girl!' she'll say, no matter what somebody else might be saying, and 'Oh you bad, bad boy!' A lawyer could have a personality that can command the attention of a boardroom but if he stands up to command Nurse Pugg his buttocks are revealed in the back and his knees and thighs in front. Speaking without getting up an eloquent lawyer will be addressing a moving target and might say: 'Now, just a minute, miss!' with irresistible authority.

Nurse Pugg can be depended upon to respond with a kind of patter she's perfected, like this: 'Miss? Who's a miss? I'm not a miss, I'm a hit! I'm a big hit, ask my boyfriend!' And she will say, breezing by: 'I'll be back with a pill to make you less grumpy, you naughty boy, don't forget what you were going to tell me!'

When she briskly washes their private parts she'll put them at ease with cries of: 'Oh, this is embarrassing! What would my boyfriend say?' She'll also wipe their noses absent-mindedly. The experiment would see the group of corporation lawyers examined upon admission to the Nailer and then examined again after two years, which is the average lifespan of a Nailerian. Jack feels certain that the standard test for senile dementia (including simple questions like: What year is it? Are you married? How old are you? Where are you now?) would give some of the smart lawyers a few problems.

Nurse Pugg, who is the best nurse in the Nailer, sees signs of everyday humanity in her patients as a source of humour. This is also what makes a chimpanzee a droll creature, its similarity to the human. A patient who might show some enjoyment of a meal, which does not often happen in the Nailer, by the way, is a marvellous glutton, Charles Laughton playing Henry VIII. Everybody hurrying must have an *important appointment*, because in the Nailer there's nothing to do. She will chivvy groups of inmates as *idle lazybones*, reminding them that they have no jobs or roles.

The topper is always the fact that when a male and a female patient are seen together *they're lovers*. That's the big boffo side-splitter, where the resemblance to the human for Nurse Pugg seems most striking. In that sexual domain Nurse Pugg stirs them up regularly with arch accusations of passion, promiscuity and fantastic goings-on. Of course the joshing is derived from her understanding that sexuality among her charges has been utterly extinguished. Somebody older than Nurse Pugg, somebody who listened sometimes, might have been able to learn that nature rarely acts so abruptly. Her spirited forays and shrieks translated for some of the patients into reminders that they were dying. There was often pain in the *they're lovers* game, or as Nurse Pugg saw it cranky refusals to join in the fun.

Mrs Delgardo wasn't always able to avoid the day nurse's steamroller jollity. Mrs Delgardo is a lady, not by birth in a family hierarchy but in the shaping of her character and manner by her experiences over the years, a system of adjustments and abrasions that can produce the most effective gentleness, outer grace combined with inner strength. Some books have been written about Mrs Delgardo, and much poetry was dedicated to her in her day. Age has taken away the Delgardo beauty of face; the body is gone too and now there is just a thin frame in a dressing gown, with only the pale clear eyes remaining, and her mind.

Nailerians are naturally peripatetic. The borrowing and returning of magazines, the little searches for trifles, and the idle journeys to and fro are the occupations of the day. The frail folk were often on their feet, supported only by walkers or canes or crutches. So Jack had made himself a place to lurk in a corner of the day room, not wishing to be responsible for carelessly sending some brittle body crashing to the tiles. The sides of two armchairs enclosed Jack in his corner. It was one of his places of rest in the Sutton, a lair or oasis stop. He could read there, hunkered with his cloak in a tent over a book in a restful green dimness like a desert nomad waiting out a sandstorm. He sometimes napped there, undisturbed. Occasionally he was hit by orange rind or an apple core tossed by some inmate who didn't feel like making the trip to a trash container.

Jack heard the chinks and rattles as Mrs Delgardo's group lifted the aluminium covers from their plates.

'Macaroni and cheese again. Oh dear,' Mrs Delgardo said. Since it was her nature to command men she said: 'Mr Smith, can't anything be done about this food?' Mr Smith mumbled an excuse, that it was a long journey to the telephone, after which there was the difficulty of getting somebody on the outside line who could understand him without teeth.

'I do wish we could have a chop or a beefsteak now and then. Can't you do something on the stock exchange, Mr Dolly? They're giving us cheap food. I suppose what they save on our meals they put in their profits account, is that how the the bookkeeping is done, Mr Dolly?'

The group had been together for a couple of months now. The men were beginning to understand an endearing characteristic of Mrs Delgardo's, her assumption that they were still people of influence. But Mr Dolly said: 'I don't have any money, Mrs Delgardo.'

'None of us has, Mr Dolly, or we wouldn't be here. Surely you don't need money for the stock exchange?'

Jack didn't bother to raise his eyes when he heard quick brisk footsteps, having seen the performance before. Dr Gerald A. Nailer advanced into the room with lots of young tousled hair freshly shampooed but uncombed as if he had been up all night attending the sick. A stethoscope swung from the side pocket of his open white coat. He did the tour wearing a smile of crinkly humour, the trustworthy grey eyes roving with great general compassion but not settling upon individuals.

'Oh goody, here's doctor!' said Nurse Pugg.

'How are we all today, Nurse Pugg?'

'We're all just hunky-dory, doctor!'

'No little problems, Nurse Pugg?'

'Not the tiniest one, doctor.'

'Did we all go poo-poo in the potty this morning, Nurse Pugg?'

'As good as gold, doctor.'

'I'll say bye-bye then. Busy day!'

'Bye-bye, doctor!'

Nurse Pugg heaved a happy sigh. She enjoyed the doctor's visit, which however, had not interrupted Mrs Delgardo's train of thought. She could be heard saying now: 'Yes, we probably do need money, if only to send out for some food or we'll starve to death. I certainly can't eat this lunch.'

'Get hold of the telephone, punks they use today can't understand English. Hung up on me four times.'

'Well, please keep trying, Mr Smith, we all appreciate your efforts. What about the stock exchange, Mr Dolly – will you use London or New York, or can money be made from Toronto?'

'Mrs Delgardo, I can't do anything.'

'But that's nonsense. You're a stock exchange man.'

'Very kind of you to say so. I can look back now and spot places where I made mistakes. It's easy now. I never believed much in the automobile. That was a place I went wrong in 1911. Then aeroplanes in 1922. Such a crazy idea. How could I advise people to invest hard cash in them? *Flying machines!* Then some of my clients wanted a few electronics companies in their portfolios in 1945 but I talked them out of it. Computers in the fifties, same problem.'

'Well, Mr Dolly, you were probably wise. Those things have become most successful, of course, but many people were ruined by them. I can think of several great fortunes that were lost in speculations in motor cars and aircraft. Are you asleep, Judge Wainwright?'

'Resting my eyes.'

'I saw an interesting report on your General Schata in the newspaper today. Is he a Bolshevik or a Fascist? I can never remember. He says a country's honour is like an individual's – much more precious than life. I wonder what he means.'

'He's not my General Schata, Mrs Delgardo. I wish you'd stop calling him my General Schata. I detest the man.'

'He thinks honour is sanctified if it's protected with blood. According to the report in today's newspaper. Can you tell me what that means, Judge Wainwright? I'm curious.'

'I haven't the least idea,' the judge said coldly. 'I suppose he isn't talking about his own blood. Would you excuse me please, Mrs Delgardo? Mr Da Luca likes to have the comics back after lunch.'

'But you do defend General Schata, don't you? You always defend him.'

'No, I don't. He's a legal head of state, that's all. I defend what's legal, Mrs Delgardo. It's a habit of mine.'

'Put a little boom-boom in his limousine,' Mr Smith suggested. 'A couple of pounds of that Czech plastic should do it, the yellow stuff, a gunpowder fuse. Draws a crowd, though, gets the police too excited. Long-range sharp shot. Or poison's good – nothing the matter with poison if you can get close.'

Mr Smith was reading the fashion section of the morning paper. He took an interest in the prices and designs of expensive furs, though their resale value as loot had fallen dramatically since he'd been inside. One of Jack's projects was the improvement of Mr Smith's eye glasses. Jack got the lenses at Currier's Mode Optical, where he also kept a supply of identical frames set aside so that he could switch bifocals on Mr Smith when he was asleep. Mr Smith was now reading fashion articles that caught his fancy, where previously he could only read the full-page furriers' ads and the large-layout headlines. The next step for Jack was the upper lenses, to give Mr Smith better eyesight for distance.

Conversation died while the inmates applied themselves to the food. Jack came out of his hiding place. Mrs Delgardo was austerely reading a little volume of poetry, with her luncheon tray untouched. Mr Smith sat by the window with his head bowed over his plate, using the upper lenses to eat by since the portions at the Nailer are small. Mr Dolly was eating also, but glumly, and casting respectful, unhappy glances at Mrs Delgardo, while Judge Wainwright had completed the first few steps of his journey to return the comics to Mr Da Luca, which would take nearly half an hour there and back, on two cherrywood sticks.

From the window Mr Smith sat at it was possible to see a part of the world outside the Sutton. Through a vertical shaft between the soaring blocks of the Parthenon Tower a busy highway on the Ottawa outskirts was visible as if framed, with toy cars and trucks and tankers carrying folk and freight in and out of the nation's capital.

Jack intended to drop in on Elmo Apse's lunch of bread and grapes, cheese and wine, to see if the rat man's guest would be Mrs Albreda Hoeglin or someone else. Albreda was the civilizing influence, Jack thought, but the beneficiary was probably younger. Elmo Apse would behave according to his character and his nature.

First Jack went shopping in a drug mart on the Concourse, looking for items that would introduce elements of reality to a pink lover's world, some-one young. Denture adhesive, haemorrhoid suppositories and rectal itch ointment, perfect. He slipped into his roomy pockets a bunch of varicose vein stockings, hairpiece deodorant and a packet of colostomy bags, adult diapers and a hernia truss. He found something for back problems, a grue-some girdle, the straps and buckles of which were terrible enough to bring the balloon down all by themselves. Then while the pharmacist on duty was demonstrating a clock radio elsewhere Jack wrote up a number of labels for prescription medications to treat ailments of a fanciful nature, using vita-min pills and liquids to fill the vials. Two capsules every day for Awful Dropsy. Gargle depilatory for mouth hair. One tablet after meals to control foul wind discharge from the ears, apply the lotion directly to the syphilitic chancre, coat the gangrenous toe twice daily, et cetera. Not that he expected anybody to stop and read it all or study the exhibits and be appalled. Much of the time lately Jack was working just to please himself.

He had noticed this about his outlook in recent days, that he was devel-oping a clown's attitude toward life-and-death matters. He thought he might be on the mend.

Chapter 4

Mr Goof-it

BECAUSE OF HAVING learning mixed into his growth through Horsy Stacpole instead of segregated at an impersonal and often hostile place called a
school, and because of the breadth of Horsy's curriculum, Jack was a well
educated lad. Well, it was a private education, a one-on-one classroom – we
could all have been well-educated with that advantage and privilege.

He intersected with the board of education's official programme regularly, sitting the examinations and writing essays and answers in copperplate
script, very rapidly. He had a feeling at these times that the authorities were
aware of him as an unhappy boy, and compiled special simple examinations
for him in kindness.

Jack's father's greyhound business started to make good money as soon as
the first litters were trained. The success could have been a result of how he
exercised the animals, rather than from the breeding itself which was ortho-
dox. He ran them over landscape that was contoured like an egg carton,
rock-strewn and treacherous, with rabbit and groundhog holes everywhere
for unwary runners to snap their legs in. When dogs who'd grown used to
this terrain saw a French track for the first time, a broad sickle of sward that
was totally flat, no skunks or porcupines to distract, no swamps to swim,
some dog idea of heaven in their minds was realized. They were able to zip
around the French courses at record speeds.

It happened that Mr Clemmaknohke's success in the dog business did
not suit his wife, Jack's mother. She'd been willing to join him in the wilder-
ness while he worked an itch or fad out of his system. The idea of a permanent exile with him and his dogs, with Jack and the wild and shabby Horsy
Stacpole, appalled her.

One day Hahka Clemmaknohke drove Jack's mother to the station with
all her luggage. That parting itself was civilized. There were promises of
frequent visits. Jack's mother protested a few times that she wouldn't need
so much money, a few thousand to get her resettled in Montreal and then as

income a third of the net yield from the dog business. She had their old apartment above the shoe store free of rent and expense.

But lawyers had to enter the picture for the divorce and after they bowed out Jack's parents hated each other. Now just like a normal child Jack loved his parents, but Meg Clemmaknohke didn't want a child with her in her new life. His father's routines could accommodate Jack on the farm without inconvenience, for as long as the boy cared to stay. But his father had no time for Jack, nor any interest in him.

Jack had nowhere to drop an anchor and no assurance of his substance. How does a person provide himself with a background from such circumstances, a place and tribe?

His father's grandparents had come from the Balkans, from a coastal duchy named Taleaturova on the Black Sea between the Bulgarian and Romanian borders. Taleaturovans included, among others, Bulgarians and Romanians, who of course in turn were composed of diverse races and numerous former tribes.

So it was true that Jack had the right to a kinship with the Taleaturovan culture, whatever form it had taken. This never attracted him much. Before the First World War, Taleaturova could only be found on expensive and detailed maps. After the war, following Romania's acquisition of Bessarabia, Banat and Bukovina, and even prior to its yielding of parts of southern Dobrudja to Bulgaria, Taleaturova could not be found on any maps at all. The people and the land continued to exist, no doubt, but they had become invisible to the rest of the world.

That farm where Jack spent his childhood is in the township of Elzevir and Grimsthorpe near a county road called the French Settlement Line. French settlement had indeed occurred in the area a century earlier. The farmers there now are all English though, with names like Marshon and Leveck, Sanpeer and Dellacraw. The house itself is a solid limestone structure, very like the prosperous farmhouses that are common much farther south.

It had been built in the later decades of the last century by a wealthy Belleville merchant, a widower whose large family of daughters married indigent and unscrupulous men. The merchant, it was said, wanted a place of retirement remote enough to protect him from the frequent visits of these families, their sharp interest in his health and their gifts of home-cooked food that tasted strange. The last stone was hardly mortared in place when the strange heirs managed to agree with each other long enough to ask a court of law to commit the merchant to an asylum, and the court readily agreed that building an expensive mansion in such an unimaginable place so far north was an act of lunacy. The unfortunate merchant was committed and his assets sold. All the in-laws of the daughters moved in together, and interbred and poisoned each other and drank themselves to death as was customary in those days in that part of Ontario.

Jack's father bought the house and land at a good price in 1969 from the remnants of a sect called Noah's Children who had acquired it with the understanding that they would be responsible for repopulating the world after every city on earth was destroyed by flood in 1968, which had not occurred.

There were times as a child when Jack thought he might be a greyhound. He did observe, though, that he was fed inside the house, sitting up at the table, and slept in a bed and not in the kennels. And that Horsy Stacpole didn't give the other dogs rides on his shoulders. But in times of depression this evidence of his separateness wasn't reassuring. Jack worried then that he was an inferior kind of greyhound like the sick puppies who were sometimes given beds inside the house in winter. He moved clumsily, uprightly, instead of lithely on all fours, and was carried on Horsy's shoulders because he had only half the regular number of legs, and he was fed inside the house because he couldn't get his flat, defective face into a dog dish.

Jack's father, who was ugly, didn't allow mirrors in the house. It was likely that Jack's pretty mother kept a mirror or two under lock and key. One day he realized that the repulsive mask he sometimes saw distorted on the inside of a darkened window or on shiny kitchenware was himself. He saw the face with frightening clarity for the first time, when he could barely walk, in the rearview mirror of his father's truck. He cried with precocious fear, although of course at that age he had no standard of comparison, except to dogs and grown-ups. There were bleak incidents, as when he first laid eyes on the pretty children that his school books told him were the other humans of his age in the world.

Jack inherited all his father's ugliness and got nothing from his mother's side. It's not just a lanky, gangling body that happens to be out of fashion – indeed Jack's is the thin hairy form of the spider. There's a melancholy bottom on the face, weighting the jaw and lower lip and leaving big stalagmite teeth exposed. The eyes can suggest guilt and dark intentions because of their simple placement in his skull, close together and barely separated by Jack's prow of nose, and their colour, a brilliant black. On his best days he'll get a second look from policemen and the security folk in the Sutton.

He had to practise patience with his fellow man, to give them time to get to know him. He's good to know. It isn't so difficult now for Jack, since he succeeded in developing vanity, as soon as he understood what it was and that he needed it. The fact he learnt is that so-called character weaknesses are often more helpful for survival purposes than the nominal character strengths. In Jack's case that splendid weakness vanity provided him with useful illusions, as it does for plenty of people, which are as good as truth. In the vital realm of appearance, vanity picks the lowliest up, telling them over the years that they aren't so bad, and maybe even rather attractive with those green stumps of teeth, the palaeolithic forehead and invigorating halitosis and whatever else they have to their disadvantage in a world that projects ruthlessly perfect norms. No virtue performs as well.

On his way to join Elmo Apse's luncheon date Jack stopped at the apartment of Ralph Jim Trasker the TV evangelist. From Ralph Jim's study came a regular heavy thumping noise: *whack, whack, whack*. The shower was on and Jack could hear the TV sound from Paul's room. Paul is Ralph Jim's son, who's ten years old and at this time of day should have been at school. Sue Ellen, Ralph Jim's wife, was taking the shower and Jack sidled into the bathroom for a few minutes to watch. When Sue Ellen shut the water off and stepped out of the tub Jack left and looked in the study.

Ralph Jim had placed a Bible on a folded blanket on the carpet and was kneeling on the floor and lashing the book with a length of lead pipe. There was fury in his punishing arm and sweat on his forehead. Jack had seen the exercise before. As John Lennon of the Beatles so truthfully remarked, everything is the opposite of what it is, isn't it, Harry? Ralph Jim was a busy showman on a full national network with his mind in the heavens usually, where it was supposed to be. Bibles to him were as mittens to a child in kindergarten. He bought them by the carton but a TV evangelist can't go on camera carrying a new Bible. When Ralph Jim went on camera he would be carrying an old beat-up Bible, a long-time survivor of constant use and frequent loving hugs.

The book's case cracked open and a signature or two of pages spilled out on the carpet. Ralph Jim assembled them reverently and hung the lead pipe, which had a loop of string on it, to a cuphook on the side of his desk. His script in one hand and the Bible in the other, he began rehearsing stances and punchy exhortations. Jack went into Paul's room and found the fat boy sitting back on his spine wearing jeans and a denim shirt, watching the TV screen with red eyes. A box of Kleenex was by his chair.

'I just came in,' Jack told the boy.

'Oh hello, Jack,' Paul said, not turning. He knew he couldn't see Jack. 'I have a cold. What time is it?'

On the TV screen an alert and amiably well-spoken individual walked along a vaulted corridor delivering a lecture on the architecture of Venice. It was an educational channel. The Traskers had a Family Edit switch on their TV that censored channels. 'Twelve,' said Jack.

'That's what I thought. Where are you?' Paul threw a TV guide into Jack's lap. 'The turtles should be on at twelve, shouldn't they?' Jack confirmed that. The child stared with rheumy dejection at the screen. 'Imagine somebody who'd rather watch this garbage. This is like being at school. Then they put on all the good shows at night, but I have to be in bed at nine.' Jack agreed again, the TV shows that would appeal to a ten-year-old are reserved for prime time. He went across to the TV and switched Family Edit out. Jack had a sense of the fat boy as a battery chicken, spending his childhood penned in this expensive apartment in the Parthenon Tower of the Sutton. The Sutton as a whole is certainly a gigantic and nearly fabulous evolution from a village market. However, the Tower is not an evolution from a village. Ralph Jim and Sue Ellen had no circle of friends in the Parthenon Tower and didn't know their next-door neighbours' names.

Their social arrangements were more sophisticated. Paul's weren't, however. For sure he did not play in the Tower with the village children of his own age. For Paul as a rule there was just school and homework and TV.

'We could watch a *Flintstones*,' Jack said, running the remote. Paul wanted to watch a *Happy Days*. The boy was in the onset of pubescence with its great mysteries spreading in his mind and body. Up to a month ago he'd been a solid Fred Flintstone fan but lately he was beginning to pay solemn attention to sexual relationships as these are taught on the *Happy Days* reruns.

Sue Ellen did her best. She bought her son healthy fruit juices and made him salads and provided him with charts and advice about calories and weight. But she's no match in influence for the teams of intelligent people who work for the travelling medicine show. Paul looked at a world of actors who were his own age in magical situations which awaited him somewhere outside his parents' apartment and discipline. These friends wanted Paul to join them in their lavish land of cereals and colas, yummy spaghettis, cookies, french fries, chips and nachos, burgers and bubblegums, and a hundred snacks of enchantment and fantasy fast foods. Sue Ellen often cries out in despair: 'The big boom's not good for you, Paul. Have a glass of orange juice!'

'Fonzie just snaps his fingers and the girls kiss him.'

'Well, *Happy Days* is a comedy programme, Paul. That is meant to be funny. Kissing girls in regular life is complicated.'

'I guess. I like the way Fonzie does it.'

Thirty seconds of the big boom message doesn't wipe out everything Sue Ellen says to her son. She could step in with a thirty-second message of her own and keep his mind in balance. She doesn't have a million-dollar budget to get to the boy though. What wipes her out as an influence is Paul's actual imprisonment in the apartment, his being chained to the chair in front of the TV. That form of brainwashing was pioneered in the Stalinist prison systems and has been adopted for TV by the big boom people. It's a matter of flashing lights in the face, the creation of boredom and anxiety, guilt and desire, and then promising forgiveness and freedom or threatening punishment and dire outcomes, the whole routine being mercilessly repeated in an unvarying pattern over long hours until it makes score marks on the mind.

At the end of the show Paul swung his legs off the bed and stared unhappily in Jack's direction. Said he: 'Jack, I don't want to know about bottery, okay?'

Jack muted the commercial and threw Paul the remote. He didn't wish to appear to be a hard salesman of adult ideas, so he gave a mild answer. 'Well, it gets you out and gives you reasons for climbing hills and crossing rivers, that's all. I wouldn't want to know botany either if I had to study it from a book.'

'Climbing hills and rivers is what I don't like about bottery,' said Paul. He then lay back on the pillows again, honking into a Kleenex in his left hand and running down the channels with the remote. But he kept the sound off, which encouraged Jack, who told himself: I shouldn't shy away from this child every time we meet. I know what to do for him. I've seen it done before. I should commit myself here, to this, instead of spending time on questionable routines and duties like that stupid Robin Hood stuff.

'It could be something else. There's good rough country near enough, no more than five miles past the stables. What about captains, do you like captains?'

'Policemen?' The kid was defensive and uneasy but trying to be polite, talking to Jack and watching the channels change.

'No, I mean captains of the ocean sea. We would travel long distances on foot, of course. But you wouldn't have to walk it all. Also, you might have great treats – not every day, naturally, but often enough. I can't say what the great treats might be because only you would know that.'

However, young Paul Trasker had no interest in these treats. He turned his head toward Jack to answer, extending his neck like an aggressive bird.

'I don't want to know anything about captains of the ocean sea, okay, Jack? Or bottery, or Jesus either. My daddy talks about Jesus, so I don't need someone else to talk to me about Jesus, okay?'

Being a courteous youngster by nature he was then instantly conscious of having spoken rudely and he added, heaving a discontented sigh: 'I know you're only trying to be nice, Jack. They think I'm still a baby, you see. I'll be okay when I get bigger.'

Jack's most troubling feeling about Paul Trasker came alive here, that when he looked at the fat lad he was looking at himself as a child in the coils of pain. The release from the same coils was freely given to me, he thought, getting nervous, and I owe it now. I should repay what I owe.

Paul found another *Happy Days* on one of the higher channels. The sound came on, politely low. Jack when he spoke had to talk over the voices of the happy kids and their happy parents and he felt somewhat loud on his own account also.

'How will you be okay when you're bigger, Paul? TV won't be any better when you're fourteen. You'll have read five books, two of them by Stephen King. Memorizing poetry is gone, so you'll never in your life have lines and verses popping into your head to cheer you up or help you out. You won't know what the capital of New Zealand is when you're fourteen if you're a regular kid, Paul, or where Ceylon went to, or Siam – which isn't so bad, but you also won't know who Cicero was, and that'll be hard on you. You'll need a calculator to do basic math and a CD-ROM player to use an encyclopaedia. Everything you learn will be from pictures, a TV or a computer monitor, so you'll be normal high-schooler, which is a stone age adolescent. How will you be okay? Your intelligence would like something to do but it has nothing to work on, has it, because you haven't put much of anything in your head. My guess is you won't be the Fonz when you're bigger, if that's what you're hoping for. You'll be lucky if you're Fred Flintstone.'

Paul did not respond to this. His aspect was rheumy and disconsolate, but not more so than before. However, the TV sound came up a couple more decibels.

Jack had been when he was Paul's age given a rapture that can happen in childhood but never again, like a wine tasted in a dream which can't be found in the real world. But it's in that world somewhere because its colour can be glimpsed now and then out of the corner of an eye. Sometimes in sadness a hint of its taste will appear, on the tongue or in the mind.

This had been young Jack's by gift from the wild old preacher Revd Stacpole in tramps over the egg-carton hills of Elzevir, in the lessons that were like stories and puzzles to be enjoyed and solved and, copiously, in the three great treats of the child's life then. The second of these, in the order that they could happen, was a chocolate chip ice-cream sandwich from MacMurray's store in Queensborough. The first was the ride on Horsy's shoulder when they fared too far and Jack's skinny legs quit on him. The third and rarest great treat of those rare days was the two extra hours that Horsy now and then agreed to stay of an evening when Jack's parents would be late home.

Any one of these three gifts could make a whole day blissful for the earnest child. He thought of them protectively as gifts. They had to come to him of themselves. Horsy wasn't allowed to know that the horsy ride was a great treat – he would do it more often if he knew, and ruin it.

Sometimes on a long excursion – especially during botany lessons with the nimble preacher darting from one interesting plant or shrub to the next, exclaiming and discoursing, his shiny old cleric's suit flapping and his rough-cut hair flying – Horsy could forget the small boy's legs for a while. Jack was forbidden by his own rule to ask to be taken up. Neither did he allow himself to betray any sign or stumble of tiredness.

Then inevitably Revd Stacpole would recollect himself, and bend to peer into Jack's ugly little mug, fretful and questioning. 'But my dear child, how can you bear it? You've been afoot since two o'clock and we've walked hundreds of miles. Well, dear me, that's much too far a ramble for a small fellow. Come on up here, up, up! Now! Next question! Through the village or across the river, which way home for us?'

When that bridge or village question came it was often within a flow of other questions – 'What colour would you call this jessamine, white or yellow?' – to which Revd Stacpole didn't necessarily await answers. Jack always chose the bridge. The village was a part of a gift and had to come freely. There were other parts too, like whether or not they went into the store. But once inside the store the teacher was wholly dependable. Unfailingly he ambled over to the freezer and reached out their two treats, the chocolate chip sandwich for the child and a caramel cone for himself.

Revd Stacpole's promises were likewise always scrupulously kept, both large and small. Decades went by before Jack understood that being a keeper of promises, especially to children, has more in it of strength of character than of courteous behaviour. For Jack's father, taciturn and selfish, promises were only talk and all talk was cheap. His mother often used promises as utterances of generosity and expressions of her mood and she was annoyed that she should be reminded of them later – as if they were no more than contracts – when her mood was different.

In one of those haphazard little vignettes without context and tintype tableaux that Jack's memory offers as its sparse record of his life, Revd Stacpole speaks as follows: 'Tomorrow will be arduous for us I'm afraid, young lad.

'I told them I'd be at the Hazzards Corner church for one. But if you can survive the hike out there I'll take you up for all the journey home. Then I must call in at MacMurray's for my paint brushes. Your father picks your mother up at the station at six, so I will stay to eight. We'll survive it all I'm sure if we rely on our strength of mind.

'I'll be strong as a horse tomorrow, and you must be brave as a lion. That's our plan. When you wake up in the morning be sure to remember that you'll be a lion all day. Asiatic, not African. I'll be there at the usual time after I've had a pail of water and a few mouthfuls of hay.'

That meant all three great treats to come in one day. That day was tomorrow, which would happen soon. His happiness was a lump in the child's breast, not unlike pain. The dream wine was so heavy in his mind that he had to let his mouth hang open to breathe air.

Yet those brief hours of the enchanted day were so profligate with rapture that more came to him. There was a girl in yellow he thought of often at that time. He had childish wishes about the girl in yellow.

He wanted her to believe him taller than he was, and stronger, and more heroic; which less than an hour later the girl in yellow did believe, looking directly at Jack on that misted summer day. Moreover she spoke gently to him. It was the best moment of Jack's childhood and, as it turned out, his life.

Paul had been scowling into his Kleenex, waiting on a commercial. Now having come to a decision he put the mute on *Happy Days*.

'Jack?'

'Just on my way out now.'

'Wellington. Sri Lanka for Ceylon. What else? Oh yes, Thailand.'

This chastened Jack of course, but he wasn't much surprised. The teacher in him was delighted. He uttered a few whoops of praise and took his leave, but turned at the door. 'What about Cicero?'

'Never heard of her. Yabba-dabba-doo, okay?' Paul Trasker lay back on the pillows and made his satisfaction at Jack's departure very plain with a noisy exhalation of relief. Then he turned the sound on *Happy Days* up full.

He had wanted the girl in yellow to believe him to be a solitary walker of the country lanes and courser of the Precambrian hills. It was a childish wish, but he was a child. Later he learnt that mature men of enviable aplomb do require that women cherish much more fantastic beliefs about them. He is on Horsy's shoulder and they're approaching a cedar fence that encloses a backyard patio with a swimming pool. The pool identifies it as the country cottage of town people. They pass the fence, just on the other side of the Black, when they take the bridge route home.

Jack's head bobs past at the level of the fence top. It is his habit to glance to his left at the people in the backyard. Usually it's a man and a woman, elderly and indistinct, on chaises. Sometimes there's a girl and a dog with them. He can always remember that she wears yellow. Her hair is dark and lies on the back of her neck in a single plait. If the girl is there Jack will lean forward against Revd Stacpole's head and swing his elbows. She looks up at him with respectful solemnity, squinting against the summer sun which has laid freckles across the top of her nose. She's about ten.

Jack's intense infant hope is that these backyard folk, especially the girl – since they can't see the horsy – believe him to be out alone. That would be so magical, he thinks, such powerful homage, if their respectful looks did come from such a belief about him, as he passes. But she just mutely stares, so he can't know.

For the next scene Mr Memory, who usually uses old 1920s sixteen-millimetre if he uses moving pictures at all, is focused and detailed. He has splurged on colour film and excellent sound is included. Revd Stacpole's ancient walking boots are noisy on the lane gravel. On the patio all three are present. She sits beside the man's chair with a picture book on her lap. This is where Jack's memory of yellow comes from – a yellow dress with a big collar and sleeves, and yellow buttons at the wrists and neck. Nothing would have happened as usual, except that today the woman is dozing. The girl reaches across and touches the woman's knee.

'Look, grandma, look! It's the tall boy!'

The woman, though, mumbles and doesn't awake. The man's newspaper is taken by a puff of wind and he struggles to fold it. Only the girl watches the tall boy who, as someone weary now from the long day and with miles still to go, meets her eye and ventures a small tired smile to acknowledge her reference to him. Whereat she shyly nods and in a small polite voice she says: 'Hello.'

He had tomorrow, which was already hurting his breast bone with happiness. The new event was a miracle gift, so large and rich that it stunned the youngster. His mouth hung open and his eyes shone. The joy of the moment was so luminous that as a man he could reach back and get ease from it. When they passed there next the house had reverted to the habitants. The fence was gone. Four old Chevy trucks were parked on the patio. The pool well had been stacked with winter firewood that included the fence cedar.

Ralph Jim wasn't in his study; he was in Sue Ellen's bedroom. The door was locked from inside and Jack had to try a few keys before he found the right one. Ralph Jim had Sue Ellen against the wall naked, with her terrycloth robe in a puddle on the floor. The evangelist was bent into his wife, his mouth down on one of Sue Ellen's plump breasts, his hands spreadeagled along her rump and upper thighs. Jack said: 'If you wouldn't mind saving it, Ralph Jim. I have to get to a lunch and I'm late now.'

Sue Ellen disengaged herself and put her robe on, not provocatively but not hurriedly either. She knew that she was okay. She gave her husband a peck and a smile of promise for a future occasion and said: 'Hello, Jack.' Ralph Jim, not so acquiescent by nature, stared blindly down at his empty cheated hands. 'Oh, Jack,' said he then. 'I'll be with you soon. I wonder if you'd be kind enough to wait in my study. This is my wife's bedroom. I'll be out directly.'

Jack did not reply. 'Are you still here?' Ralph Jim asked.

'Yes.'

'We can talk in my study.'

'Lead the way then. I haven't arranged any time in my schedule for waiting.'

You have probably seen Ralph Jim – he pronounces his name Rafe – if only in the instants before turning him off. He's a short man in real life. The mane of white hair and the swimming, dependable eyes were at the level of Jack's chest approximately. If they custom-made people especially to fit TV camera lenses they would make them Ralph Jim Trasker's size.

In the study Jack said, aggrievedly: 'I'd like to know how come you can grapple Sue Ellen every time the whim moves you. I'd like to know where your reserves come from. Some nights myself I'm too worn out to kick my shoes off.'

'You interrupted a tender moment. God, I hate that. I hate it.'

'It makes me wonder whether you're pulling your weight.'

'Sue Ellen always seems to have her clothes off when you announce yourself, doesn't she, Jack.' The evangelist's honest face was flushed. There was a film of anger and protest on his eyes. His hands were down by his sides with the elbows bent and the fingers open and trembling as if still reaching with desire for some softly silken thing.

Apart from not pulling his weight, according to Jack's suspicions anyway, the bad habit of Ralph Jim Trasker's life was swearing. When he was in a wrathful mood he swore; it was his way of letting off steam and yielding to evil. He wasn't, though, a convincing user of strong language, and could never for instance manage the brutal explosion of lower lip from upper teeth that gives the consonant bulge in *furk* its awful force. Ralph Jim's version was softer than the word as it is pronounced by hardened regular users, with an elision of that guttural which is the true heart of obscenity to many minds. What Ralph Jim said was *fork*. His body punished him for this evil speech. He got belly aches. His stomach began secreting guilty acid even as the first terrible syllables fell from his lips.

'Jesus sees you all the time.'

Ralph Jim said: 'Jesus is different. Jesus doesn't talk. I don't have to drop whatever I'm doing for Jesus. I nearly had a forking heart attack. The last time Sue Ellen was doing her freedom yoga, no clothes. The time before was the body shave – that's a very embarrassing memory, Jack. Didn't you give her the sun-lamp, in fact? I can't remember a visit of yours when she had her goddamn clothes on.'

The perturbed man took a daily journal from his desk, shooting looks of pain toward where he thought Jack's voice came from. Ralph Jim's mobility of countenance, his expressiveness, is his great attraction in the TV medium. He looks grey and mature and yet at the same time boyish. The public responds to wisdom and it responds to cuteness. His boyish aspect was emphatic now, that of a thwarted youth, the smooth face congested, the eyes rebellious and the mouth trembling and sulky.

'You think swearing makes you macho, don't you, Ralph Jim.'

'No, I don't. I don't.'

'You're afraid folk will think you're a sissy because you're a preacher, aren't you.'

'No, I'm not. That's not true. I don't care what people think about me. I honestly don't.'

'Well, the swearing doesn't make you macho.'

'I don't care. I am how I am. I'm a sinner. I never said I was perfect. I'm not trying to impress you with the swearing.'

'That's good, because it doesn't impress me. It doesn't make me think of you as macho. You know very well that swearing's not good for you, it tears your stomach up. It's a regular vice, like drug addiction or alcoholism, isn't it. First it ruins your body and then it begins nibbling on your mind. First it gives you a gut ache and then it starts making you crazy.'

'I don't care if somebody thinks I'm a sissy.'

'That's good.'

'He'd be wrong, though, that's all. I'm not a sissy. I used to play a mean game of street shinny when I was a kid. I broke my leg a few times, I broke ribs, I thought at one time I'd go in for pro sports.'

Jack didn't speak. Ralph Jim found his page in the diary. Said he vehemently: 'There's all the forking difference in the world between a spiritual visitation and somebody who appears behind your shoulder at a private conjugal moment and tells you to save it. All the difference in the world.'

'I'm pushed for time, Ralph Jim. I have to go to a lunch.'

'All right. Tell me – what's the nature of your power?'

A wrong answer to a question like this could make Ralph Jim unhappy for days. Wrong answers were those nearest to Jack's understanding of the truth. Jack's experience was that short replies were the best. Ralph Jim could meditate on the terse responses and come up with answers that fitted his needs.

Jack said: 'My power is very limited, there's practically none in fact. Its nature has to do with light.'

'You told me that the power is so great it is incomprehensible.'

'No, I didn't. I said I wouldn't try to explain the phenomenon because it is difficult to understand.'

'I could understand it if I got a simple explanation.'

'Well, I can't give you one. Some things can't be explained simply, Ralph Jim. Most things worth knowing can't be explained simply. For instance? What can't be explained simply, you'd like to know, okay. Most large objects, say anything in the nature of a cosmos or a galaxy. Or any aspect of a large object, let's say light from the sun. The subject isn't simple and so a simple explanation won't work for it. That's why we have myths, to make simple explanations work. The strange part is that myths are full of monsters and giants, yet in the real world we had predators so big that they wouldn't fit in the Concourse today, and they could get enough to eat. The sun can make that happen again, Ralph Jim, but it isn't a simple process, in the why and how and what. Giving people simple explanations is like telling them lies, most of the time, if you want my opinion.'

Ralph Jim's hand of its own volition moved to the trusty Bible on his desk. 'We have all the explanations we need.'

'Okay.'

'The simple answer is that you're spreading light?'

A whimper was forced from the lips of the invisible presence. 'No. I didn't say that, Ralph Jim. Here's what I said.'

'Never mind. You have a luncheon engagement. I can subdue the demons. I can wrestle 'em.'

The preacher's hand moved from the Bible's binding to his stomach, just beneath the ribcage. The acid was roiling there. Said he, reading from the diary: 'You could take Mrs Kaldy, at ten-thirty a.m. next Friday.' He added: 'We're making very good progress with Mrs Kaldy. Her needs are simple and we're fortunate in being able to satisfy them.'

Jack remained silent.

'You're doing a fine job.'

Still nothing from Jack. 'Are you here?'

'Yes. It's always Mrs Kaldy for me, isn't it? I come in today and you have the time and energy for frolicking with your wife. Do you ever take Mrs Kaldy yourself any more, Ralph Jim?'

'Indeed I do. We're making progress.'

'You're still writing yourself in for Mrs Kaldy, are you?'

'I had two appointments last month. You had two. We're doing fair shares with her.'

'I had three last month.'

'Well, give or take one or two, it balances out. The important point is that we're making excellent progress. Her self-esteem is rising and she's improving in all other areas of her life, which is what always happens when basic needs are regularly attended to. Feed the hungry, clothe the nude.'

'I get the feeling sometimes I'm carrying Mrs Kaldy on my back all alone.'

'Well, you aren't. I've got one for Aphrodite the Narcissist.'

'When?' Jack asked at once very eagerly.

'You're so human, Jack, aren't you,' Ralph Jim said, kneading his stomach where the post-swearing acid flowed and burned. 'The Narcissist at the same time Saturday, or do you need a break in there?'

Aphrodite the Narcissist is the occupant of apartment 1318, a high-priced condo that's packaged with a winter unit in Florida. Her rooms are furnished in French regency rococo, chairs and couches with scallop-shell backs and flowing silk wall-hangings. The bed is oval and has a luminous blue canopy. A mirror's inlaid in the canopy top with two hinged wings that are adjustable. On the floor is a perfectly white lambswool rug. Aphrodite is usually to be found lying on the snow-white rug playing with her coal-black poodle, Mr Poodle.

'Saturday's fine. I never claimed to be better than human, keep that in mind.'

'I remember. Don't say anything more.'

'All right.'

'I feel sick. My stomach. Oh, my stomach, the pain'

Jack felt that he'd picked up a useful smattering of medical lore, including psychology, from hanging around the Nailer and the Medical Wing. 'See how it is,' he explained to Ralph Jim, 'the relief gets shorter, the punishment longer, the side effect balloons all out of proportion. Pretty soon it'll be hardly any relief to speak of from the swearing, and an acid stomach like rats eating you in there that hangs on for days. Then you're getting crazy too, you see.'

'No need to disturb Sue Ellen on your way out, by the way. She'll be dressing.'

'I know she'll be dressing.'

'Well, if you would be kind enough not to disturb her,' said Ralph Jim, speaking quite stiffly.

Jack's relationship with Ralph Jim Trasker was like that, variable in the amount of mutual respect that existed between them, high on one side when low on the other, and vice versa. Most days Jack felt that Ralph Jim was a slot of genuine sincerity in the TV listings, but he thought on occasion too that he was wasting his time, working for just another fake of the airwaves. Ralph Jim could be glum, and tight about Sue Ellen and Jack's access to her, as he was now, but then on days that he felt joyous he could barely be restrained from falling down and kissing the sailor man's feet. Jack slipped into Sue Ellen's bedroom before leaving but she was already wrapped in a dressing-gown and bent with absorption over a small silver tray of bottles and brushes, painting her toenails.

Every medical service known to the science is available in the Medical Wing, which Jack crossed into after stopping for a black coffee at Rob's Snackery. You can purchase an excellent set of transplants in this centre if you're in the market, from a penis to a mop of hair. Or you can have your face improved, or your personality, or your sex. You can have nearly anything your heart desires. Indeed back in the seventies you could have had a new heart, while it was a fashionable operation, but today we don't have that particular option. We'll probably have it on offer for you by the time skirt lengths go above the knee again. You may purchase Teflon replacements for the valves in your old heart meanwhile, and they have a choice of systems for reaming and blowing out your heart arteries, should that be your need. The Sutton Medical Centre doctors are famous for charm, so it is all accomplished with the minimum of cost in anxiety.

On his walk along the Concourse Jack was surprised to see the Wake-Up Man at work already. Usually the Wake-Up Man didn't put in an appearance until the late afternoons. He was standing outside a patisserie eating croissants daintily from a paper bag. He said to the crowd, as Jack came within earshot: 'All you people! Stop thinking about sex and money and let's get on the ball here, okay?'

He chewed quietly until Jack was abreast of him. A well-groomed salesman from Dobbin Tailors was making long busy strides in the same direction. The Wake-Up Man said to the salesman, since Jack was invisible of course: 'Sooner or later they'll bury you in the ground, or else they'll burn you up and put what's left of you in an urn. How does that appeal to you? Why don't you slow down a little and give it some thought?'

Jack's never been attracted to cynicism as a state of mind, although like everybody else he has dark moods. He doesn't believe, for instance, that mankind is the wickedest form of life on earth. Certain arachnida in the spider group are much more wicked by instinct and what's worse they make no effort to improve themselves. The world could have become a place of unimaginable horror with those spiders as the dominant species instead of the smart monkey. Even as an invisible man who drifts through locked doors and sees everything Jack can still feel plenty of affection for the two-legged species on a good day.

Still, one doesn't need to be of a mind with Douglas T. Harder – a grouch and snarly misanthrope – to believe that a woman will, from time to time and from natural instinct, check out a man's bathroom medicine cabinet if she's given a chance. She will always do this, as the stars wheel in the firmament, as tides ebb and flow, as the creatures of the earth are born and die. In the Hoeglin bathroom medicine cabinet Jack found a fever thermometer, Band-Aids, Rolaids, mineral oil and Q-tips and a small bottle of aspirin. So neat and blameless a medicine cabinet isn't natural, Jack thought, and no woman deserves to be so disappointed in here, as he filled the narrow shelves with his ugly purchases from the drugstore.

The invisible man was in good time. Apse had assembled the lunch on a tray in the kitchen, with the grapes in a Hopi bowl for dessert. His guest might have been late, but Elmo Apse was at ease as usual, smoking a panatela and reading a magazine. Other people did not affect the ceremony of this man's life.

He presently put down the magazine. In the kitchen he reached a cocktail shaker out of the refrigerator and poured himself a small one.

Jack was a little surprised, at first, when Apse opened the door to a dumpy girl. What's this, Jack asked himself, is Apse now on a person-to-person relationship with the female sex? But then he saw that the girl wasn't dumpy, only fashionably dressed. We were having a fashion for clothing in layers. She peeled off her dumpiness in layers of shawls, scarves and wraps, and she turned out to be a pretty girl with a snub-nosed face, apologizing for her lateness with merry carelessness. Her manner was one of control, a kind of nervous self-confidence. She wore a plain blue dress of calf length with wide sleeves and flat-heeled shoes. Her hair was dark brown and straight, tied with a fillet.

While she sat and chatted imperiously Jack took advantage of Apse's absences in the kitchen to tousle the girl's hair. He threw bread crumbs in her lap. He also jogged her elbow, so that she spilled some of her martini on her dress. He wanted her to go into the bathroom to tidy up.

He'd left the bathroom medicine cabinet door in there wide open, so that she'd be reminded of her instinct to check it out. Indeed she faced and saw the shelves as soon as she was across the threshold, and she did rise on her toes to peer and poke. With a student's gravity, she unrolled the truss. Going pale, she choked back a scream. 'Ecch!' the girl said. She read the labels on the odious products one by one. 'Gross, gross!' she murmured, aghast, and 'Oh help, no!' and 'Awful!' and 'How wicked!' She looked sick and alarmed.

Jack waited confidently for her to flee the dire place. Instead when she had examined everything she closed the cabinet door and began to tidy her dress and comb her hair as if she'd been given no message. She studied her snub-nosed face at close range for blemishes, wanting it to be more attractive. When she left the bathroom at last he heard her cry out in the forested living room: 'I love your place, Elmo! So natural!'

What does it take from the pharmacy to cure the madness of romance, Jack asked the tiles, stepping out of the tub in wonderment. He thought of himself for the moment as a shadow of a real man, somebody attempting to be a participant in an event that's more serious than he understands. Was Apse's girl stupid or innocent? He joined them to listen to her. Her manner was unchanged – proud, even vain, and filled with uncertainty. Her name was Sarah. She was an art student, playing hooky from an afternoon of drawing cats. She was allergic to cats, she told Elmo Apse, who showed no interest whatsoever in this confidence. Her mother was a difficult woman, she revealed – treating Sarah as a child was the problem here. The girl believed it was a sign of immaturity in mothers, their unwillingness to accept the fact that their children have become adults.

At this time Jack worked within the Sutton according to the wishes of a Mr Goof-it, and in these duties for Mr Goof-it he hasn't much need of props. On his Robin Hood days for instance he simply took money away from banks and other institutions of concentrated wealth and gave it to individuals who appeared to have more need of it. Done that way, there is no drama in the Robin Hood business. It's a clerkly job, subtracting from one balance, adding to another, bills out of a bank vault and into some shabby pocket. He doesn't own a bow and arrow. But for use on different solemn occasions he is the proprietor of what's called a whoopee cushion, acquired from Yesterday in the West Plaza Walk. A good whoopee cushion will change key and contain watery flopping diminuendo notes, as of cow pats falling on concrete. The model Jack owned was a superior one, not a simple sac but an instrument similar to a set of bagpipes. It was an antique, from about 1830. The sound occurred as air escaped through three tubes of polished wood and could be modulated on brass keys.

'So much lovely green,' the girl said to Apse, who had ignored her since he put her things in the closet. 'Did you do this yourself?'

Elmo Apse didn't answer the question, being too much at ease. He said: 'Fill your glass again, Sarah?'

'"There is something about a Martini, a tingle remarkably pleasant,"' the girl Sarah said, a little loudly. '"A yellow, a mellow Martini, I wish that I had one at present."'

'Yes or no?'

'It's a rhyme by Ogden Nash. My father loved him. I grew up with those crazy verses. "There is something about a Martini, ere the dining and dancing begin ..."'

'Or there's white wine. Would you like to sit down?'

'Yes,' she said, and sat down. 'A Martini, please, Elmo, not too much gin. Richard Armour! My father loved him too. We still have a pile of those old magazines at home, the *Saturday Evening Post*.'

But Apse had no interest in Sarah's father or in old *Saturday Evening Posts*. He went into the kitchen and she stood up at once and looked out the window, then turned away, her dress swinging, and plucked a magazine from the coffee table and flipped the pages. She sat down again.

Jack, though he was beginning to understand Apse's charm for women, was in an intolerant gloom-laden state of mind. He put the whoopee to them right away. It isn't an instrument that requires timing or judgement or nice shades of calculation. He positioned himself outside and behind the kitchen door, so that the girl would think Apse was responsible and he would think it was she. Jack's cloak is no hindrance – it does not muffle the whoopee sound but rather spreads it like stereo. He caught their attention even as he inflated the bag, his breaths into the pipes sounding like preparatory gasps. When he released the first tube the blast was unbelievably loud, of a quite stunning vulgarity and nauseatingly long-winded, with Jack's fingering of the brass keys providing treble passages and a horrid brass cadenza.

Elmo Apse and his date Sarah stopped moving while the sound went on. The girl with her *New Yorker* froze utterly, showing dismay and anguish. She rushed out of the apartment. Apse on the other hand was simply annoyed. He searched under the sink and came up with a can of Freshaire, spraying the room angrily, the chemical piny air making Jack cough into his hand. In the kitchen Jack poured the contents of Apse's martini glass down the sink, and spread his cloak and unzipped his fly to fill the glass again to the same measure. He flicked the outside dry with a napkin, a waiter's gesture. Sarah returned and said all in a bright rush: 'Oh hi, sorry to disappear, I thought I dropped something out in the hallway on my way in.'

She did not comment upon the sudden atmosphere of a pine wood, though it was a choking one. Apse ignored her words but he sprayed close to her on either side of her shoulders with Freshaire, four long bursts. She blushed and coughed. He then quite rudely handed his guest her martini. He took a swallow from his own glass and spat vigorously.

'This is piss,' Apse said.

'Oh no,' she said, sipping. 'It's good.'

'Yes? Mine is piss.'

Apse's thin bearded face with its large teeth was expressionless as usual but could it be that his eyes now were slightly inward-looking? It was always hard to say and Jack was a wishful thinker. Sarah was the one who concerned herself with investigating glasses, pitcher and bottles. Apse uncorked the wine, which he tasted, and brought the lunch in.

Jack might have started Apse thinking – or might not – but that seemed to the sailor too small a result. What months of work like today's would it take before Apse began to experience little inklings of self-awareness? What years to make a conscience? Jack suspected that Mr Goof-it could be mistaken in assigning the substance of his own mind to the general population, and especially to Elmo Apse. Sailor Jack's life work only makes sense if Mr Goof-it is correct in seeing the people as made of one substance. Apse in this view of human affairs will be reduced by visitations to worry, to the biting of the nails of his forefingers.

So far so good, there's a shaking man here who fears terrible unseen forces. Could be that he'll get around to wondering next why they're picking on him in particular. Was it something I did? He might begin to ask himself such questions. Let's look at it another way, a voice inside suggests to the rattled man, an awful thought, what if we haven't had this figured out right? We've been whistling along with the idea in mind that pretty much anything that doesn't land us in jail is okay to do. What if this isn't the case? What if there's some overriding *system of justice* at work?

That man could be Jack. But Jack thought it would never be Elmo Apse, who didn't seem to be made of the same substance. He was of whatever fish are from, or shuddersome reptile forms, or perhaps hard-shelled creatures like lobsters and insects. Even as Jack considered this matter Apse was at ease again, telling Sarah about his trip to Italy. He hadn't liked the food – too heavy. The architecture was elaborate enough but seemed to be wholly and consistently, Apse thought, based on superstition.

Apse could talk about himself at length; in fact he insisted upon doing so. When anybody tried to reciprocate with stories about themselves, however, Apse would become violently bored and querulous. Just now Sarah had some thoughts on Italian architecture which Apse did not listen to.

One more detail: in his story to Sarah about Italy Apse had been there alone, though he spoke to her without reserve about girls who had joined him for parts of the trip, but according to what Jack knew of that Italian summer Elmo Apse had taken the tour as a guest of a woman named Auburn Barker, who after watching too many soap operas wanted a romantic escapade while her husband was in Wellesley Psychiatric with depression problems caused by overwork. This matter had some rough symmetry to it, the husband's work habits having driven her to the soaps in the first place.

Perhaps Sarah's usual place was at the centre of interest, with small talk about her allergies, little quotes of comic verse, memoirs of her father. With Elmo she had to learn to be a listener. He didn't offer her a choice of role. While the two finished lunch Jack sat opposite them on a settee under a small tree.

He wasn't having a particularly good day. But Jack has heart. He's a believer in putting out more effort when he appears to be losing. He wanted to attract Apse's attention.

If you thought when you first heard Bible stories – though there isn't a reason why there should have been Bible stories in your background, it is just that they were in Jack's, lavishly – of floods and fires from the skies that the Jehovah of the tribes was intemperately cranky, then you haven't properly understood the difficulty of attracting somebody's attention. Here there is a requirement of dialogue. The hardest part is persuading the person addressed to look up and say: 'Who, me?' To which the response: 'Yes, you. Pay attention.' follows.

Serenity, ease of conscience, guiltlessness, can make a man deaf to the most specific signals; there was always this practical reason for flights of thunderbolts and chariots of flame from the skies and for the shaking of towers and cities down to rubble.

Now the soft blanket of mist against the ceiling gave Jack the idea of speaking to Apse from a cloud. He hoisted his thin spider form into the branches of the tree and hung up there, looking down.

'Hey, you. Elmo Apse.'

Sarah immediately stared upward at the ceiling. Apse turned a slow head toward the apartment door.

'Mr Goof-it's justice has a terrible bite,' Jack said. 'It doesn't compare to anything that's been around before. Listen up, Apse. I'm talking to you.'

Then Sarah asked timidly: 'Who, him?'

See now the reason for plagues and pestilences, in the difficulty of attracting the attention of somebody of Elmo Apse's substance, whatever it may be. Words are only air in the trees, the noise an insect might make landing on a leaf if it had survived the Bug Death insect massacre. Even having been hailed by name from the room's high place Apse didn't feel guilty enough to say *Who, me?*

Jack, having considered other utterances, decided to forgo the further communication of warnings. He climbed down from the tiny cloud. He spread his cloak's wings to make a threatening wind on the way out. He slammed the door resoundingly also, just to let Elmo Apse know that Mr Goof-it's man was human and vicious, not a goatmilk-drinker's fantasy brimming with forgiveness.

Chapter 5

Lovers

THERE'S A LOT of resistance among scientists to the idea of invisibility. Maybe that's because invisibility is a very old fantasy of nonscientific minds, like flying. Jack knows one way of making himself invisible – he's sure there are others – and he's been around scientists long enough to be unimpressed by scientific prejudices and superstitions. The truth of the matter is that the institution of science has the same enthusiasm for change, reform and innovation as the institution of monarchy does. Scientists numbered among Jack's acquaintances, while they are all worthy people, deeply educated along narrow paths, and even with a capacity for optimism in a world that they have managed to make curiously temporary, are not abundantly endowed with imagination.

One of the celebrated men of science who told Jack that invisibility was impossible, that he would never get it off the ground so to speak, was Curtis Sevigny. Curt Sevigny, a thoroughly vain person, was known as Sweetboy by his staff. He doesn't have a part in the story except to demonstrate a state of mind. Sweetboy was much shorter than average in height, with red hair in tight curls and a handsome red beard. He looked like a dainty Viking. His family was French and had been settled in the eastern States before many of the Indian tribes.

Sweetboy had two closets for his clothes in his bedroom, and there was one smaller closet allotted to his wife, who nevertheless had to be always vigilant against her husband's encroachments on her racks. New clothes arrived for Sweetboy regularly from his tailor and shirtmaker, and elevator footwear from his shoemaker, as male fashions changed, undetectably for most men – an inch on a cuff, a softer roll on a collar, a newer brown for glove leather.

The furniture in his house was custom-made too, proportioned to his small size. His dog was a miniature animal. When he was at home, Sweetboy looked to be in normal ratio to his surroundings, but naturally everybody else, including his wife, was then clumsy and oversized, awkwardly ducking under lamp arms or perched on the small chairs and making them creak.

Once while looking through film files to check out solar wind experiments on the moon, Jack and Sweetboy were watching the NASA record of the first moon landing, a much more detailed tape than the one available to the general public. Sweetboy was running it through his tape handler. At this time Jack's invisibility principle, as he'd developed it for an orbiting camera, was similar to Apollo 11's pictures to earth when they were arriving live, a matter of two fairly crude electromechanical devices connected by high-frequency pulses. With Jack's project only one device was needed and it erased rather than assembled pulses. A light source added other amplified frequencies that could be tuned to colour and focused to make the camera see around solid obstructions to its view. He mentioned this novelty to Sweetboy, as colleague to colleague, but made the mistake of using the word *invisible*.

Sweetboy frowned jealously, an angry little Norseman. 'Well, that idea isn't worth a darn,' he said. 'It's been around and around lately, hasn't it? It comes in cycles. Irving asked me what I thought not long ago. I had to tell him the truth. I said, it's not worth a darn, Irving. I'm telling you the same, Jack. We're scientists after all,' Sweetboy said, stretched on his back on his recliner, watching the spaceship landing on the moon, 'and there are physical laws that don't change, never mind what the comic books say. Forget about Buck Rogers meets the Invisible Man, unless we find a way of repealing some of the laws of physics. Columbine's a woman,' said he irritably, 'but you should know better, for God's sake. You're a brilliant scientist.'

On the tape Ed Aldrin, a whitely glowing boxy person, ambled around cumbersomely on the surface of the moon. Ed set up a particle collector to measure solar wind, a device with a sail antenna that had been developed by one of Sweetboy's teams back then.

The particle collector was visible to Sweetboy, who had held it in his hands. However, he saw it, breaking the activity down, through the action of very high frequency waves. This was also how Jack could make it visually disappear. But Jack did not discuss invisibility further with Sweetboy, who was disposed to reject comic-book fantasy. Sweetboy didn't like the comic-book word spaceship either. He used forms like lunar module when he talked about the spaceship.

Sweetboy always liked to keep it clear that Buck Rogers had not preceded science in the matter of making a landing on the moon.

Jack had known Sweetboy at the Massachusetts Institute of Technology and for some years they ran across each other at conferences and seminars. Sweetboy Sevigny never lived anywhere else except in Boston, and he never moved from the first house he bought there. He was always Jack's mental marker for modern scientific man, our late twentieth-century version of medieval religious man, for whom unorthodoxy is a crime and an undisciplined imagination is the very devil.

Jack was working on earth satellite cameras for Technoptrax at their research facility in the industrial park in Belleville. There were two men and one woman in his lab. The younger man was Ian Peveril, a Cape Bretoner who walked as if treading the deck of a schooner. Ian deliberately retained his slow, foreign, Maritime ways, just to let people know he was a transient in Ontario, interested but condescending, like a royal visitor who has come from a far better place and will shortly return there.

George Wienewski was markedly a foreigner too. George had made his way up from the bottom, the Toronto slums, and was ill at ease as a member of the professional class. He drank to feel comfortable and in his cups had a habit of talking vigorously about *real people*, who existed in the old neighbourhoods, as he distinguished them from *fakes and phonies*, by whom he was latterly surrounded.

The woman was named Columbine.

At this time Jack was at an unattractive stage in the development of his character, split right down the middle. His instincts and learnt behaviour were in conflict. He was brimful of Christian tolerance, from the powerful influence of Horsy Stacpole, but also alive with what could be called Christian sin. As a result of trying to obey his old teacher he was acutely sensitive to the feelings of people he didn't know, and would for instance apologize to folk who jostled him on the subway, whether or not the collision was his fault. He would listen attentively to other people's ideas, in this way hearing, most of the time, thoughts that came straight off the previous night's TV shows. His meek manner made him the prey of all the sour sitters at public desks and behind bureaucratic wickets who have cheaply come to contempt for humanity. Because his own face was meek the faces he dealt with on this side of the split were as a rule set in critical lines, and impatient, and severely uncomprehending.

His rowdy hurtful side, as he thought of it at the time, was in Jack's case rock hard, unsmiling and quick to take offence. When he was like this anybody who jostled him in a crowd got an elbow in the ribs in retaliation, irrespective of age and fragility, and smart remarks from government employees sitting behind desks did not hang in the air unanswered. This side was deeply fond, not of mercy and kindness, but of bars and public dancing and women of the night. It brawled and challenged and didn't think of the human mass as brother. But it wasn't real, this side, he felt, it was temporary and regressive – Jack was confident at the time of his first outing with Columbine that he could subdue and master his unruly nature, and thus become a *better person*.

One day Columbine and Jack were detached from satellite camera projects, most of which were meteorological, and were given a defence contract. The defence department had cameras that could take a crisp snap of the lettering on a match folder from a hundred miles up, but tree foliage was baffling them in a particular Central American trouble spot. They wanted a device to take pictures of hostile guerrillas, terrorists, who had a supply road through a tract of tropical jungle under dense foliage cover. Jack took an interest in the colour of the foliage and its reflection of light.

He averaged the jungle green in different sectors of the terrain and from a pattern of altitudes. Since the idea was to take photographs he started thinking about a light source that would illuminate the dark jungle floor beneath the trees. He put together a system. It had a number of innovations, one being that it appeared to bend light. This was the kind of heresy that offended men like Sweetboy, although a bend in light hadn't bothered Einstein. He built a model in cooperation with Columbine, who was a physicist specializing in geometrical optics. It worked – matter-of-factly photographing objects that stood on a table behind a solid green screen. Columbine was delighted. She threw her arms around Jack's neck and kissed him. She admired his mind.

Though Columbine wasn't a beautiful woman she could be extraordinarily beautiful on certain occasions, and at these times plenty of men would try to catch her eye or to impress her with conversation about themselves. It seemed to depend on her mood. At times some force came from within Columbine that transformed her. Clothes and cosmetics didn't appear to affect her appearance much, for Jack anyway – indeed for the sailor she could look very plain while trying diligently to look good, having come from the hairdresser, say, and wearing her most expensive dress and fussing at a mirror with brow liner and lipstick and so on.

Jack was often, during the working day, surprised by this grace that came to Columbine, and its power unsettled him.

They went to dinner to celebrate their discovery. They were in Ottawa at the time with other Technoptrax people attending a seminar at Carleton. Jack's good side was dominant, smiling and tolerant and goatmilk-meek. He arranged to meet Columbine in the Sutton complex, at the Hunters' Club Room, a pricey and flash place in one of the mezzanine grottoes off the Concourse. There are English fox-hunting prints on the walls, with hunting horns and foxheads and brushes mounted on plaques. The bar is the John Peel Lounge.

Columbine arrived late and wore a dramatic cloak falling in yellow velvet folds with a heavy silver clasp. She looked quite different from her self in the Technoptrax lab. Her dress was a paler version of the same pink-and-yellow colour with ribbon lacing in front. Jack complimented her chivalrously on her appearance, since she had clearly put effort into it. She smiled and bobbed her head, surveyed their surroundings briefly and gave him all her attention thereafter.

She chatted about H.G. Wells's invisible man, who was named Griffin and deranged. 'Of course the formula was horse and buggy. Especially the chemistry, strychnine and opium and chloroform. He did have a light supply like yours, didn't he, though? An ethereal vibration he called it.'

'Like ours,' said Jack courteously.

'He imagined it very well. You know what I think, Jack? Anything that can be imagined can be done.'

Their waiter was an incomer from some Mediterranean country, maybe Spain, and chunky, about three inches shorter than average in height. Those are the three inches that eat the soul. Jack found his eyes being engaged with resentment by the brown eyes in the carved walnut face while the man was some distance away. The waiter studied Columbine quite frankly when he reached their table, so to speak thumping his chest and spreading his tail feathers. Had Jack happened to be out of grace he could have handled an incident like this in an instant. Well, when the sailor was black Jack the sinner, he was never bothered in this way in fact. This was a burden of Christian Jack, whose habit it was to respond to glares of resentment with a smile of Christian fellowship and who paid the price for that.

'We seem to have produced a camera that sees through solid matter,' Columbine said, 'and that's the same thing to my mind as making matter invisible. Just think of the military implications! We could equip an invisible army, Jack. An invisible army with invisible weapons.'

She knew at least as much about the subject as Jack did, but her enthusiasm was taking her somewhat ahead of the reality, which was that the camera only took photographs. The light source was the innovation. The invisible army would need monstrous controlled light sources in the sky overhead or they wouldn't be invisible. Columbine's grandfather had been a leader of a sabotage cell in the Polish underground and a big problem for the Germans in his locality in the Second World War. At the end of the war the Communists murdered him, as Columbine told the story, because he was too unswervingly Polish. She had photographs of her grandfather, a blond youngster with a tough grin. Columbine was much more extreme than Douglas T. Harder as an anti-Communist. When she talked of destroying Communism she didn't refer narrowly to the ideology but to the Communist countries and the inhabitants.

She began ordering her food and drink at once, because that was her nature. Their waiter tossed his head, flinging back a quiff of blue-black hair and said, amazed and jocular: 'We have good fresh shrimp today. How would that be for the gentleman. Shrimp?'

This was tricky, in that the waiter had been listening to Columbine but with the question he turned his stare on Jack, making the last word either a question or a characterization, hearer's choice. Jack's ethical, well-behaved self was still dominant. He did notice, though, that the waiter was tickling the disorderly side of his nature, inviting it out. He refused the shrimp with a smile and ordered soup. Columbine drank both gin and wine and talked about refraction and reflection, two important principles of invisibility.

Watching Columbine eat raw herring was fascinating for Jack. She would raise a large piece to her mouth, using the thumbs and forefingers of both hands. Her teeth were small and opalescent and made short work of stripping the fish. She could have eaten old boots with those teeth. She put the strip of herring into the pouch of her cheek then so that she could chew while talking, before swallowing and reaching for more.

The waiter had meanwhile brought Jack four and a half shrimp hooked dispiritedly on the rim of a glass dish, which contained a pool of water. There was a tub of dried-out sauce too. Staring at this, Jack understood that the water represented a bed of ice. Floating on it was a fragment of lettuce leaf that had browned at the edges and was smeared with old mayonnaise.

LEO SIMPSON

What would Horsy Stacpole have me do here, Jack asked himself, conscious of chaos of mind and blood where there had only been ethical choices as to behaviour. The ethical system of his life, when he had it in hand, was meant to stand securely against ravaging armies who might in their normal function rape and murder his wife and children. It shouldn't be screaming to abdicate because a waiter took the trouble to look in the kitchen garbage for an old lettuce leaf.

Jack said to Columbine: 'I could try to find out what's bending the light – what seems to be bending the light – but it won't be anything new. The circuits are new designs but we're using just regular hardware. It only works on the green. Maybe we're getting super transparency, not invisibility.'

'There's more. We have a holographic effect in some of the pictures too. Those little terrorists look like frozen statues.'

'Oh yes. I was wondering, could that be just high definition photography? The lenses cost about a million each.'

'No, we're getting real depth in the objects. It's real, Jack.'

Columbine had taken a cigarette from a Rothman's pack. The waiter suddenly appeared at Jack's side and leaned across the table with a matador's arch of the hips and gravity of face. His muscled backside intervened across the table between the two diners. He flicked a gold lighter for Columbine and she nodded to him and said: 'Look, could I ask you to give me a break, please? I'm trying to eat in this rotten place. I'm trying to eat the rotten food and have a drink or two and talk to this guy here. I'm sorry if you're having your period or something but leave me out of it.' She said to Jack then: 'Sorry for the interruption, it isn't your fault. No, high definition would be a form of transparency. But I couldn't measure refraction and there's definitely no reflection, none. We have to be looking at invisibility.'

Jack continued this conversation with Columbine while in a state of stress his eye kept drifting sideways to the wounded waiter. The man went into an anguished sentry-walk in front of the service trolley near the kitchen door. He had sprung a sheen of sweat on his forehead. First he strutted backward and forward with a fantastic display of maleness, a rooster parade, arms moving like two sabres, pelvis rotating and legs flexing and stamping. He brushed away approaches by other waiters. When this had gone on for some time his body suddenly collapsed into an opposite manner. His walk then became the slither of a guilty mongrel. He seemed to grow puny and hollow-chested.

He made abject noises of approval while he took Columbine's dinner order. He hung on Jack's words. Then he switched back without warning to his haughty style, slapping the wine list on the table, flicking a finger confidently at recommended items, crashing plates together and performing veronicas with the napkins. He went away.

Columbine ate a whole boiled lobster. When she'd picked the beast's carcass clean she fell silent, her tawny eyes brooding. Jack always finds it hard to remember Columbine's face in detail, because of its changes. He has some photos that show serious eyes and a large mouth and nose, nothing much of the real person in fact.

She stretched like a cat and with her thumb she absentmindedly unlaced the ribbons of her dress.

At this stage Jack was unsettled because of the waiter. Jack was thinking dutifully, which can feel like real thought. Jack thought: this waiter is just as much a creature of earth as anybody else. The waiter was Jack's brother so now Jack wanted to feel a bite of conscience or some twinge of breached integrity. But his best self felt only a renegade peace.

Columbine talked then about a new bestseller that offered ultimate information on human sexuality, with statistical tables. She advanced the opinion that there wasn't such a thing as complete information on this subject. Nobody ever understands it, said she, cradle to grave, if we did we wouldn't always be interested in the subject, as we are. We can only make wild guesses as we go along, ordering our behaviour according to fits and spasms of intuition and speculation.

She glanced around, scrutinizing their companions in the flash dining-room. Her eye fell on their waiter, catching him as he snapped into his slinking mongrel manner. He cringed at her from across the room. Then her eyes returned to Jack again, with determination. She said, forthrightly: 'You're the ugliest man I've ever met, Jack, and it doesn't bother me. But do you think you could drop the creepy lover-of-mankind horseshit? That's what bothers me.' She leaned across the table and picked up one of his fingers. Her tawny eyes were almost closed. 'I have an idea.' This idea Columbine had was very plain. She breathed lobster and wine, lemon butter and gin and brandy on Jack. 'We're a hardworking and successful team. Why don't we take tonight and tomorrow off?'

So with yellow laces trailing from her pretty breasts, Columbine, burping on expensive food but otherwise a model of grace, led the way from the

Hunters' Club Room. The waiter stood near the serving trolley quite some distance from their route of exit, staring along his nose at them. Jack wanted to be away quickly from the wretched, hurt man. To his dismay Columbine chanced to see the fellow watching them and instantly sheered toward him. She's going to apologize, Jack thought, but it would be much better if we just cleanly left this place. He followed her to add his support, reaching also for his wallet, though he had already added a heavy tip to the check.

The man stood to attention as Columbine approached him, folding his arms on his chest. 'I want to ask you,' she said, her own hands clasped together, leaning toward him across the trolley with elegance and fragility, a ballerina from a music-box, 'if you are homosexual by any chance? Because I have a homosexual friend and he likes short partners. I'm not saying,' Columbine explained carefully, 'that he's fond of midgets. He's a dear man but he isn't tall, and so of course he prefers lovers who are shorter.'

Beads of sweat broke out on the Napoleonic forehead as the man stared into Columbine's eyes in silent maniacal choler. She said with the same careful seriousness: 'I hope you don't mind my asking? I happened to notice how short you are, and the way you walk, and those tight pants.'

Jack couldn't understand why Columbine was doing this. He was astonished by what seemed to him behaviour that cut exactly against the grain of mercy. Politicians had puzzled Jack often enough in the same way, juggling budgets in the billions, spending freely to buy guns and rocketry and then taking particular pains, angrily as it always seemed, to cut off the supply of free orange juice to orphans. The waiter's lips opened and closed a few times without sound. He was moved by emotion so powerful that Jack couldn't even guess at how it might feel. He said: 'You whore. You're all whores here, it's sickening to a man's stomach. You eat like dogs, you have pigs for men, and you think dollars will buy everything. Get out of here, you whore. Cover up your whore's body and get out of here. Take your pig with you.'

Jack put his wallet back in his pocket. 'I see. You're telling me that you're not a gay person, is that it?' Columbine asked the question with a great show of aristocratic civility and a pained, perplexed smile. 'These European accents,' she said over her shoulder to Jack, 'are very attractive but I can't make head or tail of what this little person is saying, can you?' Then she said to the waiter in an admonishing tone: 'I certainly hope you're not homophobic. That isn't acceptable here. Being gay can be a matter of pride, you know, heterosexuality isn't the one and only thing. There's a new book out you should read.'

'Columbine,' said Jack.

'You God damn whore,' the waiter said, much louder, as they moved away. Columbine turned at the doorway, which Jack was glumly holding open, and addressed the fellow again from across the full width of the dining room. 'If you don't like it here,' she called, as if making a sincere enquiry, while every diner in between looked from her to the waiter, 'why don't you go back to your own foreign country, wherever it is, your country of origin?'

All the diners' heads then turned to the waiter, to see if he would offer an answer. However, he only made a small basket of the fingers and thumb of one hand, drawing two words – you whore, Jack assumed – silently out of his mouth and flinging them toward Columbine.

'Men like that are hard on women,' she said to Jack as they made their way across an edge of the prairie-size Sutton parking lot. 'Cock-proud bastards. God knows they've been hard on me.' Her car was a two-seater Porsche convertible of iridescent yellow that looked too tiny for a highway. Jack's own car that year was a Renault.

He had moved from the laboratory at MIT into a practically identical laboratory at Technoptrax's Belleville facility without much change in his life except that he was being paid a huge salary for producing his papers and studies and running and devising tests. He worked hard. He smiled when he was good and on other days he patronized a disc jockey tavern called Lulu's. He wondered from time to time if he needed to be married. He was an over-age, gawky student, a rumpled absent-minded person who perhaps needed a wife to sharpen him up and straighten him out.

In anticipation of what a wife would require, should one come along, Jack had bought himself a fine old Victorian brick house on Belleville's east side. This house had three bathrooms, five bedrooms and other dining and reception rooms which he rarely went into. They had been furnished under the supervision of a beautiful, businesslike woman named Margo from Coco Chanel Interiors of Montreal. Margo phoned Jack every six months to ask if he felt like doing something new and next time he thought he might. A local firm, Housewives Ltd., sent four teenaged boys twice a month who noisily went through all his rooms with carpet sweepers and vacuum cleaners. Another minimum wage group, Quinte Roofers & Repairs, had a contract to repair and paint and clean out eavestroughs, and he had another group that kept his garden up and mowed his lawn. Jack lived in one bedroom and the den. The den was a room off the front hallway with a pool table, music system, computer and desk and an armchair and TV. He was amassing a reel tape collection of the works of Bach and Schumann just then, and building a model of the New Bedford whaler *Sam Koets*, 1835. Jack did wonder when he lived in the Belleville house, though not with any particular discomfort, in summer especially when fine weather broke through his work-absorption, whether he would move through his lifespan in this fashion, growing old at Technoptrax, in the bedroom with some weekend visitor from Montreal or Toronto, or one of the crowd from Lulu's, at the computer, in the garden.

He hesitated at Columbine's toy-like yellow auto, which she had insisted he drive from the university, but she didn't hand the keys over again. She pointed at the passenger seat, saying: 'I'll take my baby back now. You rest.'

Well, he was disappointed, having enjoyed his turn at the controls of the powerful little machine, which had challenged his sense of *car* as something that ran economically and didn't make demands on an owner's time. Jack brooded too on the drinks he had seen his colleague consume, but as to that he was a fatalist. Whether or not he died soon wasn't important. He would be dying and when it happened it would seem too soon. The tops of the car's tires were higher than his head. The two giant searchlights cut blinding cones in the dark at road level. It occurred to Jack that if Columbine became his wife she would want to keep this car; it wasn't at all the same kind of machine as the Renault. Would there be other changes in the nature of his life that she might want to make?

He had thought his own handling of the Porsche had been daring. Now, though, his shoulders were pressed hard back against his seat, as they left the city streets through some magic portal and dropped on a ramp toward four lanes of traffic. Concrete skimmed by a few centimetres below his elbow. As a dreadful impact at the access seemed certain, Columbine relaxed and glanced behind at the lights of the Sutton, steering with one hand. When she talked she wanted to engage Jack eye to eye. 'I used to know this place, I mean before they sent in the bulldozers to build the Sutton. Sharon it was called.' Jack's main feeling was still of calm broodiness, but he did wonder if there would be much pain. His sense was of unforgiving speed while the cars that rushed toward them remained as solid as a wall. 'Biblical name, good honest people. Give way, you selfish bastards.'

When they intersected with the flow a gap opened, which seemed to Jack a lucky break, since Columbine had made no driving adjustment. Tires squealed behind them and right away she wanted to be in the leftmost lane. She lit a Rothman's one-handed, eyes squinting at the smoke, twirling the wheel by palm pressure and then using the hand with the cigarette to shift. 'God, these Ottawa drivers. Why do you think we allow people to do that, flatten a nice town out of existence and build something like the Sutton?'

She cut to an exit ramp at the last moment while Jack with intense interest watched the swaying cliff of an eighteen-wheeler's cab lunging to stay clear to his right, the driver prostrated on his wheel and fighting a jackknife. He said: 'I don't know. It's not something we can do anything about.'

'Are you sure?'

'Yes. It's like, why do we pay baseball players six gazillion bucks and so little for poets, which is a moral question on an economic subject. Where are our priorities? is what you hear too, when you hear that question. Well, certain people are willing to pay baseball players six gazillion when they expect to make eight gazillion on the deal, maybe even ten. Poets will start getting the same money when they start earning the same numbers.'

'Yes? So where are our priorities, Oprah?'

'I don't believe we change much, to be honest. Our priorities don't change, our natures don't change. The people who suffer anguish about our priorities don't have the capital, not usually anyway. The people who have the capital are very clear on the subject of priorities. What we do morally is very primitive. It's like watching a storm, seeing the trees being blasted, the houses being flooded or washed away, and so on. We can't prevent specific bad parts of a whole phenomenon. The whole phenomenon's always been the same, the way we behave. We have less control and a much larger scale now, of course.'

She was offended, throwing him an angry glance, eyes still squinted against the cigarette smoke. 'Is this a sermon, Jack? I'm not in the mood for one of your creepy sermons. Sharon was a nice town. I had an uncle in Sharon when I was a little girl. We're not building towns like Sharon any more, and there aren't any more men like my uncle, so don't tell me we aren't changing. He built a dollhouse for me – he was a craftsman carpenter, a beautiful woodworker – and also he taught me how to ride a bicycle. Then when I was a young lady he taught me how to drive a car. He was gentle, Jack, and he was funny. There won't be his like again anywhere, he went first and then Sharon went, I mean we fed it to the bulldozers. The only thing my uncle wouldn't let me do was play with his stamp collection. Then when he died he left it to me, it's six albums and worth a lot of money. Six fat albums of stamps and they've always taken up more space than I can afford but I don't grudge them an inch and I wouldn't sell them for ten times what they're worth, not if I was starving to death, Jack. Some smart developer bought Sharon out, I mean he bought the mayor and he bought the councillors. Then he bulldozed it down and built the Sutton. Do you know why?'

'Sure. If you mean – '

'Because we're stupid, that's why. Half the time we don't know what we're doing, the other half we don't care.'

'That's a very primitive point of view,' said Jack, who was still broodingly detached while Columbine was getting angrier. 'Historically we've always behaved much the same way.'

They were staying at the Louis Neuf, a good small Ottawa hotel named for a saint. They went to Columbine's suite which had a separate living room and a balcony. The carpet was a knotted beige and there was a cocktail table of dimpled brass, burnished but rough as if hand-beaten by a worker who was short-sighted and in a lot of pain. Jack noticed a couple of convivial wine glasses with dregs of red in them on this table. The ashtray had two panatela stubs crushed out in it beside a bunch of Columbine's Rothman's butts. He knew she'd lunched at the university. She'd drunk a few glasses of wine with somebody in the afternoon, for the time it took her to smoke five cigarettes, her guest meanwhile smoking two small cigars.

Columbine stepped out of her dress and underclothes while she punched buttons on the FM and moodily lit a cigarette. He looked at the lean perfect body and understood that it was much more beautiful than any others he'd seen. He'd heard enough about the wonder of love, but he wasn't prepared for its sexual power. She looked at him enquiringly as she disappeared into the bathroom, asking: 'What?' Her voice came out from inside with reverb: 'Make a move. Take your clothes off, there's a good lad.' He did so in the bathroom, where there happened to be a full-length mirror to show him his own spider body as a wicked contrast to Columbine's lovely one. He had brought his wrong self, the Christian smiler, to this engagement, and bones in pallid parchment. Love was now making matters worse, much worse. His black eyes glittered in fear, and Jack's mouth was spread back from his uneven teeth in a rictus, the frozen grin of a split man. As a smiler he couldn't think of anything to say to Columbine. He also didn't know what to do with his hands while he wore the wrong face. There were two beds and he began to fold back the duvetyn cover of one, starting to examine his own immediate thoughts in order to think his way into an answer to what seemed to be deportment problems.

She attacked him from behind, making Jack think for a moment that a mugger had got in. Columbine fixed her mouth on Jack's, her left arm around his neck while she groped him with her right. Then she heaved him on his back and jumped him, with her legs apart. He noticed from a distance her transfer to lovemaking of her direct style in eating and drinking and driving the yellow car.

Jack's response was defensive, fighting Columbine off to get more time for thought. His thoughts had been interrupted. Then his hands went to her thighs by themselves because they didn't understand the confusion. Columbine quietened under Jack's hands. Her eyes became pagan dark.

He was impressed by the utterly personal nature of their nakedness. Simply touching Columbine's nipples with his fingertips made her look far too vulnerable, as if his fingers were rocks and the nails dangerous blades. He later moved down the bed, a very lighthearted disciple of Horsy Stacpole's, and rested his ears between her thighs. Columbine began to chide Jack from the headboard, though certainly in a languid and complacent manner interrupted by silences and small pleased gasps.

'... no, don't do that any more. Oh, yes, do that for as long as you like, for ever. God, you look so awful down there, do you realize how much hair's growing from your coccyx? I suppose you wouldn't. I've never seen so many bones. Wouldn't you prefer to have the light out ... ?'

It was a fond and affectionate address, with a nut of truth at its centre. Jack was ugly and bony and spidery. She was the beauty of the world and the night. His mouth was slack now and his eyelids heavy. As soon as he entered Columbine he blacked out. When he came to he saw her hair flying underneath him like fronds of seaweed. Columbine extended her neck while she twisted her head from side to side with her eyes closed. The drift of her hair lost its underwater quality, becoming even softer and more distant, with an appearance of being inaccessible to him. Even though he was connected to Columbine most personally her face and hair made a strongly spiritual impression on Jack, as of high fine-drawn clouds he had watched when a boy, his fingers dug into the earth to hold him on the planet. She was slippery with sweat.

They went to sleep together. In the middle of the night Jack awoke and stumbled into the bathroom, feeling very strange, exuberant and respectful, as if he had been popped by magic into a better world. He sang a verse of Horsy Stacpole's favourite hymn, 'As the Faithful Heart, His Grace Abides'. That sounded much too unctuous, though, in the newfound better world and soon he walked down the Broadway of long ago. It was one evening in July.

> *As I walked down the Broadway!*
> *One evening in July*
> *I met a maid and she asked my trade*
> *And 'A sailor john!' says I!*

He brushed his teeth with Columbine's brush, in the strangeness and bright light studying the yellow glitter of his incisors through the foam of Crest, an old gapped and leaning tooth fence. He wasn't thinking now, and didn't miss thought. Back in bed he reached for Columbine again and she came into his arms pliantly at once. 'Oh dear,' she said in happy tribute. Her hips in Jack's hands were smooth and cool.

The next day they stayed in the suite. They splashed together in the shower where Jack found out that Columbine hadn't lost her violent style overnight but would have to be coaxed from it. He had merrily splayed her against the wall. While Jack was soaking her pubic hair she responded with an arm-lock on his neck to raise his head. They fell over the bathtub rim together. Hitting the tile first, Jack's skinny hip went numb. Columbine was in superb condition, unlike Jack, and skied and played squash in winter and spent summer holidays in the Quetico bush in a canoe. She pinned him to the bathroom floor with a shout of triumph. Sharp pain followed numbness and he became aware that some of the wetness he struggled on was blood from his body. By making a ferocious effort he was able to roll them into the hallway, where unluckily the sliding door of a closet had been left open. They ended up in darkness inside, Columbine uttering mad yells and yips while a wire coat-hanger on the floor forced its spike into Jack's bleeding shank. It left him with a serious scar, a long raked cut, quite deep in the centre where the hook first went in.

They spent the rest of the day on the carpet, or on one or the other of the beds and watched snatches of TV now and then. Jack coached Columbine in the rules of patience.

In the evening she lay on the bed naked eating a plate of the Louis Neuf's ballottine of duckling with her fingers. The plate was resting on her stomach. Jack's plate was on his stomach too but he was wrapped in the sheet and using a knife and fork. What brought the subject of marriage up was that she tapped a greasy finger importantly on Jack's chest. 'You are a terrific lover, you ugly bastard. You are okay. We're lovers now, is that a good deal for you?'

'I was thinking of getting married.'

She looked slightly disappointed but didn't stop chewing, saying: 'Shit, I didn't know, who is she?'

'I meant to you.' Jack glared upward at the ceiling with rancour because nobody likes to ask questions that they know will get a disappointing reply. 'I have a house.' He described the house briefly. 'The car I have won't appeal to you. It's a practical car.'

She did stop chewing then and Jack turned. She was watching him in consternation and for a bare second he thought it would be a tactful reply. But Columbine's nature as a barbarian was too strong.

'No, that wouldn't work,' she said. 'I've never looked forward to having babies. Marriage is for having babies, the way I was brought up. I don't need babies right now, so a marriage doesn't make much sense for me, and also,' Columbine said with a serious face to Jack, 'they'd be awful-looking babies wouldn't they? I can't see myself being depended on by a litter of helpless rug rats.' She dumped her plate on the floor and began to unwrap Jack's sheet. 'This is very good, the way we are now. It's strange you should ask, though. A domestic urge is unusual in a man. Were you an orphan, Jack? No,' she said as Jack made to reply. 'I don't feel like hearing about it at the moment. Maybe another time, when I'm in a different mood.' She wrapped her arms around his waist. 'I'm going to fight getting tied down to one person. And so will you, Jack, if you're smart.'

Chapter 6

Other Lovers and Heroes

JACK'S LIFE improved markedly while he and Columbine were lovers. It happened at a sacrifice of more gobs of his belief in the matter of humanity as a brotherhood. Indeed it began to seem to him clear that he could further boost the improvement in his personal life in proportion to a decrease in his tolerance of his fellow man. No conscious sacrifice of principle occurred, as far as he could judge. He sometimes thought he was simply growing up late, undergoing the completely natural process of losing illusions and sensibilities. He did retain average imperatives of charity, generosity and the like. However, he never knew whether these were his nature, or habit, or the preservation of something of Horsy Stacpole out of love.

His affair with Columbine made a social animal of the boy who had once thought he was a dog. He was often in Montreal and New York with Columbine, and in the university towns of England and Germany too. He attended many receptions. He began picking up some polish from the social grind. Earlier he'd been accustomed to dealing with women as creatures to be found in bars. Now he talked to every woman as if she were Columbine and the manner worked in a rough fashion, though he made a few spectacular errors. Women were all quite different, though they projected a sense or illusion of being similar to each other. They seemed to have a need to be perceived as similar, maybe for the same reason that so many millions, male and female, pulled on blue jeans in the mornings, in order to veil their individual natures inside the denim horde. When Columbine saw the interior of Jack's house on Victoria Street in Belleville for the first time she collapsed on the living room settee – matching the curtains, Margo had said, picking up tones from the carpet – and laughed until the tears came. He was able to deduce from this that Columbine and Margo of Coco Chanel Interiors were quite unlike each other.

On the subject of how men and women dealt with him, Jack's favourites were those of Columbine's kind who admitted they were looking at an ugly-faced scientist but then followed that with other judgements about him. He didn't much care for the diplomats, who saw nothing unusual in his appearance, nor for the art appreciators who had ideals of human appearance, on a strictly aesthetic basis if you believed them, to which Jack didn't measure up. He wasn't comfortable with expressions of sympathy, which he construed as claims of superiority: he never believed he was a worse person than people he was uglier than, but they did. The way it went for most of the crowd at Technoptrax and at other businesses, after they bit the bullet and got to know Jack they forgot that he wouldn't win any beauty contests.

But Jack as a pair with Columbine came to puzzle certain other kinds of men. Well, some wore one earring. Many were part-time athletes and workout junkies. Then too in the same constituency were the dreamy men of face and form with gold necklets and shirts open to the third button on their chests even at the office, sheepskin overcoats in the fall, a wardrobe of leather through the winter, a ten-year-old classic sportscar on the driveway. He'd catch them shooting hard glances at him.

He was a challenge to how they knew the world worked. He was a big itch with dreamboat guys, who scratched it tactlessly, force-feeding the matter of looks into lunches and coffee-breaks at the lab, and any standups he happened to join in Columbine's company at receptions, as of talking about the joys of jogging to an amputee. Suddenly Jack would find the subject of physical appearance in the conversation as a value ranked high above character, talent, good judgement and any other virtue that comes to mind. 'We had this quarterback in high school, couldn't throw but he was a really good-looking guy,' a really good-looking guy would say most earnestly, looking at everybody in the group except Jack. 'Well, in this one game....'

Keep in mind that Jack was new to the world as the rest of us know it. Now in the matter of our respect for personal appearance he was forming a sense of the larger world as much more in thrall to fantasy than Hollywood is. Moreover Hollywood has solid economic reasons for everything it does, which you can't say of the larger world. He therefore does think of Hollywood as a centre of knowledge – sort of a Harvard of the coast – and of the world outside the tinsel town as flaked and offwhack. In one place human illusion about such phenomena as the cute wink and the charming grin and their associated idolatries and instincts, the rule of the charismatic personality, how trust is placed and why, are subjects of regular conferences and painstaking study, and heavy money is wagered on what powers they can wield. In the real world beyond Hollywood's magic walls these influences come and go unacknowledged, like sprites and goblins and other visitors from fairyland.

Columbine usually dropped in to Jack's lab at day's end and they went together to the parking lot. She might put her arm around Jack's waist or hold his hand. So obviously minds were cracking, the wicked witch of the north was in town again, the system was breaking up. This is a time for men who understand the world and have big dollars invested in Jim's Gym and their hair to get some answers.

Jack was brushing green dye out of his fingernails at the end of one day when a colleague he hardly knew, a plastics technologist with a trustworthy athlete's face, took up a position at the next sink, having apparently followed Jack into the washroom. The man wore a ditch-digger's denim coverall with buckles of white gold, jade buttons and the name Nino Ricci stitched on the right breast pocket-flap. 'What does she do, that girl in optics, Columbine, is that her name?' this man asked, turning an enquiring eye on Jack with the most charming of man-to-man smiles.

'Contract projects,' Jack said sedately, though with enough reserve to convey that he was unaccustomed to washroom interrogations. 'We do the contract research. Excuse me.' He put the brush down and reached for a towel.

The plastics man's violet eyes were shadowed as he turned the taps on and he looked down at the filling sink thoughtfully. He was, Jack understood, seeking reassurance. 'You're lucky, she's very beautiful. I've seen you around. Live together too, do you?' the man said lightly and lifted one tough eyebrow.

This wasn't unlike the meeting with the waiter in the Hunters' Club Room, a random encounter of strangers. Jack could easily have seen a brother to be comforted and spared confusion. However, the sailor man is not himself free of fantasy. Right now he'd been in Greenland waters since June and seen no whale. The barrels were empty and the winter storms would soon be rising, and he'd sold his hard weather tackle to buy gin and rum last time ashore, a bad habit but it was his nature. He was working with the wrong green, or the electronics weren't tracking properly.

He stood up tall at the rail, squinting at the horizon but glancing too at the poor island savage adorned with shells and gewgaw beads. He'd maybe seen too many of these simple people. He pulled down on the towel roller, uttering a salty chuckle as he dried his hands.

'Livin together?' said Jack, and squinted one-eyed into the simple face. 'Ar, if ye like to call it that, matey, but it ain't jest the livin together, pretty as that do be, it's more the lickin and kissin an fondlin that hardly never stops, an the gushes like a school a whale. I do seek er perfeck woos with these yur hands an she screamin higher'n a gull, an swoopin on me much the same. 'Tain't only livin together, the suckin an foggin an such that do occupy her an me. It be a sight better'n livin, sinkmate, any kind a livin, take my word. It be a wonder o the world.'

The man pulled the plug without asking anything else, bending down at the shoulders with darker gentian eyes to see the swirl of water, a small vortex to look at.

The Sutton suits Cleveland Dan. The only facility it doesn't have that Dan would like is a dump. Cleveland Dan spends lots of time in garbage dumps and he's an expert on them – such a dump had undependable open hours, another was good but distant, this one wanted to be a recycling depot, that one was trying to be a barter centre, and over here you have odd attendants, sky-high dumping rates, or some other problem. Dan likes an old-fashioned dump.

He thought the Sutton should have included a dump facility. It ingested hundreds of truckloads of merchandise every day, and what were the residents supposed to do, eat it? Where could it all go? For active consumers who lived in the complex the normal collections, only two a week at best, weren't able to handle the outflow. Cleveland Dan fed as much merchandise as he could back into the system as trades, but his apartment space did keep filling up. When the whole complex was replaced by the newer model, he felt, there should be a permanent conduit to some outside pit attached, perhaps to a landfill area in the farmland beyond the Annex. Every organism had to have a rear end, after all, that was logical. A landfill just beyond the Annex could charge sensible prices for helping to clear the logjam in the Sutton at the consumer level.

He had the carpeting ripped out of his place on a regular basis. And he wasn't the kind of man to get down to the level of trying to resell used carpeting, the installers carted it away as part of the deal or if they didn't Dan had to take it to the dump. He bought two new cars a year – this is just background on Dan, he didn't dump his old vehicles – a sports model, German usually, and a big old chromy four-by-four American wagon for trips to the dump. Twice a year he rearranged the walls in his tenth-floor apartment when he upgraded his sound and video systems. There was always a rarer CD or DAT player, an amp with better specs or a nearer-to-perfect speaker system waiting to be moved in. The other furniture came and went like the seasons. In recent months the end of the era of turntables had been announced, and he'd moved out three. Just at the moment his big Panasonic is a year old and needs to be returned to Stax or Metro to make way for the Sony triple, the one-piece three-gun with the VHF remote. He had had the same pictures on his walls for a couple of months as we look in on him, from the Poussin Studio, French clowns and jockeys and ballerinas, and Dan was getting a little tired of their faces and postures.

Cleveland Dan had tried other places to live and other kinds of lives. Once he'd even enjoyed the table saws and garden tractors of the suburbs, but found that as playware they made demands and created guilt. His marriages had failed him in exactly the same way, newness and fun followed by demands and guilt. Five marriages had gone busted on Cleveland Dan before the warranties ran out. In his amiable fashion he was prepared to try again should another good woman come along. But he had trouble settling down with a woman for more than ninety days or so. There was always a newer woman he saw he liked better.

He was a rightwinger politically, though this political view wasn't held with passion or any high thoughts of his birthright of freedom. It was just pretty clear to Cleveland Dan that the leftwingers would think nothing of taking his money away and making him go out to work every day.

Metro Electronics on the North Plaza is Stax's main home-entertainment competitor. On a midweek morning of early summer, May, before the school holidays, business was slack in the Sutton in the golden age of retailing and Dan had the whole Metro showroom to himself, talking to Bernie Katz. In fact Wolf Stoglow who owns Stax is a good friend of Bernie's. Bernie is now trying to sell Cleveland Dan an overpriced speaker system he has on his hands. But he wasn't pushing the speakers seriously. He knew why Dan was in the store.

'They've been on the market for two years,' Dan objected. 'I had that system when I was married the last time.'

'I can get it for you for fifteen hundred, Dan. What did you pay two years ago, three thousand?'

'Thirty-five hundred,' Dan said, very happily smiling at Bernie who's a tall fair man in his fifties with square rimless glasses he wears low on his nose. Bernie had on a tropical suit in a light orange with a white belt. Metro's selling method is no-frills and Bernie keeps the aisles stacked with boxes from Japan and Korea and the floor littered with urethane spacers and excelsior.

'I had to take out two walls to match sound levels. I have an idea that's where the marriage started to break up, you know,' Cleveland Dan confided to Bernie Katz. 'My wife had to sleep with the kids while they moved the walls. She had a couple of weeks in there to think about everything. She's breathing gyproc dust and there's the sawing and scrugun noise, and then of course her bedroom got cut in half and she lost her closet when they put in the subwoofer. I'll say this, that wall change gave me the best bass I ever had. The midrange was funny though. Tammy Wynette got all recessed and Kenny Rogers had too much sizzle on his top end.'

They were sitting on a couple of demonstrator speakers near the big open windows drinking coffee from styro cups. As Cleveland Dan chatted with Bernie there was an addict's zing in his blood. He had the life of a drinker raising the first beaker of the evening to his lips, a gambler stepping off the plane at Las Vegas on a good morning. The few people he saw passing on the North Plaza were beautiful for him and defined on their edges with hard light like angels. Cleveland Dan is about to buy a thing. He took a swallow of his coffee which was lukewarm and watery. It was the best-tasting coffee he'd had in a week.

'Yes, with country you're sure looking for honest top end, but weren't you using the Oracle at the time, Dan? That's strange, I never heard anything but good about the midrange out of that system with the Oracle. What was your tonearm and cartridge?' This was just talk from Bernie who was waiting for Cleveland Dan to mention the Sony fifty-inch with the VHF remote. They chatted in an idle manner of well-loved cartridges and tonearms and record decks in days past, the last of their kind. Cleveland Dan seemed ready to move off. He said, one foot on the floor: 'I was in Stax yesterday. Well, I was passing by and dropped in. Pete there, I don't know if you know him, said four thousand for the three-gun Sony they have in the window. Four large. I might go outside the complex if I can't do better.'

Bernie became angry at once. He jumped off the speaker, nimbly stepping to the cash counter where he began to leaf through price dockets. 'What the hell do you go into Stax for, Dan?' he said, pretty offended. 'God,

I don't know about people. I guess they must like throwing money away. That's a salon, isn't it? That's a high-end audio salon they're running up there. Concourse rents,' said Bernie with automatic contempt, noticing that Cleveland Dan had taken two hundred dollars off Stax's quote, 'and listening-rooms, service centre on the premises, who do you think pays for it? Six salesmen in new suits and they're working for nothing. They have the Sony triple in the window. It's a fifty-inch three-gun monitor television receiver with very high frequency hand control, that the one?'

'That's the one, Bernie.'

'I'd have to get an okay from the manager,' said Bernie, who owns Metro, tapping his calculator. He was enjoying himself quite as much as Cleveland Dan was. They are partners in one of life's zestful dances, trade, which is always good fun. Sometimes Bernie gets the better deal, other times Dan, according to rules of desire and retail economics that nobody really understands. Bernie's bread-and-butter sales are made to Sutton transients he sees just once. He's like a freelance shepherd shearing passing sheep. He likes doing it but it doesn't keep him on his toes and dancing. So he loves Dan. Naturally Dan loves him too. 'You can take that unit home for thirty-seven fifty.'

'Round her off at thirty-five, Bernie. I'll write you a cheque.'

'Dan, I'd be delighted to, I'd like nothing better, but thirty-five's right on our cost. We can't make a living.'

'Well, for the difference,' Cleveland Dan said, relaxed on the sharp cusps of pleasure with equally brilliant edges yet to come, practically feeling the lovely new switches yielding under his fingertips, 'I can get their three-year service at Stax. Say I write you thirty-six, straight cash. I'll take a chance nothing goes wrong with the TV.'

Bernie picked up his coffee and took his seat on the speaker beside Cleveland Dan again. His appearance was unhappy and indifferent. Cleveland Dan shot a glance at him to check on the sincerity of this mood. Maybe it was the real McCoy, maybe not. His big pink face glowing with pleasure and friendship Cleveland Dan said: 'You have one in stock?'

'In the back,' said Bernie. He can't afford to stock big monitor TVs. But he could borrow one from Stax.

'Well, I wouldn't want to argue about fifty bucks if you can make the delivery today.'

'Thirty-seven?'

'Thirty-five fifty.'

'Thirty-six fifty, plus a couple of dozen new tapes,' said Bernie. He had a lot of rewrapped old ones. 'That's a hundred bucks right there in brand-name tapes.'

They looked into each other's eye in joy, Cleveland Dan's ginger eyebrows up on his forehead, Bernie's polished eyeglasses alight and his lips drawn back in a grin of love. 'I'll write up the ticket, Dan,' he said. 'You're going to like that TV, nothing else on the market holds a candle to it.'

Cleveland Dan, having fired up a cigar, walked two or three inches above the ground out on the North Plaza, feeling the new Sony triple in the pit of his belly. His head was as light as a child's pink balloon. He saw only two other people on the plaza walk and when he turned into the North Mall he found it empty except for the Wake-Up Man. Cleveland Dan tapped the ash from his cigar and gave the Wake-Up Man an absentminded smile.

'That's very good,' said the Wake-Up Man without breaking step going by, his lorn eyes on a spot half a metre or so above Dan's head and speaking, as always, in a civil tone. 'A man smoking a fat cigar, grinning like a fool and pretending life's wonderful. That's exactly what we need to get us out of this mess, people smoking fat cigars and looking happy. Wake up, sonny.'

Nobody at all was in sight when Cleveland Dan a few minutes later heard a sailor's shantey coming toward him, sung with gusto in a tolerable light baritone.

> *My flashman he's a Yankee boy!*
> *With his hair cut short behind.*
> *He wears a pair a long seaboots,*
> *An he sails on the Black Ball Line!*

He bumped hard into somebody, a shoulder-to-shoulder collision. But he couldn't see a person. Normally he bumped into people only on Saturday afternoons, if he happened to be making his way through the Sutton to the Parthenon Tower elevators while the big signboard was active, and all the radios and TVs were dealing out sports results, so that he had to walk with his eyes closed down to slits and a finger in each ear if he wanted to enjoy the games on tape on Sunday morning when Ralph Jim Trasker and the men with the Dixie accents held the live channels as a fortress wall to wall. But now his eyes and ears were wide open. He heard a couple of closing lines:

... oh, you New York girls!
Can't you dance the polka?

The song ended on this question. A voice exclaimed: 'Wow, a clean hit a-starboard! Hoo, down ee goes, he's sitting on his brains again! Who rammed me? Ar, beggin your pardon, Dan, me own fault an none a yourn.'

Cleveland Dan put his cigar to his mouth and took a puff with interest. He could see only the vacant spaces of the morning-time mall all around him. 'Spankin along under full sail, no lookout. I wur thinking o a wench. Part o me day come the second watch an no pleasure in't believe me – a turrible rough-weather duty it looks like. But hey, shrivel me balls, Dan, I've never seen ye better. Good colour an cut to yer jib. A seegar, a spark in yer eye an a spring in yer legs. Yer an example t'the world, Cleveland Dan. Bought summat at Metro I'll be bound. Circuits an wheels in a box from Bernie Katz an look at ye. If Gabriel blew his horn this very minute an everythin wur proved true, the justice above ourn, there's some a the righteous o'the earth entering their reward as couldn't show so much pleasure as your doin. Why? Because it ain't in their souls, Dan. Yer an example t'the world.'

Cleveland Dan said with curiosity but no surprise. 'I can hear you but I can't see you. Do we know each other?'

'Course there's some as would say we're carryin ye on our backs, Dan, we're workin our fingers t'the bone fer ye.'

This sounded aggressive to Cleveland Dan. He asked: 'How's that?'

'Yer a draggin anchor, some'd say. Put your like all away an t'heavy cream'd shake down in t'milk. The rest of us could see our work in our pay.' Jack spoke with disgraceful hypocrisy here since he's just as much a drone of the Sutton as Cleveland Dan is. He doesn't do any work, as most people understand that misused word. Jack was brushing his cloak, smudged with dust from the fall. It showed as grey streaks hovering in the air, like small galaxies made of motes suspended in a sunbeam.

'Oh yes?' Cleveland Dan said, talking to a ventilation grate he noticed a few steps away, and the digging worker or Post Office repairman who had to be down there. 'Well, let me tell you something. It's money that makes the world go. Not work. You guys are always complaining there aren't enough jobs. But suppose you got the jobs but didn't get paid? I'll bet you wouldn't want the jobs. Would you? You wouldn't take the jobs if there wasn't a pay day at the end of the week. So when you guys ask for jobs what you're really asking for is money, isn't it. In my case,' said Cleveland Dan trenchantly, 'I have my own money, so you don't hear me whining that I can't find a job. It's people like me that keep the economy running and when it stops running we're in big trouble. Little kiddies who don't have enough to eat,' Cleveland Dan explained, 'and people who have to keep driving last year's car. You guys should think of the nation's economy the next time you feel like going on strike. Ask yourselves whether you love your country or what.'

There was no reply to this argument from the person he'd buffeted though Cleveland Dan thought he heard a sigh moving away from him. As he continued on his way with his cigar the belligerence was instantly switched out of Cleveland Dan's mind. He was thinking of baseball upcoming on a fifty-inch screen. He couldn't have been happier.

Three nuns all in white turned into the North Mall off the Concourse, chatting together in French. The two on the flanks were unusually large Oriental nuns with steel-framed glasses. The middle nun was bigger still and could have weighed as much as 150 kilos. She had a round red face and a shark's mouth that was busy chewing. All three looked not at Cleveland Dan's face but at the cigar in his hand when he stopped them.

'Watch out for two men down there, sisters,' said Cleveland Dan, who's a kindly chivalrous person. 'Some heckling's going on today. Nothing dangerous, but keep an eye out. The Wake-Up Man and a union guy.'

This information amused the Oriental nuns who feinted a couple of blunt, playful judo chops at each other. The middle nun spat tobacco juice at Cleveland Dan's feet and, shooting a cuff of her habit back, tapped a finger on his chest. 'You think it's fair, my friend, forcing us to breathe your second-hand smoke?' said she. 'Take some good advice, kick the habit. If I can do it, so can you.'

In fact Jack is fonder of Cleveland Dan than he is of much of the Sutton's characteristic life. A phenomenon that somebody takes true pleasure in can't be all bad, Jack thought, meaning the Sutton, separating truth from imagination in this judgement. Even the bloodiest wars are remembered with intense nostalgia by whole generations of men who were lucky enough to come out of them alive. The wench on Jack's mind when he bumped into Cleveland Dan was Imogene Wedekind.

Here's his problem with Imogene. See what you can make of it. She's more intelligent than all the men in her life. She is also a fastidious person who never in the morning puts on yesterday's linen. Likewise you will never in Imogene Wedekind's speech hear such phrases as *if you will*, *point in time*, *bottom line* and *at the end of the day*. She won't argue against an observed tendency with the comment that something *does not a* something *make*. She very seldom uses the word *ironically*, its correct application being so rare, and she understands that *gender* isn't a nicer way of saying *sex*. Yet she's spirited and warm by nature and in her youthful years.

One of the mating ceremonies that kept nudging Jack and suggesting itself to him as helpful featured a top-hatted gentleman in the old days drinking champagne with a sprightly miss from the *corps de ballet*. Who, Jack asked himself broodingly, taking a shortcut through the empty North Plaza, would be our own time's male equivalent of those chorus girls of yesteryear, for Imogene? Not too bright, over-adulated by a faithful band of followers, showered with gifts, healthy and physically attractive and strutting their stuff regularly for an entranced audience ...? The connection came to him brilliantly, out of the blue.

Athletes, cried Jack innerly, enlightened. The TV athletes! Of course! Imogene should make her choices from the chorus lines of the puck and ball shows! Like the top-hatted gentlemen she would be looking at bodies firstmost, seeking intellect elsewhere if she sought it at all. She might like Hughie Brewer, who was a sultry blond, or Kevin Bastien – well, thought Jack, why not go all the way here, why not Jean-Guy Pickett the Golden Great One himself – it was just then that he took Cleveland Dan's hard blindsider and went down on his butt.

He had stopped by the Nailer on his way out to breakfast. Mrs Delgardo's group was playing Probe. That's a sight of rare melancholy, adults playing board games at eight in the morning. Mrs Delgardo and her people were planning to put the last will and testament fakement to Mr Nightingale, son of the newest inmate. It is a scam, if you are interested in the terminal-care underground, pioneered in the Sunset Home chain in New York State in the late sixties, that worked its way up the eastern seaboard through the Boston branches of Amazing Grace Realty and Nursing Services Incorporated. It got into the Maritimes in the eighties and into Quebec from Allcare of New Brunswick, and had recently crossed into Ontario from Hull.

'I can't do everything, Mrs Delgardo,' said the former criminal Mr

Smith, who was using the name Fetherington. 'If I'm handling General Schata then somebody else should be looking after Mrs Nightingale. Fair's fair.'

'Have you a T, Mr Fetherington?'

'Eh?'

'Mr Fetherington?'

'What's this Fetherington?'

'Mr Smith, do you have a T?'

'Eh? Oh yes, sure. You had me fooled with that Fetherington.'

'And a D?'

'No D. Sounds like some kind of fictional name, that's what fooled me. Sounds like a name somebody made up.'

Judge Wainwright had been napping in his chair. He came awake and peered at his Probe word.

Mr Smith said to Mrs Delgardo: 'Can't Wainwright here handle the Nightingale job? He sure could use the exercise.'

'No,' said Judge Wainwright. 'I provided you with a legal will form. That's so near conspiracy it's a matter of opinion, and it's all I'm doing.'

'Well, you can buy them in a store. That's no great help. How come,' said Mr Smith, appealing to Mrs Delgardo again, 'he's allowed to keep his principles? He's retired.'

'Yes, Judge Wainwright, we are living in peculiar circumstances. Can't we have new rules now?'

The judge had his eyes closed.

'What about the food, Mr Dolly? It's awful, we're not even getting macaroni any more. Just the meat loaf, made of dirt.'

'Sawdust,' said Mr Dolly. 'Well, not wood sawdust. It's some kind of hard plant fibre. The grit comes in the eggshells sprinkled on it, gives you fibre and grit. Birds love it. It's used in batteries to feed poultry. The dietician says we'll be staying on it as a staple if there aren't too many bad reactions.'

'Have you been able to phone the stock exchange, Mr Dolly?'

'I'm doing my best,' Mr Dolly said, a little defensively. 'Vancouver mines, mostly. I'm looking for short-term gainers, with no working capital. That's basically trying to pluck hard cash out of thin air. Have you got a C?'

'Yes. Money talk is so fascinating.'

'And another E?'

'Yes.'

'Delitescent, Mrs Delgardo?'

'Yes! You're so intelligent, Mr Dolly.'

Speaking out of the side of his mouth, which didn't move, Mr Smith said: 'Listen, Mrs Delgardo, just in case the intelligent one here comes up empty, don't forget we can put you on takeout food any time with the money you gave me for the other job. There's more than a few barbecued chickens and pizzas in that stash.'

'No. Certainly not. Mr Dolly is seeing to our food.'

'Yes, well, if you say so. I can't believe you're this far down, Mrs Delgardo,' said Mr Smith respectfully. 'When I was in Havana in the thirties every time I picked up a newspaper some king was giving you jewels. Or racehorses.'

'Yes, they were wonderfully romantic days. But I have only Rudolph's brooch now. I promised him I'd keep that forever.'

'Never could see the guy's appeal, speaking frankly. The one I liked best of his was *Blood and Sand*.'

Judge Wainwright snored lightly. Mr Dolly was depressed. 'It's very sad. Everything trickles away.'

'Oh no,' said Mrs Delgardo, scanning her cards with a lively eye, ready to play the new game. 'Not in the least. I never bartered a luxury for a necessity in my life. Except for Rudolph's brooch I gave all my jewellery trinkets to a very nice boy I met on the beach at Cannes in 1966.'

'All of them, Mrs Delgardo?'

'He was a very nice boy.'

Jack let himself into Elmo Apse's place like a thief and saw the bowl of grapes on the table untouched and the empty hock bottle. A couple of panatela stubs were squashed in the ashtray. Clothing had been flung on the couch, unidentifiable in the morning grey. Jack turned on the light and saw the girl's slip and dress.

He pushed his way through the forest fronds to the bedroom. Apse had the sheet pulled up to his chin, for which Jack was grateful in a detached fashion. Apse naked was no way for a sensitive invisible man with edged memories to start a day. The Ogden Nash girl, Sarah, was half covered by the sheet and lying on her back. She wore a proud expression in her sleep. One hand rested as if by custom between her legs and the other was across her ribcage, under breasts round as melons with small purple nipples.

Because of the body's response to a strange presence, something Jack was used to, her eyes snapped open. Of course Apse slept on. She looked around the bedroom in alarm and then relaxed sleepily, turning to study Apse. Here Jack would have appreciated seeing a critical scrutiny, or some sign at least of sensible judgement being conducted. He was morosely irritated to see nothing in the girl's manner toward the sleeping man except pleased tenderness, as of a child contemplating a kitten. She curled a finger in his hair. She tickled Apse's beard.

'What time is it?' Apse asked.

'It's getting late. I have to go now, Elmo.'

However, it was clear even to Jack, standing across the room in the doorway, that Sarah didn't have to go but wanted to be coaxed to stay. She was in bed with the wrong man for that game. Apse yawned and scratched his chest and reached for a smoke. Jack took a seat on a plant bench inside the doorway, a dissatisfied sprawl, not bored exactly but with a strong sense of seeing a rerun of something he hadn't liked in the first place.

When Sarah went to the bathroom she turned on both taps so that Apse wouldn't hear unpleasant sounds from in there. She brought her clothes from the living room into the bedroom and then stopped, deciding that getting dressed so soon would be an unsophisticated thing to do. She wanted to be a cool femme, naked in the morning at her lover's place, it was just that she didn't know how to do it. She began to comb her hair, sitting on her side of the bed. But the sweep of the girl's back from shoulder to waist was so artlessly clean that Jack sprang to his feet from the bench, throwing his arms apart and his head back, mouthing an appeal to an imaginary umpire up past the Hoeglin ceiling: 'What kind of perverted shit do you call this, eh? Eh?'

'What, Elmo?'

'I didn't say anything.'

'So when will I see you,' she said, at last beginning to dress, putting the question with an admirable air of command. 'Tomorrow's no good for me. I have the gallery on Thursday.'

'Saturday?'

'That'd be great.'

'I'll pick you up. I love you very much, Sarah,' Apse said, showing his large teeth in a smile, a wide grin that looked like love and seemed to have soul in the eyes. She said primly at once: 'It's too early to talk about love.'

Nevertheless she was thinking about love herself. Jack didn't know just then whether this was good or bad for her. Naturally he could do nothing until he'd made that decision about Sarah. Conscience and compromise were too much alike, thought Jack, looking into the serenity on Sarah's face, which was hidden from Apse by being turned toward Jack. They were very like forgiveness too, and forgiveness – the kind Horsy taught, the Christian version – was so often a twin brother of wretchedness that only a man who resisted forms of weakness and weighed all his acts could be sure he knew he was doing the right thing.

Jack was at Arpinall College, a divinity school in Cambridge, Massachusetts, before he became a scientist. After a year he understood that his education by Horsy Stacpole wasn't complete, or was complete for a nonexistent world, with mythology occupying too much territory. He was the superior of all his peers in education but he didn't function well among them with what he thought he knew about life. He was like some humanitarian symbol in an idealistic story. He credited people automatically with extensive principles, and intelligence, and honourable motives. He actually shouldn't have been let out in the world alone without a keeper or bodyguard.

The big problem was Horsy Stacpole's education of Jack in the system of Christian ethics and moral thought as a practical basis for the conduct of a life. As a theory, a resource of knowledge, this system usually doesn't do an individual any harm. Indeed, an ability to distinguish between good and evil can be quite useful in a career, in jurisprudence or teaching, say. But Horsy always made a distinction between fact and theory in what he taught. When Horsy Stacpole taught Jack botany the lad accepted the teaching trustfully. The next lesson might then have been Psalms, *The meek shall inherit*, and naturally with the same trust and no other human contact Jack felt that he was hearing about a process as inexorable as photosynthesis. Matthew was Horsy Stacpole's favourite apostle, the author of possibly the most misleading instructions ever set to paper for a young man seeking to find his feet and balance in the American free-enterprise system. In his freshman year Jack was as true as an arrow to Horsy Stacpole's favourite Matthew, five forty-four, which goes, unbelievably: *Love your enemies, bless them that curse you, do good to them that hate you, and pray for them which despitefully use you, and persecute you.*

He began his first year of human fellowship living according to that rule with a roommate named Dungannon, a severe and haughty boy who precociously looked like a bishop. Pretty soon Dungannon was shaking thumbtacks under Jack's bedsheets and tipping glue into his typewriter and squeezing Jack's toothpaste all over the bathroom floor and throwing his texts and notes out the window, apparently in response to something Dungannon saw in meek Jack that was deeply loathsome. Later Dungannon also spread odd accounts of Jack's private behaviour around the college, feeling free to invent incidents of ritual sacrilege and devil worship. On the rare occasions Jack was spoken to on campus he was sometimes asked about his mother's brothel.

A number of special and restrictive rules for scholarship students appeared on the notice board on Jack's floor in his first year. The same notices weren't on other floors, and Jack found out by chance that he was the only man on a scholarship in the residence. When he went to keep appointments with his professors they didn't answer his knock, though he could hear them moving around quietly behind their doors. These teachers, oblique and civil men, seemed to be in possession of information about Jack that went beyond Dungannon's stories. He now and then received private lectures, on such subjects as hypocrisy, vainglory, sanctimony and humility, given to the full class but directed at him, with the professor standing in front of Jack and holding his eye. It had somehow been predetermined by the faculty that he was a liar and would cheat on tests.

His papers were returned uncorrected. Occasionally there was a note, as of somebody pouncing, demanding a source or an author's name which Jack had thought too obvious to supply. His one gloss of congratulation on a paper ran as follows: *I haven't been able to discover who the real author of this fine essay is, Mr Clemmaknohke. Well done!*

The college cafeteria assigned Jack a special small table near the cashier, where the guard could watch him. His card was checked every time he used one of the libraries. He was on some kind of blacklist at the student council office where they refused to accept him for volunteer projects, hobby groups, fundraisers, team support events et cetera.

A rapist-murderer was active that winter in the Brighton area of Boston and two campus security men visited Jack to ask him about his movements. Jack was able to supply them with alibis, but Dungannon butted in too with information the investigators didn't ask for, notes of the time it would take to reach Brighton from Cambridge by speedy car and helicopter, a theory that Jack had a twin brother, ways that the time of a violent death could be faked to create an alibi by a cunning psycho killer. Toward the end of the school year the Book-of-the-Month Club cancelled Jack's subscription, refunding his money without an explanation. By then Jack knew that he wanted to have a career in a discipline where ideas that didn't check out could be discarded. He had felt some depression in his first experience of living with others according to Horsy Stacpole's rules and felt strengthened by the thought of a new beginning.

He saw a relationship at Arpinall that caught his interest, carried to his ears at first as conversation about one person named Adelentom. This turned out to be the lovers Adele and Tom. Jack observed them for a week, measured by the time it took him to read Joseph Butler's *Analogy of Religion*, a book he could only think of finally as bumptious naïvety. He did his reading in good weather outside, seeking solitude in Longfellow Park or along the banks of the Charles, where professors could not accuse him, as happened sometimes in the main Arpinall Library, of shameful pretence of diligence. He ran across the lovers because they wanted to be alone too and used the same paths.

On the positive side, Jack didn't doubt the mystical and heroic stature of true love: man and woman could aspire no higher together, thought he. Adele was a radiant, chubby girl who seemed to dress expensively. She had warm eyes and saw the world with kindness. Her nature in manner was gay, in opinion merry. Adele had a gift of honest vivacity, gaiety without the stress that's sometimes its prompter.

Tom was less prone to smiles, a man with a narrow face, thin lips and watery blue eyes. His hair was brown and untidy, sparse on top at twenty, and he usually wore a tweed jacket with a woollen tie. He carried a canvas satchel slung on his shoulder wherever he went. He kept magazines in it, and poetry, texts, pencils and notebooks, candy and keys, and even so his jacket pockets always bulged full. With his male friends Tom was shy and silent. With Adele he could talk confidently and articulately, and he could tell jokes.

Adele brought this change to Tom instantly, by her presence. More than once in the week Jack saw Tom kicking along a path to meet her, smoking a cigarette and listless after a day's classes. Then when he saw the girl Tom's back straightened, his step quickened, his head lifted and his eyes shone, and he was a whole new man.

Tom was to every other eye a somewhat seedy lad, scruffy, woolly, not well bathed, but for Adele he was a splendid knight. Tom's opinions were the best word on any subject for Adele. He was a gift from the sky for her, Jack thought, who was nineteen himself and at that age able to judge others quickly to his own satisfaction. Without Tom Adele would be a Rubens beauty misplaced in days of righteous thinness. Perhaps she would be unhappy in the hostile world, applying herself to penitential diets and lured away from grace by chocolate cake, with laughter that was more stressed and an outlook less kind. In the same way, had Adele not come along, as Jack decided, Tom could have been condemned to his abashed self indefinitely. Tom smoked a lot of cigarettes and there were people who would call his satchel a security blanket. He might have gone on through his life in silent oppression, maybe adding a bottle to the things he needed in the satchel, and boxes of pills and powders too even, until the satchel couldn't help him any more.

In a romance they would both have been beautiful. That would have made their love look truer, in a romance. But Jack was far enough ahead now to understand that it would have made their love look fake to him. Moreover, had just one of them been beautiful the young sailor lad would have been sceptical about the other one. As matters stood he did believe in them. He believed he was seeing a sacrament, and that Adele and Tom had lucked into the mystery of fire and music for which civilizations had fallen, the great madness of the heart.

But then down at the commonplace level Jack, who was living there and a toilsome life it was, noticed that the name Adelentom, when Tom wasn't present, was used contemptuously. He wasn't respected in the community of his friends. He couldn't belong to it. Tom couldn't participate in spontaneous plans, for trips or parties or contributions of time or money, because he wasn't free to pledge himself. Tom always had to check with Adele, and so to his peers he came to seem a slavish fellow.

Jack was on the last pages of Butler, meaning that he was soon to bid the lovers farewell. He couldn't help thinking of two imperfect trees in a forest remaining upright and healthy only because they've fallen against each other. More seriously, unless Jack was mistaken their relationship had taken on even more of a glow in the week he'd known them. They'd become more in love, and Jack didn't like what that implied. The phenomenon was capable of change. Something that improves can degrade.

In his final week at Arpinall some time later Jack was having a sandwich and coffee at his island table in the cafeteria when Dungannon came in with a dozen or so members of the Philosophy Club. 'There he is,' said Dungannon in his silver pulpit voice, stabbing a finger almost in Jack's face with his eager followers gathered behind him. 'Stalked Adelentom through the park and took photographs. He's demanding money from Tom and wants to sleep with Adele, or,' said the future bishop to the philosophers with a worldly laugh, 'vice versa. We're getting up a petition to have his table moved into the kitchen and I'd like you all to sign.'

But Dungannon was already in Jack's past. Now he believed that a person could not be redeemed by love. He could only try to become a hero, which meant that he could probably never allow himself to become a lover. The story always ends when a hero becomes a lover, because that is when he stops being a hero. It was obvious enough to Jack at nineteen that on a late movie a gunman with holsters tied down wouldn't be able to bring a hush of respect on a town by riding into it if he happened to have his true love riding on the pillion of his horse with her besotted arms wrapped around his lean gunman's waist. The sailor lad thought he would be in control of his own life as it unfolded for him.

Chapter 7

Zapping

THE NOVELIST and column guru Douglas T. Harder inducts new followers on Thursdays. They are met in town for a personal audience at a bar near the paper, and then it's into cars and on to Harder's apartment in the Tower for an evening of philosophy. Harder's talk on education, one of his favourite subjects, includes slides of illiterate student papers, vandalized classrooms, security guards in school corridors with revolvers on their hips, and tape of teachers on picket lines. Later on he reads from his work.

He'd never been to school himself. Living life had been his education, as he often said, with an implication that nobody else had done this. But he did see himself as an ascetic scholar, nourished by mind and aphorism and disdaining comfort for the body. His furniture was strikingly spartan, meant to make an observer ask the question – why do we all need cushions and tassels and colour schemes and such, if an eminent writer and thinker like Douglas T. Harder needs so little? He had an idea of himself as a pre-Christian hermit of the Celts in a cave. The simplicity of his own needs was as frequent a subject in Harder's columns as education and the vices and shortcomings of the rest of humankind.

The new guests on Thursdays weren't surprised to walk into a very plain place. Some were initially shocked, and embarrassed, because they had nearly all grown up in houses with solid and tasteful furnishings, tassels and colour schemes, and on first view an ascetic's habitation looks like shameful penury. When the bottom family in your group earns its low ranking by having couches and carpeting that are a little frayed, or the wrong colour, or from the wrong store, it's a test of intellectual rigour to adjust to no carpeting and no couches and no visible brand names. An important distinction between a pauper and a guru, however, was usually perceived by Harder's new followers after a few moments of adjustment: the one who lives an involuntarily thin life will often make most pathetic efforts to improve his poor state, and these efforts rather than the meagreness are his marks of shame.

Harder's cave was just as he wanted it to be, with books and dog-eared quarterlies on the chairs and floors. Books are the beauty of a home, Harder was fond of telling fans, to let them know that they'd come through the doorway of a superior free spirit and not some bollockless bachelor asking them to excuse the mess. He had had two failed marriages and often wrote with insight about wedlock.

There were a dozen kitchen chairs from the Salvation Army in the living room against the walls to be pulled out by the group as needed, and two black-oak church pews, one against the wall and its mate under the window.

These walls were faced around the room by brick-and-plank shelves. Harder's apartment was on the eighth floor and didn't have curtains on the windows. Very good light washed across a floor that was actually just the plywood installed in the Parthenon Tower as a carpet base. Austere construction-industry hieroglyphics like BC FIR and *Con. grd GIS* could be seen stencilled in places on Harder's floor. In this way his mind was free to soar above carpet care.

'I haven't time in my life to read the books I want to read,' he had written. 'So why should I squander time on housecleaning? And I haven't enough money to buy the books I want to buy. So why should I pay out money to have housecleaning done for me?' The bar counter projected from in front of the kitchen entrance and was stocked with bottled waters and essences of garlic and carrot and white-label cans of tomato juice, palely honourable under lighting designed to bathe the hues of liquors and wines.

Jack spent most of the morning humping materials into Harder's cave. It was labour, and Jack whistled halyard shanteys to keep his spirits up, getting down to a job he'd been postponing. It was subtle work too, and thankless, say like advancing literary models that need to be preserved even though they're noncommercial and the labour is too fine to be noticed. Look at any human person, moderately independent, as the hero of his own movie. Well, he is, apart from the basic skeleton and flesh, self-chosen. He treads his very own stage floor – paying rent or mortgage on it – and the backdrop of walls and windows are likewise his, the fabrics too and the shadows and the lighting. He chose them, or agreed that they should be chosen. He chooses his own costumes. He speaks his own script. He is every day a new offering from Self-Created Productions Intergalactic.

Moreover, if his importance grows so does his dramatic content. Truly lofty folk are allowed to practise twenty-four-hour posturing and mummery, and indeed it is expected of them, and cheered and clapped by the rest of us.

The sailor's labour today was simply the alteration of the Douglas T. Harder movie from Socrates to a sitcom. He'd had to stop postponing some small-scale jobs like this because General Schata would soon be in Ottawa, and he expected to be busy on a larger scale when that happened.

The controversy about the general's visit had now begun to occupy newspaper space and air time in the capital city. Conservatives didn't especially like Schata's record but thought he was taking one or two unfair hits from what they liked to call *overheated liberal rhetoric*. He had had a few problems he was trying to iron out as best he could. The liberals, strongly denying ever using warm language, explained that everybody could see General Schata for what he was, a bestial thug and crazed monster tyrant and a bloody-handed maniac; also, on other days, a rabid killer and a deranged psychopathic hoodlum. The conservatives usually then came back with the thought that the general was a dependable customer for our raw materials. He didn't owe our banks any money, and what more could you expect of a foreign country?

Harder is a leading conservative voice. He is in fact so far ahead of conservative opinion that most of it likes to claim to be unaware of him. He admires Schata's record and cites it often. Stray tales of punitive massacres, executions and torture-prisons he brushes off as special-interest exaggerations and propaganda of the outlawed previous regime. Hasn't Schata succeeded in abolishing free education, welfare, the deficit and the trade unions in less than two years? Hasn't he passed firm laws against poverty and parasitism? Had he or had he not achieved full employment for his people, zero unemployment?

Naturally there were liberal rebuttals – putting poor people in concentration camps isn't your ideal anti-poverty programme, said they, nor can massive slave labour be accurately called full employment, and Harder was a grovelling fascist pig – but the fact here is that the guru had a thousand words five times a week for his opinions while the other side had to take its chances that what they believed to be the true stories on the general would somehow come through the great ink-wash and halogen glare of modern news transmission.

Harder's fans weren't well understood by Jack. He could recognize the transients, nervous youngsters of both sexes undergoing their time of change, who having cast off lines from their parents could be taken in tow by any strong grapple. And he understood nostalgists of childhood – of magic neighbourhoods without foreign intruders, and with their own long traditions, who liked Harder's tough talk on immigration policy – Jack could comprehend these folk, while primly withholding sympathy for their opinions. But the guru's core groupies were more alien to Jack's understanding than cats. They looked like any crowd, a line-up at a movie or the column shuffling its way past the checkout at Wonder Food Mart, but to the sailor they were creatures of mystery and enigma. His best guess about them, which didn't explain anything, was that they were in pain. Their confusion made them angry, he supposed, anger being a normal expression of bafflement. Harder offered easements for bafflement, heroes and scapegoats and simple little stories which eased the pain, so they went for it.

In the morning he used a rented polishing-machine on the flooring, applying plenty of wax. The result, polished plywood, looked satisfactorily brave and effortful. He tied a few bright plush cushions on the oaken benches and put a five-dollar rug from K-Mart in front of each bench – one blue and yellow, the other black with gold tassels. In the bathroom Jack thumbtacked a dozen or so joke cards on the walls, and installed a musical holder for the toilet roll that played 'Johnny's So Long At The Fair' on a harp.

For the bare walls in the living room he had brought along a couple of bright posters, one of two kittens in a boot looking out over the laces at four puppies worrying a slipper, and the other showing a blue sunrise in a misty primrose landscape, the phenomenon as a whole viewed from the bottom of a winding pathway that ran through a grove of immature silver birch trees.

The two heaviest items Jack carried in were the TV floor console and the Lay-Z-Lounge. The TV was a model from the early sixties, and was actually not even in working order, but Jack liked it because it said *TV* louder than anything the Japanese were supplying in the nineties, and for its awful power to dominate room-space, however large. He put the TV in the middle of the room with its wires trailing to the walls. On the right side of the Lay-Z-Lounge Jack scattered bags of Cheezies, Toasted Onionchips, and Pizza-Flavoured Snax. On the left, empty ginger ale splits, rye mickeys, beer cans and a tumbler he'd rinsed in milk. Jack had been saving *TV Guides* for a couple of months, waiting to do this job, and he skimmed these on to the floor around the other junk.

After lunch he was still whistling, though somewhat weary by now. He'd brought curtains for Harder's bare windows, of balding blue velvet, all the wrong size, with stain-spots, which he hung unevenly. He purloined all the philosopher's quarterlies and poetry magazines. To replace them he'd brought along lurid periodicals with titles like *Hot Lesbies* and *Mud-Wrestling Mommas*. He pillaged the plank bookshelves of their classical literature, sticking in instead a hundred or so practical nonfiction paperbacks with titles such as *Teach Yourself Aggression, You Can Be a Better Speller!* and *How To Act With Girls*, which dated from the fifties and which he'd bought as a lot for three dollars at one of the Sutton's craft and charity sales.

Harder's study contained a chair, a desk and a filing cabinet. Jack didn't have changes to make in here, where the guests wouldn't penetrate. He sat at the desk to take an honest rest, and found himself looking at a note the philosopher had made on a 4x6 card: 'Men of Business and Feeding the Third World'. It had the appearance of an article or a lecture title to Jack.

He thought he could imagine how a talk by Harder with this title would go. Slide photos of the men of business who might help, guys who knew how to spin straw into gold and whose careers of undeviating self-interest benefited the rest of us, then the usual slides of black kids lining up with bowls to get a ladleful of lumpy white stuff. A rundown of taxpayer cost per capita of this white stuff with no end in sight. Please observe that every child has his/her own dish – could not the private sector help us to recover some of our investment by confiscating these containers and marketing them as grape servers or finger-bowls?

Douglas T. Harder as Jack saw him was a sitcom kind of person, a juggler of thoughts dug up like bones, secondhand revelations and insights, old beauty and integrity, yesterday's passions and chivalries that weren't available to the general population any more because of existing only in literature and not in pictures that could go on TV. He was a smart dog making a living in the entertainment business.

He's a man of clerkly appearance with well-groomed flesh and fingernails, white hair in waves, a mouth turned down by thought in a dry lined face and brightly-absorbed eyes behind glasses that are often held together by bits of tape. He has a high-pitched voice and foppish mannerisms – meeting somebody new he uses two hands to make the greeting, the left on the person's shoulder, the right held at chest level with the thumb up and the fingers pointed down. His writer's costume as a rule is a black turtleneck with tight slacks, but sometimes he appears in a very old moth-eaten sweater and bigwale cords. Formally he comes in a grey lounge suit with a pink shirt and a bow tie. His usual social expression is a priestly smile, as of a grave man among triflers who has a wire open to a more substantial idea of life.

Jack's custom was to take precautions for maintaining darkness when he made his duty calls for Ralph Jim Trasker. He is of course as visible as anybody else when he's naked. But when he went out on visits he could hardly do the work without doffing his invisibility rig of cloak and headgear, gloves and sneakers.

Mama Kaldy happened to be in the bathroom of apartment 1314 when he entered. Jack could hear her splashing around like a hippo in there. Today she was working her way through the sleepwalking scene from Verdi's *Macbeth* in her terrifyingly powerful contralto. The toughened double-glazed windows of her high apartment were resonating and pinging like wineglasses.

Mama Kaldy didn't smoke but Jack went through her handbag anyway checking for matches or any other source of sudden illumination. She was sneaky, and boundlessly curious about him. He closed all the curtains. Just before he turned off the main switch at the fusebox in the kitchen he gave her a call: 'Mrs Kaldy, Ralph Jim's man! Are you ready?'

She let out a squeal of delight. The crashing and thumping sounds from the room indicated that Mrs Kaldy had bounded across the floor and jumped into bed. Jack warily approached the bed looking for a safe way in. He thought he saw her head turned away and darted forward. But then Mrs Kaldy grabbed his ankle. She savagely hauled him on to her stomach. His mouth was opened to yell in fear when the nape of his neck was seized and Mama's thighs closed on his ears. Outside noises were abruptly shut off. Jack could hear only a huge pulse and awful thunderous gurgles: his surmise was that his face was pressed hard against Mrs Kaldy's pudendum. He tried to keep his nose well up, his hands flailing over yielding rolls of mighty flesh with nothing to grasp for purchase.

Mrs Kaldy opened her thighs slightly so that he could hear her. 'Get your tongue out!' she shouted. 'I could name twenty men who'd give their right arms to be where you are right now, you small little skinny ghost fellow. Go on, get it out!'

He'd made the same mistake in this apartment a couple of times already, underestimating Mrs Kaldy's guile and brutal strength. She was, Jack thought, a bragger too. Maybe there were at most three or four men who'd want to be where he was, his nose against a moist squash, suffocating and listening to the dimmed roar of Mama's mighty digestion. Say three or four with oedipal interests, just out of prison. He thrust his knee between her calves and popped his head loose, gasping air in. Simultaneously he strove for holds on Mrs Kaldy's meaty arms which were trying to stuff his head down in there again.

'I wish I had a Hungarian man right now!' Mrs Kaldy complained. 'Oh for just one real man, a Magyar man! Listen, little boy, there aren't any men except Hungarian men, you remember that. The men of Hungary have blood like tokay wine!'

She came athwart of Jack as he lunged upward, going for a quick tranquillizing penetration. He drew back his head just in time to avoid a breast like a cannon ball as it swung past his face. She had Jack's thigh caught in one hand while she tried to grope him with the other, a move he was fending off with a knee and an instep.

'So what's it you've got there, what big thing do you have for me, little child? I can't find anything! Let me feel it! Put it in Mama's hand, there's a good boy!'

Jack thought he understood as he struggled why Mrs Kaldy, a woman with a moustache and abundant underarm hair, and a pubic boss that looked like an electrified yacht mop, found it difficult to hold on to men. She was a Hungarian chauvinist who saw lovemaking as a combat encounter. The Hungarian men Jack knew in the Parthenon Tower were prominently courteous and intellectual, and thin and brittle-looking in physique, and though doubtless there were other kinds they weren't available in her present habitat.

Fortunately Jack managed to clamp Mrs Kaldy's arm under his fending instep, and by using her raised thigh as a rail to guide him he got a lucky penetration. Mama began to calm down then, though still wanting him at arm's length to use her massive hands on his body. 'Let me have that tiny thing!' she said.

Jack had no plans for doing so of course, not to have it exuberantly crushed, gristle and blood vessels viced and damaged, nor to have the member roaringly engulfed in Mrs Kaldy's mouth where with every generous intention on her part it might in a spasm be snapped between massive teeth or sucked hard enough by those great contralto lungs, powerful as a blacksmith's bellows, to suction the scrotum sac inside out. He thought he knew how to proceed. The shifts in the hooks and clasps of arms and legs gave him a way of gripping the headboard one-handed. With this anchor he could move his legs to wrest himself free of her holds. After a few minutes Jack's use of his freedom acted on Mrs Kaldy like a shot of morphine. In fact she was a good-hearted woman. It was just that she had allowed her large spirit and strength into too many areas of her life. Jack held on up there until she slept, thinking of himself as a shipwrecked sailorman astride a whale, some panic still in his eyes and the sweat of fear drying on his spider body. He gave himself credit for seizing his opportunities and keeping his head but he knew his luck in these engagements couldn't last forever.

With so much adrenalin free in his system he must have lost consciousness briefly. He was slapped on the buttocks hard enough then to force a scream in a hiss from between teeth clenched in shock and pain.

'Say, you're a fine boy, you know?' Mrs Kaldy said. 'You're sure you're not Hungarian, hey? Boy, I think some clever Hungarian got to your mommy while your daddy was away. You have style!'

When Jack went to live in the Sutton first he didn't realize he would need his own place as a visible man. He began as a gypsy, camping in whatever Tower apartments were unoccupied, moving out obligingly every time the management rented the place. It wasn't a satisfactory life. It became clear that he needed the same stability, and comforts and possessions, as every other Parthenon Tower inhabitant.

After he got to know his way around the office files and computers he arranged a permanent apartment for himself on the eighth floor in the name of Geoffrey Oliver O'Fit, which was his way of marking himself as a representative of Mr Goof-it. He lives there in pretty good style. He has taken the trouble to arrange a few appearances for Geoff O'Fit in the Sutton offices, an amiable businessman from Boston who has contracts with the feds.

He doesn't work a regular clock. He does, though, put in an honest day, making little adjustments in the Sutton, tinkering with this and that. He has a Robin Hood routine. He tinkers and mends and does some moderate zapping. He can't be everywhere at once but he runs a tight enough ship. Nobody's perfect.

We can look in on Jack for a moment, halting in the doorway of number 816 to gaze on a monk's couch on the immediate right against the wall. Unlike Douglas T. Harder Jack doesn't entertain a view of himself as a monk, however. He knows he hasn't the control to be a monk. On the contrary, he knows he has so little control that he could fly apart at any time, and become any thing. Above the monk's couch hangs an 1881 poster advertisement of Lillian Russell in *The Grand Mogul* at the New York Bijou opera house. To Jack's eye Miss Russell looks merely healthy and plumply built. But for Horsy Stacpole, to explain her presence on Jack's wall, she was always the most beautiful woman God had ever made.

Farther right, beyond four high shankleg stools at a serving counter, you'll see a well-lighted Pullman kitchen. A glass-fronted double fridge, gas stove and vented grill, butcher block, dishwasher, and a disposal area take your eye in that order. In fact Jack can often be found in this kitchen, bruising herbs into a sauce or watching over some gold-crusted dish in the oven while he cooks down a savoury accompaniment for it on the stove top. His being a sailor man doesn't mean he must stick to a diet of lobscouse dinners. You're likely to hear Verdi or Mozart from Jack when he's in this mood, mixed in with the shanteys, as he bangs the Italian saucepans around or slices up the raw flesh and vegetables with his carbon-steel German knifeware. Alas, he often eats elsewhere, however, and his appetite isn't large anyway, he being of the spider kind by nature, in animal terms one of the greyhound breed since boyhood. On a regular basis Jack can be seen scraping dishes that have sat out their span in the fridge into the disposal. Nor does he sing at this chore but works silently, and as quickly as he can.

On your left – you're still standing on number 816's doorsill, where you were put – there's an English harpsichord, a spinet, and an antique pyrometer of cast iron and fine wire on an oak base. You're also viewing on that side a wall of bookshelves and a TV. Against the wall directly ahead, Jack's bedroom wall, he's got an audio stack and a computer station.

Right in front of your eyes, at your feet, lies a Sehna-knotted Isfahan carpet with arabesque patterning on a cream field inside a red border. Jack's red-leather rocker sits on this carpet and, by his right hand, a small cherrywood table piled with the system remotes, notepads, books, sheet-music, video and music cassettes and CD liner notes. He has a Ch'ing sang-de-boeuf fruit bowl on the table too, which he keeps stocked with Crispins or Cortlands or Macouns, or whatever local apples are available.

In case you're curious, Jack paid a big dollar for his bookshelves. Well, admittedly he wasn't using his own money, but he disagrees with the cheap-equals-virtue state of mind. The shelves are walnut and of fine workmanship, the grains matched, the joints invisible. All his technical books are stoutly bound in leather covers, and if you browse the shelves you'll see sailing and navigation manuals, physics texts and source books and what remains, a few classics, of his formerly large library of theology and religious philosophy. He also owns more than a regular share of those volumes and slim editions of novels and poetry that are remarkable for depth and value in their discipline but are by unknown authors whose fingers never did close upon a brass ring as we know it.

He keeps his invisibility rigs in the closet with his other clothes. They rotate through the wash, usually with his coloured shirts.

The spinet is a copy of one made by a Rucker, tuned to the baroque chamber pitch, a semitone lower than the modern. Building models of sailing vessels has been his hobby in most seasons of his life so far, and his current project's more than a metre tall, a ship-rigged three-masted Cape Horner that carried easterners to the California goldfields, the *Aughrim* out of Boston. It sits lengthwise on the serving counter where Jack can comfortably reach into its port or starboard. He keeps his Dremel tools and his wood billets and glues and cordage in the counter drawers.

Depending on the stresses of the moment and the time of day he'll be supine on the monk's couch figuring problems or perched over at the spinet's keys picking out some delicate air we all received as a gift, or tinkering with an elegant batch file on the computer that would compare windlass design graphics through parameters like sailing vessel types, countries and centuries, or stretched on the rocker reading or watching TV, or reaching into the *Aughrim* with the forceps or an Xacto, or in the kitchen as mentioned. That's him in there, when he's alone, and from time to time he'll entertain a guest or guests.

If you stand as you are now you'll see him munching an apple or a carrot, or sipping camomile from a bone china cup, or deep into the rum bottle. As to times, the small morning hours are when he usually watches TV, when he can't sleep, and the hours just after daybreak are given to the *Aughrim*, a mug of black coffee sitting among the glue tubes and glass papers, before the Sutton opens up its doors, while Jack's eye is still fresh and his hand steady. Evenings are given to the computer, and on slack afternoons he'll sit there too, working on little compositions of his own in the baroque style which he won't admit to, as he also denies writing poetry. But naturally nothing follows a strict pattern, and he's been known to restring rigging past midnight or go to the spinet stool early in the afternoon, staying there until an aching lower back causes him to stagger to the rocker. He's been known at a moment of unexpected collapse of control to pour a slug of rum into his camomile tea.

Jack was just living this way in old Sharon, working for himself as a freelance knight, when he met Ralph Jim Trasker, the TV evangelist, who has a son named Paul.

Now Ralph Jim's most immediately impressive characteristic is niceness. When you see him on TV you'd be a hard heart indeed if you didn't say to yourself: 'What a nice man!' Then because many people are cynical about anybody who appears on a screen with a phone number flashing on his chest you'd probably tell yourself the niceness is a fake. That's where you'd be wrong. Ralph Jim Trasker's niceness is real. He's nice most of the time, except when he's swearing, which is his only not-nice character aspect.

Ralph Jim has a serious problem as a religious professional because of his nice nature. He's too nice to make it as a saint. He is technically nearest to a Baptist but will acknowledge the integrity of every other denomination and all other religions, out to the far reaches and such fine divisions as schisms of Shintoism. The truth here is that Ralph Jim's tolerance has spread the buckler of his faith as thin as Saran wrap. It's a closed mind, after all, that makes a faithful man; bigotry is what gives the best nourishment to strength of conviction. When niceness and conscience-searching has undermined proscriptions, dissolved dogmas and dispersed rigid interpretations there's a glorious freedom from prejudice to be sure, and a mind open to every possibility of the universe. But in tolerating everything Ralph Jim can lay claim to nothing of his own. Without bigotry and intolerance he's adrift in a sea of goodwill. That is what niceness does for you.

His wife Sue Ellen is good to look at. Jack likes to watch her romping with Paul and doing housework, taking showers and so on. Her depth of sincerity as the support of the TV preacher may be questionable, however, not that that matters. Jack has an idea of her as a chameleon wife who has taken on the colours of her husband. Say her husband was a general in a war it is possible that she would be as interested in battles and dying bodies, Jack supposes, as she is now in God and saving souls with Ralph Jim. But why not? She likes to keep an eye on the money flow. Her family needs money to live and thrive. She is a woman both beautiful and realistic.

Ralph Jim and Sue Ellen had begun to teach their son Paul to pray to Jesus on his own when Jack entered the picture.

Say we look at this episode of praying to Jesus from Paul's point of view. He is an affectionate and imaginative child. He is now free of family prayer, a sonorous ritual that had no meaning for him except in being important to his parents. He seems to have more power now. He is allowed to make what Ralph Jim calls *phone calls to heaven.*

He got to an important issue right away, stating that he'd like some replies. 'If you can listen,' Paul said to Jesus, 'you should be able to talk. Say something.' Prayers had to be said aloud, which was one of the rules, so Sue Ellen was monitoring and was able to set Paul straight here, though her son wasn't happy with the explanation. It was like talking to himself, he told his mother. On another night at prayer-time he gave Jesus brand names and prices of toys he wanted in case they didn't come through from his parents for his birthday. Ralph Jim interrupted with laughter and kindness to explain a further rule of prayer, don't ask for things. But as the child frankly told his father that rule pretty much destroyed the whole point of prayer, for somebody his age, who needed lots of stuff. It left very little he could talk to Jesus about. What was left to say?

The idea of prayer as praise was explained again. Paul said he understood. 'You have nice eyes,' Paul said, at the next prayer-time, kneeling by the side of his bed. 'I like your beard and your dressing-gown. I hope the soldiers didn't hurt you too much when they killed you.' Then, irritably, because a six-year-old can't sustain role-playing beyond a sentence or two, Paul said: 'Jesus Christ, you make so many mistakes at the school, you shouldn't get praise anyway.'

This time both parents were on hand to set Paul straight. They'd been hoping, frankly, to reap more grace and joy than this from listening to their child's simple spontaneous thoughts to his God. They tucked Paul in and sat on his bed and went over the rules again with hugs and smiles. Paul was now beginning to understand Jesus as he understood his parents: severe restrictions on what he could say and do, and much difficulty in getting a hearing for his problems.

A word here on the subject of zapping. In prayers Ralph Jim and Sue Ellen overheard but didn't listen to Paul said: 'These are the people who should be zapped tomorrow. Kevin and Charlie Wittier and the boy with red hair in Miss Peters's class. You don't have to zap Kevin too hard.'

And another time he said, without conveying grace or joy, or meaning, to his parents: 'You shouldn't zap Janet so much. She didn't throw the ruler and she had nothing to do with splashing mud on Mr Welnyk's car. John is getting zapped too much too, and so is Connie.'

These zap and cease-zap prayers were understood by Jack to be the six-year-old's wish to impose order on ethical anarchy at the pre-beginner and kindergarten level, Mrs Johnson's and Miss Peters's classes, the child's observation of the unjust punishment of innocents, which is usually seen together with the wicked in great power flourishing like a green bay tree. Paul didn't go into detail when passing on his requests, as one discussing something the other party is aware of, and he was pretty curt when he had to repeat them, where Jack assumed that injustices in the schoolyard were being allowed to continue unchecked.

Ralph Jim thought he could clear up a major misunderstanding of the nature of prayer with a fable. It was a wonderful fable, ending with the neatest one-liner, causing listeners to sit back in awed understanding at last. It seems there was this boy, Paul's age, who prayed for a marvellous new bicycle. But he didn't get the bicycle. 'Jesus didn't answer my prayer!' the boy complained angrily to his parent. (Now here was the last line of the fable, from the kindly Father, the Teacher.) 'He did,' said the boy's father,' said Paul's father. 'He said no.'

The silence that descended on the bedroom was most satisfactory for Ralph Jim, a lovely stroke of parenting, and he gazed fondly on the face of his son, creased in thought. In fact, Paul's mind wasn't tranquil but in turmoil. *Where did the bicycle come from?* he asked himself, striving to know the reason for the story. A bicycle! I never asked for a bicycle! How did he get the idea that I asked Jesus for a bicycle?

Sue Ellen also thought the moment was beautiful, the small family together, the child learning prayer. Moreover, she had a practical use for it, immediately, before it vanished like tranquil evening mist – straight away she began naming relatives she hadn't seen for a while, for too long, and while Ralph Jim began by nodding pleasantly as the list grew his face darkened somewhat. He realized that for some reason they had blundered away from his shining moment of fatherly success and into a discussion of aunts' visits, a subject he gravely disliked. Sue Ellen had many, many more relatives than Ralph Jim did, elderly aunts in particular. He had a feeling about certain aunts she was naming now, who were in Ralph Jim's view hectoring tyrants and whiners, money-spongers and character-assassins, that the time elapsed since their last visits had been very brief, countable in weeks rather than months or years.

That got them into mnemonics and memory snapshots, which Sue Ellen was better at than Ralph Jim, since she didn't hesitate to invent scenes and incidents that supported her side, believing her side to be the right one. Said Ralph Jim in protest: 'Eileen? But darling, Eileen was here five weeks ago. No, I don't mean Helen – Eileen. She stayed four days. She called the delegate from the Mali mission, Bishop Sutherland, a savage and a wife-beater, and she said he should wear a ring through his nose, surely you remember that.'

Sue Ellen shook her head vigorously, smiling but showing exasperation too. They had three comparatively empty months ahead and she wanted to fit in four visits, so this was important. 'No, no, no, darling. No, Helen hasn't been here since January of last year. Remember she had those expensive fur boots and we hadn't taken down the Christmas tree? She got pine needles in her fur boots and I had to use a clothes brush to get them out.'

'Oh? Then who was that four or five weeks ago who called Bishop Sutherland –

'Darling, I don't know, we haven't invited anybody at all for more than two months. It was Lou the last time, remember she – '

'That can't be right. I like Lou. We haven't seen Lou since your mother's birthday party.'

Paul said: 'Jesus wasn't listening when the boy asked for the bicycle, that's what happened. Nobody listens when you tell them something.'

Bringing in Lou had been a mistake on Sue Ellen's part, but she just shook her head and kept going. Soon she had the preacher on his back foot once more, trying to handle her curve balls – names he'd never heard before that she was recruiting to force concessions on the others. She could produce people to match the names too, if it came to that. Sue Ellen had a half dozen or so aunts in reserve; she was deep in aunts.

'Really, my dear, I distinctly remember that your Aunt Gracie was here – '

'You must mean Stacey. Darling, you've never even *met* Gracie. She gave us the pewter goblets.'

'That boy's daddy thought Jesus said no, but he didn't say no. He never says anything. He doesn't listen to anything either.'

Only Jack heard Paul's complaint, with aunts' names now zipping back and forth like badminton birds. Jack didn't want to get into a relationship with a six-year-old. He lacked the patience, he knew, and would have problems with the language. The times were hard too, and direly suspicious of men who sought friendships with children. But he had no choice in this matter, according to how he saw himself and what he did. Paul was in his territory.

So a few nights later it happened that Paul was saying his prayers without monitors, his mother being in the laundry room sorting wash and his father working late in his study, which to the child meant that he didn't have to kneel while praying. He lay in bed with his pudgy fingers laced on his stomach. 'I traded the Bubblicious for the racer,' he said. 'It was my racer now. Then Jim chewed the Bubblicious except for one piece he gave to Michelle. She stuck that in my mouth when he grabbed the racer back. He threw the big piece on the ground. It was already chewed and it got a lot of dirt on it.'

Jack said from a corner of the room: 'Okay, so what is it you're praying for, Paul, a package of Bubblicious or a racer?'

Paul did blink, and appeared slightly shocked, but he didn't, as an adult would, scream and jump out of bed. Children have to live in busy bedrooms that guardian angels are free to traipse through, and also the Sandman and the tooth fairy, Peter Pan and the Easter bunny, as well as Jesus himself. Somebody in his bedroom was possible in Paul Trasker's mind, but though he didn't panic he was uneasy. He got up on his knees and looked around to make sure a bad thing hadn't got in. He said in a loud whisper: 'Are you Jesus?'

'No. My name's Jack. You're Paul. I'm pleased to meet you.'

'How do you do. I'd better tell my mom and dad you're in here.'

'Okay. But I haven't time for a lot of talk now. Just tell me what you're asking Jesus for.'

'I already told you. It's my racer. He can't chew the Bubblicious and grab the racer back.'

'Suppose I bring you a new racer. What kind of toy is that, Paul?'

'Don't you know?'

Bite my tongue, thought Jack. He was well aware, though, that he wasn't hitting the problem exactly on the head. He was hitting around it. 'Tell me anyway.'

'Matchbox, but with only three wheels, they're five dollars now. The Bubblicious is ninety cents. Ice cream,' Paul said, getting comfortably into bed again and drawing the covers up, 'is seventy-five cents a cone. Chips are fifty-five. A Sweet Marie's eighty cents, a slush puppie's thirty-five ...'

'Say I bring you a new racer tomorrow night.'

'Well, that's not what I was praying for. You can't ask for things. Jim should give me back my racer. He shouldn't have chewed the gum and took the racer. He shouldn't have given a piece to Michelle because if he wasn't going to let me keep the racer it was my Bubblicious.'

'Yes,' Jack said. 'I understand all that.' Jack heaved a deep and troubled sigh. 'I'll just bring the racer, I can't – well, I'll just bring the racer. I have to go now. I'll call in tomorrow night. After bedtime, and after you're tucked in,' said the sailor man, beginning to look at the problem of making appointments with somebody who can't tell time yet. 'I'll talk first. If I don't say anything it means I'm not here yet. Happy dreams.'

'Where will you buy the racer for me? Do you know that much?'

'Toy World, I guess.' Jack had become evasive, he noticed. 'Or I could look in on Toys 'R' Us on the Concourse – '

'Are you going to pay money for it?'

'No, I'm not, Paul.'

'You mean you'll steal the racer?'

'No, I – '

'Are you going to bust a wheel off?'

'No.'

'What about zapping Jim?'

'Well, no. That's something I should have explained. I can't zap people at your school. I don't go outside the Sutton.'

'You remember I asked Jesus to zap Jean-Guy? Not the little Jean-Guy, the big one. Can you do that?'

'I guess not.' Jack was now fairly depressed.

'Can you tell Jesus?'

'I'm sorry, Paul. No.'

'It's okay,' young Paul Trasker said, thinking the matter over. Then he said: 'Are you still there?'

'Yes.'

'You're not Jesus?'

'That's right. My name is Jack.'

'How do you do, Jack. What about people,' the child asked, sitting up on his elbows and squinting thoughtfully at the corner the voice came from, 'who are getting zapped too much? You remember Dougie, the little kid who wets his pants?'

'I can't do anything at your school.'

'Can you get Dougie a racer?'

'Oh, sure. No problem.'

'A Marvel racer? They're ten dollars, eight fifty-six and then the tax, you have to have ten dollars.'

'A Marvel. Right.'

'If you like,' Paul said, 'you could get me a Marvel racer too instead of the Matchbox. If you're getting a Marvel for Dougie. I'll give it to him for you at school. I won't ask him to trade anything for it, I'll just give it to him.'

'Good idea, Paul.'

'He doesn't have anything to trade anyway. He's very poor, and he stinks from wetting his pants. I'll say Jack got it for him. Would you like some praise from Dougie, if you get it?'

'No, I don't need praise, Paul. We'll have another talk tomorrow.'

'All right, after I'm tucked in. You'll bring two Marvel racers, one for me and one for Dougie,' Paul said, nailing the deal down. 'New racers,' he added. 'I won't tell my mom and dad about you.'

'Well, I don't mind. They're going to find out sooner or later.'

'Yes, but they'd make me give my racer back. Thanks very much, Jack. You're a very generous person.'

'Good night, Paul.'

There could be an argument here that Jack wasn't doing young Paul a favour because greed weakens character and self-reliance, et cetera. There's a strong body of opinion abroad in favour of deprivation for kids, with a belief that it gives them spine and makes them strong. Jack wasn't much of a believer in deprivation. He'd noticed that the deprived populations of the world aren't splendidly characterful people as a rule, somehow in subjection to a minority of folk whose greedy amassments have turned them into spineless, characterless creatures. Jack had a sense of opposites in these matters, our modern myth stock, and for instance never had difficulty in recognizing chaos in too much order. He saw Paul Trasker as a whole person. Everybody he met was complete as he stood in Jack's book.

Unfortunately Ralph Jim saw his son as something in the process of becoming something else, like an unripe vegetable. According to this parental view, Paul needed tending and nourishing for a day when he would become a man. Which day in particular it would be was left pretty vague. Indeed, Jack's domain was populated by children in adult bodies for whom that day had not arrived yet, or in their minds had come and gone, or had receded like a mirage as they aged, turning them into ever-expectant trudging caterpillars who had been promised a butterfly day as kids.

With the same plain eye Jack saw the gewgaws from the bubblegum machines that children like as only cheap copies of flash toys their mothers and fathers possess with serious faces when they can afford them, cell phones and start-ups and string jets, gold wristwatches and quartz fishfinders, diamond bracelets and sapphire rings, Lamborghinis, Versaces, precious pins and periapts, glips and silks, dobbers and leathers.

Jack got into the habit of substituting adult jewellery for the bubblepack kind to unload from his pockets onto Paul's counterpane, real diamond dobbers instead of plastic, heavy jewel-encrusted combs and chains instead of the lightweight Taiwanese junk. Well, it was easier to carry in bulk than the plastic eggs and he didn't need a pocketful of quarters on each run. Paul passed the loot on to over-zapped tads in Miss Peters's and Mrs Johnson's classes who were soon strutting around the schoolyard wearing and trading the trinkets. Presently Paul reported that Dougie, who had gotten a bad name for wetting his pants, had now taken to wearing gold wristwatches up to his elbows on both arms, and had gained a circle of sincere friends, and as a propertied person respect beyond the circle, even though in the excitement of the new life he peed his pants oftener and stank more. This was all temporary joy of course, until parents and teachers started digging ropes of pearls out of toy boxes and cutting into windowpanes as easily as into cheese slices with the diamond rings, but all joy is temporary. It was a whole lot better than doing nothing, as Jack saw this enterprise.

One night Paul asked Jack, in a stiff prayer, apparently rehearsed, for a horse. A horse was easy enough for Jack, who wasn't busy at the time. He wasn't either, though, utterly lacking in a sense of child care; with Paul's safety in mind he talked the lad down to a pony. The next problem was that Ralph Jim and Sue Ellen wouldn't believe their son when he told them that he had received a pony through prayer and needed to pick the animal up at the Sutton Livery Stable and Riding School. Jack's only thought was of getting the pony for Paul Trasker. He felt that care and the stabling and feeding, and so on, were responsibilities of the parents, to be taught to the child as part of their duties. The truth here is that the sailor man believed that getting the pony for Paul was the hardest part, and that the rest would be all enjoyment for the Trasker family.

But the Traskers, smiling and hugging Paul, wouldn't even phone the stables, which lie beyond the tennis courts and the golf course, a kilometre or so to the east of the building complex. Jack finally fetched the pony himself, an affectionate animal named Laddie who fitted comfortably into the service elevator. They should know that the pony was real, was Jack's idea, and that it was Paul's. So he left Laddie in Paul's room with a bag of oats. Ralph Jim and Sue Ellen happened to be out when Jack made the delivery, though had either or both been home Jack would have walked Laddie into Paul's room anyway. The child had prayed for a pony and here it was.

When the Traskers got home, though, only Paul was delighted. Sue Ellen shrieked and fetched a broom, with the intention of hitting Laddie with it, though the pony had done nothing more than fix a friendly stare on her while chewing. Ralph Jim began dialling the police while the child Paul tried to secure his attention.

'I asked for a horse,' Paul explained to his father. 'He doesn't have that rule about you shouldn't ask for things. We were getting little racers and the rings and watches and stuff. I wanted a real racer, a Lotus, but I can't drive. So I asked for a horse, and I got a pony. He thought I might kill myself with a horse, you see, dad.'

Ralph Jim, following his usual habit of not listening to his child, decided that though the police might be willing to take the animal in Paul's room away, the greater mysteries would remain. Who, why, to what purpose, and was there a larger meaning? There seemed to be no malice involved. Meanwhile he noticed Paul tugging at his pants leg.

'There's a horse in your room, Paul,' the televangelist explained. Sue Ellen was taking little peeks in there and shrieking. Laddie munched his oats, prepared to be friends with everybody but a little nervous about the shrieks.

'Dad, he's not a horse.'

Then the man who had built a most successful career on speaking with utter conviction about miracles spent a whole afternoon on the phone trying to solve the pony mystery. Certainly a separation of religious conviction, say the belief that the Lord can provide a pony, from ordinary gullibility is as necessary in Ralph Jim's trade as in any other, but meanwhile Jack was irritated and depressed by all the fuss and dismay. Ralph Jim preached daily about miracles and the power of prayer, and now neither crossed his mind as an answer, and eventually Jack had to get the stables to call Ralph Jim. One of the stable girls came and took the amiable Laddie away.

The situation looked better then to the Traskers. They sat down with Paul and planned a schedule of riding lessons. Well, they planned the lessons together, with Paul present, gravely consulting him about times, Tuesdays or Thursdays, or what about Saturdays, mornings or afternoons?

At the very beginning Paul said: 'I don't want to ride him.'

Sue Ellen, who had put the broom back in the closet, laughed and hugged Paul, saying: 'Oh, you scaredy, lots of children begin taking riding lessons at your age. I wanted to when I was a little girl. Don't worry, there'll be plenty of people around to look after you, darling. We won't let him bite you and we won't let you fall.'

Paul said: 'I'm not scared of him. He's a good pony.'

But by then Sue Ellen was on the phone again trying to get in touch with her sister in Victoria. The Traskers had arrived at an agreement that Sue Ellen's younger brother, Paul's Uncle Hurlbut, who had a reputation in the family as a prankster, was responsible for the pony. Sue Ellen's sister would know where Hurlbut was.

Sue Ellen raised the subject of the bridle with 'Laddie' on it a week later, after Paul was asleep. She had been about to take a shower and go to bed early. Jack happened to be hanging around. Instead she got out her sewing-machine, casting docile looks at her husband to gauge his mood. Ralph Jim sat on the couch in the living room, as he does every night, smoking his pipe and drinking coffee and reading correspondence. The TV Chapel gets over two hundred pieces of mail every day and a dozen or so penetrate to Ralph Jim, big names or big money. He was separating cheques from the letters and stacking the cash in a pile, adding the take on a calculator, not greedily but not with repugnance either. A feast was made for laughter and wine maketh merry but money answereth all things.

'Ralph, I'm worried about Paul. He has a serious difficulty in his spiritual life.'

Ralph Jim's head flinched a little and his teeth on the pipestem tightened almost unnoticeably. He loved Sue Ellen of course, but he wished she wouldn't always choose moments of serenity for the introduction and analysis of unpleasant topics. She thought peaceful times were the best times for gritty discussions. When he felt most tranquil of a day Ralph Jim would suddenly find himself handling subjects like Sue Ellen's mother's menopause or some close friend's alcoholism, or the still unresolved question of aunts' visits. Only lately had he come to understand that these shreddings of his contentment weren't just bad luck. At separate moments, when Ralph Jim's colour was high and his blood warm, when he was striding up and down the carpet, ready to tackle his wife's mother's menopause with full medical and emotional vigour, when he was eager to ask questions and anxious to listen to lengthy clinical answers, Sue Ellen always became quiet and retreated, saying only: 'I'll talk to you when you're in a better mood.'

'What serious problem?'

'He isn't praying to God.'

Ralph Jim stopped reading, putting the letter aside, though still following it with his eyes, turning a blank empty face to his wife. He isn't praying to God, Ralph Jim thought with only a little part of his mind. He isn't digging in the ground. He isn't breathing air, he isn't eating food. That must be it. 'He isn't praying, did you say, sweetheart?'

'He isn't praying to God.'

'I see.'

'Yes,' said Sue Ellen, glancing at him from her domestic chore with trusting brown eyes – they have an Oriental uptilt at the corners Jack likes – as she smoothed down a kraft paper pattern and tacked a seam. 'I'm just wondering what we should do now. It's the kind of thing that could encourage doubt. Say he talks at school and the newspapers find out. Paul's praying to somebody named Jack.'

'Jack,' said Ralph Jim. She had about a quarter of his attention now. 'Well, that's odd, but it doesn't sound serious. He plays games. He's talking to some storybook character. Jack and the Beanstalk? Jack and Jill, Nimble Jack, or he could have a friend at school named Jack. I believe he has friends at school. He talks to him here when he thinks he's alone. That isn't,' Ralph Jim said, 'a spiritual difficulty, Sue Ellen, it's a game. He'll grow out of it.'

Sue Ellen put the power to her machine which chattered smoothly down a perfect row of lock stitches. 'It was Jack who brought the pony. I know because Paul's just got a bridle with 'Laddie' in silver on the part that holds the bit, the headstall, pure silver. Hallmarked. He's always called that pony Laddie. I heard him praying for the bridle.'

Ralph Jim said pleasantly: 'I see. You think Paul's friend Jack brought the pony, and now he's brought a bridle. Did you get in touch with Butsy?'

'Yes. Hurlbut knows nothing about the pony. Paul didn't bring the bridle into his room. And nobody else went in there. I just found it on Paul's bed before he got home from school. Would you like to see it?'

'Of course, but not just at the moment, darling, I'm adding up these contributions and reading the letters.' Ralph Jim stared with longing and irritation at the nice stack of cheques and the calculator. 'There's probably a simple explanation. Also the Lord could put a thousand bridles in Paul's room if he wanted to, my darling.'

'Yes. But this isn't the Lord. As I was saying, it's somebody named Jack.'

Right here the televangelist was hooked and gaffed, strung up between boat and water. Ralph Jim had no way of returning to his cheques and letters without being rude to his wife. He got a faraway look in his eye then, escaping, and seemed to stare, roused, down an unimaginably long tunnel of precedent life, as if to the very first man who had succeeded in filling his belly for a few successive days and could therefore spare a moment to look with amazement and curiosity at his own strange fingers and could study the bizarre contours of his face in a forest pool and wonder where he had come from and what was what.

Said he, stirred: 'We know God takes many forms and many names. We know we can't be certain of anything. We know very little for sure, Sue Ellen.'

Of course Ralph Jim only knew so little because he had freed himself of bigotry. As a bigot he would have known vastly more, and for sure. Now he began pacing the room, agitated, discoursing on miracles because he was confused by the matter of Jack and the pony. When he finished the rant, since he was roused anyway he put his face down to Sue Ellen's and asked her if she had any other concerns she wished to share with him. What about visits by her aunts? He was up for that. But Sue Ellen only leaned forward and kissed him, shaking her head. Then she gathered her sewing up silently and left the room. She found Ralph Jim difficult to talk to when he was in this alert mood. But she decided she would raise the matter of Jack again when they had their next peaceable time together.

The following evening Jack slipped into the apartment at Paul's bedtime but the child and his mother weren't home. Ralph Jim was sitting at his desk in his study with an open Bible on the blotter. Jack was about to ask Ralph Jim where everybody was. At the same moment Ralph Jim said, not very hopefully: 'Well, Jack, are you here yet?'

'I just arrived this minute, Ralph Jim. Take it easy! Take it easy now, there's nothing to be frightened of.'

Ralph Jim had shot up straight in his chair. His dependable eyes went scared and shifty, darting around the room, and he dropped his head into his shoulder and cowered. His hands on the Bible trembled. He pushed his chair back then and fell on his knees on the carpet.

'Get up,' said Jack. 'I don't talk to kneeling people.'

'Are you evil?'

'No more than you are, Ralph Jim.'

The televangelist wasn't reassured by Jack's reply. He drew a sheaf of papers from under the Bible. 'I have some questions for you.'

'How many questions?'

'Sixty-three.'

'Sure. And if I answer sixty-three questions you'll come back with a hundred more. So where are Paul and Sue Ellen tonight?'

'They're with friends. I've been keeping my vigil and calling your name. I need to know your nature and your power.'

'No, that's not correct, is it. What you're telling me is what you'd like to know. You don't need to know anything.'

'If I'm to trust you.'

'I don't mind if you don't trust me, Ralph Jim.'

'What do you want from me?'

'Nothing, as a matter of fact, not a damn thing. I'm just a passerby, in your case. I guess you know I got a pony and bridle for your son because the kid leads a miserable life, and I'm expecting a request for a saddle. While I'm here,' Jack said generously, 'is there anything you'd like yourself? I'm invisible as you can see. I can move around freely.'

'There's a village on the Indus, north of Rondu. They're in the second month of a cholera epidemic. The government has the whole district in quarantine ...'

'No, not that freely.' Jack was suddenly moved by compassion for Ralph Jim Trasker. 'I'm sorry, but you haven't made a fantastic discovery in me. I'm nothing more than a scientific curiosity, like the coelacanth or a hot air balloon. I can help you out with chores if you like, and I'm good at sneaky work – stealing and robbery, in a good cause of course, and cheering folk up when they're needy and there's an easy answer, a winter overcoat, a case of Scotch. But I don't operate on a big scale. Hunger in foreign parts, suffering of innocents, war, disease, torture, injustice, the human race as a whole on the skids, all that's somebody else's responsibility, a fellow named Goof-it. I just work inside the Sutton here in Ottawa. I don't go outside the complex much either.'

Ralph Jim's face was tight in stress, his mouth pulled into the form of a smile. He walked over to the window, looking at evening clouds with his hands in his pockets. He said: 'You're probably lying to me.'

Jack was prepared to leave it at that.

He still felt sorry for Ralph Jim, though. 'I'm just like you,' he said. 'Just getting by, Ralph Jim, that's all, trying to make sense of what happens, just trying to keep my ass out of the Cuisinart day to day. You have to talk to me out loud – I can't read your mind. When I don't answer it means I'm else-where, and can't hear you for that reason; I haven't any strategies of superi-ority or policies of silence. If we're to meet again we have to make appoint-ments, which would make more sense than this method of sending your wife and children away and sitting around all evening trying to talk to an empty room.'

'Do you have another name besides Jack?'

'Yes, Clemmaknohke.'

'Clem – what?'

'It's Taleaturovan. That's a country that doesn't exist any more, Ralph Jim.'

'A very ancient country, I suppose. You have a trustworthy voice. I want to see what you look like, Clemmaknohke – '

'Jack.'

'Jack, I want to see what you look like if you're a man. That should be simple enough.'

'It's simple, but I don't owe you anything. I don't like that part about a trustworthy voice, it means somebody can have an untrustworthy voice. I don't like you wanting to see a face. I got tired of being judged on my appearance a long time ago, so you can forget it. Let's have a look at your times.'

'I'll get my book.' But Ralph Jim stayed at the window for the moment, looking out at the evening clouds. Though his hands were in his trouser pockets and his stance was relaxed, and he smiled still, he was a very tense preacher. His whole body was in a clench. He nodded to himself. Said he: 'I don't understand yet, but I hope to learn, I hope to learn much. Meanwhile I want you to know that I do appreciate your courtesy in coming here and talking to me. I do appreciate that very much.'

Chapter 8

Limbo

MR. PRENTISS NIGHTINGALE, who had scrapped his mother, was waiting and fretting with his wife at Mrs Aquerra's desk and doing the Nailer hover there after a visit that had lasted ten minutes from hello to goodbye. He wanted to ask Mrs Aquerra if there was medication his mother could be given to stop her crying.

'These places are awful. They smell of death. Look at that old fellow. He can hardly walk.'

Judge Wainwright, shuffling toward them with tremulous angular rigidity, did indeed look overdue for boxing and interment. He gripped papers in one hand.

'Do you know him, Prentiss?'

'Of course I don't know him, Eugenie.'

'He's smiling at you.'

This was certainly true, and it was clever of Mrs Nightingale to understand that that was what Judge Wainwright was doing. He was attempting a smile but his wrecked old features could only project a dreadful wall-eyed leer.

'God. I'm glad we didn't bring the children.'

'They wanted to come. Their nanny wanted to see them.'

'I'm trying to do what's best for everybody.'

Judge Wainwright reached them and addressed a question to the asphalt floor just forward of Mrs Eugenie Nightingale's toes.

'Have you seen Mrs Aquerra?'

'She'll be a few minutes,' said Mrs Nightingale.

'Have you ever heard of lucky dogs?' Judge Wainwright's head jerked a few times and then settled to a stare at Mr Prentiss Nightingale's groin and upper thighs. No answer being directly forthcoming the judge added peevishly: 'I'm talking to you, sir, pay attention. Lucky dogs, lucky dogs! It's a common expression, for goodness' sake, lucky dogs.'

Mr Nightingale laughed with desperate condescension. 'Ha ha. Lucky dogs. Sure I've heard of them.'

'You should call in at the Kanata humane shelter and take a look at them,' said Judge Wainwright, as if recommending an unspoilt holiday resort or an undiscovered eating place or other special treat. 'They all live there, the lucky dogs. A pen's all I want from Mrs Aquerra – be kind enough to hand it to me, madame.'

Mrs Nightingale proffered a pen from Mrs Aquerra's desk and the judge made a few magician's passes over the ballpoint before seizing it suddenly and thrusting it into his dressing-gown pocket.

'You're going to do some writing now, eh,' said Mr Nightingale, who had put on a wide idiotic grin. 'That's nice.'

'No, just signing,' the judge said over his shoulder as he moved away. 'I'm a witness of the will for dogs. Forty thousand bucks for stray doggies in the Kanata pound from Mrs Nightingale.'

'What? Wait a minute. Who? Let me see that.'

'It's a will, Prentiss.'

'I can see it's a will.'

'For dogs,' Judge Wainwright said. While the Nightingales studied the will form in amazement the aged jurist, who distinguished in his own mind between forging and uttering, held the papers tightly with both hands.

'I didn't know she had any money, Prentiss.'

'Well, neither did I, neither did I. This is terrible,' said Mr Nightingale, scanning the will, feeling betrayed. 'Jesus, she's leaving all this money to the Kanata humane shelter. I know nothing about this. I'm her son, god damn it. I'm her only son.'

'Well, in that case,' said Judge Wainwright reasonably, 'I don't understand why she isn't leaving her money to you. It's a puzzler. But cheer up. Maybe she'll change the will before they take her through the west door. That's the only way we leave here, you know, feet first through the west door over there and down the service elevator. The regular elevators're just for live people.'

'But the secretiveness, the ingratitude. What a disgraceful way to treat her son.'

'Lucky dogs, though.'

After Judge Wainwright left and before Mrs Aquerra returned to the nursing-station the Nightingales had completely revised their visiting schedule to Mrs Agnes Nightingale in the Nailer. Indeed they returned right away and spent another hour with her.

Mrs Delgardo's group ran a checkers play-off every week to determine the checkers champ. Judge Wainwright, playing Mrs Delgardo in the final, thought he had a good chance this time. His game plan called for early sacrifices that would give him three kings for the middle stretch. Mr Smith, not in the best of moods, was reading Mr Dolly's notes of his transactions on the Vancouver exchange while Mr Dolly looked anxious and was offering excuses. The lunch had been a special treat, macaroni and cheese, though with just a sprinkling of cheese-flavoured powder, no actual cheese, on a ration of two tablespoonfuls of watery macaroni per plate.

'Probably the original mistake was borrowing five thousand dollars from this outfit here, Sicilian Credit,' Mr Smith suggested to Mr Dolly.

'Well, I was sick of hearing about collateral from the banks. If I had all the collateral they want I'd have friends, I wouldn't need to borrow money from a bank. Then the bank tried to sell me its Preferred Customer Credit Plan, looks good, nine percent, but as soon as your balance drops below ten thousand it's twenty-five percent. If that bank was a criminal it'd be in jail. Sicilian just gave me the money, no questions, and took my name and phone number. I bought into a software outfit at twenty-six, Memory-Optimized Backups, and it went to eighty in two days, that's a profit of six thousand. But then I got the call from Sicilian and we're back where we started. How can I owe six thousand interest on five thousand principal over five days?'

'It's a per day rate, Mr Dolly. Sicilian advised you on the investment, did they?'

Mr Dolly remained silent. His head, though, sank furtively low on his shoulders. His eyes blinked and guiltily shifted between Mr Smith's face and those of the checkers players, lingering on Mrs Delgardo's.

'Strange to say I think you had a stroke of luck on the investment, you know, Memory-Optimized Backups getting a quick boost like that. It would read MOB as an acronym, did you notice, Mr Dolly? I guess not, it's a particular kind of bravado humour the Anglo-Saxon mind always finds hard to grasp. You're a little chub in these waters. My advice is to stay away from the phone from now on and thank your lucky stars that you don't have any of their money.'

'Mrs Nightingale never leaves her room. What's the matter with her?'

Judge Wainwright advanced his sacrifice pieces and Mrs Delgardo, leader of the group, picked them off like berries. She was doing everything Judge Wainwright wanted her to.

'Maybe Mrs Nightingale's a snob,' the judge suggested. 'She doesn't want to mix with us. I peeked in there. She seems haughty.'

'She's staying in her room because she's unhappy,' Mrs Delgardo said. 'She'll be out soon, now that her son's seen the will. That always works very well. She can't be a snob, Judge Wainwright. She isn't our social superior, as we used to say.'

'Well, maybe she's our social inferior. A reverse snob.'

'Like reverse racism?' said Mrs Delgardo, amused. 'That's a mysterious idea. I've never known prejudices to be reversible. There are just privileged people and angry ones. A favourite thought in Europe, oh, forty, dear me, *sixty* years ago was that only the middle people in the social hierarchy were snobs. Because of feeling insecure, you see. Aristocrats and peasants were supposed to be non-snobs as a rule of thumb. I can't speak about peasants,' Mrs Delgardo said, studying the checkers board with a sprightly eye, 'but the worst snob I ever met was a queen. I knew a number of dukes and princesses who were snobs, and two very snobbish kings, three if you count pretenders. They were all most gracious and quite charming people other-wise of course ...' Her voice dwindled and died as she lost interest in her own discourse. She asked then, with lively curiosity: 'Is anything happening about the food, Mr Dolly?'

'Well, yes and no,' Mr Dolly answered, shifty-eyed.

An announcer on the small black-and-white TV had been reading the one o'clock news. He said now: 'General Schata has begun his round of talks in Washington. His visit to Ottawa with a mostly economic agenda will take place later this week.'

Mrs Delgardo's group watched the Washington footage of General Schata, except for Judge Wainwright who took the opportunity to count his deployed checkers pieces. He was behind by five, exactly as planned. The tall sandy-haired head of state, General Schata, was shown descending from an aircraft, shaking hands with officials and paying a tribute to American democracy into a thicket of microphones.

'The question is whether they have somebody just like him to take his place if he gets popped off,' said Mr Smith to Mrs Delgardo. She had become obviously offended while watching the news clip.

'No, the man is usually the key. He takes advantage of an opportunity.

Napoleon was responsible for the Napoleonic age. The key to Russia when the dust settled after they shot Nicky and his family was Stalin. If Archie Carstrum at the British Foreign Office had listened to people who were more intelligent than he was in 1933 we would have been spared a whole generation of the most dreadful tragedy. Archie was told for years he should kill that hideous Hitler man. But no, Hitler was a weapon against Bolshevism. The British knew what they were doing. They always do of course.'

'But does killing ever solve anything?' Judge Wainwright asked this question with great severity. He had decided that his chances of being checkers champ this week were excellent, the way the pieces lay.

'It can tip the odds in your favour sometimes,' Mr Smith told him. 'You should try to keep an open mind.'

'You have to take me, Mrs Delgardo.'

'I don't think I want to, Judge Wainwright. That looks like a risky move for my side.'

'If you don't I'll huff you.'

Mrs Delgardo said, exasperated: 'Oh, very well. You're so rigid, Judge Wainwright. I'm glad I never ended up in your court after a party.'

The judge studied the board. Mrs Delgardo hadn't taken the checker he'd meant her to take. She'd also moved to the left side of the board, which was his bad eye side. That side wasn't even in his plan. 'I committed a crime this morning,' he said. 'My first crime.'

Mr Smith had begun clearing plates and cups off the table, for something to do. Mrs Delgardo hadn't touched her macaroni and cheese. She'd just drunk the apple juice. She looked pale to Mr Smith, who said: 'Let's get on the phone and order you in a bucket of fried chicken or a medium pepperoni, Mrs Delgardo. Hell, we can dig into our capital a little, we don't have to go for the high-priced model. We can get just as good a quality in the middle range, give or take a feature.'

'No, we must purchase the best obtainable. If we fail it mustn't be because we did something very stupid like cheeseparing. I have absolute confidence in Mr Dolly,' said Mrs Delgardo. 'He'll get nourishing meals for us very soon now, we must give him some elbow room.' She was peering with interest at the left side of the board, her right side, which Judge Wainwright had intended to plunder later, after he had his three kings. His traps on the other side were still unsprung.

'Don't you have to take me, Judge Wainwright?'

'Yes, I do,' said the aged judge, who had turned snappish and petulant, because he'd committed his first crime, he told himself, not because he'd never been checkers champ, and mightn't be today. 'But I don't have to take that. I can take over here as well.'

'All right. No, it's still your move. Take me again.'

'Damn. Damn this childish game. I've always hated this game.'

'But playing it makes you much more human and interesting, Judge Wainwright,' Mrs Delgardo said. 'King me.'

Mr Smith, having stacked the plates and cups and juice glasses on a tray, had spent some time lying back in thought. After a while he said quietly, into a silence broken only by the clicking sound of Mrs Delgardo's marauding checkers king: 'I believe I'll change my name to Gavrilov for a while now. Smith's okay but I'm finding the name tough as hell to grow into.'

Jack didn't share Mrs Delgardo's faith in Mr Dolly, so he was trying to figure out a way to handle the food situation at the Nailer. Stocking the kitchen could be done simply enough but obviously any quality groceries that suddenly appeared there would be returned just as promptly by the clinic for a cash refund. Take-out food that arrived at the Nailer would be dealt with in the same way. He didn't have time to distribute daily food parcels to the Nailerians. He had made trial distributions of cash to a few of the more famished inmates. Some splurged on chocolate bars and doughnuts but in most cases the money was pocketed by the relatives. 'Oh dear, where did this come from? Goodness, we'd better look after this for you. Is there anything you need?' The seat of the problem was the inmates' feebleness and incapacity. Any improved diet had to come from the Nailer kitchen, at scheduled meal-times, on their regular trays. It would be full-time work.

Jack's project for getting better eyeglasses for Mr Smith was stalled by what had been known at Brand X Cameras as a 'fixing the screwdriver delay,' meaning that the ancient maintenance equipment usually had to be repaired first, before it could be used to repair the equally antique production equipment. A dying child named Louise presented Jack with a task that intervened between Mr Smith and new glasses. Mr Smith had been friends for a couple of weeks with the twelve-year-old Louise from the St. Francis Hospice, the nearest cancer clinic to the Nailer in the Medical Wing. She was a busy child. While her tests were being done she spent days skipping in and out of the Nailer mothering the Nailerians. She combed hair and straightened beds and fetched books and bottles. In a week she knew every inmate by name. She was a particular friend of Mr Smith's.

Unhappily Louise had, in the phrase of the cancer clinic nurses, 'become terminal'. Mr Smith went to see her and found her on morphine but in serious pain nevertheless. Mr Smith was hit hard. He didn't sleep at night. Jack wanted to borrow Mr Smith's glasses, who only took them off to sleep, and that's how he found out about Louise.

Louise's was organ and spine pain and her morphine worked fine for organ pain but wouldn't get to anything worse than moderate pain in a bone according to Mr Smith, whose complaint was that healthy punks were walking around shot full of the stuff the kid needed to help her die. Mr Smith had some familiarity with heroin, the drug that could best reach her pain. He talked about it to Mrs Delgardo and the group. What it all meant was that Jack was left with no excuse for inaction on the Louise problem.

He went to see Louise in the St. Francis, a small clinic with a test lab and two floors of private wards. He slipped in at midnight and the child was, as Mr Smith had reported, very drowsy but also moaning and sweating. She was receiving diligent care. Her misery, however, was *normal*. Louise's face had caved in like a Nailerian's and she'd lost most of her hair on the chemotherapy.

This was the second time Jack had had to go outside a modern medical facility to find a drug for somebody who needed it. Once before he had had to do so, for aspirin. First he turned over all the pharmacies in the Sutton, and all the clinics. He spent most of a day looking through the apartments and condos of likely users in the Parthenon Tower. When he came up blank and angry he decided that he was being unimaginative. Heroin wasn't a rare drug. It was like a new car or stereo. A salesman sector existed that was in the business of selling heroin to any member of the general public who could afford it. You could go downtown and buy heroin.

That night Jack made one of his forays outside the Sutton, and drifted from bar to bar on the main until the early morning hours, wearing a beer-drinker's honest clothes, jeans and a sweatshirt and a dark green bomber jacket. It's a law-abiding town and puts up its shutters early. At two a.m. he was in the Wasfi Tal on the main on Laurier's lower stretch. The Wasfi Tal is nominally a social club, and Jack had a membership card if anybody wanted to see one. It's a narrow place at the bottom of a flight of stone steps, with a small blue neon sign that says 'Wasfi Tal – Club' on the outside. The tables are set against two long walls, with a strip of aisle between, and most of the light inside comes from the candles in lamps with smoked chimneys that sit on the tables. A TV over the bar at the end of the room was running a Fernandel movie from the fifties and the Pointer Sisters were on the juke box as Jack took a seat as near as he could get to the bar. The customers in his vicinity were drinking beer or eating, in groups of two and three, familiar with each other and their neighbours, as if they were local folk with a habit of dropping in here in the small morning hours on a weekday. Two men who sat separately were reading tabloid papers, one a hockey and the other a horseracing journal. He was encouraged to see a man and a woman sitting together who had coked-up noses and running eyes and whose hands on their beer glasses shook and trembled. The waiter was a stoop-shouldered elderly man with a bald head. Jack gave him fifty dollars.

'I'm in the market for a few grams of heroin, best available quality,' said the sailor in French. He opened the menu and ordered a litre carafe of wine and an oyster soup, meeting the waiter's eyes squarely while doing so.

'The house wine isn't great here,' said the waiter, speaking English. He had a fatherly, confiding manner, with benign brown eyes under big wedges of grey eyebrows. 'The regulars drink it like pop, but what do they know? Take my advice and have a bottle of Chablis with the soup – better still, forget the soup. He puts canned oysters in it, and it's not much more than stock and clam juice anyway. We have fresh oysters. Have a dozen.' He patted Jack on the shoulder and handed back his fifty dollars. 'Hold on to this bribe. Let me take your driver's licence and whatever you have in credit cards, and we'll probably need a social insurance number. I'll ask.'

He brought the bottle of wine directly and opened it for Jack. While he was doing so Jack happened to look beyond the waiter and noticed that the two tabloid readers had lowered their papers to nose level and were watching him.

The waiter looked back too, and both papers went up again. He said to Jack, shrugging: 'We see a lot of deceit and masquerade in here of an evening. Police are the worst offenders, and they don't spend a whole lot of money either, it's mostly beer and sandwiches, no matter how hard I push the Chablis and the oysters. We think Coor's Light back there is Metro and the Bud's a provincial, not that it matters one way or another. I'll send somebody over who speaks English. No offence but your French is pathetic.'

Jack ate a dozen oysters and was halfway down the wine bottle when a chunky man with a tie hanging loose took the seat opposite him. He'd brought an empty glass, and raised his brows at Jack for permission before pouring himself a fill. He passed back the driver's licence and credit cards. He had a clump of frizzy red hair over each ear and a forehead covered in freckles. He whistled along with the juke box, and gave Jack a cursory scrutiny, kneading his freckled forehead absentmindedly. He looked tired and appeared to have larger matters on his mind. 'We can't find much on you in the last two years, Jack,' said he. 'You got fired from the camera company, and then you had your nervous breakdown, and after that you dropped out of sight. Naturally I'd like to be sure you didn't become a member of any organization, say to fight crime, putting the drug traffickers behind bars where they belong, that sort of role. Will I be okay if I assume that you're an honest guy?'

'I'm too honest,' Jack said. 'It's a fault in excess, honesty.' The tired man seemed to expect more, his mildly disbelieving eyes steady on Jack's face, so the sailor added the explanation: 'Everything in excess is a fault.'

'I'd love to sit around and drink wine and talk it up,' said the man, heaving a sigh. 'I haven't had a good all-nighter on like morals and ethics and rules of thumb for personal behaviour since my second year at Notre Dame, and it's probably something my body needs, along with about a month in the Bahamas. Well, I guess you can go through. You have an honest face.'

Jack's black close-set eyes glittered in the lamp light, which also hit yellowy highlights on his fallen-tombstone teeth. The parchment skin of his nose had picked up a blue tint from a ray of the neon sign outside and was blinking on and off. He got a small warm glow inside. This was the closest anybody had ever come to admiring the sailor's face.

The chunky man drained his glass and nodded at the pair with the coked-up noses. 'Wait out here until the Mounties leave. Go through the door behind the bar.'

Jack had an hour's wait in the bar and drank another litre of wine. He went through the door and past some men who were standing there and down a corridor to a well-lit waiting room. Two other customers waited there already, one stout and wearing dark glasses and a three-piece suit of good fit and quality, the other unshaven in jeans and workboots, both leafing through copies of *Cosmopolitan* magazine. All the magazines in the waiting room were *Cosmopolitans* except for a few old *Family Circles* and *Chatelaines*. Jack sat down, irritably wondering if the waiter had understood him properly. Another hour went by. He thought of leaving more than once. Jack felt that his own time was just as valuable as any Mafia man's.

A leggy pretty girl with auburn hair in a bun who wore an office worker's dark skirt and white blouse came in from the opposite door and said: 'Mr Baggiano.' The stout man grumbled: 'At last!' He went through the door and the girl gave Jack a charming smile. 'Mr Clemmaknohke, your bill will be four hundred dollars.' She offered a helpless shrug and a grimace to show her sympathy for the amount.

The other man said to the girl in French: 'Is a credit card okay? This is my first time here.'

'No problem, sir.' Then she put two fingers to her rosebud mouth daintily, having thought of a problem. 'Mr Nones, it's a single capsule, isn't it, just one capsule.' He didn't say anything and the auburn-haired girl continued in a manner both apologetic and stern. 'No, Mr Nones, a credit card isn't okay. It's a suicide pill, Mr Nones, our rule for those is cash.'

'God damn crooks,' the man in workboots said to Jack in English when they were alone. 'They don't give a fog really, you know? Just squeeze you for all they can get.'

By the time Jack's turn came, at nearly six o'clock in the morning, the waiting room had filled gradually, with much the same kind of people who were drinking house wine and beer out in the bar, middle-aged and phlegmatic men and women who were mainly worker types but with executives included too and maybe some investors. Jack went through the door into an office where a sleepy stout man in a white shirt and open vest sat behind a desk writing in a file with a glass of milk at his elbow. 'Be right with you,' this man said. 'Excuse me for a minute.'

On the desk was a computer terminal. A huge refrigerator stood in a corner. While he waited again Jack looked at the merchandise on metal racks around the walls of the room, cartons and boxes of antacids, vitamins, diapers and bandages, toothpaste and brushes and shampoos. The office looked just like a part of a regular drug store except for an old-fashioned photograph in a broad gilt frame that hung on a clear section of panelling behind the desk, a head-and-shoulders study of a young man with a full moustache in a coat with narrow lapels and a wing collar. Jack read on the brass plate at the bottom of the frame: *Eddie Considine, 1899–1972.*

'I'm Dr Baumgardner,' the man behind the desk said, and shook Jack's hand. His smile was a shade cynical but avuncular, his broad dark face showing the kind encompassing energy and liveliness that usually signals a readiness to offer advice. His black hair was cut short and combed forward to hang on his forehead raggedly, and black-and-grey chest hair showed at his neck and chest between his open vest where the top two buttons of his shirt were undone. Like the man outside in the restaurant he moved wearily and it occurred to Jack that Mafia folk probably put in a full day. Probably there was just as much office politics in the mob as in a regular office too, and the losers took bigger lumps. 'You look to be in pretty good shape to me, Mr Clemmaknohke.'

Jack again explained his need. Dr Baumgardner clicked a mouse a few times and studied the computer screen. 'Little kid named Louise Keeling. What a shame. Well, okay, besides the drugs you need a nurse, or you need clear instructions from a nurse, because we don't know anything about the child's medical condition, and my guess is you're not up enough on giving drugs for a do-it-yourself job here, unless you spent the last couple of years studying medicine. Okay?'

'I can get one of her nurses to do this. Probably I could get one of her doctors if it comes to that.'

'Okay.' He crossed to the refrigerator and swung the heavy door open, choosing a few vials and bottles which he put in a brown bag. Then he wrote a swift half-page of notes on a pad with a fat Mont Blanc pen and stuffed the page in the bag, which he passed across the desk to the sailor. 'The bad news is I'll have to charge you two hundred dollars. That's medical grade skag you've got there and I'm giving you nearly a half ounce.'

'The girl outside,' said Jack, who didn't want any money misunderstandings with organized crime, 'told me four hundred. So don't try to save me money, sell me everything I need.'

'That's all you need, and a nurse.' Dr Baumgardner stared hard at Jack and then smiled. 'I guess I'll have to overcharge somebody else.' When the sailor didn't return the smile the doctor said: 'Don't jump to any conclusions, Jack. We have hearts of stone.'

Dr Baumgardner's defensiveness interested Jack, who remarked: 'She's just a dying person. Correct me if I'm wrong but you guys kill people all the time, don't you, and you cause a lot of other misery besides. Knocking down the price of heroin for one dying person doesn't do much.'

Dr Baumgardner gave Jack his distant smile, leaning back in his swivel chair and sipping milk. 'Any killing we happen to do is for good reasons.

Well, usually for good reasons. At a pinch we could probably explain every killing. That's more than the legal authorities can say for an army overseas. They'll just issue a general explanation for thousands of dead people. A telegram and a follow-up letter to the families. That's crazy.' Dr Baumgardner drew air in between his teeth in a hiss and shrugged again, turning two palms upward to indicate a hopeless situation. 'That's crazy, Jack. Those are real people. Like I was in the army once. I was in Vietnam. I was fighting for my country, I was ready to die for my country for a while. I swallowed the whole story. I was a good soldier. Finally I asked myself, if there was nobody in the country would I die for it? I'm talking about an empty country, a bunch of mountains and valleys and rivers, you understand, but no people. It's landscape and real estate. I thought I'd be a fool to die for a mountain or a meadow. Then I put one human being into the country, just one to keep it simple. His name could be Hank Dairyman. Why not? Now would I give my life for Hank, the only human in the country, would I die for him in Vietnam? Well, no. No, I told myself, and no again, Hank Dairyman can die for himself if he wants to, but my life is all I've got and it's mine. So make it millions of Hanks and my attitude doesn't change. I was twenty-four at the time, and you wouldn't believe how naïve. The way I stayed alive when I was in the army in Vietnam,' said Dr Baumgardner with satisfaction, 'was by telling myself that if I died I'd be dying for a guy named Hank Dairyman I went to school with, a rotten little fart who never thought about anything except making money. He got into the trucking business while the rest of us were in Vietnam and before the army let us out Hank was worth five or six million. We were saving the country and Hank was making bank deposits. I mean I didn't even like the guy. Why should I get myself killed so that Hank Dairyman could go on stacking up more and more money in the trucking business? Or,' asked Dr Baumgardner, raising his black eyebrows and leaning forward on his desk toward Jack in sincere enquiry, 'any other zitface in any other business?'

Jack understood the long wait outside now. 'Sounds crazy to me too, doctor,' he said pacifically.

'That's right. Crazy? You bet. Crazy's an aberration of sensible behaviour, it's madness, like killing or dying for no good reason. In Russia before they went belly-up over there from sheer incompetence calling the government incompetent used to be madness. They had this terrific arrangement where you could get psychiatric treatment for it free of charge.

The government paid. I'm sitting here,' Dr Baumgardner told Jack, 'dispensing drugs at a fair profit. Am I causing human misery or helping people? It's a statistical question. I'm only about forty percent illegal anyway.' He nodded at the stacked shelves of drug-store merchandise. 'Those are samples, we do a nice trade in legal goods because we own the companies. I can sell you brand-name mouthwash and junk like that at wholesale prices if you order a minimum of a dozen gross. I don't sell much heroin and cocaine in fact, it's a little pricey for this end of the main – the volume in those items is up by the National Arts Centre, mostly what we do here's the shift-worker and bread-and-butter stuff, amphetamines and tranquillizers … sleeping pills, steroids. I guess I probably keep as many people doped up as a regular doctor. Well, I'm not a healer, that's the only difference. A guy in here wants tranquillizers and I hand them over. I don't tell him he should exercise more. I don't ask him nosy questions about his sex life. If women don't like taking their clothes off for some zitface in an office who's pretending that a woman's naked body means nothing to him, well, they get their pills from me. Guys with beards too, I do a lot of business with them. The customers I sell to want to keep their beards and they don't have suits in their closets. Say you have a beard and you need amphetamines. You can get them from a doctor but first you have to shave off the beard and put on a suit. A doctor's a tightly wrapped middle-class person. So all we're really doing here is covering the full range of the free enterprise system,' Dr Baumgardner explained to the sailor. 'Then when you go up higher in my outfit, lo and behold everything's legal. Scale's the answer. Get scale and there aren't any more laws because laws aren't for organizations, they're for individual people. You can be illegal throwing a Popsicle wrapper into your local river, but pay twenty guys to dump bales of Popsicle wrappers into the river and the government'll stand behind you one hundred percent. They'll give you subsidies. That's where strength of character counts for our kind of businessman,' the Mafia doctor said, making eye-to-eye contact with Jack, solemnly. 'We don't have any laws to guide us in our operations. We have to rely most of the time on innate morality, our natural sense of what's right and what's wrong.'

Dr Baumgardner pointed a thumb over his shoulder at the Italianate portrait subscribed by the name *Eddie Considine*. 'A great man. What he did in his time was to wipe out the line that used to separate so-called crime from private enterprise. The truth is that we're all free-enterprisers, we're all engines of the economy. Eddie gave the people in my industry pride in our careers.'

'He looks like somebody I've seen before.' Jack had listened to stranger opinions than Dr Baumgardner's often enough in his time. 'From everything I ever heard I thought organized crime was bad for a country. Eddie said the stuff you do's okay, did he?'

'Well, it's okay and it isn't, like most things. Take theft and robbery. Hitting a guy on the head and grabbing his wallet or busting through the doors of a bank with a sawed-off shotgun, the law is clear if you do that. It's wrong. But look, the *legal drug lobby* gets the government to extend patent protection for what, twenty years, and you're the taxpayer. Is somebody stealing your money? The country runs short of oil again, Colombia has a bad winter, or so the story goes, interest rates are up, the market's down, you're paying an extra two bits a litre at the pump and seven bucks a pound for coffee. Same question – is somebody's hand going in and out of your pocket? Who can say? Collecting money because of a particular set of circumstances isn't stealing. Arranging the circumstances isn't illegal most of the time. That was the way Eddie saw it – we are all businessmen, and businessmen are the engine-masters of the economy of the country. Some of us are at one end of the range and some at the other, that's all the difference.' Dr Baumgardner took his glass to the refrigerator and poured himself a refill of milk. 'I don't have a conscience problem,' he said. 'My prices are competitive with the big pharmaceuticals, we're not shy about marking up but even so I can beat big rafts of their regular lines by fifteen, twenty-five, thirty percent. About the only thing the international pharmaceuticals do that I don't is publish prissy little pamphlets saying eat more bran and reduce your fat intake for a fuller, happier life. The only real problem I have is the long hours,' he said. 'It'd be nice to play a little golf now and then, or have a love affair. I'm putting in a twelve-hour day when you count it up, on the desk here or in the rear rooms where we have our hospital facilities. I can show you around if you like.'

'If we could leave it for another time that'd be a pleasure,' Jack said. 'Right now though I'd like to make it back to the St. Francis before the day shift comes on at eight.'

'I don't get all the ego-stroking a regular doctor does, either.'

'Hard to see why not, doctor,' said the sailor, remaining tactful but stopping short of an actual fawn. 'You look just like a regular doctor to me. In fact there's another Sutton clinic you might think about if you feel that this rational mood you're in just now has any future. I'd like to bring you a set of private ledgers belonging to the Nailer Geriatric Clinic in the Sutton. You can't call them up on your network, they're all private paper records. The Nailer's actually a nursing home in the Sutton.'

'We don't care about nursing homes.'

'Doctor, I'm not talking to you as a humanitarian. I know you're not a humanitarian.'

'We're businessmen. We're not any different from anybody else.'

'Dr Gerald A. Nailer.'

'Okay.' Dr Baumgardner clicked his mouse a few times. 'Well, let's see what the government takes.' He came alive a moment later, shooting an amazed glance at Jack. 'Holy baloney. Can you bring those books in later today? Just drop them off with Victor out front. He'll make a set of photocopies and you can have them right back. We never pay finder's commissions but if it works out we'll owe you one.'

As he left the Wasfi Tal Jack met the bald-headed waiter at the door. 'I forgot to ask, how were the oysters, sir?' the waiter said, the white wedges of his eyebrows coming together anxiously. 'Oh, good. That's good. And the other matter? Well, I'm delighted. Then I'll take my fifty dollars now, sir, if you'd be so kind.'

Columbine and Jack were asked to be godparents of a baby who was to be christened at St. Michael's, a Catholic church in Belleville. The parents were called Labarge: Sophronia, a friend of Columbine's, and her husband Rod. The truth here is that Jack wasn't fond of the name Rod, as perhaps had he lived in earlier days he wouldn't have liked the name Phallus. On the other hand he doesn't mind the name Dick. A Roderick or a Rodney didn't stir up this prejudice of Jack's, only the suggestion of unwilting erection and godhead that in his sour view resonated from the diminutive form, Rod. It being a prejudice, as he freely admitted, not a conviction or an opinion, he would sometimes meet individuals who by their nature clearly refuted it, nice Rods, unthrusting fellows, even occasionally in the company of short Dicks, but prejudices are never moderated by reason.

Jack and Columbine waited in the porch of St. Michael's and they both felt uncomfortable, as scientists hanging around a site of religious ritual. There were several babies with their retinues inside the church, where baptisms had already begun. A priest with a dark gypsy face performed the rite. From the boomy church acoustic vault behind him Jack heard the words: 'Begone, ye devil, for the judgement of the Lord is at hand.'

Sophronia came out of the church miserably, without baby or Rod. She was a small lively girl, usually merry, and even now she giggled for a moment before telling them that the baptism of her baby, Emile James, had been cancelled. Rod had wrestled with his principles and decided that he couldn't allow his firstborn to be the principal in a ceremony of superstition.

With the instructions to devils in his ears Jack was prepared to take Rod's side in the matter. Jack's plan for the Sunday afternoon was to watch hockey on the dish, Habs against the Islanders, a game that had started according to his watch while they were looking at falling snow and waiting for Emile James to arrive and be purged of whatever devils were inside the infant. Columbine had paper work, a draft of a schedule of experiments for the next week. They were after nearly a year together still in a state of madness and rapture. They expected to have dinner at five and be in bed by seven.

'How do you feel about this, Sophy?' Columbine asked, though.

Sophronia had begun to look like somebody who has been in an accident. Her eyes had a distant focus and the lids were dark. She said: 'My baby might go to Limbo.' And she fell on Columbine's shoulder, shaking and in pain, but not weeping.

There was a mix-up before Jack could speak. Columbine, a religious illiterate, assumed Limbo was Sophronia's home town in Greece. 'That won't be so bad, darling,' she said, holding her friend. 'His grandparents will love him.' Sophronia began shedding tears then, wailing most pitiably.

Jack sketched for Columbine the worrying part of the doctrine of *limbo infantum*, that unbaptized children if they die must spend eternity in a region adjoining Hell, which is a bad neighbourhood. Columbine looked dumbly over Sophronia's shoulder at Jack. She was bewildered. 'You mean she believes that?'

'Well, she believes it now. I don't know if she believes it all the time. Right now it's tough on her.'

'Why don't we look into this,' Columbine said.

Jack with a glance at his watch bade farewell to his chance of catching the first period of the hockey game. Columbine held the shaking Sophronia in her arms. She stroked her hair and put kisses on her forehead. 'Hush, hush, my little one,' she said. 'Your baby won't go to Limbo. I promise, okay. We'll go and fetch Emile James now. We'll do everything the way it's supposed to be done.'

Columbine's face was white. Her eyes were flat, showing a dullness Jack didn't care for, it being both introverted and animal. She was very, very angry. She said: 'Jack, get the car around here, would you.'

'Yes,' said Jack. 'Look, can we talk for a minute? This is a private family argument about religion.'

'Would you get the car, please. Please.'

That was how they came to break in with some suddenness on Rod, upholder of principle and integrity of conviction as he sat in his elegant living room in a house on Maple Drive, a tree-shaded avenue just east of Sidney in Belleville. He had been sipping a cup of coffee, eyes fixed on the TV. '... a pass to the centre, one man back,' said the TV. Rod was startled at the irruption of course and didn't have an immediate answer when Columbine, even before taking her coat off, stood over him asking: 'Tell me this, what kind of an insensitive moron are you?'

Rod ignored Columbine and demanded an explanation of his wife. Sophronia placed herself between Columbine and Rod, and being confused she also grabbed Jack's lapel and cried: 'Don't do it, Jack! He's a father now!' Jack was just keeping an eye on Columbine. He said to Rod: 'We're having a problem, Rod. Take it easy for a minute.' Hostile eyes looked back at him. 'I ought to call the police.'

As to Rod he was a man with every appearance of one who will pursue honesty at any cost. His nose was honourable, with fine nostrils that flared as he breathed through them in well-justified exasperation. His forehead was smooth, his gaze was straight, his hair was a natural chestnut thatch. He had a perfect right to say no to mumbo-jumbo in the naming of his child.

Sophronia went to check her baby. In the sort of quiet interval between antagonists that can easily kick up into shouting again Jack asked Rod for a beer. Rod hesitated, but being a gentleman he went to open a beer for his guest.

'I think I know how to talk to him,' Jack said.

'You just stay out of this, Jack.'

'He's right in my territory, with a moral scruple like that. I've been having moral scruples ever since I could talk.'

'He doesn't have a moral scruple.'

'Well, he thinks he has. It's the same thing.'

'He's a rat.'

What Jack saw as an odd sexual interval occurred here. For the church ceremony Columbine wore a white suit with a long jacket and a wrap skirt with buttons on the sides. She had undone a few of these buttons, Jack noticed, and was now showing a fair length of thigh, a softening to suit her manner, which had become mellow. Rod returned and began to speak his mind, tentatively at first and then with confidence as Columbine listened to his arguments. Her eyes were grave and she only smiled when Rod did. He didn't seem to notice Columbine's legs.

Jack took some interest in the hockey on TV while Rod talked on. In a lengthy ramble Rod conceded that the cosmos was illimitable and imponderable and that he, Rod, wasn't enough of a presumptuous philosopher to downgrade its mysteries. But he did happen to – he said that, *happen to* – draw the line at the witch-doctor mummery with oil and water and smoking incense.

Sophronia came back from the nursery, crying again and carrying Emile James, the very fellow who stood a chance of winding up in Limbo if the afternoon's business went the wrong way. He was cosily sleeping in his christening robes. Sophronia didn't like the peace in the room any better than she'd liked the earlier row, and she shouted at Rod, her English breaking under strong emotion: 'Why is it you don' wan' your baby baptize today? Why was it okay when we see the priest to baptize your baby and now today it's bad?'

Rod patiently closed his eyes. The truth of the devil crisis, which Columbine had seen as soon as she walked in on Rod, was at this late stage clear to Jack. Rod didn't have a moral scruple. He simply hadn't known when he'd agreed to the baptism that the Habs would be playing the Islanders on the day of the ceremony. This was the civilization illusion, where a man of sensibility, a clean-cut coffee-drinker who used a saucer even when he was alone, got credit from Jack for an honourable motive just because he staked a claim to one. Had Rod been a different kind of Sunday afternoon sports fan, an unkempt slob sucking on a bottle of Blue, he would have been easier for Jack to judge. He would have looked like the kind of man who doesn't mind if his wife is in terror of devils so long as he can watch a hockey game.

Columbine's opinion of the general population was always bleaker than Jack's. She always thought the worst of people. She was more often right than he was. As Jack caught up with what was happening she had risen to admire Emile James and to hug her friend Sophronia. Then Jack looked back at the visit's necessity, as she'd seen it, to yield to Rod who was the important person to Sophronia. Sophronia would send her child's godparents home if Rod wanted that. 'A spinerama move by Pickett,' said the TV. 'The Golden Great One is doing it all today.' 'Let us not forget,' said Rod loudly with his eyes patiently closed, 'that there is somebody else to be considered here. Who? Why, my son. How do I explain to him later that I put him through a voodoo rite when he was a baby?' Columbine lit a cigarette and gazed down at Rod as she shook the match out. Her mind was elsewhere Jack could see because little Emile James got a cloud of smoke in his face and coughed in his sleep.

Jack thought that the afternoon might fly apart again. Rod believed he was engaged in a debate, a tussle of minds. However, Jack knew Rod could find himself being bounced off his living room walls by Columbine, who never hesitated to extend a difference of opinion to its final expression, violence. This often came as a surprise, especially to men, who were slow to make the connection between a lithe body and physical conditioning, in the sense of a physical dimension to an argument. Her Polish hauteur was never tolerant of any opposition, not a witty insult or a patronizing raised eyebrow even, and especially not, as in Rod's case, obstructive stupidity. Columbine's grandfather after all had spent most of his short life shooting and stabbing and exploding the people he was opposed to politically.

But when she spoke her tone was sweet. 'Rod, why don't we do this. We'll take the baby to be baptized but we'll do so against your wishes. That way your principles won't be compromised. When Emile James grows up you can tell him truthfully you had no part in it. Sophy isn't asking for your participation at the baptism, are you, Sophy. What do you say, Rod? You could just wait for us here and watch TV or something.'

Sophronia anxiously awaited her husband's decision. Columbine smiled gently at him. He brooded on the offer. 'Good end to end play,' said the TV. 'Pickett's all over the Islanders, Boomer.' Rod let them take his child. Jack felt like Rumpelstiltskin. Sophronia pressed kisses on Rod's forehead. 'I love you.' He was a detestable civilized human being and one of the nastiest Rods Jack has ever met.

Still, there was just the work at the church to do now. But as Jack helped Sophronia into the back of the car Columbine said: 'Sophy, just a minute, I forgot my cigarettes. Jack, would you sit with her. I won't be long.'

Jack put an arm around Sophronia's shoulder, remembering as he did so that sound carries in snowy weather. They are elegant houses on the Labarges' section of Maple Drive but as newer structures they don't have much of the soundproofing that old beams and solid doors and walls gave their neighbours. Jack could hear the thumps from inside quite distinctly. Rod's first harsh yell of pain made Sophronia stir and protectively hold Emile James closer to her breast. 'Good game,' said Jack into the car's silence. 'That sounded like a Montreal score.'

Sophronia looked at Jack, tears still abrim in the corners of eyes as fair as Helen's might have been. 'Can't be long now,' he said cheerfully. The next yell came after a thud that shook the windows. He guessed that Columbine had dropped Rod on the floor. She did that when somebody came to expect the bounce against the wall and tried to brace for it.

Sophronia said: 'He is cry out.'

'Those Habs'll do it every time,' said Jack, feigning a lot of hockey enthusiasm, hitting the car seat in front with his fist to cover the sound of more yells drifting to them on the wintry afternoon air, on an empty street, in a slow, quiet city. 'Everybody had 'em counted out for this game. I bet Rod had, did he? Well, they're doing it again, now they've got the fans jumping and screaming.' Sophronia made no reply and to Jack's relief Columbine came down the driveway then, showing them a Rothman's packet before dropping it on the front seat. Sophronia didn't look at the cigarettes but at Columbine's knuckles which were skinned purple and bleeding a little.

Jack drove them to St. Michael's. On the way Sophronia spoke to Jack unhappily. 'No, he is support the Islanders. He won't never jump for Montreal.' The priest of the dark face was still operating and they got Emile James free of devils. They went to Columbine's place and drank sherry and ate walnuts and Sophronia was her merry self again. When Sophronia had to leave Columbine gave her sterile gauze and tape, embrocation and bandages, in a paper bag, to take home with her. Jack was interested to see that Sophronia accepted the items with thanks but no other comment, while Columbine didn't explain them. Later Jack helped Columbine with her experiment scheduling and they were in bed at seven as planned with nothing lost from the day.

Chapter 9

Recreating Imogene

RALPH JIM'S two bad habits were grovelling and asking trick questions. As to grovelling, Jack had severe reservations about gods who wanted to see kneelers and self-abasers – he thought a god like that must have all the confidence in godhead of a small-time warlord or satrap. Asking trick questions was Ralph Jim's attempt to confirm his private idea about who Jack was. When they were first together Jack often felt like a traveller in primitive lands who has been adopted for purposes of worship by a naïve tribe. He was himself somewhat to blame for this relationship, being reluctant to tell the preacher the true story of his life. You must know that a gentlemanly reticence was in Jack's bosom like his heartbeat; he felt himself to be the last man left on earth who didn't enjoy talking about himself. Everybody else in the world was in counselling or group or other kinds of confessional therapy and there was just this sailor, wrecked on a desert island more than likely, who nourished the conviction that the storms visited upon a life were private matters that a hero should be able to handle with reticence and by means of single combat.

So he made the decision to stay clear of Ralph Jim as much as possible. Then one morning Jack happened to be on the Parthenon Tower elevator when Ralph Jim got on. Jack squeezed himself back into a corner and said nothing.

Two floors down another passenger entered, a woman in her late thirties with dark curls and a trim figure who greeted Ralph Jim very warmly, saying: 'Hey, great days, it's you, studman. Someone's been hiding from Monica, haven't they. Long time no see, R.J.'

Ralph Jim said: 'Hello, Mrs Schwall.'

When the elevator door closed Ralph Jim seized Mrs Schwall and bent her backward on his elbow and kissed her. He also thrust his free hand up under her candy-stripe jersey top. To Jack it seemed that Mrs Schwall's own two hands, in a flurry, were pushing at the televangelist's chest. She broke free of the kiss and, gasping, pressed one of the service buttons, which brought the elevator to a stop.

Jack was surprised but didn't have a role in this encounter except the obvious one of protecting the woman. He said: 'Back off, Ralph Jim. Get your hand out of there. Mrs Schwall, you're safe.'

Only then did Jack notice that Mrs Schwall had pressed the stop button and not the alarm. As to other buttons, when she had seemed to be pushing against the televangelist's chest she'd undone eight waistcoat and four shirt. Even as Jack uttered his interruption she pinned her man hard against the wall with an answering kiss while she worked on his belt buckle.

'Oh, excuse me,' said Jack, feeling embarrassed.

'Jack?' said Ralph Jim, loudly and guiltily.

'Who spoke?' Mrs Schwall asked, looking back over her shoulder with tousled curls and glazed eyes.

'It's Jack!' said Ralph Jim and groaned desperately. 'I knew it! I knew it! I was right! Oh miserable wretch, oh wicked evildoer that I am!'

'This won't take a minute,' Jack said and set the elevator moving for the ground floor. It was Wednesday and on the Robin Hood calendar he had a distribution of cash to make into the shopping bags of the raggedy people who came out by welfare taxis to the Sutton for the grocery specials at Wonder Food Mart. 'Ralph Jim, my mistake. Forget I opened my mouth.'

'I want to explain, Jack. You have to understand about this.'

'That's not true. I don't have to understand.'

'Jack, let me introduce Mrs Monica Schwall, of my hundred-voice choir the TV Chapeltones.'

'Pleased to meet you, Mrs Schwall. Excuse me for butting in.'

Mrs Schwall asked Ralph Jim angrily: 'What's this conversation?'

'Monica, he's a visitation to guide me.'

'No, I'm not.'

'He sees everything I do.'

'No, I don't. Most of the time I'm not around.'

'He's a moral guardian.'

'I'm not, Ralph Jim. I just happened to be in the elevator. I was on first.'

'He was on first?' Mrs Schwall asked Ralph Jim. 'What's this now, baseball jokes? Who have we got in here spying on us, do you know him?'

'His name's Jack, Monica. He can be heard but he can't be seen.'

'Well, okay, I'll fix Mr Jack's wagon for him, the spying rat,' Mrs Schwall said. Showing the quickest belief in the principle of invisibility Jack had ever seen she made an efficient blind grope in the elevator corners and caught Jack first by a lapel and then by the throat, even though he tried to duck and dodge. 'Got the brute. Mr Jack the visitation who sees everything. Mr Pry the peeper.'

'Can he be touched, Monica?' asked Ralph Jim in awe.

'Mr Who's on first. Oh yes, I got him touched now. Let's just see if he can be kicked.' Still holding Jack's throat, she swung a knee up. The knee was aimed at Jack's groin but he'd wilted somewhat from pain and having his windpipe in the chorister's clutch and he took the kick high, on his lower stomach. He was stunned by nausea and dropped like a stone. Fortunately the elevator doors opened as he fell. He squirmed out on his belly and elbows with his mouth wide and the red veins of agony in his eyes. Mrs Schwall swept the elevator corners with her hands for him again. 'I lost him. Give him a call, R.J. See if he comes back.'

What a fake, thought Jack, a typical televangelist, a travelling medicine show fake who grabs and fondles the TV Chapeltones while his wife Sue Ellen sits at home and trusts him. In the elevator lurk as a remote invisible man Jack had seen the embracing of Mrs Schwall by Ralph Jim from a virtuous pinnacle. Now on all fours and feeling pain, and ready to throw up, he wasn't so detached. He became a wicked warlock, somebody the preacher could believe in. 'I'll wreak vengeance on you for this, Ralph Jim,' Jack shouted, although well aware that Ralph Jim had done him no harm. 'How would you like boils? Or big bleeding haemorrhoids hanging down like a bunch of grapes? Or dysentery and the stone botts and fish-skin disease? I'll make you weep, Ralph Jim Trasker, you treacherous philandering hypocrite. Expect a reckoning.'

'Why don't you come back in here and tell us about it?' Mrs Schwall invited, while behind her Ralph Jim's dependable eyes swivelled left and right and up and down in terror. Then she fended off two men and a couple of children who were trying to get on the elevator. She had already turned to enfold Ralph Jim in her arms as the doors closed.

The encounter was an instructive one for Jack who limped to his apartment and took a hot bath and tried to calm himself with Boccherini and a mystery novel for the afternoon. He cancelled his Robin Hood day at the Wonder Food Mart checkouts. He was interested in some phenomena of his elevator encounter – one of them was how quickly his own pain had been translated into chivalry on Sue Ellen's behalf. Rage from hurt and the desire for revenge seemed to claim a virtuous justification automatically – it went to respectability like paper clips to a magnet. Nor did Jack while his stomach hurt feel guilt that he'd cancelled his Robin Hood morning and wasn't down at the checkouts dropping twenties into the bags of hamburger and Kraft dinner. Indeed while Jack groaned and uncapped the Captain Morgan he remembered only how some of the raggedy Wednesday people would undo his work of a Thursday morning, coming in with faces shining in stupid honesty to return the twenties, squandering money they needed on a vain charge of righteousness. What could you do with people like that?

When the pain went away Jack didn't feel this way, however. In the evening he worked on schemes for increasing cash to his Robin Hood distributions, and other good deeds. Here again, though, he stopped to consider his own behaviour, and it seemed to the sailor that it told him this: that a properly virtuous outlook was only available to somebody with a mind in good balance and a body in good health. Which made him then wonder if virtue was nothing more than an emotion, with a tidal ebb and flow. He had previously thought of it as an attribute of character, and maybe even intellect. Following his painful encounter with Mrs Schwall he saw a just man in a simple definition as one with an instinct for justice who hasn't recently been kicked in the stomach.

Nobody behaves the same way all the time, either. Later still the delicate music began to fail to reach Jack, who had lowered the level on the bottle of Captain Morgan by a few inches, the mystery novel became trivial and his philanthropic schemes tedious. He got on the computer and began to zap the Grumrogs of Shroud with an Orgogun, shredding their cities and vaporizing their armies, creating uncountable bytes of widows and orphans without regret, glowering and mopping them up to the last straggler, making mouth noises like Pitikoo! and Fabash, you little bastards! to supplement the game sounds. He was the same man, but in a different mode. Nor had he lost his fondness for music – while he wiped out the Grumrogs, and after them the Viles, and most of the planet colonies of the Fangrokes, he sang very lustily all twenty-four verses of 'The Mary L. Mackay', giving it the full chorus after each verse, and ending exuberantly with:

From Portland, Maine, to Yarmouth Sound
Two twenty miles we ran,

In eighteen hours, me bully boys!
Now beat that if you can!
The sail crew said 'twas seamanship
The top lads they kept mum
But what drove our brig so far so fast,
Was the keg of Portland rum, me boys!
The keg of Portland rum!

Jack kept in touch with Paul at the stables and riding-school, privately owned, that drew its customers from the Sutton. The stables had been a farm in the countryside east of Sharon. The farmhouse with its three dormer windows is now divided up into business offices, with a snack bar and a sports clothes store on the ground floor. Tackle and farrier's shops occupy the barns, and there are paddocks where customers can view what horses and ponies are for rent. Beyond the barns are the rows of new stables and fenced pasture. To the west is the Sutton parking lot, as large as an airport, the low outline of the complex filling the skyline, the Parthenon Tower in the centre reaching up toward the clouds, while the good green Quebec country fades into the misted horizon on the north. A number of riding paths are maintained on the north side by the stable owners, the south being broken up by roads and ditching and snow fencing. The school operates in the summer months only, employing teenage girls who work for low pay, ride like circus performers and understand horses much better than they do their parents and boy friends.

Sue Ellen was away visiting an aunt when Ralph Jim started Paul's riding lessons. Paul did explain to his father, with composure, that he didn't want to ride Laddie – the pony was a pet, and what the child wanted to do was take his large pet for walks. When Ralph Jim insisted upon the lessons Paul did his best to oblige his father. He had courage, but his balance was poor and he kept sliding off the saddle, though Laddie did everything a pony could do to hold him on. Ralph Jim took a hearty interest for the first day or two, shouting encouragement while he sat on a fence talking to fans and signing autographs. He did look at his watch frequently. When he saw no quick progress, though, he was satisfied with dropping Paul off, seeing him safely in the care of his instructor and picking him up a couple of hours later.

Jack couldn't be reliably invisible outdoors, but he did talk to Paul sometimes in Laddie's stable. What Paul couldn't understand was, why did everybody want him to ride? He had tried his best to ride. It was difficult – he couldn't do it. But he liked his pony. Couldn't he just groom and pet Laddie, give him treats and take him for walks?

Said the helpful girl who was Paul's instructor: 'What you need is a dog, little kid. This is a pony. I don't mind, you know, I'll spend the time with you but this is a smart good-looking pony and it's a waste. Ask your daddy for a dog, why don't you.'

And Laddie made his own wishes known too, when he began to see a pattern of long stall-time and just walks every day with the little fat person who couldn't ride him. He took to shoving Paul with his muzzle, to encourage him to think of something more interesting, and that frightened the child. This big pet who shoved him was a massive, powerful creature who delicately took a carrot from the girl's hand but then crunched it between huge teeth, making the loudest chewing sounds Paul had ever heard. So the idea of a dog began to sound good to him, a small dog.

Jack had been dropping in at the Fish and Critters pet store to look at puppies. A TV preacher with a national reputation for uprightness, Jack thought, would probably let his son have a little dog if the request was made by somebody who'd seen him in an elevator kissing a member of his hundred-voice choir the TV Chapeltones.

So Jack was waiting for Paul in the stable with a book of dog pictures. He was leafing through the selection and had come upon an illustration of a greyhound, the animal of his childhood. He stared at the dog's shape with a primitive fear. The fear wasn't of the dog itself but of the memories it brought in a rush to his mind. That was the problem with childhood, routine and everyday occurrences in it were the bones of nightmares in the grown man.

'Jack?'

The child had talked. Ralph Jim held one of the big stable doors open, letting in a shaft of sunlight that made a wide golden arrowhead on the straw floor. Jack moved back from the light. He pocketed the dog book and said: 'Yes, come on in, Ralph Jim.'

'Paul's not here. He won't be coming again.'

The televangelist sat on a hay bale in the aisle between the stall, looking around him confidently. 'Whereabouts are you in here?'

Jack did not reply. 'He told me I might find you with the pony,' said

Ralph Jim. 'I suppose you misunderstood what you saw in the elevator. I mean me and Mrs Schwall. That's related to a mission I have that Sue Ellen doesn't need to know about. I'll explain, if you have a minute.'

'I was just leaving,' said Jack. 'An explanation's not necessary for me, I keep no tabs. I'm on my way to lunch right now.'

'You have a minute. Nobody's that busy. First it was because I'm a famous preacher, a woman could see I'd keep her secret. Kiss-and-tell men are a big problem for women, so I start out by looking good to them, and then there's whatever natural attraction I have on top of that. Well, they have agonies we don't know about. First they have power, and then it's taken away before they fully understand it. How would you feel if you were loot, like a bag of gold? What chance would you have of knowing who you were and what you were? Especially since most of what you hear is lies, we hardly ever tell them the truth, you know. They're flattered and rifled and betrayed. They have to show a good face, and try to keep their wits about them.'

'This is a lecture on women, Ralph Jim.'

'Yes, it's agony for them. Later on she isn't a king and she isn't loot either, the same woman. But who is she now, and does she know? The courtiers have packed up and gone home, the palace is empty. Nobody has enough interest in her to tell her a lie or to betray her. How do you think that makes her feel?'

'I have no idea, Ralph Jim, and neither do you. I hate a talk like this.'

'Some women claim they're happily married.' Ralph Jim shook his head. 'But who knows, eh? Happiness in marriage isn't the normal state, what's more normal in marriage is Valium. Right now I have eleven women on my list. Oh, we could say fifteen, counting in everybody who wants to be in. If I'm really talking about everybody, twenty-five, or including people who come and go like Mrs Schwall, forty-seven. But it could easily be a hundred, a hundred and fifty, two hundred. Jack, I sometimes think it could be every woman I meet. So much of the time I'm trying to harden my heart and protect my own family – that's where my first loyalty lies. The women are my ministry but Sue Ellen is my wife. Fortunately,' Ralph Jim said, 'I keep in good shape. For them sex is love, as it needs to be. How can you blame them?'

'I hate men who talk about generic women, as if they were a no-name product, a box of something. Let me just say this, Ralph Jim. I'm not blaming any of these women you're referring to. I'm blaming you. I'm calling you a horny stoat. I'm calling you an adulterer.'

'Now you're beginning to get the picture. I have my hands full, and I'm only one man, I need help. It isn't the fault of the women and it isn't the fault of the husbands either. You can't escape the subject by placing the blame on men. Surely you can see that, Jack? In a marriage every man fails in time. The question is, what is the nature of the failure, and how hard is the judgement upon it? Think of Romeo in his forties and ask yourself about his promises and his ardour. But judge him on some other basis and he might have worked out to be an acceptable husband. He might have become pretty good at woodwork. Or he might have had a talent for child-care, who knows.'

'It's all self-serving garbage, though, isn't it. You're not dealing with women's needs. You're a lecher.'

'I agree. I'm among the sinners, and I'm not dealing with all their needs. I'm just handling the romantic side, sex and intrigue, deception and affection. To the best of my ability, which isn't always equal to the task. They complain all the time, you know. I don't phone often enough, I break dates, I spend too much time with my wife. Am I seeing other women? I explain exactly what I do and they ask if I'm seeing other women. Of course I'm seeing other women. But they want to hear lies, they beg me to tell them lies. And why don't I ever write, is it too much trouble to scribble a few lines of a love letter …? Jack, I could be ruined! I need help in the worst way, why must I be responsible for these extra women besides my wife? I'll tell you why,' said Ralph Jim, frustration raising his tone of voice to a higher pitch, 'it's because we have a whole population of selfish laggards out there who aren't pulling their weight. We have bone-idle free riders who're using the marriage bed for nothing else except sleep. Romance, flowers, little presents, an unexpected kiss, a touch of appreciation? Never. They won't even take the trouble to talk to them most of the time. They never listen, never. They have important other stuff to do and to think about so they tune the women out, and then I've got one more on my doorstep. I need help, Jack.'

'You're not getting any from me, not with this. This smells to me like something very simple, something you see a lot of on the ground around these stables and paddocks, if you want my honest opinion, Ralph Jim. I'm not buying it as hearts and flowers.' Said the sailor restlessly: 'I'd like to go get a bite of lunch now. I haven't been eating much breakfast since Mrs

Schwall kicked me in the stomach. It's like morning sickness.'

'See, there's another problem, today I can't eat lunch. Every second day it's an apple and a handful of carrot sticks. I have to train and diet like a prizefighter, you see.' The televangelist changed down from a manner of strident frustration to a reflective tone of complaint, elbows on his knees and his hands clasped, staring into the dark corner Jack was speaking from. 'Protein, fruit, fibre, iron supplements. Brandy and amphetamines when my back's again the wall, which is more and more often these days. How long can I last the pace? Weekends are good, the families are at home and so they have other things to do. The devil jumps up on Mondays and Tuesdays, mostly. Well, Thursdays too. My producer's sister started looking me straight in the eye just today. Direct eye contact, Jack, it means she intends to confer a gift on me. You think a little punch in the stomach is bad. I have more pulls and bruises and injuries and tenderness than any baseball jock who ever played. My groin strain is pretty much permanent. I have a sore hamstring I got from Mrs Kaldy the choir trainer that won't go away.' He changed up to strident lamentation again, sounding as if he might at any moment lose control and weep. 'There's a sweet girl who is suffering like a damned soul, Imogene Wedekind, a niece of Larry Kunz my Bible-quote researcher. For the love of God, I'm only one man, where can I find the time? Now Mrs Schwall's back again, that's completely out of the blue. Her husband landed a dream job in Los Angeles but she made him move back here so that she can be near me, but now of course he's out of work, hitting the bottle and turning into a bum ... Fortunately I have a good chiropractor,' said Ralph Jim, changing down once more and trying to look on the bright side then. 'The programme's doing great, I'm making truckloads of money. We're a cable show that gets a thirty-share for religious prime, we're beating out network standards like Jimmy Swaggart and Don Summers, Robert Schuller and *Mass for Shut-Ins*. We're only a point or so behind Oral Roberts, Woody Woodpecker and Eek! The Cat. My family is the greatest family in the world. Sue Ellen is the truest and most wonderful wife a man could wish for. I have a fine son.'

'On the subject of Paul,' said Jack, 'what about a dog? Laddie goes to another owner who'll appreciate him, and your son gets a nice dog. I have some pictures of dogs here.'

'In the olden days we had these fears – well, I'm not calling them good or bad but we had them, as men and women, fear of social disgrace,' Ralph Jim said with some wistfulness, 'of pregnancy and disgrace, village gossip was a part of what kept most folk on the straight and narrow path. Now we can shift all our reproductive engines into neutral gear with ingenious chemicals. Or we can wrap our organs in various plastics, with a choice of colours. Everything that would tend to guide our behaviour has been sealed and wrapped by smart developments in modern fogging science which only the strongest of the earth will survive,' the televangelist griped. His head fell low between his shoulders dejectedly again. Then he raised just his brows and eyes resentfully, shooting a look of rancour into Jack's dark corner. 'I thought you'd be advancing the dog idea when I saw the dog book, so I'll give you my thoughts on a dog. He's a god backwards, you know. But in real life he's a urinating and defecating creature like the rest of us, he gnaws leathers and eyeglasses, he sheds hair and jumps on furniture, he claims a share of your day, he requires affection as well as dog food. Somebody has to handle that, Paul's too young, Sue Ellen's too busy already and so am I. Wait a minute!' Ralph Jim hit the side of his head with the palm of his hand in a theatrical manner, putting on an act of sudden comprehension. 'I see! *You're* offering to do those things, are you, Jack, taking care of Paul's dog, vacuuming the hair off the furniture, cleaning the messes while he's being housetrained, the walks, the baths, the trips to the vet. You'll be handling it, will you. All you need from me is my consent.'

Jack didn't say anything. You could get really tired of preachers.

'Because if you're not going to be making the sacrifices it means somebody else must do so on your behalf. There's no gift from you without sacrifice, effortless bounty is for Shriners. Okay, you went and got a dog book but otherwise where's your role? Where's your part as a bestower of the bounty? What we come to is that Paul can't have a dog because his friend Jack doesn't want to do what's necessary to let him have a dog. I hope we're clear on that. But if you're in a helpful mood, let's get back to this other matter, unhappy women. I don't have one break from unhappy women this week between Monday and Friday. Tuesday is just fogging awful. I have three on Tuesday. Awful. Miss Lorenzen. Vain and guilty, a weeper and a schemer. But,' he said in a lighter tone, maybe conscious of revealing unattractive prejudices, 'a woman is a kindly spirit, Jack. She's a gentle heart we do harm to.' He put a hand inside his waistcoat then and winced. 'Stomach acid,' Ralph Jim said. 'The doctor doesn't know what causes it. Would you introduce yourself to Miss Lorenzen on Tuesday? Say Big Bill sent you, and let her cry on your shoulder. I have two others the same morning, practically the same time. I sure could use a chance to take a shower and get a cup of coffee.'

Said Jack: 'Well, Ralph Jim, I'm beginning to see how it is with you. Anything you want to do is okay, and a noble duty, anything you don't want to do is a bad idea, and somebody else is responsible. You want to have a bunch of lady friends for visits and you don't want to let Paul have a dog. I say you are marked as a betrayer and a liar and a faithless consort,' said the sailor with plenty of indignation, 'and believe me I'll never consent to being an accomplice in your disgraceful behaviour. I'll never see your so-called crusade as anything else except self-serving hypocrisy and libertine promiscuity. That's my last word, and it's firm as a rock.'

Jack then went to his apartment to dress. Shortly afterward, eating a lobster lunch at Neptune's Cavern in the Court and trimly visible in white cords and a Senators sweater, he had to think about the government cabinet, which had a role in the Schata business. To the delight of the TV news reporters, who were mostly illiterates in their twenties themselves, the new cabinet was composed of politicians of unprecedented youth and vim. If hard work and youthful smiles could save a country this was the cabinet to do it. There would be a reception and press conference for General Schata. But the members of the cabinet seemed to Jack greatly handicapped by that innocence which made them look so good on TV. For the children men like Hitler and Stalin were characters in books, and books weren't real. Jack was beginning to look at the reception as a happy, noisy party, with presents on the floor for the guest of honour to open, anything he asked for. All the friends played games and then sat down to hamburgers and ice cream and chocolate milk. A few loud words, maybe, while they played the games, but then General Schata gave his hosts a balloon each that he'd brought, and they were all happy again. One or two members of the cabinet were sick in their limousines going home from too much ice cream but they'd had a super party with the nice man.

Jack was keeping an eye on the newspapers, wondering if Schata would be taken through the Sutton, as sometimes happened with politicians from the general's part of the world, who swept with their aides and henchmen like harvesting winds through the complex buying everything in sight. But General Schata was perhaps too serious-minded for shopping. He couldn't avoid, however, passing within sight of the Sutton on his way into Ottawa from the airport.

A loud voice from a nearby table interrupted these reflections. As it happened Jack recognized the two men seated there. He knew what they were talking about also, having been a principal in the events. Porky Barry Dalmadge, with pouched cheeks and breadcrumbs on his handlebar moustache, forked turbot wolfishly into his mouth. John Kiley, Dalmadge's superior at Morosoph Educational Supply, whose apartment in the Parthenon Tower Dalmadge had borrowed one night after he took Imogene Wedekind to dinner, was a tall large-boned man, and owner of the loud voice. He had very little hair and the tweeds he wore hung on him loosely, apparently as a result of successful dieting. He was eating squid and a small green salad.

'Six hockey pucks. An athletic support.' Kiley's eyes were resentfully on Dalmadge's side orders of fried potatoes and crabmeat dumplings. 'I suppose he takes the pucks with him to autograph when he makes public appearances. Six pucks in a briefcase, a shirt, *Sports Illustrated*. Leaving the athletic support was a mistake but he must have felt very comfortable in my place. I mean I'm surprised there wasn't a sweater number 44 in my closet. The maid's been picking bobby pins out of the shag and leaving 'em on my bedside table in little paper cups. For God's sake, Barry,' Kiley said, pushing his haggard face across the table at Dalmadge, 'my wife has a key to that apartment too, you know. Suppose she dropped in and saw a paper cup with hair pins?'

'Geez, I don't understand. It was just the one time.'

'You said you had an affair.'

'It was just the one time at your place. I mean, we were having an affair, John,' Dalmadge lied with manly *Weltschmerz*, 'but I didn't abuse your hospitality. I'd never do that.'

'How did she get the key?'

'I honestly don't know, John. Honestly.'

'They had a key each, Imogene and Jean-Guy, the twinkie feminist and the Golden Great One. It's my apartment, Barry. Sure it's the company apartment but it's mine, it's my company apartment. They were living in the place. Squatters. I should collect a month's rent from Mizz Wedekind and Mr God Damn Pickett. I should collect it from you. The maid on my floor's a black woman, big and simple, half Irish and half Jamaican. She's a religious fanatic. She doesn't like the idea of bobby pins in the shag, she hates sweeping champagne glasses out of the fireplace and she knows grass when she smells it. Then I have to give the guy a party when Mizz Poutface waltzes into the office with a ring. It's a happy ending, never mind they've already had a month's honeymoon in my apartment rent-free.'

'But you're in good with the old man, John. He really enjoyed himself talking hockey with the Golden Great One. I think he's overrated myself. Pickett, I mean.'

'I was always okay with the old man,' Kiley said, chewing squid and watching Barry Dalmadge digging in to fried potatoes while he dunked a chunk of fish in lemon butter. 'It's tough in the company apartment, my own apartment, a guest's there for the first time and he knows where everything is. The bride-to-be has a little headache from the excitement and here I am, the host, apologizing, we don't have any Alka-Seltzer. Then he goes straight into the kitchen and gets her one. That made me look foolish, you know, Barry? Like somebody who couldn't find his ass with a mirror.' Kiley swallowed his mouthful of squid and signalled for a check, though Dalmadge was hardly halfway through his own meal. 'I looked like an idiot, and that's something I don't do well. Maybe it's different with you. I wonder why she calls him Jack? It's not English for Jean. Jack is Jacques I always thought.'

'What?' said Barry Dalmadge in his old style.

'The Wedekind woman. Mizz God Damn Wedekind, she calls Jean-Guy Pickett Jack. I was wondering why. My name's John and nobody's ever called me Jack. That's three hundred calories for me,' Kiley said as he signed the check. 'You had a thousand on the rolls and butter before we ordered, so if you can get by without the dumplings, your count is four thousand. Take your time if you're still hungry.'

'Well, I'm not dieting, John,' said Barry with a laugh, correcting the haggard man's misapprehension with all gentleness.

'Oh? I'm sorry, my mistake. I thought all of us were on the lean and mean bandwagon from necessity. Personally I miss the good old times when everybody ate three-course lunches and Morosoph could absorb the loss. Are you sure? Because I'm not in a hurry. It's a shame to waste those nice fries.'

'No, I'm ready. Have you,' asked Barry Dalmadge, getting up, 'ever wanted to be called Jack, John? I could call you Jack.'

'No, I never have. Don't call me Jack.'

Mr Goof-it had arranged a change in Imogene Wedekind's sexual life, because she was too smart for the regular run of men. Jack had worked from an understanding of how the problem is resolved in the opposite direction. Intelligent males never seemed less than contented with pretty females who reached their high point of concentration while painting their toenails. It was only a matter then of deciding what pool of males looked best, and everybody liked hockey players. The match-up of Imogene Wedekind and Jean-Guy Pickett had worked out so well that Jack had player lists on his computer now, for comparison with Ralph Jim's unhappy women's roster. He was especially anxious to find somebody big, maybe a centre, could be from the prairies, who'd go for Mrs Kaldy the choir-trainer.

As Jack finished his modest meal the Wake-Up Man was being seated at the table vacated by the men from Morosoph. The Wake-Up Man ordered a Martini rocks and with gentlemanly interest began a study of the menu. His manner with his choosing of a meal was sensuously alive. He wasn't a lentil soup prophet. There did not seem to be anything in his private canon about mortification of the flesh.

His foggy mat-grey eyebrows rode high and relaxed on his face, drawing his eyelids smooth, and he seemed to sight down along his nose with affection, first at the table, then – tilting his neck back – at his fellow diners, including Jack. His mild stare might have rested on Jack for a moment. The Wake-Up Man for the sailor was always a vividly rebuking presence. Now Jack asked himself: why oh why do I continue to buy my apparel out of the Oriental sweat shops? I'm tidy and neat, certainly, good hip slacks from somewhere in Indonesia and a Hong Kong baseball top but as theatre I'm low-budget. My production values are B grade, that's for sure.

Today the Wake-Up Man unassumingly wore a white linen shirt that might have come from the wardrobe of a pre-revolutionary French aristo-crat, but which could be seen to be new, and fitted him exactly, even to fol-lowing a height difference of a millimetre or so between his left and right shoulders. Two rows of nubby pearl buttons winked on the breast seams. The doubled-back cuffs were folded into emerald links with gold chains, and fine lacework could be seen that just reached his wrists. His wide tie was a silk-and-cotton foulard of grey, and there was a diamond in it somewhere – nothing large, but Jack could see the firefly blaze now and then. Then the suit over the shirt was a muted money-green two-piece with a darker vest, and he carried his usual silver-headed cane. He'd left a white scarf, yellow gloves and a lightweight camel-hair overcoat with the lady in the Neptune Cavern's cloakroom.

The Wake-Up Man's whole style of presentation had to do with being unaware of his own appearance. He always looked outward, with intense concern. It could be seen that he would have no interest in looking in a mirror. He was art grade as theatre.

'I see you people are walking upright now,' said the Wake-Up Man to the waiter who brought his aperitif. 'You're all walking on two legs and wearing clothes. That's a good move. That makes sense. Allow me to offer my congratulations.'

'Thank you, sir,' said the waiter, somewhat amused.

'I notice everybody woke up safely this morning,' said the Wake-Up Man to the patrons of Neptune's Cavern at large. 'You've recovered from the unconsciousness of the black night-time hours. I'd like to see a show of surprise here about that. Let's see some surprise and pleasure. Because if it ever stops happening there isn't much we can do to get it going again.'

Chapter 10

Walking Down Paradise Street

JACK PAYS A VISIT every year to the place where his father breeds the dogs. His father always takes a minute to recognize Jack. Mr Clemmaknohke doesn't ask Jack to stay. He's usually taciturn and busy and, Jack can see, somewhat angry at the annual reappearance of somebody from a previous episode of his life. Mr Clemmaknohke has done no wrong, yet must endure these science-fiction hauntings by a time traveller who is a year older on each appearance. It could have been worse for him of course; he might have been haunted by a time traveller who blamed his parent for all his problems and wanted to discuss every one in detail.

Jack spends a day or two with Horsy Stacpole at his rectory in Elzevir. They go on hikes through the bush together and do a little fishing. The Black River at Queensborough is good for bass and pickerel and you can take trout from Moira Lake if you know where they are.

Horsy Stacpole looked younger to Jack every time he saw him. There appeared to be more and glossier brown in Horsy Stacpole's hair, which was as thick and wild as it had ever been. He was learning German. At a country auction in Madoc Township he'd acquired for fifty dollars what he called 'priceless treasure trove', a big old red-pine chest filled with books, collections of German sermons of the nineteenth century. There were more than a hundred leather-bound volumes of these sermons in German, Horsy Stacpole told Jack enthusiastically, and the best part was that the books themselves were in mint condition. 'Preserved by incredible luck,' the wild old preacher told Jack as they sat together on a bank of the Black with their fishing poles, 'almost as if they had never been opened.'

Jack has now arrived at a way of listening to Horsy Stacpole's views of life and the race of man. As a youth his belief in them nearly got him killed. Now he automatically applies his rule of opposites. It works for all sunny maxims. Make your own list if you like. The best things in life are – it's as plain as a pikestaff – unaffordable. Regrettably, coronets are more than kind hearts. Indeed a kind heart, especially together with simple faith, is in most company correctly marked down as a form of imbecility. Power, the preacher had often remarked, shaking his head over his copy of the *Madoc Review*, tends to corrupt.... The powerful people Jack had met weren't corrupt, though he assumed it could happen to them at any time. They were humane and charming. They were self-deprecating and witty. An opposite here wasn't hard to find, in fact was hard not to see, looking at the teeming streets, snarly folk, violence-prone and stare-eyed, the knifers and the brutalizers of old women for their thin purses, the ravagers of children. Lack of power tends to corrupt. Anybody can step on you like a bug, and most choose to. You don't get much charm from bugs. Wait as long as you like for the gracious gesture or the delightful witticism.

When he worked at Brand X cameras in Kanata Jack was in a low power state for a while. Brand X was an assembler of popular cameras from cheap Taiwanese and Korean parts, a big step down from Technoptrax.

'Mr Goof-it would never understand that,' they told Jack at this Brand X camera place when he made a suggestion of any intricacy. 'We want a model,' they said to Jack, who was the whole technical department, 'to sell to that dumb forker Mr Goof-it, so that he won't make a mistake when he takes a picture of Mrs Goof-it, the big bimbo, and all the little forking Goof-its. We want to make it out of parts that cost pennies and go together fast.' Every year they added new features to the line of models. Jack's technical tasks were a matter of integrating these features into the line, always with Mr Goof-it's basic stupidity in mind. If Mr Goof-it was given a flashy chrome lens cap on the Truematic he would forget to remove it so he had to be offered a buzzer or a winking light on the deluxe model as a reminder. Of course he didn't need either of these features in the first place for lenses that came into the Brand X warehouse at a hundred dollars a gross.

A popular sales department image was of Mr Goof-it as a lunchpail gorilla, affluent and strike-happy, with dangling arms and short legs and no forehead, who belonged to menacing tribes with names like AFL and CLC that congregated in dockyards and steel plants. Who was in all respects untrustworthy but who in a manner of speaking could be made to trade for glass beads. Jack didn't have prejudices of this nature, to the best of his knowledge, and when he thought about it he had the impression that Mr Goof-it was probably evenly layered through the population. Brand X honoured no warranty claims and conducted no market research but a high proportion of the warranty registration cards that came into the Brand X post-office box number were filled out in the careful big handwriting of children.

Mr Goof-it was always an invisible presence at the Brand X meetings. Everybody pretended he was the lunchpail jerk, which seemed to provide the most comfortable working climate for the Brand X groups, all men and tending to be grade twelve to first-year university dropouts. As the suggestions for moving the line were thrown on the table these merchandisers had to look inside themselves and give the matter of a simple nature some thought. Where else could they look? They searched themselves for the Neanderthal, the ancient hunters, the makers of tools from stones and bones, everything they believed Mr Goof-it to be. With jokes and shrugs they tried to imagine how it would feel to be naive, to believe what was written in the newspapers and uttered on TV and what was promised by politicians, to have a sentimental credulity about justice and order, the saving grace of love, the sanctity of truth, the inevitable punishment of wickedness, et cetera.

Mr Goof-it had times when he could be seen in dumb grinning wholeness by this method. Somebody had found him inside. The sales of the Brand X models took a jump then. The older merchandisers only nodded saying, okay, right now we have the market, let's jack these prices up. The merchandisers in the middle began to look at boats, and the young ones thought they had the popular camera business figured out from A to Z.

But then Mr Goof-it would whimsically change, rejecting models he should have liked, halting the assembly lines, creating big cold pile-ups in the warehouses. He struck the buyers of parts abroad with uncertainty. He wrecked the confidence of the salesmen on the retail rounds with dire rumours of takeover and ingestion by some big shark, and reigned over weeks of panic at the worker level where the talk was of layoffs and plant closings.

Just one bored yawn by Mr Goof-it, the contemptible Mr Goof-it, could do this at Brand X. Intelligent and civilized people lost their livings because their idea of themselves as simple folk had slipped out of mind while they were thinking on a more sophisticated level.

The sales chief at Brand X was a man named Jim Doser who was called Bull. He was weighty but energetic and ran up and down stairs instead of using the elevators. Bull wore plaid waistcoats and striped shirts with the sleeves rolled up. He had black hair plastered sideways on top of his head. He conducted meetings in the Brand X corridors, catching people on the run, beige folders under his arm, pink telephone slips peeping from his shirt and waistcoat pockets and usually a ballpoint clenched between his teeth. When he was in his office Bull just stayed long enough to take a phone call or to look for a paper on his desk. Then he was out the door and on the go again.

One afternoon Jack found Bull Doser at his shoulder in a corridor, talking indistinctly through an Erasermate. Jack was on his way home. But he must have been feeling better because he understood that he was having a meeting with the sales chief. He was able to understand too that Bull was talking about the Brand X Instant Picture. It had become cluttered with an accumulation of bright junky sales ideas over the years, buzzers, flashing lights, timers, cranks and resets and remote functions, cigar lighters, lint filters, nail files. Now the Instant Picture model had moved beyond what Mr Goof-it could afford and what he could understand. So Bull wanted a new instant picture snapshooter for Mr Goof-it, something sales could start from scratch on, adding a lens defroster or a bubblegum dispenser every year as they went along. 'Give me something different in a camera to get us started with Instant Picture Pro, young fella,' Bull said, patting Jack on the shoulder before veering away to pound up a flight of stairs, 'something new, eh, but remember our rule – keep it simple. There's a good lad.'

Jack understood what the sales chief wanted. This was another good sign. He'd been dead lately, the walking dead. For two months he'd been listening to people without hearing them, as if they were speaking a strange language, or ghosts moving their mouths without making sounds. He wasn't sleeping much and felt tired all the time. In bed, though, he was alert, dozing sometimes then waking as his eyes snapped open and his mind roved with its dreadful routine and persistence over the figures of his pain.

Just eating presented a big obstacle. In his worst state Jack had to make the decision that to buy food he would need to go to a market. In the market he looked at the shelves and had to stop and decide that paper towels and detergents weren't food. He found a shelf of canned meat and bought a dozen cans of something, tuna as it turned out. On his next trip to the store he had learnt what to do. He bought a dozen cans of tuna.

By the time Jack started at Brand X he could muster enough concentration to hear and answer questions. This took effort though. He had to exert will power and bring his mind into focus in order to do it. He was only a shadow of the man he'd been at Technoptrax, as an employee. Brand X saw Jack as a person with heavyweight credentials who'd become a zombie but who was cheap and could do the job. The Kanata company had many such bargain employees, broken in spirit and confidence for one reason and another. Up to the corridor meeting with Bull Doser he'd been making his way at work on free memory, formulae and procedures tumbling readily from the reservoir within whenever required. Where there was no memory he was helpless. He couldn't imagine, and he couldn't deal with new thoughts, because nothing except thoughts of Columbine's death would stick in his mind.

But he found he could think about Bull Doser's project, probably because the answer to it came with a memory of Columbine when she was alive. It went back to some of their early time together.

One camera principle Mr Goof-it always found hard to grasp was a light supply affected by both the lens opening and shutter speed, and many Brand X models had automatic flash, and automatic switching between daylight and flash. Jack thought he could simplify this by providing just one light source. He would use a special kind of light control he'd developed while working with Columbine at Technoptrax on high-altitude reconnaisance cameras. In this control system the light itself moved, shifting photo subject views from one eye to the other. Jack's idea here was that if he could make the light control work in one of Brand X's cheap cameras he could give Bull an Instant Picture camera that would take three-dimensional snapshots, something that hadn't been available in popular photography up to now.

At Technoptrax Jack and Columbine's work had been called controlled light optics, CLO. It was a matter of controlling a certain frequency by using a higher one, exactly as a transistor radio is able to pull music out of empty air. He was dealing with the light frequency spectrum, roughly three hundred gigahertz to three hundred thousand terahertz. X-rays are above that, then gamma rays, which are simply X-rays on a higher frequency. The control was oscillating energy, in fact, though some physicists like to talk of it as subatomic particles. The control made light bend. A solid subject within the CLO field was lighted from the front and sides and then the light, bending, collapsed together to produce a view around the subject to the background. When the background was filled in completely the subject, naturally, became invisible. What Jack and Columbine had done with this at Technoptrax was to make jungle foliage cover disappear, so that reconnaissance aircraft could photograph rebel movements under the cover.

Now he wanted a strong and simple colour range for Mr Goof-it's Instant Picture camera, and he was guessing about sixty percent green. He began in his Brand X lab by setting up a test series that reduced the above-light energy in measured steps. He was looking for something tuned to the point where the subject stood forward boldly from the background, just before it vanished. He put together a CLO model and began testing on film.

He had the green spectrum on an easel against a white wall. On the same board was a card with the primaries red and blue, and their complements cyan and yellow. This didn't work. He started getting bands of white in his green bands, and he got moiré and other disturbance of the green bands adjacent to the white.

Looking just at photos he couldn't understand where these whites were coming from for a while, there being no white bands anywhere on the board. Then he remembered the invisibility barrier, comically striking his forehead with the heel of his hand, since we're all bad theatre under stress – he was looking at rectangular photos of the white wall behind the board. He'd have to back up and go through the series again.

He hadn't seen the invisibility effect since Technoptrax, though, and he studied it with interest now. He lit the board with his CLO generator and peered through it at the wall behind. The effect was of a rectangle missing from the green spectrum. It was so uncanny that Jack had to go and tap the white panel with a finger. The section was solidly there, but his finger appeared to be tapping nothingness.

He made other CLO models, boosting and attenuating, looking for ranges and limits that he could put in a computer as numbers. That specific green range always vanished quickly – it was the cloak of invisibility. The generator's power wasn't stable in those first models but he was able to see that CLO light itself was as pervasive as air, not simply an energy wave or a beam. For one experiment, jotting down an attenuation scale, Jack set up the CLO generator in a janitor's closet in a hall a couple of corridors away from his little lab at Brand X. He closed the workroom door. He took the test board into an equipment room and closed that door. The green remained invisible. Distances and obstructions did drain CLO energy, however. Much later, working for himself, Jack was able to draw up a table of equivalents, between distance and obstructing forces and materials, and CLO energy required. In the open air invisibility was intermittent, flashing on and off in random patterns. Jack's light wasn't a good competitor with natural light and other cosmic energy forms.

On the Mr Goof-it Instant Picture project he backed up a good safe distance from the invisibility barrier and put a dumb light source in a rough-up from a Brand X Instant Picture camera. The camera worked. It took bold, good-looking three-dimensional pictures, on instant-processable film, and cut the film and ejected the prints through the slot.

It was Jack's first original design in many months and he liked it. He found Bull Doser on the loading bay with a Parker T-Ball clenched in his teeth and a cell phone clamped between chin and shoulder. 'These look great, son,' said Bull, thumbing through Jack's sample 3D photos taken with the new design, four of the warehouse cat, Tums, and a half-dozen of the Brand X parking lot. 'Whose Jetta is that in Mr Gagnon's spot? Look at these pictures. Wooey. We can sell this product, can we ever. If if if if if. Let's see what you got here.' He turned Jack's rough-up camera back and forth, making mental substitutions of cheaper parts. 'Three inside assemblies, are there? Cheese, that's rich! They were mailed on the twentieth and you got them the next day and signed for them,' said he into the phone. 'Yes, I know you're not complaining. You got nothing to complain about, Gerry.' He popped the aluminium back off the camera case with the blade of an old pocket knife. 'No, this don't work.'

'It do work like a charm, Bull,' said Jack mournfully, though he knew what Bull meant. 'An it be yourn free if ye want t'spend a ha'penny or so. It be free by nature, like air an sunshine an electricity. Give it to pore Mr Goof-it, why don't ye. He do work hard an all he gets fer fun is the woeful TV picture shows.'

Bull had meanwhile hung up on Gerry and was dialling out again. He probed inside the rough-up with the T-Ball point. 'Your fargle here's five dollars thirty to six-fifty,' he said to Jack, 'so it retails out to say forty-five, and we want to sell the whole camera, with a case and a strap and packaging, for under thirty.' He talked on the phone for a minute, looking idly at Jack's model in his hand before tossing it in a trashcan. 'Our end of the camera business is a big dogfight,' he explained to Jack then, not unkindly. 'We aren't in business to finance people's inventions, and we sure aren't in business to improve the quality of Mr Goof-it's life, we're just trying to get ahold of our share of his money. Check with me again when you have some-thing that works, and,' said the sales chief, 'you could put a sock in the sailor talk, too. Hardly anybody around here can figure it out, Jack.... They put beer in his saucer on the four to twelve, just to see him stagger, that's how he puts on the weight. That's why he likes the stomach pills.'

The final words from Bull were directed into the phone, but Bull at the same time handed back the snaps of Tums the cat, which Jack could then see were of an overweight animal, morose and dyspeptic in all four poses. He didn't even trouble to retrieve his rough-up camera from the trashcan, although he had liked it very well no more than five minutes earlier. It had been a gift for Mr Goof-it, who to tell the truth is nothing else except the commonalty of men or by the same argument the god Mr Goof-it has created as an ideal form of himself. Jack didn't feel he could afford to waste any more of his lifespan working to improve Mr Goof-it's comfort and wel-fare. He had his own future to think about.

An invisible man is a man of power, Columbine had said long ago, quot-ing H.G. Wells, when she was enthusiastic about invisibility as a weapon against the folk who killed her father.

Maybe Jack wasn't recovering after all.

It could be that Jack never did recover. All the invisible men so far have been mad.

His first invisibility rig included a CLO generator that rode above his head on a shoulder harness. It was cumbersome, and made no sense at all in the Tower, where he needed to go through many doorways, but it worked and gave him invisible mobility. He used it temporarily in the Sutton to make cash withdrawals from banks. He used it for a few weeks in out-of-the-way maintenance store rooms while he rewired the main light systems. Later, when he had the leisure to peruse and revise tenders he had this work done by the Sutton's regular electrical contractors and lighting equipment suppliers. It was just a particular way to wire a lighting system, so that every one of the five separate maintenance and janitorial companies that worked the Sutton provided Jack with a CLO environment. Well, the CLO habitat was more expensive than regular wiring for filaments and fluorescents but what replacements and repairs don't get more expensive day by day? The rest of the setup went very well, though before he got all the new lights installed and tested he had a few unsettling experiences of walking from invisibility into sudden visibility, particularly in the Parthenon Tower apartments which are more hived with walls than the Sutton shopping areas.

He was a frightening sight when he materialized unexpectedly. Grown men had hopped in the air on both feet and screamed when it happened. Dressed in his invisibility rig and in plain view Jack unfortunately looks like a comic-book Algae Monster, or the Slime Creature. The head covering is thin nylon, flimsy enough to see through, headgear as worn by stocking mask bandits. The cloak reaches to his ankles and has slits for his hands, and capacious pockets to carry off whatever he steals. These and the shoes and socks and gloves are all dyed green, do-it-yourself work by Jack. They have a matted, viridian appearance, as if grown from monster seed in ocean trenches. Nobody of harmless intent needs to be that green.

For practical reasons he has two green rigs. One goes into the wash every Sunday night.

There was a time when he thought a store-bought green would be okay if he allowed a generous wave length when choosing the spectroscopic position on the line spectrum at the CLO end. The problem with this was that it made innocent bystanders, or parts of them, invisible accidentally. For instance on one quiet shopping morning in those early days Jack's eye was caught on the Concourse by a young girl wearing a green sundress. She was looking at shoes on the Bata entry display. What captured the sailor man's attention was her midsection, all the area of her sundress, which shimmered in the CLO field generated by the store's display lighting. Blast me eyes, this can happen all over, thought Jack, this won't do, the green's got to be thin as a hair or thinner or we'll have folk jumping in and out of view like frogs.

Sure enough the girl moved a step and her midsection vanished; the crowd by chance at that moment contained a large mill of young men, who stared hard and murmured in wonderment, which the girl turned and noticed, the turn bringing her dress back into normal light again. The dress seems to work fine, thought she, pretending not to see the stares, now if I could just find a pair of heels to match.

The Wake-Up Man was among the crowd, in a dark blue Chesapeake Yacht Club blazer with grey flannels and Florsheims, having come out of Bootle's bookstore tilted somewhat to starboard by the weight of a shopping bag containing a half-dozen or so of the new novels and poetry collections. 'Yes, those shoes are nice,' he said in his courteous tones, nodding at the Bata display while the crowd still mumbled and stared. 'I like to see people wearing nice shoes, in all walks of life. But where do you suppose they'll get you in the long run, nice shoes?'

His little homily was lost on the object of the crowd's attention, who had happily slipped inside the Bata store, having spotted a pair she wanted to try on. The people moved about their affairs again, though one or two stopped, accosting strangers, with questions like Did you see that? and What happened? One young lady of uncompromising manner declared that it was an outrage, and a disgraceful way to sell shoes, forcing a model to parade in the open without a dress; she did not say without a dress or a body, which would have weakened the censorious force of her protest. She added that there were children present. Jack was depressed now, with more finicky adjustments to make on the CLO generator and nearly a hundred generators already installed to replace. His own opinion is that a view of nakedness isn't even a factor in the corruption of children, or indeed of anybody else. Nakedness in most cases is a cheerful state, while corruption is a process and a dismal one.

Jack had been in a cheerful state one time in Toronto when he had a fatal encounter with corruption. It was a matter of happening to meet a man, Elmo Apse, in a bar.

The bar was the Anne Boleyn room in the Sheraton Centre in Toronto. Columbine had planned early Christmas shopping in Toronto and she had also arranged meetings with friends from her school days. Early on a Monday afternoon they arrived and unpacked and went into the bar, which was nearly empty.

Elmo Apse was sitting with a girl at the far end of the room and his eyes followed Columbine, who was sparkling and big-eyed, since she was beginning a break she'd been looking forward to. She didn't see him just then. It was mid-October of what had been a wonderful year. She had a dinner party on her social schedule to which Jack was invited, and then other events and reunions, ranging down from the dinner to a ten-minute coffee break at a hospital cafeteria with a schoolmate who had become a medical administrator. Her time was all mapped out with Columbine's characteristic efficiency. She had even scheduled certain hours for spontaneous behaviour.

Some events included Jack, but he also had his own plans for the week, not so crowded – some appointments in the suburbs with importers of test equipment, and a couple of lunches. Their excuse for the trip was a trade exhibition at the Sheraton Centre, which they would visit together. Also, and this was a subject of jokes between them, Columbine wanted a ring of a particular warm jade, a promise ring she called it sentimentally, instead of a diamond ring for a mark of their union, and they would shop for that together too.

Apse's place in the bar was a few tables directly behind Columbine as they happened to seat themselves. She was talking earnestly, seeking Jack's understanding of a time of singular vitality in her life, with her own circle from within the tribe of these friends she would revisit.

'I was as close to them as I've been to anybody until I met you,' she said. 'The only other two people I was that close to were my father, and I never knew him, and my uncle in Sharon. We worked hard and we had great times. The advanced arts and sciences, boys and beer, ball games and good causes, the kind of education that teaches a woman everything she will ever need to know. I've learnt nothing new since. I expect to forget more than I learn from now on.'

Jack was uneasy. This was a scene he replayed a thousand times later in the dark hours, and he always remembers his own unease. It wasn't premonition, it was the understanding that Columbine was vulnerable. He joked about the jade ring because Columbine had been a tough person up to then but the person who wanted a promise ring could be hurt. She had been balanced and self-sufficient through their early times and now suddenly they were in a city of alien air and she was talking about cherished friends that she depended upon for who she was.

'They are all so wretchedly successful, Jack, that sometimes I think it's pure chance – they each won heaven's lottery, maybe. But I really think it was us, the stuff we learnt together and how we talked together. We talked about everything, no hold backs, that was the education we gave ourselves. Christine is the chatelaine of what amounts to a castle in Rosedale. She has young girls from the West Indies living in the attics who do all the housework for her. It's just disgraceful, she has no sense of shame whatever, she enjoys every day of her life and she looks great. Heather's in Forest Hill with two young children. There's going to be a lot of parenting and schooling talk from Heather – well, she always talked that way, long before she got married, but now she knows more so she talks more. It doesn't matter if you're not interested ...' she said to Jack, who was letting his eyelids droop and his jaw sag. 'This is all about me, so you have to know it because now it's all about us. Biker was what we used to call Bianca – it was a ten-speed, not a

Harley, she was years in advance of the bicycle craze. Bianca's the only one of us who isn't married.'

'Well, you can relax with Bianca,' Jack suggested. 'Compare experiences and try to figure out what you're doing wrong.'

'You see, you're a still a very weird man, aren't you,' said Columbine. 'You have a remarkable mind, but at a deeper level it's adolescent.' She took his hand on the bar table. 'Who isn't married at the moment, I meant to say. I was invited to all three of her weddings but I could only get to one. If I went out to the hotel newsstand right now I'd probably be able to bring you back a couple of pictures of the Biker. She was the tough one of us. My end of chit-chat with the others will be just fine. They're locked in the seraglio, and now I will be too, we're all on the same level, and we all knew we would come to this, except Bianca. I mean, shacked up in Belleville with some guy; she won't understand that. I guarantee you she'll want to save me from it.'

Elmo Apse had turned around in his seat to keep an eye on Columbine. He thought he knew her but wasn't certain yet. The girl with him had narrow dark eyes and a pale face with blond hair in a fringe on her forehead. She looked sad to Jack, who had noticed the couple, and naturally she didn't share Apse's interest in Columbine. So here is our mariner with his steadfast stare on a horizon of fair weather but coming up on a reef line.

'Bianca was the first person I ever met who talked about prenuptial contracts, although one or two men,' said Columbine, irritated by the memory, 'have mentioned them to me since. Usually it's a man who wants them, but I remember the Biker explaining the idea to me when she was barely eighteen. She said, I'm going to take the guy to a lawyer's office, Dad's would be best, and have him sign legal documents. About his property, and any money he has, and who owns the children, like a will you see, in the event of the death of the marriage. Then, Bianca said, if they get a divorce he's left with a tidy pauper's life but he knew about that in advance. The way she talked then, it was to help his concentration on Bianca, and to stop him thinking about divorce without an excellent reason. She's matured a lot since. The mistake women make, the Biker always says,' said Columbine, still affectionately holding Jack's hand, 'is to try to screw money out of the guy when they're having the divorce. That's the wrong time. He's hopping mad then and he hates her, not a nickel for that awful bitch, he says. Biker gets a lot of marriage proposals. When a man wants her to marry him, she says, he's as near to perfect as he'll ever be. He'll never be that close to perfect again. He's kind and considerate. He thinks of her when they're apart. He says he's in love forever. Now that's the right time. That's when he should be taken to the lawyer's office, the Biker says.... What do you think, Jack?'

'I agree with her right readily,' said the sailor promptly. 'Her thoughts are like a lighthouse in this foggy bar, your friend Bianca, why if her views prevailed we would have a much more weighted society. Men and women would be unhappy, but what of it, they're unhappy now. Take him directly to a lawyer's office – at his moment of warmest ardour, if that can be done. He should be taken deep into the recesses of the oldest and most powerful legal firm Bianca knows. Her father's sounds perfect. He should be presented with an iron-clad document, as thick as the Old Testament. That would be the way to do it. Yes. That would be a an excellent test of his sincerity and the durability of his affections.'

'But is that a healthy way to begin a marriage, Jack?'

'Very healthy. It weeds out so many unsuitable guys. Make the contract tight enough and you could get the perfect husband, the only man for you. Everybody else would bail out.'

'No, I mean seriously, I worry about the Biker, she always says she doesn't want to be a trophy wife, but that's what always happens to her. If she could get her mind off contracts wouldn't she be able to look for something else in marriage? I don't know what, something better than money and property and a nice guy, at the risk of sounding naïve? It could pass her by if she isn't on the lookout, and then what? What was the thing about summer's lease?'

'No idea. There's a man behind you staring at you.'

'Summer's lease hath all too short a date. She ends up as a sad old divorced lady.'

'Don't forget rich, Columbine. She has paid sensible attention to contracts, and now she is a sad old rich divorced lady. The state she missed out on according to your idea would be that of a happy old married lady, or I guess a happy old widow, but how many of those do you see? Be realistic. Old ladies are naturally cantankerous and disagreeable, that's their natural temper. If they're cheerful it's because they're on drugs. She's going to be grouchy anyway, and if she's rich she can get away with it. I believe your friend Bianca is sensible and wise, Columbine. I'm looking forward to meeting her, moreover, and congratulating her on her good sense and wisdom.'

Elmo Apse had sauntered across. He bowed from the waist with both hands deep in his pants pockets. 'I wasn't sure it was you,' he said. The lovers unclasped their hands. Jack thought at the time that Columbine had some trouble remembering the man. He knew later he was wrong about that. She said: 'Elmo, for goodness' sake. What a surprise.'

Their brief conversation followed the pattern for chance encounters, what they were doing, where living, what friends were still around or moved away. Elmo Apse's handshake was deliberately firm. In his talk with Columbine his face changed expression in the same way, deliberately, by an act of will. Jack could see him deciding to smile before he smiled, and deciding to look interested before he did that. When he said goodbye to Columbine he leaned forward carefully and squeezed her shoulder. Then before he returned to his companion he gave them both a smile, one each and separately delivered.

Childhood days occur in a more powerful world than the real one.

Childhood is when sorcery is at its most intense, as everybody admits. Ordinary people are taller, and goldener, and crueller, and more frightening. Folk carried forward from the childhood world can be a letdown as a consequence; but they can sometimes bring their powerful sorcery with them all intact.

That was what Elmo Apse did, as it happened. Elmo Apse had known Columbine in the enchanted forest. They'd walked to school together now and then. A passing wizard saw them one day on the golden forest path, while Columbine's face was turned to Elmo, shining, and sparkles flew from his magic wand.

Now in the Anne Boleyn Room something spellbinding, the awe and grace of Elmo Apse as she'd seen him with her shining child's face reached out and claimed Columbine again. It hung a weight of chains on her. That had been a cruel wizard back in the forest.

At the dinner party Jack was seated beside Christine, a lean vigorous woman with sun-bleached hair and a forthright way of talking. Before they went into the dining-room Christine told her guests, four couples, two elderly ladies and a middle-aged man in a wheelchair, that she hoped they would find her food worth picking at but that she hadn't been able to bring herself to pay the fancy prices the government stores were asking for French wines, hence the Californian Chablis and the Inniskillen red. In tête-à-tête table talk with Jack the hostess managed to find out a lot about him without showing much curiosity. Jack sometimes felt trapped during long dinners but he enjoyed Christine's.

Their party at Heather's followed a day Jack spent in the industrial out-reaches of Rexdale. Columbine had had her lunch with Jane. When Jack got back to the hotel Columbine was lying on the bed drinking Scotch with the TV on. This was the afternoon they were to buy the jade ring, but Colum-bine had drunk too much. She held and kissed Jack and told him she loved him. She insisted that he take his clothes off and get into bed. Then she fell asleep. Jack took his equipment literature from his case and began looking through it, his mind offering him undefined shadows of concern. He hissed song snatches quietly through his teeth as he worked, until he began to find depressing ideas – which he hadn't noticed before – in even the classics.

An' I'll give ye fair warning before we belay –
To me way-hey, blow the man down.
Don't never pay heed to what pretty girls say!
Give me some time to blow the man down!

Heather it turned out was cramming all her Christmas entertaining into one evening. Prosperous people stood toe to toe in every room of her house, a multi-roomed mansion on a Forest Hill hilltop with a lawn the size of a meadow and a backyard that stretched down into a valley. Columbine had drunk most of a bottle of wine before they left the hotel, so Jack was nursing a club soda when she went to find Heather after they arrived, nudged by the eddies and morose of mood. One realignment of the crowd brought Elmo Apse sideways through a doorway.

'What a crush,' Elmo Apse said to Jack, looking directly into Jack's face though without meeting his eye. Apse then raised his chin as if posing for a photographer, also tucking a thumb into the armhole of the waistcoat of his three-piece pinstripe to balance his stance. He seemed to Jack a man of poses, who made a ceremony of movement. 'Well, you managed to get a drink. This is us at our worst, isn't it? To look at us now you'd never guess how successful we are.'

While Jack wondered what to reply, because he'd never heard anybody boasting on behalf of a Forest Hill group before, Apse went on, the volume of his words waxing and fading in the roar of talk around them. 'I mean *the whole human race*. We're *enormously* successful. Think of what we did over the years, like discovering how to *hunt with stone axes*. We came out on top in the end. People don't seem to realize what a *victory* that is.'

He was talking with some animation, and posing physically, but he didn't appear to be drunk. Jack had never learnt how to deal with people who introduced large subjects into small talk. 'Yes, we won our battles with the animals,' he said with a civil smile and a nod.

'Not only *animals*. Other tribes of *humans, too*. Thousands of other tribes. *Neanderthals!* All of us here are descendants of the winners. The *play I'm working on now* tells the whole story – from the *Stone Age* to the *present day*. We're the conquerors of the planet! I said *we're the conquerors of the planet!*' Elmo Apse had raised one arm triumphantly. 'But,' he said to Jack as he allowed a tow of bodies to bear him away, '*you'd never think so to look at us here tonight!*'

When Jack met Heather she stared at him with open dislike. It was a shock – he'd enjoyed Columbine's friends so far and had been looking forward to meeting Heather. Her face was round as a china doll's, with that same prettiness, big cheeks and a tiny pursed mouth. She was surrounded by courtiers. Her style of talk was rapid and exclamatory, with frequent citings of the opinions, customs, habits and utterances of her husband, Allan. 'Well, the mystery man, how are you, Jason?' she said to Jack. 'We must have a long talk, so that you can tell me all about yourself, when I'm not so rushed off my feet.' She turned away. She was sipping from a liqueur glass and not particularly busy that Jack could see, though he had little desire for a long talk with Heather, and none to tell her all about himself. Later he chanced to be in a group with Allan, a sandy-haired man in a brown suit who spoke sparingly and had a marginally guilty manner because of being a pipe-smoker, which his wife hadn't mentioned among his faults or virtues. He had a system of holding his pipe down by his side, and then turning his head away with his chin raised whenever he put the stem to his mouth for a puff. Allan would have been an acceptable Forest Hill host but of course his character of calm reserve had already been breached by his wife. Allan hates this, always does this, never does that, and believes as follows. The other guests in the group knew too much about Allan and dealt with him disregardingly, though the man Allan himself spoke little and listened courteously while Jack was in his company.

Heather bothered Jack, because she suggested a certain blindness of affection in Columbine, and just then he was sensitive to Columbine's affections. How come Columbine liked Heather?

He spent the next morning at the exhibition in the Sheraton Centre, returning to his room in the early afternoon for a session on the telephone. He was on his way out again when the phone rang and a woman asked for Columbine. Jack said she was at lunch, his mind on his own affairs.

'Tell her I managed to get off for Saturday.' The woman said in some irritation: 'She did go out to lunch today, then? That's marvellous. The way she sounded when she kissed me off I thought she was dying. I mean I was considering sending flowers. Is that Jack? Tell her she's a pain in the ass, will you, Jack. Making a space on Saturday isn't easy for me. Who did she stand me up for?'

Jack knew who was calling then. 'You're Bianca, right?'

'Right. Hello.'

There was a pause. Jack said: 'I thought she was seeing you today. She hasn't mentioned anybody else to me. When did she call you?'

Jack could hear an awakening caution on the line. Bianca's tone of voice brightened, and he imagined somebody who spent important stretches of her day on the telephone, the receiver clipped between shoulder and jawline leaving the hands free, an art of escaping entanglements. 'Hello, hello? Good, you're still there.... No, no, she didn't call me. My real problem is that they give me these tiny scraps of paper with messages, those sticky little yellow things, and either I lose them or.... Would you just tell her I'll get back to her as soon as I know what I'm doing here? That would be great, Jack, thanks.' He hadn't moved when Bianca hung up. Just before the disconnection he heard the tiny voice say: 'Shoot.' The receiver buzzed in Jack's ear for a while before he got his thoughts collected and replaced it.

But as soon as our packet was clear of the bar –
To me way-hey, blow the man down.
Her mate knocked me out with the end of a spar!
Give me some time to blow the man down!

Nurse Pugg at the Nailer was a believer in cheerful TV for the inmates. Her idea of cheerfulness was female game contestants turned into hysterical creatures by greed. 'Security for General Schata's visit to the sanctions and tariffs conference in the nation's capital,' said the TV primly, however, as Nurse Pugg looked in to check the day room, 'is the tightest we've seen since

President Reagan's visit to Ottawa. We take you now to Gingerly Grimble on Parliament Hill. Gingerly?'

Mr Smith had detached himself from Mrs Delgardo's group and was following the news show with a rheumy eye. Nurse went over to get a proper programme for him. 'There's that dull old news again!' she shouted cheerfully to Mr Smith, attacking the channel changer. 'Here we are, Trash or Treat!'

In the game studio a Hispanic woman with a large bosom was kissing the show host who smiled down his chin at her with contempt. 'The barbecue and jacuzzi and a trip to the Bahamas if you burst all the balloons, Maria,' he said, pushing her away and hardly able to conceal his disgust. She screamed and tried to throw her arms around him.

'I was *watching* that damn news show,' Mr Smith complained. As usual the toothless old mouth hashed the words. Nurse Pugg turned the sound up for Mr Smith, on the basis that somebody who can't speak clearly won't be able to hear well either. She looked around to see if there was any other cheerful thing she could do in here.

It should be said that the TV was now a brilliant modern large-screen monitor. In the past week gangs of workmen had invaded the Nailer. Thick new carpeting covered the floor. The Salvation Army junk was gone, replaced by coherent systems of lounge and recreation room furniture in tasteful shades. The day room windows had been enlarged to let in the pleasant golden light of day.

Organized crime in fact had arrived and taken the nursing home away from Dr Nailer, groups of men without conscience, rapacious and capable of sickening cruelties. By their calculations the Nailer would yield as high a profit as a well-placed brothel, even allowing for the renovations and the running costs of a kitchen that served good food. Give a little, get a lot, the thugs thought. If they stayed with the slum habitat and dog food catering of Dr Nailer's proprietorship somebody was bound to raise a fuss sooner or later and close them down.

Mr Smith eyed the distance to the TV and, shaking his head and muttering curses, turned toward the table, a pleasant birch with place mats now. The group was seated on leather chairs, Mrs Delgardo buttering a crusty roll. The lunch being distributed by the new kitchen staff, ribald middle-aged women who were all full-figured and wore heavy makeup and tight clothes, markedly pensioners from a branch of the entertainment business, was a small T-bone with mushrooms and cauliflower, roast potatoes and a chef's salad.

'But don't you see?' Judge Wainwright was on his moral hobby horse, appealing to the group's reason and sense of justice. 'Nothing ever changes! The human plight isn't relieved. We have this hopeless, amorphous idea of torture and suffering and victims. But kill the oppressors, free the victims, close the torture chambers, and what happens next? Human nature's the culprit, not particular people. After you've done the work they crop up again like dandelions on your lawn, new oppressors, victims, more torture, suffering. It's never happened any other way. Shuffling the cards,' the good judge said, 'has never made a difference in how the game goes. It's always the same in the long run.'

'And she's the same old deck every time,' Mr Smith agreed, having arrived. What he actually said was: ansheesh the shame oleck harry hime, and the table took a moment to ponder the words. Mr Smith regretfully pushed his steak aside and began to gum a sprig of cauliflower.

Judge Wainwright said: 'That's exactly true, Mr Smith. Then why go on with it?'

'Don't ask me. I'm only doing what Mrs Delgardo wants done.'

'Mrs Delgardo?'

'It isn't a rational act, and I never said it was, Judge Wainwright.' Mrs Delgardo spoke somewhat testily. 'Taking the philosopher's view is only an excuse for doing nothing. We are behaving with human passion, Judge Wainwright. It is our prerogative. The trouble with your rational schemes is that everybody doesn't follow them. General Schata doesn't. He acts as his nature impels him to and so must I.' She said to Mr Dolly, with a clear indication that the subject of General Schata was closed: 'This is excellent food, Mr Dolly. Well done.'

'Thank you,' said Mr Dolly, nodding gratefully. He said then, turning his round honest face to Mrs Delgardo: 'But I can't remember what I did. It's so easy to forget these days. What did I do?'

Mrs Delgardo gazed at Mr Dolly with concern as she chewed her steak in tiny mouthfuls. 'But that tasteless macaroni, Mr Dolly, the eggshells and the other rubbish they were giving us to eat? It wasn't so long ago. I was hungry every day.'

'I remember that part.'

'Well, good. I asked you to do something about the situation. The food now,' Mrs Delgardo said to Mr Dolly with a grateful smile, 'is very good indeed. I knew I could depend on you but of course you've been much more successful than I expected. Thank you.'

'You're very welcome,' said Mr Dolly, vastly pleased and trying not to show it. But he remained puzzled too, deep down. He resolved to go through his papers again and try to figure out what he'd done right.

Mrs Delgardo turned back to Judge Wainwright in gracious enquiry. 'Mrs Nightingale's health is much improved, I understand, yet she still doesn't leave her room. I wonder why that is.'

'Well, I can only speak rationally,' said Judge Wainwright with a sarcastic laugh. 'Therefore I don't expect my opinion to carry a lot of weight. If Mrs Nightingale leaves her room and joins us, if she becomes part of our life here, it means she belongs here. But she doesn't feel she belongs here. She's acting,' the judge said, 'as her nature impels her to. Stupidly.' He threw his napkin down, somewhat toward Mrs Delgardo, challengingly. 'Checkers after lunch?'

'Tristan, if it's my choice,' responded Mrs Delgardo with a wide smile, apparently not noticing the tiny failure of good manners on the judge's part.

During the nights at the Nailer now Mr Smith rehearsed the Schata assassination at the window of his room, with Mrs Delgardo and Mr Dolly as lookouts. The Schata limo would be within Mr Smith's view for about three seconds, he thought, but that counted two seconds for the limo's long hood and the chauffeur's seat. The general's head would be within Mr Smith's line of fire for a bare second, maybe even less. The weapon he'd acquired didn't have a maker's name or any other markings on it. Assembled it looked like the skeleton of an M.14. When it was broken down the parts fitted into a laptop computer case. He had two rounds of 7.62 mm ammo – with under a second to blow General Schata's head off this was twice as much as he'd need if all went well.

In the rehearsals he assumed a shaky crouch at the window, with a stop-watch on the sill, leading passing cars and clicking the trigger on the empty chamber. Sometimes when Mr Smith squeezed the trigger he said: 'Gotcha.' Quite as often he cursed or wiped a tear from his eye, making an excuse. Or else he simply stared, having forgotten what he was doing. His glasses were correct now. But even so (as Jack knew) when Mr Smith peered through the scope he saw cars out on the highway five hundred metres away that looked blobby at best, like microbes wriggling on a plate.

Jack had done some tinkering with the scope sight in the lab at Currier's Mode Optical. He thought that with everything done to help him Mr Smith's chances of hitting the general were about fifty per cent now.

What might give Mr Smith better odds? A glassful from the fountain of youth, for sure. Or else something that felt the same, momentarily, a small taste of hope that his physical disintegration wasn't as straight a downhill slide as it looked. Jack believed he knew how to get some of Mr Smith back. That might be all that was needed to push the odds up to eighty per cent.

But maybe it wouldn't make much difference either way. As Jack read the newspapers the world was in a hard phase and forms of benignity were out of fashion. Terror was as widespread as it had ever been in the marching path of bloody armies. The old plagues and diseases, contrary to rumour, had never died. The news of sieges and famines and massacres kept coming in on the wires and was expected to continue. Old atrocities were being repeated as they were rediscovered by the new generations, who were nothing else except the worst we could be, the living age's form of the savage dead and depraved generations from the darkest times. Worse and bloodier men than could be seen smiling in TV news stories had never lived. We're not learning anything, was how Jack felt, we've taken ourselves from Elmo Apse's heroes with stone axes to the dread-inspiring metal grace of space cruisers without getting a single new idea. Whereas Mrs Delgardo saw an assassination as an act of passion, in a less sentimental way Jack thought of it as a little exercise of censorship.

By tradition censorship is a perquisite of power. The New Phoenix Theatre in the Sutton won a censorship battle with the bureaucracy when it put on a musical comedy based on the life of Adolf Hitler. The reviewers cheered the show on. 'A brash and youthfully iconoclastic smasheroo.' 'History loses, entertainment wins.' 'The Charlie Chaplin monster is given a human face in a feast of fun and song.' The first week was a hit. There was talk of Broadway next backstage. Jack went to the second week's run with his whoopee cushion bagpipes. He worked the rig on the stage, mingling with the chorus, and the familiar whoopee sounds in high-tech amplification just buried the sprightly music, emptying the house. It was a cruel destruction of fun and dreams of course. But who ever heard of a musical comedy based on the life of Adolf Hitler? Jack felt that he could make this kind of call just as competently as the customs administration or the theatre review board or anybody else in the bureaucracy.

Chapter 11

The Rat Art Man

AFTER COLUMBINE left Technoptrax and moved to Toronto Jack was brought to some awareness of the company he worked for. His working method up to now had been absorption in the problems they gave him, a productive fog of absentmindedness. Now he was dealing directly with senior folk. He remembered names for some that he'd gotten from Columbine but most were strangers to him. He made his mind up about these people, who they were and what their authority might be, while they spoke to him.

At the end of January he was called into the office of Alexander the Grate, by Columbine's naming scheme, a tough little man with a red face, a trimmed grey moustache and bushy sideburns that looked like handles on his bald head. Alexander the Grate said he was concerned about Jack's work.

Jack was hanging on to a hope of recovery. He was suffering a hurt he couldn't put a name to, like a dumb animal whose young have been taken away but who doesn't know what's wrong. He waited to heal, putting all the strength he could command into maintaining will power. He made his life outside of Technoptrax as active as it could be. During the winter he saw a succession of girls but these affairs didn't outlast the snow. By spring he was in the habit of spending weekends in Ottawa on the same quest, looking for somebody like Columbine. Then when the buds were well out on the trees of Belleville Jack thought he was beginning to think straight again. He could go for an hour at a time without an ache. Alexander the Grate, who had fretted at the beginning of winter, went back to his old style of giving Jack a big ruddy-faced smile when they chanced to meet in a corridor or elevator, and otherwise leaving him alone.

He was good for Technoptrax that summer and Technoptrax gave Jack a focus for energies that might otherwise have turned inward and harmed him. He was spending fourteen hours a day at work and was weeks ahead on all his projects although the company was handling a big log of European contracts at the time. Most evenings he was to be found at a Meyer's Pier hangout named Spangles, dancing with inelegant elasticity, sweating the day's last flaws of strength from his spider body. He went where the crowds did in the evenings and slept about four hours out of the twenty-four. He took two showers a day and cultivated a crisp, modish wardrobe, with laundry delivery of shirts, three-piece executive suits for Technoptrax and a haircut every two weeks that included styling. He patronized a professional manicurist for the first time, and began to pay attention to shoe fashions and leather quality.

He had favourite places in Ottawa on his weekend trips. One of these was the Sutton, where Jack was impressed by the astonishing effort to cover all human need. Babies were born in the maternity wards of the Medical Wing, and were taken out through the main entranceway into the big world, maybe to return regularly as time went by, and aged people died in the Nailer and were discreetly wheeled into a side parking lot through the west door and returned to earth.

Columbine called from Toronto late on a Sunday night in August. Jack had just come from the station. He had made himself the last drink of the day.

She sounded uncharacteristically tentative. 'It's been a long time,' Columbine said. 'There isn't any reason, is there, why we shouldn't see each other?'

'No,' said Jack.

'I thought you'd keep in touch, at least. I don't know if you're dead or sick or anything.'

'No, I'm just sticking to the way we left it,' said Jack, who was speaking with some care. 'Nothing's new with me.'

'Yes, but this doesn't make any sense. We can see each other. We can talk to each other. Why don't you come and see us when you're in town?'

So Jack said: 'Us?'

'Well, yes, for Christ's sake. You can come and see us. I'd like to see you again, Jack. I don't have your talent for turning myself into stone. What harm would it do if you dropped in for a cup of coffee or something?'

Columbine seemed to Jack to be talking at random. He said: 'Are you all right?'

'I am perfectly fine. I have human emotions, unlike you, that's all. I think it's okay to talk to somebody on the phone if I feel like doing that. I mean there's such a thing as friendship. I don't believe in your lovers or heroes horseshit.'

'Well, that wouldn't work for me, though,' said Jack, with as much tact as he could summon, dealing on the telephone with a thoughtless impulse and nothing else. He said, though he remembered Elmo Apse's name very well: 'How's what's-his-name, face, has he found a job yet?'

'He wasn't looking for a job, Jack. He was working on a play.'

'Oh yes.'

'He's been doing a lot of painting lately.'

Jack thought of happy kindergarteners with their fingerpaints. 'But he's serious about the play, is he?'

'For God's sake. He's *serious* about everything, Jack. It's difficult for him here. All his contacts are in Montreal – well, he even has some out in Van. He was hoping to make a breakthrough in theatre but that's an old crowd here, nobody wants to take a chance on an outsider. He did some fine painting a few years ago. He's gone back to that now. I know what you're thinking but it isn't true, Jack. Elmo has heaps of talent. You should see his art photography.'

'I guess. My interest in the guy's never been like, a fine-tuned thing.' Jack looked at his watch. 'He's not home right now, face?'

'He's away for a couple of days. He has to travel around and try to sell what he does.'

Jack didn't say anything. He had an image, maybe a memory of a movie. There was a huge attic with the sun sending square shafts down from the skylights. Easels with canvases stood in the slanted light. Other paintings in baroque gilt frames were stacked against the walls. Elmo Apse wasn't present but Columbine sat on a little stool in the sunlit room forlornly, waiting for him to return with a buyer.

She said: 'I shouldn't have called. I meant well. I do think of you all the time, Jack.'

'Same here,' Jack said.

For the rest of the summer and through the fall months there was no more contact between the sailor man and Columbine. At Technoptrax he was given two new helpers, which with Ian Peveril and George Wienewski added up to four official assistants. Jack was then appointed chief of the department. His promotion was announced at a short congratulatory party in Alexander the Grate's office, where set out on the board table was one bottle of expensive sherry on a tray with crystal glasses. The celebrants got one glass each and no refills, and listened to a short speech of congratulation to Jack from Alexander and a few modest words of thanks in response from Jack. Then everybody clapped and lined up to shake the sailor's hand. He was privately told by Alexander that he'd be able to purchase stock in Technoptrax in the new year, the amount to be determined by the board.

Jack could name about half the folk present, seeing them all together like that. He noted that there were actually two directors with beards – this cleared up some confusion because he'd been dealing with them as one person who had two titles and oddly assorted needs. He inwardly identified Stewart the Pretender, a sunburnt man who maintained a wide, jovial smile and wore a red blazer and a tartan tie, and Henry the Ape, slouched and rumpled with black brows that overhung his eyes and seemed to need combing out. Jack did remember too – and he never in his career came closer to being an office politician at Technoptrax – that there was a higher power above these three, much higher, who had also been given some monarch's name by Columbine.

And sure enough not very long afterward, in the late winter of the new year, three months after Columbine died, Jack was summoned to a remote office behind a mahogany door, with an anteroom where three elderly secretaries sat like guards and stared angrily at Jack. He had never seen the man beyond the mahogany door as far as he could remember. Small in stature, the man sat rigidly behind a bare lustrous desk. He seemed to Jack very tense, and he was also angry.

He wished Jack a dry good morning and began to make quick conversation, about company affairs, seemingly, though with hostile comments and sharply malevolent glances included. The sailor was relieved when the man opened a drawer and took a file out and passed over a sheaf of papers for his signature – it was something Jack could do, whereas the man's talk and questions were beyond his power. While he was putting his name to a receipt attached to a cheque it occurred to Jack that in the last five minutes or so he'd probably been fired from Technoptrax by the angry, clerkly man behind the desk. He still couldn't think of the man's name.

Outside in the director's lot, trying to remember where he'd parked, the name suddenly came to him. Irving the Terrible! He thumped a fist into his palm in triumph when he got the flash, and shouted *Hah!* aloud. By then

Jack's hold on reality was very insecure indeed. He was so detached that he continued to feel pleased with himself as he drove out of the Technoptrax company parking lot for the last time. Thereafter he went on the skids.

The sailor's downfall, which took him from Irving the Terrible's office to Brand X cameras, began with an early Christmas card from Columbine. It was an inexpensive card showing a family of squirrels wearing sweaters and scarves in a toboggan which on the inside said only HAPPY HOLIDAY! FROM: _____. She had written her name in the space provided, and underneath: *Come and visit me in the holiday some time.* He was happy to see that the note said me and not us.

Jack and Columbine's separation was nearing its first anniversary. In the mood Jack was in when the card arrived it seemed possible that a childhood crush which could attach a barbarian like Columbine to the kind of man Elmo Apse was might not last beyond a year.

He reached Columbine's place a week before Christmas in a snowstorm. He knew Toronto well enough but he had trouble with the address, in the northwestern part of that city. The streets all looked alike and lay between main arteries. Getting on the wrong one-way street meant being swept out of the district. It was a second-floor apartment in an Italian neighbourhood, yellow brick with a small lawn in a neighbourhood of rental properties, brick and frame houses and apartment buildings. He looked at three doorbells with name cards. Two Italian names were in faded old ballpoint. ELMO APSE had been produced by a laser printer in big block letters with serifs. That is very artistic, thought Jack, who had driven more than two hundred kilometres through blinding snow and wasn't relaxed, probably Times Old Roman or some such. Or Bodoni. He had himself hard-braced for meeting Columbine again.

However, it was Elmo Apse who answered the ring and took Jack up a flight of bare wooden stairs. Apse was solicitous and ready with manly small talk about driving conditions and traffic. 'I'm afraid Columbine isn't here to welcome you,' he said over his shoulder, climbing. 'She said to tell you she had to go out. She'll be back soon.' The door at the head of the stairs had another ELMO APSE card on it. 'Sorry. The amenities don't include a guest bedroom, Jack. It'll have to be the pull-out there, but we'll make you comfortable enough. Just sling the suitcase in the corner. Now, what can I get you to drink?'

A log flickered in the fireplace. The main room had a long couch, an easy chair and an Indian rug on the hardwood floor. Jack heard carols playing. A Christmas tree with presents beneath it stood in a corner. The kitchen was through a round stucco arch with a corridor through a similar arch opposite the entranceway. It seemed to Jack a warm and modest place. He left his bag by the door. He did take his overcoat off but he expected to be putting it on again very soon. For the visit Jack wore one of his well-cut executive grey suits, though with a festive red tie. He had brought some presents of jewellery for Columbine.

'We're offering Martinis. I make a great Martini.'

'Well, okay,' said Jack, with an austere nod. 'No olive or peel in mine, heavy on the mix.'

Elmo Apse went into the kitchen and brought the drinks back, giving Jack a glass ceremoniously. 'I think you'll like that.' He dragged a footstool forward with a long leg to perch opposite and somewhat under Jack who was seated angrily on the couch. He put his own Martini on the floor and clapped his hands, rubbing them together comfortably. 'Well! Here we are.'

'How's Columbine, Elmo?'

'Winter sniffles, otherwise just great.' He gave Jack a smile. 'We have this problem, it's why you're here I guess. She doesn't like my promotion trips. I have to go out and hustle, in my line there's a limit to what can be done on the phone. You know women,' he suggested with a little shrug, spreading his hands and showing his teeth again. 'I told her I might have to be away over Christmas. I suppose she called you and complained.'

'No. Nobody complained to me, Elmo.'

'Well, that's the situation. I'm being straight about this, you see, Jack. Nothing's decided yet, I'm waiting for a call now. But say I take off and leave you with her. That's asking a lot. Maybe I'll stick around here now you've arrived. We never had much of a chance to get to know each other.'

Jack picked the neat curl of lemon peel from his glass and dropped it in Elmo's ashtray among the panatela stubs. He shook his head irritably, wondering why Elmo was talking to him. 'No, I'm not looking for a chance to get to know anybody. I don't think of myself as a friend of the household, a blanket and a cushion on the pullout, you understand.'

Elmo laughed, although Jack wasn't smiling. Perched easily on the footstool and leaning forward with his elbows on his knees to converse, the man was behaving as if they were already good friends. 'I think I know what's bothering you, and what I want to say is that it shouldn't. Let me tell you what happened between us, Jack, you and me. That was a primitive event, so I understand it. Either of us could have won, but it happened to be me. In a sense the two of us weren't even involved. She was with you and she looked attractive to me. I can't even remember why now. That's the mystery of the primitive. The lights in the bar maybe. What she was wearing at the time.'

Jack stood up without replying to this and went, rudely questing, through the arch, finding a bathroom at the end of the corridor. He splashed handfuls of cold water on his face and tried to think. When he got back Elmo Apse was imperturbably smoking a fresh panatela. 'Columbine was happy that afternoon,' said Jack. 'That's what always bothers me most about what happened in the bar. Everything else is bullshit. She was happy.' He had never known how to talk to simple people.

Elmo nodded slowly, humouring Jack. 'I sure as hell would like to get away today,' said he. Then he had an idea. 'I'll show you some of my work.'

'No, thank you.'

'You'll like it.'

In a slow ceremony Elmo Apse repositioned the footstool and took his glass into the kitchen. 'The idea is to make a myth of the whole primitive story, in historical perspective,' he explained. He went through the arch and called out cheerfully. 'Like a saga. A parade of primitive events.'

Jack thought of putting his coat on and bailing out directly. But he asked himself: What is this? He shouted down the corridor: 'Listen, don't bring a play out here. I'm not going to read a play.'

Elmo brought out art, a square string-bound portfolio about the size of a school atlas with black board covers. ELMO APSE on the front of course, very large type this time. Baskerville maybe, Jack thought, still buzzing with adrenalin from the drive through the snowstorm and trying to stay alert. He looked at a painting composed like a stained-glass window, small pictures contained inside thick lines. It seemed to be a serial story. The draftsmanship wasn't precise but he thought he saw rampant jungle animals and turned to the next picture. A naked man with a club upraised occupied one of the panels. Getting the idea, Jack began snapping the paintings over rapidly. Villages, men in armour, wars, then either towers or rockets. Symbolism probably, he guessed. Many of the little pictures were abstracts, and he guessed too that the artist would be happy to explain what they all meant or didn't mean. Elmo Apse had gone to fetch other work but returned with quick steps when he heard the snapping of drawing paper. He carried a beige file folder. Jack gave him back the portfolio. 'Very nice.'

'The detail's interesting, if you have the eye.' Elmo Apse was amused. 'Do you know anything about art, Jack?'

'I've seen that kind of thing before, many times, Elmo.'

'You think you have, do you.' He was even more amused. He put the folder on the couch beside Jack, who ignored it. 'Doing the work isn't enough, we have to do the politics too. This week it's in Montreal, lots of money, all kinds of publicity, most of the big names. They're an elitist crowd so I could be wasting my time. I mean Montreal's the place to be this week but it'll be somewhere else another week. No great urgency.'

'I'm a believer in elitism, Elmo,' said Jack, looking at his watch. 'It gives mediocrity something to aspire to.' He had meanwhile become aware that a deal was being offered by Elmo Apse. But Jack couldn't see what his side of it might be. 'I don't know anybody who could help you sell this stuff.'

'I wouldn't expect you to, in Brampton or wherever it is you are.'

'I wouldn't buy it myself in a fit.'

'Well, that's good too because there's no way I could let you have this. I need it to go somewhere where it will be seen, since it's major. Fill your glass again, Jack?'

A part of a photograph had slipped out of the folder and Jack lifted the cover to see the rest of it, with the thought that photos offer reality, even when they're art. They were photos of rats, thin and savage-looking creatures with matted grey coats and black unblinking eyes. The folder contained six of these, eight-by-tens of rats in close-up on a hardwood floor, in a corner of a room. It was the room they were sitting it, or one with the same baseboard.

Elmo stretched out a leg and hiked the footstool forward again. Jack's drink had a fresh shaving of lemon peel in it, and he plucked this out and threw it in the ashtray. 'Well, at least I can be positive about these, Elmo,' he said. 'I hate them. I'm aware that rats exist but I don't care to be reminded of them while I'm sitting having a drink.'

'That's good, you're making progress. There's hope for you, buddy.' Elmo Apse smiled and, leaning across, hit Jack's knee with his fist encouragingly. 'You see, I'm dealing with terror in my rat series – it's called *corneredrats*, one word, small c.' He tapped the folder, looking straight into Jack's eyes. 'We're bigger than rats and even so most people are afraid of them, which is what you're saying when you say you don't want to be reminded of them. With rats it's always only a question of size – think of the fear problems we'd have if they were the size of horses. So what we do in the art sense, we photograph the rats and then blow the photographs up to a size bigger than we are. That gives a whole new perspective.'

'Why?' asked Jack.

'You mean how?'

'No. I was wondering why.'

Elmo Apse said regretfully, as if Jack hadn't spoken: 'What you see there with those six pictures is just notes for the series. I'll need much better equipment before I can do the quality blowups.'

Jack now opened his eyes wide, showing aggressive, jocund enlightenment. Said he: 'People will buy these rat pictures for their living rooms, am I right, Elmo? First they get the Ethan Allen furniture and the Yapur rugs, and now they need the final touch for the walls, and here you are with just the thing, larger-than-life-size rats in black and white....'

The phone rang but Elmo Apse let it ring and pursed his lips and blew softly to indicate weary patience. He said to Jack: 'Art, for your information, my friend, is a synthesis of life. It is anything life is.' He put his glass carefully on the table. 'It was never just something to hang on a wall.' He stood up while the phone rang and toed the footstool to its place in front of the easy chair. 'A reminder of terror is art,' he told Jack, moving slowly to the kitchen doorway, and reaching inside to take a receiver off a hook there.

'Elmo Apse,' said Elmo Apse into the phone and listened. 'No, fifteen hundred for the stamp collection is firm – it's been appraised at three thousand. I'd like a quick sale but I'm not giving it away, it's an old collection but in perfect condition. I've got receipts and provenance for every stamp in the album, Joseph. Well, forget the train,' he said. 'It's Christmas, you know. No, the late train's too slow.' His eyes were on Jack now as he spoke. 'Yes I can. I can make the four o'clock flight if I get a cab right away. But I don't have enough money at this end,' he said, as much to Jack as to the phone. After which he took himself into the kitchen with the phone and lowered his voice to a mutter.

Such a simple deal hadn't crossed Jack's mind, straight cash. He had three hundred dollars in ready cash in his wallet. The phone call was a long one. Before Elmo Apse hung up Jack had begun to worry that the man would miss his flight.

In the transaction Jack suggested a loan, which Elmo Apse would return by mail. A difficulty arose as to the amount – Jack offered two hundred dollars but Elmo Apse, showing no self-consciousness and indeed interrupting Jack to bring him a fresh drink with lemon peel in it, thought he'd need five hundred for expenses and incidentals, to be on the safe side, as he said. He was much at ease, smoking his cigar and talking money with Jack. He paused too to bring luggage from the bedroom to the apartment door, a couple of very large suitcases and a valise, which seemed to the sailor a lot to carry on a visit of a few days to the art cliques in Montreal. Their deal was struck for two hundred and fifty only after Jack let Elmo Apse see the inside of his wallet with the fifty that remained in there. The rat artist didn't say thank you for the loan. Nor did Jack entertain an expectation of getting the cash back in the mail.

When the door closed Jack ducked under the Christmas tree and threw all the presents out on the carpet. He prowled the floor, reading tags, finding four from Columbine to Elmo. Two would have been plenty, surely. But there were six from Elmo to her – that cheered the sailor for a moment. He sat on the couch and tore the wrappings off Elmo's six gifts to Columbine, which were all clumsily wrapped, the paper bulking on the corners and forced down with a lot of Scotch tape. The first present was just a red-clay vase. Jack opened the second and found a candy dish or an ash tray, and the next was a coffee mug. What might have been a trivet or pot rest followed, and then a second vase, and lastly a little pot with a lid. Six gifts that could easily have been one, clayware.

He was puzzled, looking at these items. Like a chess player he moved a vase to stand beside its mate, seeing that they were both red and nearly the same shape, and possibly intended to be a pair. He didn't understand why Elmo Apse would expect Columbine to want these ugly things as presents. The vases were noticeably of unequal heights. The round candy dish was trying to stretch itself into an oval on one side. The lid of the pot didn't fit very well. What did they mean?

Jack turned a pot over in his hands and there it was, the answer. ELMO APSE, and a date. Elmo Apse was a potter as well as a playwright and painter and photographer, and these were his pottery creations, wrapped as Christmas presents and left under the tree to delight his wife while he was away in Montreal. The date would be, Jack supposed, for future collectors and curators who might wish to know exactly when Apse was in his lumpy vase period, and when in his sloping trivet, and in what month and year he produced the skewed marmalade jar with the rocking lid.

He turned a shifty eye toward Columbine's presents to Elmo Apse. Four weighty boxes neatly wrapped and square-cornered, with bows and bright-hued string, but then of course she wasn't an artist. Jack ripped the tidy wrappings off right away, scattering bows and paper around the floor. A camera system. A Nikon body. Lenses. They gleamed splendidly in their boxes and tissue paper. This was exactly the kind of thing Jack hadn't wanted to see. Could I be a worse fool, on this fool's journey, he asked himself. Could I be a weaker wretch, reading unwritten messages on a cheap card. He held himself tightly, hands crossed on his chest, because his unruly emotions wanted justification of themselves with yells of pain and streaming eyes.

Worse than misconstruing the card was being in the woman's house, awaiting her return. There was nothing for Jack in the house, nor would there be when Columbine returned.

Before he moved, though, Columbine came through the door backward, carrying packages. At first sight Jack took her for a stranger with a key, perhaps the cleaning woman. She had become smaller. When she turned around he saw a sallow face. Her eyes were lustreless in hard bone sockets, and scarcely brighter when she looked at him in delight.

But she didn't have much to say to him, naturally. Columbine provided Jack with conversation about Christmas crowds and the traffic situation while she put the groceries away. Her movements were all quick, the fluid grace was gone. This jerkiness and her shrunken size and the banal talk brought powerful ghosts back for the sailor. In his bag he had a necklace of heavy silver with agate stones streaked in blue and green. And a necklace with the same weighty silver links, lumps of polished jade held in their claws. They were presents to bedeck a woman with a barbaric nature who, as it appeared now, no longer existed. Jack decided that he would have been nearer to her need had he brought nourishing soups and cooked food, sleeping pills, cheerful reading material, a hairdresser.

'What on earth's happened here?'

She was looking at the scattered gift-wrap. Columbine wore a white shirt and grey slacks. She bent to collect the torn paper, somewhat aimlessly, watched by Jack who was tight as a wound spring, showing her a genial social face. Her shanks had gotten thin and when she stooped too low she was taken by a coughing spasm. Winter sniffles.

'You did this you nosy bastard,' she said to Jack. 'Imagine opening somebody's presents. I'd forgotten what a crude bugger you are.'

Being near him just then Columbine put her arms around Jack and held him. He could feel just the hard nervousness in her body. After a moment she said: 'I need you more than anybody. I'm hungry.'

Jack made her an omelet and a few strips of bacon out of the fridge while she repaired what he'd done under the tree. She didn't comment on the pottery. She cut into all the food on her plate and then ate hardly any of it.

'When did he leave?'

He told her.

'Who called, do you know?'

Jack shook his head. 'I'm sorry, Columbine.'

'It doesn't matter anyway. Nothing makes any difference.'

While Jack was with her that afternoon she remained in the present in their conversation. All he had of her was in the past. She had a part-time job in a university lab. She talked about that at some length. Jack was now in a nightmare. No terror of the dark night could have been worse for him than this ordinary afternoon and its dull talk. He couldn't manage to talk about himself but he brought her up to date on Technoptrax affairs, insofar as he was aware of them. He didn't mention his promotion – that was a simple byproduct of the pain, which couldn't be mentioned.

Columbine wanted to make a friend of Jack. After she did that she would be able to discuss Elmo Apse with him. She'd had the same desire when she called in the summer, he supposed. He turned her away as a friend, genially deflecting her suggestions and advances.

In the evening they watched *A Christmas Carol*, Tiny Tim in Camden Town piping bravely in his upper-crust accent, crutch under the wrong arm; wretched Scrooge hauled from his rest three times in the small hours, bullyragged and reviled by revenant tyrants of the mass sentimentality and finally terrorized into a state of gibbering philanthropy. Jack finished Elmo's vodka and started on a bottle of the rat art man's rum.

While the Cratchit family admired the big turkey, Columbine said, loudly: 'He keeps saying he may not come back. That's really the only problem I have when he goes away. This time he's going to be away for Christmas, and he might not come back.'

Jack got his bag and coat. 'Well, I'll be at the Pellidore for a few days. I'll call you tomorrow.'

She said: 'Jack, I'm really sorry we can't talk to each other.'

Said the sailor: 'It's nobody's fault, Columbine. Nobody did anything wrong. Nobody's to blame.'

She stared at him for a moment with her gaunt face, as if she meant to answer or argue but then only nodded, turning her head away.

Outside the snow still fell, gusting along the streets and sidewalks, little pellets that stung the eyes and froze in the hair. Jack spent the rest of that night listening to the music and drinking rum in the jazz lounge of the Pellidore on Charles Street, a shabby old hotel with nothing to recommend it except the jazz and a convenient downtown location. It was a forties place, fated to come down soon to make way for a condo development. The Pellidore had the French atmosphere he was used to, an unhurried pace and regular guests and customers. The barmen were tolerant of idlers – he could read a newspaper there and order a drink or a coffee according to his mood. Girls came in at night and they had their regular customers too. In a short while some of them were telling Jack their troubles. He didn't mind buying drinks and he offered a ready ear, with nothing better to do.

Columbine called in the early morning the day before Christmas Eve. Jack in his sagging old double bed had a thick head and a nauseous stomach and foul mouth, which was his regular waking condition in that interval at the Pellidore.

'He's home,' said Columbine. She was whispering close to the phone mouthpiece. 'Jack, Elmo's home now. He got in last night – this morning. I'm fine. You can go home, Jack.'

'What time last night?'

'What time? I don't know, about one. I was asleep. Look, why don't we keep in touch with each other? If I need you I promise I'll call you in Belleville. I promise, Jack.'

'Well, I'll be here at the Pellidore for a few more days,' said Jack. 'Call me here.'

He had to wait for the coffee shop to open. He spent some of the morning looking up bus and train and flight times. There wasn't much from Montreal that would deliver a man to Toronto after midnight; no flight, and the day train arrived at Union Station at ten. Naturally the man might have arrived at any time, and spent any time he wished in the conduct of his affairs before getting home at one in the morning. But the sailor was of the opinion that a man like Elmo Apse might be cheap enough to time his homecoming in the expectation of finding two people in bed together.

It was Jack's opinion moreover that Elmo would be leaving Columbine again, and probably very soon. So he remained in his room with the rum bottle and TV at night and occupied himself on Technoptrax business during the day with a pack of disks and a laptop. The phone rang just before noon on Christmas Eve. She was choking on what she thought he should know first, the stray things that came to her mind.

'He said I was a liar,' Columbine told Jack. 'He had clothes at the dry cleaners, that was the only reason he came home.'

On the way uptown Jack gunned his little Renault through the stops and reds, spinning the front wheels on crusty slush when he went around corners. He saw himself as the worst lover of a woman who had ever lived. He was neither a lover nor a hero, though he had always known that once a man became a lover he must from that day onward be one or the other, or nothing at all.

Columbine had asked other people for help before she called Jack. He found an Italian couple in the apartment with her, dressed for going out, the man in an old sheepskin jacket, the woman wearing a pink cloth coat with a fur collar. 'What can we do, eh?' the man said to Jack, almost shouting, a hard-eyed working man, darkly balked. 'Nothing for the police. He didn't steal, he didn't punch her out. She's doing stupid things now, the lady. She's talking about she needs to wash the floor. This is something nobody can help her with, she's acting crazy.' The woman was reserved, feeling less involved in the emergency than her husband did.

When they had gone Jack called an ambulance. Columbine didn't want to leave the kitchen. She had taken several saucepans from a cupboard and was trying to fit them into the sink. 'He hates you, Jack,' she said, as if Jack should care. 'He hates me too, you know. Nobody told him any lies. What I can't understand is how he got the idea that I told him lies.'

Columbine's presents to Elmo Apse were gone from beneath the Christmas tree. He had left the clayware.

'He threw the toast and eggs on the floor. When I finish the dishes I need to clean up that floor.'

He had to take her in his arms, and then he had to hold her stiff body down on the couch until she consented to relax. Her forehead was very hot. When she fell asleep it seemed to Jack to happen too suddenly.

The heavy-set ambulance men brought snow and cold into the small living room and the smell of wet serge uniforms. Columbine's eyes were still closed but her lips had started to move. The ambulance bounced heavily going south over the Bathurst streetcar cobblestones. She opened her eyes after one of these jolts. 'He meant to stay, I mean why would he come back from Montreal just to collect cleaning? Slacks. A summer jacket.' Not so long ago Columbine would have readily understood a man like Elmo Apse.

Jack was gripping both her hands. 'That's the way. You're starting to feel better already.'

'I would have sent them anyway. He said everything was okay when he called.'

Columbine's thoughts and fever were fixed on what Elmo Apse had said, which she tried to reconcile with events. Jack believed that anything Elmo Apse ever said would be whatever it was in Elmo Apse's interest to say, at any time, and that events told a separate and simple story. The rat artist had taken two large pieces of luggage out of the apartment while Jack was present. On the phone he'd been arranging to sell Columbine's uncle's stamp collection. He would know about the expensive camera and accessories under the tree, since that was his nature, but hadn't taken them, and so Jack had understood Elmo Apse would return, for that cache anyway and whatever else he hadn't been able to take on the first trip. The reason for the going and coming would be to give Jack and Columbine a chance to couple. Having already received two hundred and fifty dollars from Jack for three days' rent of Columbine, he had possibly expected to be able to negotiate five or ten times that amount to finance his permanent departure, or as an outright sale. This might then be the reason for his rage, and throwing the toast and eggs on the floor, that Jack and Columbine hadn't behaved like cats or dogs, primitively. Probably it offended the man's artistic beliefs, Jack supposed, as well as denying him a portion of loot. But over all Elmo Apse had looted Columbine with fair thoroughness. He had taken most of what she had.

'Jack? Jack, what did I do wrong? Look, I'll tell you every single thing that happened. You tell me what I did wrong.'

If he had come back from Montreal he had meant to stay, she believed. Columbine was in hysteria and essaying rationality. The sailor believed, with a simpler view, that the whole Montreal story was fable and that Elmo Apse the primitive had been elsewhere in Toronto, probably in a new lair with a new mate, and had now returned there. He said: 'Don't try to talk, sweetheart. We'll talk about everything later. We'll go over every detail together.'

This seemed to satisfy Columbine and she closed her eyes when Jack kissed her damp forehead.

The ambulance bounced heavily making a left turn across the streetcar tracks into the hospital entranceway.

'Jack? See me through this.'

'You bet.'

The waiting area of the emergency area put Jack in mind of an airport on a busy day. Holiday time. The ambulance men quickly transferred Columbine from their stretcher to a hospital gurney which they set against a wall. The clerk at the desk had just been brought a mug of coffee. She allowed her coffee to go cold while her fingers flew like a concert pianist's all over her terminal keyboard. She kept a phone at her ear at the same time. 'We're backed up a little here,' she told Jack. 'I'm getting you an orderly, and he'll take her through directly. Dr Wootton says he'll be waiting for you on the ward. Take care now.'

This was getting the breaks, thought the sailor man who was among those who had heard accounts of bureaucratic bottlenecks in hospital emergency departments. No more than half an hour had passed since he had phoned for the ambulance. He had to lope to keep pace with the wiry, aged orderly who wheeled Columbine at speed along corridors and through a number of double doors and into an elevator. They got out at a nurse station island between two rows of wards. Some patients in dressing gowns were strolling outside the wards. One nurse was on duty inside the island at a desk laden with document trays and a stack of beige folders. A plastic name-plate on her uniform breast said A.B. SIERACKI. She took the gurney and a folder from the orderly, saying to Jack: 'There's a waiting area just through the doors at the end of this corridor. We'll look after her now – the doctor is on his way.'

The folk in dressing gowns showed an interest in Columbine as she was taken into the examining room by the nurse, who closed the door. One old woman caught Jack's eye and shook her head, whether in sympathy or as a diagnosis he couldn't tell.

When Nurse Sieracki came out again Jack asked: 'What's the matter with her?'

'Mr Clemmaknohke? If you'd like to go down to the waiting area I'll have you called when she's ready to see you. Just on your right after you go through the doors ...'

Nurse Sieracki was in her thirties and had a student's open face. Her thin body operated gracelessly but with efficient large movements and a lot of energy. She wore soft, heavy shoes and big-lensed glasses tinted blue and her hair was pulled back into a blue plastic barrette on the nape of her neck. Jack said thank you to her but went into the examining-room. Columbine in a hospital gown was sleeping on a stretcher behind a screen, her head raised high on two pillows. He felt her forehead which was dry and still very hot. Her body under the gown was as dry as paper. 'Hang in there,' Jack said, casting an eye around the shelves where the instruments were laid out on towels. He found a jarful of thermometers and while he waited soaked one of the towels in cold water at the sink. The displaced instruments clattered when he pulled the towel out, which brought the nurse back in while he was bathing Columbine's face.

'You can't stay here.'

'Look at this. Her temperature's over forty-one.'

'Yes, well, we know that. Now you're going to have to leave her with us.'

'She's getting up near enzyme damage and she has no way of cooling down. Can you get me a few aspirin?'

'Jesus Christ. Of course I can't get you aspirin!' But then she came and stood by the stretcher, laying the back of her hand against Columbine's fore-head.

'You're not her husband, are you?'

Jack shook his head.

'Well, look, I can't give out medication until Dr Wootton sees her, you understand that, don't you.' She was dismayed by Jack, an unkempt man, distraught and wild of face. He saw her step back from him, and became quiet right away, taking in deep breaths. Jack spoke as gently as he could to Nurse Sieracki then, and smiled meekly, and pleaded with his eyes. Said he: 'If she doesn't get treatment for the fever she's a goner, as you know, nurse, doesn't matter what else is wrong, as you're aware. Obviously you can't unfry an egg, can you, an overheated enzyme's like a fried egg, probably you got all that in your first year, the progress of a fever. You can't turn it back into a raw egg again. So look, why don't we give her something for the fever now before it's too late?'

He didn't know why he was fixed on the fever problem. It was just one of several worries in his mind, but in his grief he needed a clear direction to hold and follow.

Meanwhile ward bells were summoning the nurse, whose manner was overridingly one of preoccupation even while she talked directly to Jack, looking at him. He was immediate as a problem but far down on the list of Nurse Sieracki's priorities on this shift. He heard a loud plaintive voice calling: 'Come here, please, nurse, quickly! Come quickly please!' She was clearly overworked.

'You're going to have to get out of here, or I must phone the man to take you out, Mr Clemmaknohke. What are you, brother, neighbour, what?'

'Hard to say. A friend, I guess.'

She stared at Jack, and then nodded. 'All right, I'll bring you some alcohol.'

Half an hour later no doctor had put in an appearance. Columbine's temperature remained too high. Since he was bathing her with alcohol he thought the fever wanted to go higher. Nurse Sieracki looked in, making long strides in her big shoes, and said: 'The doctor will be along in a minute.'

Fifteen minutes passed. He went out and punched the elevator button. Nurse Sieracki was standing at her desk with a chart and she turned and eyed Jack over her shoulder, hoping he was leaving. 'She's dying,' Jack said to the nurse, who lowered her eyes. Jack jogged down the long green corridors. Outside the hospital he saw nothing except mesh fences and car parks for a while, then the drugstore on a distant corner.

Nurse Sieracki was with Columbine when he got back up, taking her temperature again. 'Excuse me a minute,' Jack said politely to the nurse, shifting her aside. He dumped tongue depressors out of a glass and filled it with water. His hand shaking, Jack spilled aspirin on a towel and pounded them to powder with an auriscope. Columbine swallowed the drink, which he was glad to see. Her lips were white and continued to move when he laid her head down. 'Some kind of pneumonia, is it?' he said to the nurse. She hadn't tried to stop him giving Columbine the aspirin. 'What do you think?'

Nurse Sieracki shook her head impatiently – it was too general a question. She straightened the towels and put the supplies and instruments back in place, and then said to Jack, sharply: 'What do you know about the bites on her back? Look here.'

Jack could only think of insect bites. The nurse rolled Columbine toward her and pulled her gown apart to show him a cluster of horseshoe-shaped wounds under Columbine's shoulder blades, each the size of a shirt button. 'We used to see these on children and infants in South Africa, in the black townships. Where is it exactly she lives in Toronto?'

Doors slammed and clattered and a voice echoed down the tunnel of the corridor as if coming from a loud hailer. Two doctors had emerged from the elevator at last, moving unhurriedly toward the examining room. Dr Wootton wore a business suit under his white coat. He was a stoop-shouldered man with pepper-and-salt hair which ran over his ears at the sides and fell forward in a thick lock on his forehead. He was the one doing the loud talking. The other doctor was Japanese and unfortunately Jack had seen this man often as a prison commandant in the Second World War, giving the orders for executions and cuts in rations and death marches. A line of individual hairs ran along the bottom part of his long upper lip over a gigantic eye-tooth overbite. He peered at Jack through bottle-glass spectacles. 'How do you do, sir?' The Japanese doctor was very sleepy. He yawned continuously, holding his hand over his mouth. He could hardly keep his eyes open.

Dr Wootton gave Jack an absentminded nod while he glanced at the nurse's notes. 'Dr Fuchida is with me today,' Dr Wootton said, not addressing anybody in particular while he signed the chart. Then as if he had left something important unexplained he added vibrantly: 'From *Japan*. Tokyo University.'

Jack asked: 'How is she?'

'She's very thin, isn't she,' the doctor said, thoughtfully rocking on his heels and staring at Jack's right ear. 'It doesn't look as if she's been eating well at all.' Without saying anything Nurse Sieracki rolled Columbine toward her, opening the gown again. Dr Fuchida leaned forward, bringing his thick spectacles to within a few centimetres of Columbine's shoulder. 'Rat bites,' said he, nodding at the nurse. 'Get them to check for *spirillum minus* and *spirochaeta morsusmuris*.'

'A *rash* of some kind on her back,' Dr Wootton said, reverting to loud-hailer volume, overriding the commandant. 'He's finishing a tour in the States. Two days here, then Vancouver and back to Tokyo. More a matter of stamina than anything else, hard to say what good these tours do.'

'What about her temperature?' asked Jack.

'Yes, well we'll have a better idea about everything a little later. *You* could go and get yourself a cup of coffee if you like,' the doctor suggested to Jack, looking at the sailor's face for the first time, frowning and taken aback when he saw the fury there. 'Or better still, why don't you give us a couple of hours and we'll know more? Ask for me downstairs at the reception desk. My name is Dr Wootton. Ask them for Dr Wootton.' He said to Nurse Sieracki then: 'I'll take a look at Mrs Cavioli while I'm here. Dr Suter is tied up at Sunnybrook for the rest of the day. And I can't promise I'll be in tomorrow, I'm afraid.'

The staffing numbers on the ward had somehow improved following the arrival of the doctors. Nurses in pairs and threes moved with purpose up and down the corridors. An orderly came back with Nurse Sieracki and wheeled Columbine into one of the ward rooms. Three nurses helped her prepare the bed while Jack hovered at the room doorway, peering in. On their way back to the elevator both doctors smiled at Jack, who didn't smile in return.

Nurse Sieracki was now following a policy of pretending not to see Jack. He knew he was visible, however – one of the new nurses took the time to point him in the direction of the waiting-room, saying: 'You can't stand around here, sir, it's against the rules. You can't wait here.' Another nurse called out *'Excuse me, please!'* every time she passed him at the doorway, although he was never in her way.

When he finally got into the room Columbine's bed screens were drawn. Her small lank-haired head rested deep in a large pillow and she was still unconscious, breathing lightly.

She had two liquids going into her wrist and a nasogastric tube taped to her cheek and chin. Jack, hovering, watching Columbine's face, found a space to stand in at the foot of her bed, shoving the bed tray and a sphyg-momanoter trolley aside to make room for a chair – he was expecting a long vigil. But even before he brought the chair Columbine's lips fell open and remained apart with the top lip drawn back from her teeth. Her teeth went dry as he watched.

Later on, and not long later, Nurse Sieracki helped the wailing man to the elevator. He couldn't see where he was going through his swimming eyes. She said sincerely: 'I'm very sorry, Mr Clemmaknohke. I'm very, very sorry.' She was one of the few people Jack had met who pronounced Clemmaknohke properly, as his father had pronounced the Taleaturovan name.

Two undersized Barnes Security men got off the elevator when the doors opened, and one said: 'This the man, Anna?' She made no reply and Jack rode down alone. Down he went, sinking surely downward, all the time searching, searching with his feet for bottom and never finding it. There was no surcease and neither was there an end, though the jolly tar probably died before the doors opened and he exited the elevator.

> *The sailor man cried help but he drifted with the tide,*
> *In the lowland sea that is so deep and wide,*
> *He did sink beneath the lonesome lowlands;*
> *He did drown beneath the lowland sea.*

Chapter 12

Wreck

SUPERSTAR VALUE DAYS on the Concourse was the important midsummer festival, not as lavish as the Summer Funerama but with better buys in sports merchandise.

We used to have the closeouts on the summer sports lines in that season too and markdowns on the new fall inventories.

In the three weeks the Concourse was hung with the Superstar banners everything from winter sportswear to a ready-to-assemble summer cottage was to be had at a tempting price. The banners feature an attractive shopping family, a mom and dad, a boy and girl and dog and cat, surrounded by their bargain spoils, down-filled overwear, Icelandic sweaters, tents, barbecues, skis, snowmobiles, RVs and fishing rods. Hovering over the family in a kind of celestial box there's a sports Superstar. The Sutton brought in four Superstars every year, usually two hockey players and two baseballers, to draw the crowds to its Superstar Value sale.

Those big banners weren't false promises either. Everything you saw on a banner was available to you in the Sutton.

If you happened to be an anonymous male face in the mill you could pick up the dog and cat from Pets 'n' Critters, and the blond wife, with a little luck, from Compu Dates and Mates. Say you were pushed for time to complete your poster family there was every chance you could acquire a couple of kids the fast way too, by leaving your name and a deposit at Murdstone's Adoption & Fostering Services in the South Plaza Walk.

General Schata was to pass the Sutton on his way in from the airport early in the afternoon. The featured Superstars for the day were clean-cut Greg Bolitho of the Expos, who was on the fifteen-day DL, and the Golden Great One, Jean-Guy Pickett of the Expos, just back from a long Caribbean honeymoon with Imogene.

The company of athletes agrees with Imogene and she's developed an eye for male beauty. This would be comparable to a man of mind and substance, an intellectual or some such, who of a sudden sees that a life with chorus girls needn't be a frivolous way of spending time. Imogene now has a regular box on the first-base line of the Big O. She's looking forward to winter nights at the Forum.

The celebrity platform, hung with flags and banners, is on the aisle outside the One Stop Jock Shop, and from there the Superstars announced the prize giveaways every day. A crowd was already gathering at the platform, where cords of baseball bats and hockey sticks were piled, autographed by the two sports greats. During Superstar Value Days more than at any other time of the year male shoppers outnumber females and the unwrappable sports implements are a hazard on the Concourse. Youths have a habit of stopping in the open spaces to swing their autographed bats and sticks. Jack liked to be visible when he went through the Concourse in this particular season.

He was on his way to the John Peel Lounge to eavesdrop on a conversation between a mother and her daughter.

The loudspeaker music didn't reach up to the Nailer nor did the bargain-hunters' cries. Silence there made it possible to hear tiny sounds, a slipper dragging on the carpet, the turning of a newspaper page, drops of rain hitting the window. Mr Dolly sat in the day room, hands on the table, looking with blind grieving eyes at his cup of coffee. Judge Wainwright joined him, carrying his own trembling cup. 'What was all that whispering last night?'

Mr Dolly said: 'Ambulance.'

'Oh dear.'

'They took Mrs Delgardo through the west door last night, Judge Wainwright.'

Judge Wainwright stirred his coffee. The silence returned again until Mr Smith arrived, carrying a newspaper and a paper bag. 'This rain's a problem,' Mr Smith told them. 'Visibility. I'd say our chances were about even before. With this rain, who can say. Thirty per cent? See, it upsets timing too – the traffic out there bunches up and changes speed.'

'Have you heard?' Judge Wainwright asked him.

'Yes. I was,' said Mr Smith, 'with Mrs Delgardo last night. She was scared, naturally. She asked me to pin the Valentino brooch on her nightdress. She didn't say much, the whole thing only lasted about five minutes. I was on my way to the john and she called out.'

Mr Dolly and Judge Wainwright leaned forward to listen because as usual Mr Smith's gummy mumble was tough to understand.

'I told her my real name.'

'Name, did you say?'

'That's right. That was the only thing I could think of, to give her.'

'Nice thought, Mr Smith,' said Mr Dolly.

'I was glad I did. Her mind was okay for a while. Of course the name didn't mean anything to Mrs Delgardo. It's my real name, that's all. My name isn't Smith. The next minute she was still looking at me but she didn't recognize me. She had no idea why she was wearing a brooch. That's the way it goes.' Mr Smith put his head down on his paper bag and began to cry.

After breakfast Mr Smith occupied himself with the newspaper and a road map and notebook, making calculations of times from the airport. The other two feeble old men watched him without saying anything. 'Mr Smith,' said Mr Dolly presently.

'Forget it, please, Mr Smith,' the judge said. 'It's all over.'

'How's that?'

'The assassination, Mr Smith. Ridding the world of General Schata. We won't be pretending to do that now.'

Said Mr Dolly: 'It was always Mrs Delgardo's idea. Now she's gone, you see. We have no reason to try to rid the world of anybody.'

'Well,' said Mr Smith, looking at his two friends in severe perplexity, 'I don't see how you can forget so quickly. He tortures children. He makes the parents watch. For punishment, she said, not just to get confessions. The general's men don't need confessions any more, that's what she said. Surely you remember? You must remember the story about the crying babies. The women and children who ran from the villages after their men lost the war?'

'We can't do anything, Mr Smith.'

'He's not so unusual, you know,' Mr Dolly said, more than a little depressed. 'Plenty more just like him. All over the place.'

'The women's breasts dried up because they couldn't get enough food. The babies cried at night. The patrols went out after dark and listened for the sounds of babies crying. They never brought back any prisoners. I'm surprised,' Mr Smith said, 'to hear you say we have no reason to pop the general. That's a big surprise to me because you heard the same stories I did. She was a good lady and she wouldn't lie to us. What is it you're trying to tell me now? That Mrs Delgardo lied to us?'

Judge Wainwright said: 'No, Mr Smith. We're just trying to make you understand that Mrs Delgardo's dead.'

Mr Dolly said: 'That's right. Mrs Delgardo's dead, Mr Smith.'

'We know you liked her.'

'We were all very fond of Mrs Delgardo, Mr Smith.'

'They don't allow tombstones in cemeteries any more.' Mr Smith opened his paper bag and looked inside sorrowfully. 'Not for people like me anyway. I'll get one of those brass markers in the ground like a car licence plate. Well, people walk all over you,' he said and smiled into his bag. 'Now they can do it after you're dead too. No special messages allowed either, those plates aren't custom jobs. If I had a tombstone, though, what I'd like it to say is this: He was true to his friends.'

Mr Smith delved a number of curious items from the paper bag, laying them on the coffee table in a line.

'We're wasting our breath, I think,' Judge Wainwright said to Mr Dolly. 'General Schata's not the issue for him. It's Mrs Delgardo.'

'This here is a smoke bomb. Firecrackers – you've seen them before, and this thing's a shriek alarm. Same idea again with this, noise, more smoke. I need you two to set these off down here while I make the shot upstairs. It'll take about twenty minutes altogether, waiting for the guy and then disassembling the piece and hiding the parts.' Mr Smith said with his collapsed jaw outthrust and watering eyes: 'If that's too much to do for Mrs Delgardo, now's the time to tell me. I'd like to make other arrangements.'

Judge Wainwright gently removed the paper bag from Mr Smith's clutch and took him by the hand. 'Come to the window.'

All three shuffled to the window, Mr Smith reluctantly because he knew the judge had good sense and rational arguments on his side. Rain was now gusting across the lower rooftops, pattering heavily against the glass.

'Tell me what you see down there, Mr Smith.'

Mr Smith fumbled his glasses onto his nose. The pall of rain made a grey blur of the stretch of highway that was visible between the gap of buildings. He could make out the autos shuttling across the gap but he couldn't see anything of drivers and passengers. Even so he said: 'I have a better angle upstairs. This rain mightn't last. Maybe I'll snap off a lucky shot. How do we know we can't make it if we don't give it a try?'

Judge Wainwright and Mr Dolly didn't answer. They were sorry for Mr Smith. The three were staring silently out into the hopeless rain when one of the Mafia's blowsy nurses brought Mrs Nightingale into the day room on her arm. The nurse had a sense of filling a vacancy when she led Mrs Nightingale to their table. Mrs Nightingale didn't resemble Mrs Delgardo in any way. She was tall with heavy bones and a somewhat guarded face, while Mrs Delgardo had been petite, with bones as small and light as a bird's.

Mr Dolly said: 'Good to see you up and around.' And Judge Wainwright gave her a welcoming smile. 'Mrs Nightingale, you've come to join us. How kind of you.' But Mr Smith, holding his paper bag in his lap, only nodded politely to Mrs Nightingale. He watched her with resentment as she was seated in Mrs Delgardo's chair. Then Mr Smith opened his newspaper and hid his ruined face behind it.

Toward the end of the morning a peevish row broke out in the Nailer around the TV. The World Hunger Telethon came on the air at noon with Burly Broom as host. For the Nailerians who followed the soaps and games the telethon was a nuisance event, an annoying loss of one channel. But a gang of inmates who didn't watch the regular programming were trying to horn in and wanted to spend the whole day watching Burly Broom and his telethon guests.

The new nursing staff got into an arbitration wrangle. Instead of making a clean decision for one side they came up with a compromise that satisfied nobody, with switchings back and forth during pledge appeals and commercial breaks, and monitoring of the highlights of soaps and games. Burly Broom's first guest was a young comedian, to break the ice. Of course around the TV in the Nailer the intruding gang's seizures of laughter were unnaturally loud, even when they didn't understand the jokes. And the partisans of regular TV were just as noisy, groaning and snarling and asking each other what was so funny.

Nurse Pugg would have stamped out these flares of individuality with massive jollity. She would have banished Burly Broom and his telethon. Wasn't a telethon a deviation from normal daytime TV, and therefore an uncontrolled occurrence, and thus a threat to good order in the Nailer?

Alas, alas, but Nurse Pugg's reign at the Nailer ended before you reached this page. She's been taken away.

Here's what's known. Dr Baumgardner's group, criminals and racketeers, transferred a bunch of superannuated females out of Windsor and Hamilton into Ottawa to do the nursing at the Nailer.

It could be that no note was made of the nurses who stayed on at the

Nailer from the previous ownership. Or, more likely, the hard-faced new owners shrugged, saying, Who cares? and, What does it matter? Most of their human resources decisions are ad hoc and swiftly executed.

A visiting auditor reported an asset, meaning Nurse Pugg, that appeared to be prematurely written down in the books. He clipped a Polaroid of the plump blonde to the report. She was matched to a vacancy that popped onto the computers simultaneously at the Amusette de Missy Mimi in New Orleans, an entertainment hotel off Royal in the Vieux Carré that includes an oyster bar, a massage salon, a Japanese bathhouse, movies, and poker and blackjack. Nurse Pugg was punched out of the Nailer and taken south the same day.

Horrors, you may exclaim, another life destroyed by a bureaucratic pen-stroke, another human soul condemned to degradation, albeit in a Superstar city with a climate that makes sense as a human habitation. But wait. Say the new blonde is assigned to the Japanese bathhouse. Then surely Nurse Pugg's bouncing breasts and bantering style, and her deftness with soap and water, are guarantees of popularity and fulfilment in her new life. Why not look on the bright side?

'Take one of his pieces and compare it to early Iroquois,' said Sarah Kiner, Elmo Apse's art student girl friend who liked Ogden Nash. 'The similarities are uncanny. They're incredible. That's an expression of universal consciousness, mother.'

Mother and daughter were adventurously trying the John Peel Lounge's house sherry. Jack was a table away with his ears tuned to the conversation. Superstar Value Days. Hearty sportsmen ordering beer outnumbered the females in the bar. For camouflage as he listened Jack had his eyes fixed on a paperback, which happened to be *Invisible Man* by Ralph Ellison. In the concentrated act of listening to Sarah and her mother Jack was reading one passage over and over: 'When one is invisible he finds such problems as good and evil, honesty and dishonesty, of such shifting shapes that he confuses one with the other, depending upon who happens to be looking through him at the time.'

'Stirrup cup, sir.'

Sarah's mother, a woman in her forties, had a tanned, intelligent face and wore a diamond pin on her ruff shirt collar. Her light blond hair was pulled back to show earrings set with small pearls. Jack's impression was that Mrs

Kiner would be a serene navigator in social situations where people could be dealt with at arm's length. Listening to her daughter, she displayed composure and sympathetic interest. She did, though, stub out all her cigarettes with hard, impatient fingers when they were half smoked.

The John Peel Lounge's stirrup cup is a mull of Niagara Falls wine and Etobicoke vodka served in a fake pewter mug: acidic and close to undrinkable but an infallible lifter of depressed spirits once in the bloodstream. Jack was on his third, smacking his lips on the metallic sediment, aluminium solder molecules stripped from the inside of the mug by the warm alcohol.

'I bet if you compared European finds from very early times the pottery would look like Elmo's too. That's too much. That's fantastic. That's the most incredible thing I've ever heard of.'

'Yes, it is remarkable, darling.' Mrs Kiner smiled at Sarah, whose pretty snub-nosed face wasn't excited by the phenomenon she was explaining, but defensive and stubborn because her mother was conducting a boring interrogation.

'I suppose the arguments about that sort of thing are complicated....'

'Yes, they are.'

'... unless it's something like making clothes. Maybe the early Iroquois just weren't good at pottery, darling. That's what happens with dresses, if you have a bad design and a bad cut. Don't ask me why it is but they all look alike.'

'God. Oh God. That's so typical, mother. Dresses. I'm talking about the whole of civilization, not dresses. I could scream. He's had articles written about him. There's one out this month. 'The Fountain of Creativity', which is *about* universal consciousness, and it mentions Elmo and two other artists who aren't as good as he is. It's written by an important name in the world of art that you've never heard of.'

'Well, he's had years of practice, hasn't he, darling? I suppose he had a struggle for recognition when he was your age. As a young man. This is awful sherry. I don't mind you spending the day shopping with him. Men don't usually enjoy shopping, so you're lucky. There's a big sale on too, a sale for men, apparently, very strange. But I suppose they know what they're doing.... That's why you've come all the way out here to the Sutton from Vanier, is it, for the sale? If he's living on Rockwood it's miles out of his way too. He is still living on Rockwood, is he, darling?'

'Yes, mother. Yes, yes, yes.'

'Let's say I pick you up right here at, what, three? Four? I know I'm a nuisance, darling. This is exactly why I didn't want you to go to art school in the first place. Music or dance would have been so much better for my nerves. I'll meet you here at four, that gives you three hours. For your shopping with him. With this man. Could I just say hello to him or would that embarrass you?'

'No. No, you can't just say hello to him. God, mother, I can't stand it. I have a mother who drives me to dates and wants to pick me up. I don't know anybody who has a mother like that.'

Her mother gave the girl a sympathetic smile, dropping her cigarettes and lighter in her handbag and snapping it shut. Her scrutiny of the check was careful, so that she spoke next in an absentminded way. 'What a large place this is, the Sutton. What's that word you use? Humongous? Yes, what a humongous place, to be sure. There's no location, is there, but so many people do seem to live here now, how can you argue. How expensive are the apartments here, do you know, sweetheart?'

Mrs Kiner's suspicions were on the mark in fact. Buzz Hoeglin, having been home briefly, was now in South Korea. His wife Albreda's off to Montreal again. Elmo Apse isn't living on Rockwood in Ottawa, he's living with the plants in Buzz's apartment in the Parthenon Tower.

Jack lifted his eyes from his paperback, scanning the room for a waiter who would be happy to bring him another cupful of the vodka mull. He didn't especially wish to be drunk. It was only that he felt uncomfortable sober. Good and evil were changing places for Jack just as Mr Ellison said they did. This made it difficult for him to act. He felt he might not have the stomach for some things Mr Goof-it could want from him now.

'I give *up*. How come we're talking about apartments all of a sudden, mother, what's so interesting about *apartments*? I told you I'm going shopping here. It's a shopping centre. Apartments! How did that subject enter the conversation, would you mind explaining? No, on second thoughts, don't bother, I know the answer! I'm still a child to you, aren't I? A ten-year-old child.'

Mrs Kiner bent to kiss her daughter's forehead, smiling with serenity and saying nothing as she went on her way, though it is true enough that she had a fixed image of Sarah's maturity, as to awareness of life's hazards and knowledge of men, but it usually floated between five years old and eight. Given the chance she would have embraced ten gladly and slept better on it and smoked less.

Jack an hour later, invisible, made his way into the Sutton's shadowy underworld. The best way underground at the Sutton is through the back rooms of businesses with a high turnover of product, so that they don't lock their stairway doors. This time he went down through the kitchen of Rob's Snackery. These days he was in a time that tested his blood, of always knowing exactly where Elmo Apse was, and what the man was doing. Jack just looked and nodded as a rule. Sometimes he sighed or shook his head in despair. He did know that Elmo Apse would sooner or later earn himself a direr response. He couldn't guess when.

All the far reaches of the Sutton, including the Parthenon Tower and its parking basements, and the many avenues of concourses and malls, sit up on subterranean concrete catacombs through which run the capacious water and sewage and fuel pipelines. Within the central areas of the retail complex these caverns are very large. Sometimes they have finished walls, heating, elevators and storage bays. The underworld doesn't exactly replicate the world above, though. Insurance companies hardly exist down here, and you won't find banks and auto showrooms either. Or Lucky Luke, lottery ticket vendor, or Diamond Lil Jewellery, which in the bright world above sit on either side of Art Revival Furniture. Down below Art Revival occupies all three storage areas, and a couple of others on the opposite side too.

Still, the Sutton underworld does exist as a rough shadow of the glittering enchantment overhead. Say in prehistoric times, long before folk built anything other than stone altars and mud habitations, some grunting visionary smoking bits of plant or mushroom got a flash on the marvel of the Sutton in the future he could have – with a sharp stick in sand, charcoal on a smooth rockface, or whatever he had – drawn a version of his dream that would resemble this lower place, a roughed-in world. It was an outline on a cave wall backlit by the dance of a fire.

Jack followed a flashlight beam, passing along concrete hallways that were lighted at intervals by floods in wiremesh drums. The familiar names down here showed in Jack's beam as painted black stencils or stick-on yellow letters. Suzy Cheer, Wal-Co, Gambos, The Pantry, K-Mart. He was also passing through changes in temperature, depending on what use the leaseholders made of their underlie, and as it happened much of the lighting down here was neglected and cobwebby and pre-CLO. He couldn't be sure of his invisibility. He could see his own nose at times, and his feet as he stalked in and out of the pools of darkness. A watcher might have observed the occasional shimmer of a green man with his head bent trudging through the shadow malls, new out of the green deeps it might be thought, making a way on dry land for the first time. The creature born in the sea, formless first, a tadpole next, then finned and tailed – here he comes now with arms grown from the fins and legs from the tail, ready to deal with moral conundrums!

The underground of the Wonder Food Mart in the Sutton is the biggest food warehouse you've ever seen and stretches out below the front parking lot for nearly half a klick. It is able to absorb a double semi from the national warehouse in Oshawa every day and distributes to all Wonder Food stores in the Ottawa-Hull market, which gives you some idea of capacity. We aren't merely dump and pick-up either. We'll hold and release according to demand, sales promotions, supplier write-downs et cetera. For a few days the vasty place can be packed high and tight, with hardly enough room to turn a forklift. Then it's empty and you're listening to the clank and echo of the rollway treads and gazing at vistas of empty warehouse with nothing to break up the void except floor-to-ceiling pillars at intervals, a few of the two thousand whitewashed legs the Sutton stands on.

Temperature control in the Wonder Food Mart cold rooms is full range – a head of lettuce goes in one bay, frozen fillets in another – and the inventory computer tracks everything. There's a pest problem down here, however. The downside of an out-of-town location is that you're situated in country-side. Hundreds of wildlife pest species make their home in the countryside.

Wonder's manager, Mel Cole, is a wildlife tenderheart and retains Humble's Humane Control to keep his underground free of skunks, coons and squirrels, bats and porcupines, birds and rats and mice. These crea-tures, as Mel hears it, are taken across the river and deep into the Quebec forests where they're released and live happily ever after. On the same con-tract Mel gets bonus control of termites, moths and silverfish, weevils, roaches, ticks and spiders, which are mostly urban pests but are part of the Humble package. It's a joke at Humble Humane that Mel had to be talked out of an idea that this group too should be captured alive and released into distant forest greenery.

The exterminator's vehicle is an old unmarked Jimmy that appears on the loading dock at odd hours of the working day, and its employees are two slow milk-eyed youths with Walkmans attached to their heads. The senior youth is usually pushing a Wonder Food Mart shopping cart when Jack sees him – it will have a few enclosing traps and sacks of dead pests in it from time to time – and the other patrols the underground aisles carrying a mop and a bucket, sometimes stopping to swab down a wall. How far these two go into forests Jack can't say but he thinks not far. He's become friendly with a plump raccoon, Bandito, who though a beast of mood and temper like the rest of us, never looks to Jack fatigued by travel or as if he's swum the Ottawa. When found by Jack's flashlight beam Bandito is either ankle-high in Snickers wrappers or squinting out indignantly – hands grasping the wires to either side of his criminal head – from one of Humble's humane cages.

On this visit Bandito was away. His hangout area was clean, the candy cartons unbroken and the rectangular enclosing trap awaited him in a side aisle, intelligently baited with a Snickers bar. The façades, the merchandise stacked in walls, hadn't changed much in this section since Jack's last visit, and he knew exactly where he was. He paused between stacks of Oat Crunch to let a lonely forklift trundle past on the mainway, turning his flashlight on again when the darkness closed around him. All sounds down here were of an underwater, reverberant kind. The dominating noise in most areas of the warehouse was the regular thumping beat of the big roll-way escalator that ran up and down between the receiving terminal below and the bays of the Wonder Food Mart loading dock out on the Sutton lot.

That rollway belt is made of linked aluminium plates about two metres wide, and looks like a monster tank tread, textured with holes and spikes and eye-bolts. The escalator can carry its full length of two-ton skids, more than thirty, with no strain, up or down.

The port to the outside, where the treads stop climbing and start to run level, is screened by heavy canvas drops to keep the weather out. However, the outside weather does get inside on a busy day, and the floor area under the rollway tends to be a damp and smelly grunge pit most of the time. Carton and sacks break now and then too and whatever spillage can't be pulled away with box hooks goes down between the treads. Once every few weeks the motors are switched off and the Wonder Mart stockmen work a couple of overtime hours in under the belt with shovels and brooms and hoses. A chain-link fence system separates the rollway from the storage area, with no access except through the fence gates.

Jack is now making his way toward this feculent estuary. He is a wisp of greenish fog in appearance, probably picking up some light reflected into the alleys from the mainway fluorescents.

Elmo Apse had one of the chain-link gates open. He was sitting on a busted pallet at the end of an alley of Cheerios. He was partly lit by the roll-way floods in a white shirt buttoned at the neck and black slacks, somewhat clerical. The thump of the machinery this close was an assault on all the senses. The concrete floor trembled. No other souls were in the vicinity.

Jack watched and breathed. Then he called out. 'Matey! What's it ee be looking to catch down yur?'

Elmo Apse heard Jack's shout and lifted a palm to him – hold on a minute – but didn't look round. He had a couple of enclosing traps between his legs. He dipped a lump of greyish meat from a Ziploc between thumb and forefinger and fixed it to the trigger pan of one of the cages.

'Looking fer a kitty, are ye, a lost kitty?'

Apse had an animal travel crate beside him on the pallet of a size to suit a cat or a small dog. He had a gym bag too, and a broom and a rake. The foul state of this area of the warehouse also raises a question, in Jack's mind anyway, about the intactness of Wonder's cement-block foundations under the escalator. How well are they withstanding the pounding and vibration? Most of the Sutton's sewerways do run out to the lagoon from this side.

What the art man Elmo Apse had done so far was to gather in several Humble rat traps with his rake. These were killing traps, springbows, your household mousetrap in the jumbo size because even Mel Cole doesn't argue against the killing of rat pests. Apse had hauled in a few full traps and tripped the others – Jack could see three dead rats in traps from where he stood. Now Elmo Apse was substituting humane enclosing traps for the lethal springbows.

In fact he'd been at this work since yesterday, patiently exchanging and baiting. Jack saw movement inside the travel crate.

'What ee be castin fer, fish? No fish down yur.'

Apse paused then and turned his head, as usual with a mannered slowness, a deliberate ceremony, to look into the mouth of the alley. He could see nothing. A little baton of green haze coloured the air between the Cheerio stacks.

'Turn the light off, please! What do you want? I have permission to be here.'

Well, that hadn't been hard to come by and Jack can state the exact price paid by Elmo Apse for permission to catch rats: two Ozzy Osbourne CDs and a pair of Blaupunkts for the Jimmy.

'Turn the fogging light off. Who are you? What is it you want?'

'No birdies either, matey, oney the coons an squirrels, an a course them rats you got. I did warn ee fair an square,' Jack said. 'Fair an square, I gave out a honourable warnin which ee didn't pay no mind to. Mr Goof-it takes a nard bite.'

He came from the recess of the twilit alley into the bright day of the roll-way floods, which weren't a controlled light source. He made a sudden astonishing appearance like a stage ghost shooting up out of a trapdoor, and he had that terrifying aspect he'd always believed in, thinking of this moment. Jack was an awful comic-book avenger come to life, a monstrous apparition sent into the Wonder Food Mart distribution warehouse by some unconsidered god. He shone out a vivid green colour from shoes to head, cloak and trews, socks to gloves, his face a fearsome mask. The arms that yearned toward the ratman's throat dripped long Dracula sleeves.

For a moment, seeing this, Elmo Apse was appalled. His eyes went big and his shoulders fell, cowed. But before Jack could grasp his throat Elmo Apse recovered, reaching into his gym bag and taking out a hammer. Jack's heel came down at the same moment on one of the squirmy dead rats. His leg turned, pitching his body into the rollway.

Elmo Apse shouted: 'I know who you are, you fog, what do you think I am, stupid? Did anybody ever tell you that this is a free country?'

Jack's left ribcage hit the tread edges first, most painfully, causing him to gasp aloud, and his hands made a grab at the rollway to save his face, since he was falling. The treads lifted and settled as they ran, clanking, according to the belt's sways and heaves, and could very easily chop off a limb or any collop of flesh that got into the gaps. Both his hands luckily slammed down on plate centres, but Jack's cloak was pinched and held where his ribs had struck.

He had to move with the rollway then, at a fast walking rate, until he could divest himself of the cloak. That particular two treads didn't jump again and were as unhelpful and perverse as are all inanimate things in a crisis, grasping the green polyester tight while the neighbouring plates merrily jumped and fell like fish.

Elmo Apse's shouts rose above the thumping metal and the motor din.

'... gave you the right to come in and out of Albreda's *nosing into my lifestyle? This is the nineties!* We're going to be seeing the last of nosy little creepers like you who want to tell everybody else what they can and what they can't do. We've had it up to here with your tired liberal horseshit!'

At a lopsided trot Jack tried to free an arm from his sleeves. He couldn't get any slack. Very soon, if his situation didn't change, he'd be hoisted off his feet. Up at the port his body would hit the cement-block wall. The big rollers would chew his legs off.

One sleeve free would be enough, so Jack canted his upper body leftward as he moved, seeking any moment of looseness of the cloth. It was wound on him like a straitjacket. His mask was obstructing Jack's view sideways so he pulled it off, leaning into the treads.

Elmo Apse was provoked to deeper passion by the sight of Jack's face. He made a quick run to catch up and then swung the hammer at Jack's head, a blow of great force and fatal intent. When he tried to dodge – he couldn't see all the way over his right shoulder but his assailant was almost level with him – Jack's ribs went into the treads again. *AAARGH!* gasped the sailor man, redness floating up in front of his eyes, *aargh!* that be agony, that be. That be pure agony. Maybe this'll be my death now. This yur winder engine below the food store.

Still, his mind was cool. He could see that the treads gripping his clothing were jammed by the bulk of cloth itself. It needed an upward tug. But now under Elmo Apse's onslaught he had no chance to make such a nice disentanglement. Apse had exploded like a box of springs, striking blindly at his gyrating enemy and shouting curses. Then he got picky, peering and capering, looking for a good part of Jack to hammer, striking metal when he missed. Clang! and the sailor bent his hips, and clang! and he brought an elbow up to deflect Apse's wrist. Fuff! then, and Jack took a terrible hammer blow on his right hip. Being left without an alternative, plaintively groaning and short of breath, he dived up on to the rollway, released the straitjacket easily, and took himself with a frenzied crab's sidle out of Apse's reach. Clang! went Apse's hammer, just missing Jack's foot as he was borne away.

Jack felt that he'd been unlucky, in that Elmo Apse happened to have a hammer in his bag – in fact it belongs to Humble's senior youth, who uses it for bopping any rats who survive the springbows. He'd been unlucky also to lose his footing by stepping on the dead rat. Falling against the rollway was a bad break too, as was the injury to his ribs. And thereafter having his cloak grabbed by the rollway treads could be counted as another stare of disfavour from fortune.

A quick handful of mishaps, yet we scientists are so wonderfully free of superstition, thought he frantically, that we shrug off all pattern and consistency in bad luck. Jack resembled a giant spider more than ever now, spreadeagled on the jumping clankers, just moving off the last horizontal roller and onto the bottom roller of the incline. His clinging spider form began its lumber upward toward the screened port on a rise of about thirty degrees.

A man gets out of bed on a day, mused the feverish sailor, and his shoelace breaks. It is a signal, an alarm call – maybe Jack had some unstable bubbles in his blood from the sudden shocks, though his head remained clear – and what does experience tell him to do? Experience tells him to get back into bed and stay there. Being so wonderfully enlightened by science, however, he knows better, and forges stupidly through the day, which – he's never surprised by this – is a terrible morass of mishaps and continuing bad luck.

An unexpected sleepiness fell on Jack, weighting his eyelids. He thought a bone atop his right buttock had been broken, a rim of the pelvic cup. Also, with every breath he drew a blade of pain cut into his ribcage. Shouldn't I learn from experience, he asked himself, gasping and yawning. Why can't I learn from experience? Other people say they do.

Instead I embrace scientific enlightenment, which tells me that the shoelace breaks because it is worn and ready to break. The events of the rest of the day that follow are separate and separately connected. I embrace that. I'm a scientist.

I just need to play through these setbacks like a hero. This was hero's work. Did Cuculann flee from single combat after taking a couple of unlucky gashes? He could not and did not. Nor did Diomedes or Roland or any of the others, though they all surely saw their share of times when the javelins were fumbly and flew awry. The sword wouldn't leap, the bowstring snapped like a bad shoelace....

He was nearing the port screen, a hang of thick vinyl flaps with heavy brass selvaging. He could have passed easily beneath the bottom of the screen along most of its length. However, on his particular course two of the flaps hung lower than the rest. He turned his head away to take the brass tips on the shoulder. Much to Jack's amazement then he found himself staring into the angry oval of Elmo Apse's face, glaring at him wrathfully over the rollway edge. The sailor realized that he wasn't moving much faster than a quick walk, and his rise wasn't steep. He was fortunately still out of hammer reach.

'... does it have to do with you anyway, you or anybody else?' demanded the ranting head, '... like I have news for you, Mr Such-A-Nice-Guy, Mr Scientist, this is a free country we're living in here! What *I* do is none of *your* fogging business!'

Jack felt that he should respond with equal passion. But he could think of nothing he wanted to say to Elmo Apse. He yawned a couple of times. Elmo Apse's head kept up with the sailor, bobbing and mouthing. Jack shouted: 'Yer a hard fella t'like, ratman!'

The oval disappeared soon after. Just wait, I'll be back down there with you in a few minutes, thought Jack, do or die. No reason why not. Then reverting to the earlier thought, his mind being strangely lethargic: I'm probably already elf-shot. I go back down there and I'll be shot again and again and again. That's the way it has always happened to me before when I was elf-shot. Of course Jack's elf was as invisible as the malevolent little life-forms that scientific men used to carry into operating rooms on their hands and aprons. Hard-headed folk always laugh when we try to talk to them about invisible creatures who do harm. The elf perhaps sits on Jack's shoulder, although that's pure guesswork. He takes an intense interest in whatever the sailor does, for reasons we can't expect to know. Zap and the shoelace snaps. Zap and a slop of hot coffee hits the thigh. The elf waits and watches to see what the man will try to do next. Usually he stays with Jack all day. Sometimes he'll get bored after he's had lunch and he'll go on his way, wherever or whatever that might be.

The top half of Elmo Apse's head popped again into Jack's view. His right hand still brandished the hammer.

Said Apse: 'It's high time we cleaned house, god damn it. We shouldn't have let your kind into the country in the first place.'

Hard to say what kind that might be, thought the salt, taken aback by the reminder of the hammer. Ugly people, maybe. Second-generation Taleaturovans. First thing I do when I arrive down there again, get the hammer away. It's a brutal implement. I didn't know he had a hammer. I would have given my monster attack more thought.

Now Apse's left hand came up in a large overhand cast, like a pitcher delivering a knuckleball. He delivered the rat-rake, which reached Jack easily. A couple of tines of the rake bit into Jack's calf, a couple or three more went through his pants leg, grabbing the cloth securely. Apse hauled on the rake and Jack began to slide down and leftward.

Well okay, he agreed, we can do it this way. It's much riskier for me this way, but fine. He rolled over and sat up as best he could on the jumping treads and pulled his feet free of the rake head. Standing next, he was beset by waves of nausea but found that his injured hip bore his weight tolerably. He thought – a strategy. But a strategy didn't come to mind as he lurched back down the rollway all stiff and straight on his right side, attempting to correct for the free fall of his body leftward. The treads bucked open and shut like massive metal jaws, and he had no control of where his feet went.

He was beginning to lose all balance on the clanker slope when Apse came into view once more, poking the rake at Jack's legs. Apse had a strategy: grab him with the rake, hit him with the hammer. Jack turned full left and piled onto his enemy, snarling and cursing. Apse gave ground, somewhat surprised, and the sailor got a two-handed stranglehold on his throat, pushing in hard and continuing to utter howls, shrieks and other animal sounds. This went on for a while until of a sudden Apse put his lanky body into a galvanic heave, breaking Jack's hold and pushing him into the rollway again. Jack's feet flew up and the back of his head hit the aluminium with a merciless crack. He felt himself to be very heavy in weight for some reason. Damn elf, he complained innerly, looking at unrelieved darkness with his eyes open.

Jack was heavy because Elmo Apse sat astride his stomach, as he saw when his vision cleared. Much to Jack's alarm he saw also that Apse was still in possession of the hammer. Now Jack's left hand was a captive of Apse's knee, while his right lay flat on a tread under Apse's elbow. Up went the hammer, but even with Apse's shortened grip on the handle there wasn't room for a deadly swing. Jack raised his shoulders and crowded into his enemy chest to chest. The blow grazed the side of his neck. A tread was hit and clanged like a bell. Then he saw that Apse brought back only a splinter of the hardwood handle, a broken-off wooden bevel.

Sweat drops stood out on Elmo Apse's forehead and dripped into his beard. His eyes showed white, his lips worked as if on a mouthful of tough meat and his teeth, always large, looked dog-sized now. He muttered directly into Jack's face: 'We'll get rid of all of you people, you can take that to the bank. Your days are numbered.'

The remains of the hammer didn't look promising from Jack's viewpoint, being a wooden stake, a vampire killer, spade-pointed. Apse's next move was

LEO SIMPSON

to stiff-arm Jack at the chest to give himself striking room, plunging the
stake at his throat. This released Jack's right hand and raised Apse to a
kneeling position. Acting on simple instinct the sailor brought his right arm
up to take the stake in his forearm.

They went under the screen at the same moment. Jack passed clear. The
brass selvage whapped Elmo Apse under the chin and he got scraped off and
bowled backward. What a lucky break, thought the sailor, amazed. What a
fortunate deliverance.

He rode out under the blinding light of day, relieved, woozy, swooning.
Here all the treads lay flat again, following a path of horseshoe shape with a
truck dock along each of the long legs and a dolly ramp at the toe. Jack sat
up and looked to right and left. If he stayed on the rollway he'd be taken past
two empty semis on supports on one side, a sealed reefer on the return. He
saw a lunch-break group on the dock near the far trailer, one man reading a
tabloid newspaper and another lying supine with his eyes closed, using his
folded jacket for a pillow, and three in loud combative conversation, laughing and extending their necks at each other like angry geese. None looked at
Jack, on his elbows clanking toward them. Down at the dolly ramp an
elderly man in a Wonder Food Mart blazer struggled alone to cover a stack
of cardboard cartons with a tarp. A black-edged ridge of cloud was rolling in
on the Sutton from the west.

Jack swung his legs off the rollway and stood on the dock, crying out in
pain: '*Ow! Hoowah! Harr!*' He peered back at the screen, wondering if Elmo
Apse would be coming through, and saw that a couple of the treads were
wedged open and immobile, gripping the hammer head with its broken splinter of handle. Abreast of Jack the rollway hiccuped and softly popped the
hammerhead into his hand, an easy catch from the elf. Oh, much indebted,
thought he, thank you abundantly. Greatly obliged for your assistance.

He assumed that Elmo Apse had gone down the aluminium slope all the
way, like a Slinky toy. Maybe he'd killed himself. If not, let's give him five
minutes here, if he meant to ride the treads back up. Jack gaped patiently at
the screen. Jack's right eye shed copious water, having been hurt somehow
in the mellay, and he had to blink and mop while he kept his vigil. Elmo
Apse didn't come up, though. So now Jack would have to go down, via the
elevator in the upstairs stockroom.

But before he took a step he was arrested by an extraordinary sight,
which he recognized instantly as a hallucination. At the bottom of the dock

steps, directly in his path, stood a man of great height and girth wearing a military uniform. He was in conversation with another man, equally tall but of lesser paunch, in plainer dress. The first man was clothed in a red tunic, yellow jodhpur breeches with red pipes, and black patent-leather shoes. He wore six rows of ribbons on his left breast, and a black leather belt, brilliant as his shoes, twenty centimetres wide, with silver buckles embossed with crests. The collar of his red tunic was a gold-braided choker, and much more rich gold braiding sat in pendant clusters on epaulets, giving him the shoulder span of a pro lineman.

He would be a general from one of the small central European countries, early nineteenth century, Jack thought. His complexion was high, his eyes a watery green, his moustaches thick as a blackbird's wings, waxed and twisted upward at the tips. He looked somehow familiar, also. A pre-Bismarck cavalry commander in a compact German duchy, guessed Jack, taking pride in his quick adjustment to the hallucination. He's having a talk with a Cromwellian figment on the dock here.

The other man was attired in a clean brown uniform – a collarless shirt with two breast pockets and flaps, a brown cloth belt, puddler pants that had pockets stitched on the thigh fronts as well as along the hip sides, and brown-and-white low cuts. He did indeed have a Puritanical aspect, being narrow of face, intolerant at the mouth line, and pale. Jack observed too, though, that his plain uniform had an unusually large number of pockets. Two more vast pouches became noticeable on his back hips as, having seen Jack, he turned a little away from him. He seemed to be a Puritan but he was costumed for the kind of acquisitive life we live in the Sutton.

His accent was English regional, it seemed to the sailor, who thought he had heard the same slow cadences in dramas on PBS. Or maybe Welsh, well-pitched, with easy command of tone and modulation.

'You're begging for affront, my stout Tybalt, with a design that remains correct when purposely turned upside down,' this plain man said. 'Because you are inviting accidental as well as intentional insult. Any boater you see flying you may be abusing you, for all you know, flying you inverted and giggling up his sleeve....'

The cavalryman protested: 'It's a delicate argument, Prynne, but I can't see what's so traductive if the design remains correct either way. How can you be upside down if you can't be upside down, how can you be a victim of outrage?'

'I'm not, Tybalt, of course not, if we credit folk with good intentions at all times, which I don't do. The commonest intention is to jeer and ridicule and revile. My view would then be that I am being insulted at all times if my design remains the same whether I am right side up or upside down. And I won't stand for it, of course I won't. Somebody flying me upside down and laughing up his sleeve, some quick-money little bugger in a cigarette boat. I won't stand for it.'

Tybalt, who despite a fiercer appearance seemed the milder of the two, noticed Jack, stared hard and then grinned in recognition.

'National flags,' he explained. 'K–Mart has them on in the Superstar sale. Some fellows on Silver Lake are flying them upside down.' He stared hard again, past Jack's shoulder, his eyes bulging more than ever. 'Watch out behind!'

Jack took a hard slam in the spine that sent him reeling against the dock and then a hit on the chest. Elmo Apse had ridden up on the treads after all, having been delayed below in a search for a weapon to replace the hammer. He'd found an effective club, a length of broken two-by-two from one of the skid walls. Much to his disgust Jack was violently flung back on to the roll-way again, cringing when the clankers started snapping at his flailing arms and feet. Then his breath was abruptly cut off. Apse's wicked eyes and animal teeth were hard in his face. Apse's spittle fell on Jack's eyes. Apse was using his new club to press a crosscheck on Jack's windpipe.

Along the near leg of the horseshoe they travelled, struggling, round the dolly ramp and back. The tabloid reader lowered his paper to watch them go by, and the snoozer too raised his head to view the action. The arguers took an interest instantly, shouting, Kill him, why don't you? and, Go to it, boys, and, Kick him in the culshies, you moron.

This time Apse was ready when they hit the selvaging, dropping his head like a charging bull and tossing the brass weights off his shoulders. 'Are you beginning to understand me?' he asked of Jack. Some more of his drool fell on the sailor's eyes. 'This is real, what we're doing now, all the rest is sentimental bullshit.'

They transferred to the down slope and Elmo Apse rode it like a cowboy, leaning back on his hips and then forward again. Most of his body weight came down on the wooden club that lay across Jack's throat, so then Jack brought his right hand up to cuff Elmo Apse's ear with the hammerhead that the elf had given him. It was a slap of full force with the iron, though a lighter blow would have done the job. Elmo Apse flew off without a sound.

Jack continued to ride down backward, head first, choking and gasping. He was looking at blind fields of red stars and exploding white sparklers. He drew in air in chestfuls, blowing like a horse to keep his trachea open. When the treads ran level he got off at once.

A long watch later, as it seemed to Jack, and he is holding on to a standpipe by the down escalator, gargling cold water from somebody's coffee mug. He is resting. His breath comes hard still and his ribs ache. His hip too. His right eye won't open, puts out water in a salty stream and feels as rough as a walnut. However, the trauma to his throat has completed its swelling and he's still able to draw air through his windpipe. He holds to the pipe for dear life.

The warehouse now returns from the lunch break. Somebody bellowed an order. A forklift motor kicked on. Jack heard a steady tap coming down on the rollway, like a funeral drumbeat – it is a tread held up by one of Elmo Apse's shoes. Apse is lying formally on his back on the treads, both hands extended by his sides, one hand still loosely gripping the two-by-two skid rail. All the left side of his face had caved in and was rose-red and speckled with ivory bone. The other eye was open and watched Jack. Elmo Apse moved past the sailor with noticeable ritual, to the dirgeful rap of the tread, going down feet first, ceremoniously.

Oh, ye pinks and posies, whispered the salt. He got a higher grip on the pipe, preparing to cast off. As we were ploughing round the Horn. I wished to God I'd never been born ... He tried a shaking step, and found he could still put weight on his hips.

Now one more haul and that'll do. We are the boys to pull her through. He could move without falling. Elmo Apse passed formally out of sight. Oh ye pinks and posies, muttered Jack, hoarse of voice, go down ye blood-red roses. He set a shaky course toward the main corridor out of the Wonder underlie.

Go down.

Chapter 13

Flinty Men and Timid Beauties

SOME IMPRACTICAL IDEALISTS and liberal crybabies were expected to mount a protest against General Schata's visit to the capital city, so a score or so of Douglas T. Harder's admirers were getting ready to show the general a welcome. The author and his disciples thought General Schata should have, as Harder put it humourlessly, some moral support. He didn't particularly want to be seen in public carrying a pro-Schata banner, since that might be narrowly construed by his enemies. He did, though, direct the placard-making workshop and he paid for all the materials out of his own pocket.

The writer was in optimistic spirits all morning, serving coffee and cans of pop and encouraging his people with pats on the back and earnest little pep talks. It is a basic group of skin-and-weight-problem youngsters, many not as fixed in sexual direction as their parents would like them to be. Now today some are fearful of crossing the line that divides an intellectual position, with pizza and a beer, from *action on the streets*. But most are true blue, to their credit, looking forward to the demonstration and their appearance on TV.

On the way through the Concourse toward the parking lot they flourished their placards and cried slogans with innocent cheerfulness. Harder walked a little apart, head down, wearing a serious face. When he came by Stax TV & Stereo the big Sony in the window happened to be showing a group of children crouched in African dust and dying of hunger, one of the graphics for the World Hunger telethon. No sound from the TV could be heard outside the window but the pathetic picture stopped the writer. 'See how we're playing into their hands?' he cried to his group. 'We're giving them our airwaves for their propaganda. Who's paying to have this shown on our TV?'

Harder's people gathered at the Stax window, quietening to look at the dusty children, who were replaced by Burly Broom on the screen. 'That's only the WH telethon,' a young woman who was familiar with TV matters told him. 'It's not a *political* appeal, Mr Harder. It's television. Burly Broom is just trying to make world hunger famous, like Jerry Lewis did with muscular dystrophy.'

Naturally Douglas T. Harder had to take the time here, before they moved on, to set her straight. Everything was political, world hunger being one of the most powerful political questions on the international agenda. We were being invited to spill our strength like water into the vast African dustlands.

On the Sony, Burly Broom introduced his next guest. 'World hunger's a mountain of a problem. But as we all know, faith can move mountains. Ladies and gentlemen, the Trasker Television Chapel and Ralph Jim Trasker.'

'Thanks, Burly.'

The telethon didn't have the slick editing of a multi-camera tape that you get on a regular Ralph Jim Trasker production. This one made him look pale and lacking in dependability. The TV Chapeltones seemed a little straggly on the stage, like a police line-up of night ladies, whereas usually they were seen standing at different heights on bosky steps and celestial balconies. Nor were the viewers getting the benefit of a muted organ on a background track. Which were all understandable shortcomings on a live telethon.

But as Ralph Jim stood at the microphone, much else could be seen to be amiss. His tie was ineptly knotted and he'd been running his fingers through his hair. The famous Trasker style was a confident stare into the camera but now he avoided its eye. Then too, the Bible he carried was a mint copy, fresh from the carton. Nobody had read this book before, ever. When Ralph Jim by habit laid the spine on his right palm the pages didn't reverently fall open but remained as tightly closed as a clamshell in tribute to good stout bookbinding.

The pale man spoke into the microphone half-heartedly, tucking the Bible he'd never read under his arm, his blow-dry hairset awry in strange horns and spikes. 'We could try a prayer if that's your desire, Burly,' he said. 'I can tell you now it won't do any good. Nobody's done more kowtowing and pleading for grace and favours than I have. I wish I could think of a time that it changed anything. I mean I make a good living, I have no complaints there.' He scratched his head and looked at his fingernails to check for dandruff, the thought of the good living brightening his mood just a little. 'The money's the best part. That's fine. Well, we all get discouraged in our work sometimes I guess. Today's a real fogging downer for me,' Ralph Jim admitted honestly. 'I'd like to be able to do something for World Hunger besides a guest spot, or kicking in a few bucks. What I'm supposed to be doing now for the problem is saying a prayer. Making powerful medicine. If it works I guess we won't even need the money. Will we, Burly? We can all keep our hands in our pockets and just enjoy the show. Maybe we should get a guy with a bag of feathers and a rattle out here and try that too. Can you hear me? This isn't going to work, Burly. We can beat Jerry Lewis by a million dollars, which we don't have a hope in hell of doing on these pissant local channels and the money won't even scratch the surface of WH. It's just batshit, Burly. We're fooling the people here.'

Burly stepped into the picture sweating with rage and fear and tried to shoulder Ralph Jim away from the microphone. The pale evangelist glumly resisted, setting his feet, and then gave the show host a winsome smile. 'Now I'd like to say a few words about Jesus, Burly.'

In the control booth they just waited. Talking about Jesus was what Ralph Jim had been invited on the telethon to do. Burly Broom, however, had seen plenty of show people cracking up on air in his time. He recognized the snake look in the eyes. Off camera, Burly jumped up and down, prancing on bent knees like a chimpanzee to get the floor director's attention. He kept making the throat-cutting sign but who in the control room looked at him? Nobody. In the booth they didn't take direction from the emcee.

The passersby outside the Stax window saw only Ralph Jim mouthing silently on the big Sony. Overhead, in the Nailer, they were getting sound and he had an attentive audience.

We can be up there right now. The burden of feebleness seems to weigh with particular heaviness on the group today. Mrs Nightingale has taken Mrs Delgado's chair. Just returned from a long journey to the washroom, a walk that fully tested his strength on every step, Mr Dolly was sitting forward in despair with his elbows on his knees because he knew he had to go again. When his strength couldn't handle the washroom trips he wouldn't be able to be in the dayroom any more. Judge Wainwright slept with his mouth open. The stringy tendons of the judge's neck were stretched to one side and a pulse in his throat could be seen faintly beating.

Mrs Nightingale thought the people she'd been put among were too old for her. She had only Mr Smith to talk to just now. Mr Smith's paper was politely lowered but his face made it clear enough that he didn't feel like con-versation. 'My family's been extremely good to me,' Mrs Nightingale was tel-ling Mr Smith. She said with a frown: 'It's very surprising in a way, because I didn't think my son had the character. A sense of responsibility is a matter of character, isn't it. That's what I was brought up to believe, anyway.'

'We should try to think the best of people.'

Mrs Nightingale considered this idea, although Mr Smith had spoken automatically. She said finally: 'No, that wouldn't work at all, Mr Smith. We'd make so many mistakes we'd be miserable and disappointed most of the time, wouldn't we. It would be worse than always thinking the worst of people. Oh, do please read your newspaper now. I'm bothering you.'

'A bit depressed today, that's all.'

Then feeling guilty for his inattention Mr Smith offered a section of his newspaper to Mrs Nightingale. She shook her head. 'Thank you, but I've already seen today's paper. That's what made me angry this morning. I came out here because I was so angry I couldn't bear to be in my room. That wicked man Schata is coming to our shores and we're rolling out the red car-pet for him. Somebody should do something about General Schata,' said Mrs Nightingale, speaking somewhat mechanically in her turn. 'He's a foul monster, and I wonder what the people in Ottawa think they're doing, not that they ever know.'

Mr Smith had come upright in his chair, and now he threw his paper down and bent toward Mrs Nightingale with so much passion burning in his old lizard-lidded eyes that she shrank back a little in alarm.

'That's an interesting point of view,' Mr Smith whispered, shoulders hunched, darting hooded criminal glances from side to side. 'What exactly did you have in mind, Mrs Nightingale, hey? Hey? Hey? Talk to me!'

Over at the TV Ralph Jim was still grinding out the bad news for the WH Telethon audience. He wasn't saying *fog* now. His teeth and lips were com-ing firmly together to spit out an accurate pronunciation of the awful forbid-den word: *fork*. '... don't go to church in the Mercedes and you've never rented any porn tapes from ADULTS XXX EXTASY. Who the *fork's* going to wel-come you into heaven on that basis? Why? Why,' the mad-haired evangelist asked, 'will Jesus raise you into glory after your ten-thousand-buck funeral if you were alive and didn't give a shit while WH was killing a million of his little kiddies every day? Nobody ever asked you to get a handle on a situation like that, I suppose, did they, nobody you can think of? I guess Jesus must be a redneck white guy. We'll be okay with him, he's just like us, we'll go from good times here to forking better times up there, no problems. Jesus doesn't want us to throw good money away on milk and rice and shit like that, he wants us to buy a new boat. If we're talking about anything here,' said Ralph Jim, letting his voice drop to a conversational pitch for a moment, 'we're talking about the power that moves the seven-tiered galaxies. You should give it credit for a little intelligence. It's probably smarter than you are, you know, not dumber. Jesus isn't a feel-good pill to cure the blues. He's not an invisible friend by your side like *HARVEY THE GIANT FORKING RABBIT.* He's –'

Somebody in the control room decided here that Ralph Jim was probably becoming too hostile, and using too many forks, besides which his makeup was running and his hair needed combing. His microphone was switched off. A delay on the picture followed, with the evangelist flinging taboo words at the screen, pain in his snake eyes, the lights shining pitilessly on his wild untrustworthy hair. Then another camera took over, panning into Burly Broom sitting on a baby elephant, ready to introduce a circus act and wearing a smile as big as a slice of watermelon.

In the Nailer audience a bronchial old man wheezed: 'I've heard of him, Ralph Jim Trasker. Never seen him before. Not bad, eh?'

The judgements were mixed. 'That's disgusting language to use on TV,' said a woman with bandaged legs. 'Good cause or not, there's no excuse for it.' Some of the inmates agreed with this. Some said they'd heard the words before and felt no worse for hearing them again. A view that Ralph Jim Trasker should be banned got a mutter of support too, as did an opposed feeling that everybody was entitled to an opinion. 'Always thought he was kind of a jerk,' said the wheezy old man, watching clowns tumbling across the screen. 'That's not such a bad show he puts on though. Compared to some of the other garbage.'

The underlie of Mandrake's Funeral Services is next door to Olympia Antiques & Junque. Jack put his key in the padlock of Olympia's big double gates and stepped from the corridor's weak light into darkness. His flashlight was gone and he had to feel a way across the Olympia warehouse to the switches near the stairway. He held a hand against his eye which wept both tears and blood. Whenever the sailor set his full weight on his right foot a knife of bone in his ribcage stopped his breath.

The lights showed him property that had survived its owners, a vast hoard of old furniture silted to the roof on three walls, with hundreds of lamps and clocks, and dishware in cartons, on tables in the centre space. On the other side of the mesh fence the light reached Mandrake's more orderly stock, rows of coffins on trestles ready for the elevator trip up, occupancy and interment.

For Jack down here it was a matter of finding a particular armchair that had been in the Nailer under Dr Nailer's ownership. He searched for an hour, grudging every minute. Up in the real world General Schata was expected in under three hours at Ottawa International. A Major Barkman, escort commander, had in the previous week fitted the military and police components of the armed cavalcades smoothly together. He was already at the airport conferring with the general's embassy and security staff, and as soon as General Schata alighted from the aircraft would bring the limo and entourage safely into the capital from the airport. Minute by minute the sailor quested, with patience and diligence, limping from point to point, tugging away layers of the salvage to see what lay beneath, painfully scrutinizing each pile with his one good eye. The old Nailer couch was the first thing Jack recognized. He pulled it away to look behind. Two other couches and then lo, the chair, the third up on a stack of four against the wall. He rested for a moment, wondering how seriously he was wounded.

This particular chair forms a background to a cameo, one of Jack's last observations of Nurse Pugg in action in the Nailer. In the cameo the nurse strikes with duty as a mugger does from an alley. The aftermath of confusion and loss is much the same too. A woman of gentle temperament named Miss Lion has fallen asleep in her chair in the day room, mouth open and dribbling a little, as often happens to Nailerians. Breezing by with the noon tranquillizers Nurse Pugg put the brakes on and cried: 'Don't swallow your toofens, Miss Lion!' And she reached an expert hand into Miss Lion's mouth, removing both dentures. Clop, clop. With the briskness of habit the teeth are then tucked down into Miss Lion's chair between the side and cushion, Nurse Pugg continuing on her way, no doubt with some tiny fluffy intention of letting the sleeper know later where her teeth are. It doesn't surprise Jack when the nurse forgets to do this. He did watch in enlightened awe, however, as Nurse Pugg dealt with Miss Lion's distress that same evening. The lady is now robbed of clear speech. She is quite as mumbly as Mr Smith. 'Don't worry, Miss Lion, for goodness sake!' Nurse Pugg cries when the gentle inmate seeks to enquire about her teeth. 'I can't understand a word you're saying, but whatever it is we'll do it, so don't worry!'

He dipped his hand down past the saddle of the dusty chair. Jack found a set of uppers first. He groped deeper and found another set of upper teeth. Despondently he put his hand in again, breathing with difficulty through the knife of bone in his side. Then he brought up yet another set of upper dentures, and after them a couple of pencil stubs, one *Seventeen* magazine and half a *Woman*, two caps from ballpoint pens, three pennies, a rusted nail file, a handful of ancient peanuts, a bottle of four-hundred IU vitamin E, nearly full, and an old pocket comb. Nothing else. He paused to recollect then, and looked at a mind's-eye picture of Nurse Pugg's act again, noting her reach and how far forward she had bent to stow the teeth. Then he groped a couple of handbreadths farther back, instantly finding a second saddlebag that contained a ball of wool, four snapshots of the same family group, an empty Scotch tape dispenser, a teaspoon, and, lumpily together, the three missing lower sets. The sailor stowed them gratefully in his pocket with the first three. He would wait for better light to mate them.

Next he had to get into an invisibility suit and proceed to Mr Smith's room in the Nailer.

He's there now, waiting for Mr Smith, an invisible green handkerchief gently against his rough walnut eye, sitting on the floor with his back against a corner, and he's taking careful breaths, long and deep, that are like gasps. These inmate bedrooms are three by four metres, with white walls, a closet, a chest of drawers, a bed and a lamp. Mr Smith had added a woven cloth mat from Zeller's at his bedside and a scenic Royal Bank calendar on the wall, for the personal touch. Mr Smith's room had a window, also, looking out between one of the Parthenon Tower wings and the big grey air-conditioning plant atop the North Plaza. The highway that would take General Schata into Ottawa is a smudged line up near the windowtop. This is the assassin's window.

The old man shuffled in backward, peering up and down the corridor outside, then closing the door. Turning, tottering, with top-heavy head and shoulders well forward, he went directly to the window. The rain had slackened, leaving a veil of haze.

Mr Smith peered, blinked a few times, then took a solid grip on a window rail and peered again at the distant highway. He couldn't see much detail out there through the veil. His hand trembled as he plucked his glasses off to clean them. He turned to the chest of drawers for a handkerchief. His eyes opened wide.

Three tumblers stood on the chest by Mr Smith's bed. Three sets of dentures said cheese to him.

He bent a rheumy scrutiny on each in turn. The first hardly got a glance, the second seemed to take Mr Smith aback and bring an extra tear to his wet old eyes. Who knows why? Perhaps he'd had a soft spot for Miss Lion too before she was borne toothless through the west door. He reached casually into the centre glass and glopped that set on to his gums without ceremony.

Ah! breathed Mr Smith then, with satisfaction that came up from his belly. 'Good, good. That's good,' said he aloud, running his hands over the new outlines of his face. His spine lost its shoulder curve, lifting his chin first, then his whole head. Mr Smith worked his jaw muscles and closed his eyes, digging his thumb and fingers into the back of his neck. The stringy neck was somewhat stiff from lolling hangdog since he'd lost the teeth. He kicked his slippers away, then tucked his shirt into his belt and took the belt in a notch. Then he got the handkerchief from the chest of drawers to wipe his eyes and polish his glasses. This time for some reason when Mr Smith's eyes were dry they didn't water up again: they stayed dry and beady.

Now his moves of hands and feet were blunt, careless even. He'd become less gentle by the looks of him. His face had planes again and he had become heavy-jawed, with the hollows gone from his cheeks.

He was at the window, vigilantly staring out. He looked at his watch a few times, and seemed to be making calculations, as traffic wriggled across the horizon. Jack for a while was puzzled by Mr Smith's interest in a Shell flag on the roof of a gas station in the window's lower right, until he realized that it was the only windage check in the frame.

Something odd happened here, though not a big part of the story. Mr Smith's face at the window was lighted for a moment by a cloud-break, and looked to Jack like the profile of a pagan king on a coin. He had seen this man before. He had been close to him, but in a different context. But they hadn't spoken to each other.

It came to him – a picture. The redrawn Mr Smith was the man in the portrait of Eddie Considine that hung in Dr Baumgardner's office in the

Wasfi Tal down on the Laurier main. Put Mr Smith in an old-style coat with velvet facings on the lapels, and a celluloid collar and broadstripe four-in-hand. Take half a dozen decades off his age. Mr Smith is Eddie Considine, famous in his time, sacred in memory to his tribe.

Presently Mr Smith is on his knees, pulling a section of baseboard away from the wall near the bed. There's a five-centimetre gap between the ply floor and the wall panel and Mr Smith – Eddie – pushes the panel back and lifts out the case that contains the M.14.

It troubled Jack more than a little to find a famous man, generally considered dead and gone, still alive; and not only alive but struggling like the rest of us to handle small details as they are thrust at him. This opens up glory, triumph, fame, legend, and most of history to serious question, the sailor brooded. It is very inconvenient, since we depend on death to understand each other. We are lectured constantly about the lavishness and kinds of new information available to us but notwithstanding our richnesses of information hardly anybody knows what's happening, or needs to happen, or what's been done or remains undone. Or who has left town and should return, or who should be tarred and feathered and driven out of town, and who we can trust to make those decisions for us in our situation, a poverty of information, an absence of clear knowledge. I hope this doesn't mean, worried the sailor man, feeling warm, that I can expect to meet folk like Scott Fitzgerald as an ancient pensioner sweeping the Concourse, his legend incomplete while he does that, or Charles A. Lindbergh, fallen on hard times, driving the Ottawa shuttle. I hope most fervently I can still enjoy a sandwich in that parkette on Nicholson when I'm in town, sitting in the shade under the statue of Mackenzie King, without the risk of seeing Rex himself on the bench beside me, ancient and depleted, munching a burger and crumbling some of the bun for the birds....

Jack was fading in and out. Also, the breathstopping spike in his side hadn't gone away. He thought he might give Dr Baumgardner a call and get some medical attention in case he was at risk of fading permanently.

Mr Smith had now gotten all the sniper rifle's parts in order on the mat. Its breech of black-varnished metal lay in place across the handguard liner, and the barrel extension was threaded and ready to be joined to the flash suppressor. Two rounds only in the cartridge clip, which if all went well would be one too many. Mr Smith with quick vigour, bottom lip jutting, commenced in a series of hard snaps and clicks to fit the parts together. He

was an old man but he looked to Jack while he assembled the rifle as inno-
cently absorbed as a child with a Lego set.

'Good afternoon, sir. How do you do?'

A couple of hours later Jack is awakened in a regular hospital bed in one
of Dr Baumgardner's rooms in the back of the Wasfi Tal. He's been under
for more than an hour. His ribs are now encased in a canvas corset. His rent
skin and flesh have been stapled back together by Dr Baumgardner, who has
promised an early report on Jack's condition. Jack's hip is numb. His right
eye is covered by a king-size sterile gauze pad fastened with generous rips of
tape to his cheek, nose, and forehead, so he takes a minute to apprehend a
visitor. The man is leaning with one elegant elbow on a stack of cartons of
Motorola cell phones that occupies the wall to Jack's right. Farther down the
wall are cartons of Panasonic portables and auto stereos. Then two big
freezers in the corner – ice-cream storage according to the doctor, Freeze
Glides.

Jack's bed is separated from the left wall by a night table. He can see cartons of Sony mini-disc players as far as the door to the adjoining storeroom.
The corridor door faced him directly.

'... me to introduce myself. My name is George Pardiwala.'

He has already met Mr Gump Gauthier and Mr Lars Kjarsgaard, the
other two occupants of the adjoining room, which has three beds. In Dr
Baumgardner's system that's a semi, Jack's being a private since he has his
own room. Freezers and cartons of electronics are deemed not to count. ('All
a freezer does is take up space, it doesn't threaten your privacy and peace of
mind, does it. It'd be different, wouldn't it, if we had our beef and pork car-
casses in here, on hooks and racks, that's not something a patient wants to
see coming out of surgery.')

'I was asleep when you arrived. Rude of me, apologies, no excuses.
Nothing's been done to me, you see, nor will it be, not here anyway. Strange
to tell, my surgery is scheduled for next week at the Ottawa hospital called
Memorial. I will have a private suite there, of course. Don't you feel that this
is an odd place?'

'Water,' the sailor whispered.

'I'd say it's a very odd place. Do you know there's a night club down at the
end of the corridor? There's nude display. We have three beds in our ward,
though Mr Kjarsgaard isn't using his much. A big vegetable freezer and

hundreds of cartons of DATs, digital tape decks only. More tape decks than I've ever seen in my life.'

'A Coke. Doesn't matter if it's not diet....'

'Well, sir, am I looking like a nurse to you? I hope not.'

By forcing the right side of his head and bandaged eye deep into the pillow Jack at last brought his visitor into view. He could see Mr Pardiwala from head to toe, albeit in a horizontal frame. Handsome as an actor the man was, with narrow features, a fine sable moustache, high cheekbones and splendid milk-white teeth. He wore brown slippers of fleece-lined glove leather and above them – moving right to left in Jack's monocle – a sky-blue sleep suit, a Fraser plaid dressing gown of fine quality with deep pockets, and a knubby silk scarf.

He looked to Jack quite healthy. He was an oil industry technician.

'Two days ago – in fact about this time of day exactly – I was resting on my coffee break. The coffee is tasting strange. I must have collapsed. My next recollection is of coming to in our plant's sick bay – I'm talking about Calgary, you understand. Just imagine, by air ambulance across the prairies and Ontario, for three hours and who knows what expense, just to reach that one man, at Memorial Hospital, who has the best understanding in the country of polyps on the spleen. Oh my, yes indeed, we have excellent health coverage in my industry. Just superb medical care and protection. My coverage is actually for a private suite. I believe I'm in a holding pattern at the moment only. That's my impression. I am only waiting for a suitable private suite to open up at Memorial....'

The medical attendant on afternoon duty, Nurse Koo, arrived on the ward now. She bore a most astonishing likeness to the young Ingrid Bergman, strengthening Jack's suspicion that Dr Baumgardner and his people are cast in their roles, like a movie, and not the kind of random assembly that's got in real life. She wears a starched nurse's uniform from the fifties, a blue seersucker dress and a white apron with a hook-and-eye belt and bodice. She is adorable. Her manner is wide-eyed and serene, but fretful too from time to time, meaning that she must worry about important matters – maybe involving a young Cary Grant – that are her secrets and nobody else's business.

She was destined for Jack's bedside bearing a large glass of ice water and a tumbler on a tray. Mr Pardiwala intercepted her, however, putting questions about his own needs and wishes. She gave him her attention instantly, showing big-eyed concern.

Jack watched the beads of water on the outside of the pitcher while he waited, and the clutter of ice-cubes on top. He moved his tongue around his gums and the roof of his mouth, trying to get some spit started.

Mr Pardiwala's questions all contained more than a few subordinate clauses. He ran down his medical history too, as a reminder. A couple of times Nurse Koo hefted the drooping water tray with a smile and a mute appeal that she be allowed to place it on Jack's bedside table. Mr Pardiwala ignored this plea. Indeed he moved to position himself more directly between Nurse Koo and Jack. He was first in line, as he saw it. Other people must take their turn.

'... you see the coffee is tasting strange – a disarray of the sense of taste is an important symptom of a polyp on the spleen, as my condition was explained to me. Dr Vic Ogliaruso is the doctor's name at Memorial ... can we talk directly to Dr Ogliaruso? That would be best. My coverage is for VIP medical treatment but here I am in this strange shabby place only, and why? There's a bureaucratic blockage somewhere on the lower levels. It's always very difficult – let me give you a tip from my experience in these matters, which, regrettably, is extensive – to free up that kind of an obstruction from below. It must always be done from above, you see....'

Adding to Jack's discomfort while he waited was his knowledge that Nurse Koo in fact understands no English but won't admit it. She brings a manner of unfocused pleasantness, with tender nods and warm smiles, into play whenever she hears English, as she was doing now in her accostation by Mr Pardiwala. It adds density to the fog she hides her real self inside. Other languages Nurse Koo doesn't understand include French, according to Gump Gauthier. He believes she is unaware of every language used by humankind; his theory is that she's a blessing to the men of earth, largely holographic or hallucinatory, from another galaxy. She's much too delicately charming, he thinks, to be of us, making the same small talk, reading the same subliterate newspapers and watching the TV we do.

Mr Gauthier is a hockey goalie of the pre-mask days, with a seamed and scarred slab of visage and a head of grey bristles. He coaches a team of the provincial pro league that chances to be owned by interests that include the proprietors of the Wasfi Tal. He had fractured his knee cap in a practice.

He's an ardent admirer of Jean-Guy Pickett, and boasts that he coached Jean-Guy for a season when the Golden Great One was a lad. He's also a conversationalist, a gardener – kitchen herbs, cannabis – a food fan, a separatist and a musician. In hospital he's fallen into the role of Stoic, letting the youngsters see that a busted leg doesn't put a real man on his back. While he awaits his turn under Dr Baumgardner's knife Gump Gauthier refuses to stay abed but limps between wards and conversations on a cane, white-faced with the agony. 'Sure, it hurts bad,' said he. 'Hurts like hell, that damn knee, but no point giving in to the bugger, eh.'

Naturally the food in these back rooms is out of the Wasfi Tal's kitchen. That day's lunch – served just before Jack was taken out for urgent emergency repair – had been a particular Maritimes fish stew, prompting the comment from Mr Gauthier that the chef had used cod instead of haddock, or black cod, what in the Newfoundland islands they called the *ane*; and he'd substituted gurnets for the red mullet. But Mr Gauthier had ordered Perigord goose liver and a few crackers with a glass of red instead of dessert, and that had been excellent, true Guyenne taste and a fine country vintage. Highly recommended, said the netminder.

So now it was with this treat, a generous hunk of goose liver, crackers, a huge balloon glass brimming with country red, that Mr Gauthier limped in from the kitchen. He put the flat of one hand on Mr Pardiwala's moving mouth and shoved him smoothly out of the way. On Nurse Koo he bent a ravaged and worshipful gaze.

'She is heaven's bounty, can't you see?' he admonished Mr Pardiwala. 'She's a god damn real angel maybe, this lovely creature. Don't talk to her all the time about your damn polyp. I told you before.'

Nurse Koo put Jack's ice water on his table and gave Mr Gauthier a tender and wide-eyed smile, though nothing more in intimacy than Mr Pardiwala had gotten. Her big blue eyes misted up then in abstracted recollection of private matters – her problem with Cary Grant – and she was absentminded while she tidied Jack's bedclothes. Her starched apron and bodice swished against her seersucker stripes as she departed. All three men watched her leave. Mr Gauthier sighed, exhaling noisily, severely anguished by the beauty. The sailor was impressed also but he took in long draughts of ice water too, and munched on a cracker.

Said Mr Pardiwala, shaking his head, 'Oh you fellows are such impractical romantics! What's to be done with you? You live in the greatest country in the world, and this is how you spend your time only, is it. Chasing after the pretty girls, drinking alcohol beverages, watching the TV amusements! How you waste your opportunities, how you fritter your golden hours. Now me, I am of a more serious mind, you could call me a pragmatic reformist in this fine land. Well, that's what I'm calling myself, a pragmatic reformist, a practical man who sees much that is good but also pauses to ask: why can't it be better? So I'm a participant in the great game of democracy as an issues petitioner; I have special interests in that field only, issues, politics, and I have numerous talents too. On a good day in my workplace I am putting a thousand signatures on an issues clipboard. Then all the documents are going out through my PC on the weekend – one copy board of directors, copy federal energy authorities, environmental boards, three levels of government.... See what I'm driving at? That's democracy. That's active involvement, by a pragmatic reformist. I am also having a great talent for persistence, oh yes, I am gifted with the courage of persistence, because you do step on toes, people would wish you to cease and desist. Why, I've had phone calls from eminent officials, senior people, you understand, and they always finally ask that one question, *What is your interest in this, Mr Pardiwala?* And I must always humbly reply, *Sir, I am simply a pragmatic reformist only!* Sadly there is no such freedom in my native country – in the land of my birth they are still far too immature for democracy. My own country's leaders, unfortunately, prefer that the man in the street is having no active role in affairs of state, you see. Yet here where every kind of participation is encouraged you are all so very apathetic toward great issues, so dull and so lazy only, if you'll forgive me saying so. You prefer the instant amusements, don't you, the frivolities? Flirtings with Nurse Koo, watching TV, cracking open the bottles of beer! How is it you can live that way?'

Now Mr Kjarsgaard made an appearance at the doorway to the left of the auto stereos. He's a muscular, low-built patient with a jowly clown-white face and a cottonball fringe over each ear. His left arm lay halfway in a sling and he wore Air Nikes and navy rugby pants and a blue-and-white striped T-shirt. Seeing Mr Pardiwala Mr Kjarsgaard gave a little jump of dismay on both feet, instantly veering back into the corridor.

Mr Pardiwala started after him, loudly crying: 'Hold up there, Mr Kjarsgaard! A word only, if you would be so kind!'

Mr Kjarsgaard was the type of patient who in convalescence becomes a ward volunteer, changing sheets and pillow-cases, sweeping floors and distributing drinks and snacks and urinals, all done in his case with one good hand and the elbow of the other. He'd taken a couple of bullets in the arm, Mr Gauthier said, in a shootout with a carload of Quebec provincials. But he seemed to have an old intimacy with Dr Baumgardner, and they could often be seen in animated conversation together, obviously about matters that were more important than bullet wounds and hospital routines. Notwithstanding his helpful practices Mr Kjarsgaard was a crafty and uncommunicative individual, shy of eye contact, with a habit of staring down hard at the toes of his Nikes while anybody spoke to him.

It was Mr Pardiwala's belief that Mr Kjarsgaard was an insider in the councils of the Wasfi Tal, and he would corner Mr Kjarsgaard at every opportunity, when Dr Baumgardner was unavailable, to ask if any news of his surgery had come from Dr Vic Ogliaruso at Memorial. Mr Kjarsgaard's usual responses were in temporizing snarls and mutters, and curses in a Scandinavian tongue.

'Like I recall a couple guys had their spleens taken out, you know, Jack,' said Mr Gauthier now. 'Like you can take a spleen out and throw the damn thing away. I don't understand a specialist in spleen polyps, if you can throw the whole part away anyway. I had the choice last winter, exhaust problem in one of my old junkers, eighty-two Pontiac wagon, the guy at the shop says to me three hundred to fix your cat converter, which is a platinum-coated part, you know. Then he says, your other option is I'll take it out for forty bucks, give you sixty for it. Hard choice, eh? Very rare, getting something for nothing that way. Like separatism, what's always happened up to now, in this world anyway, people die to free their countries, they make very big sacrifices, for generations usually, men and women and children, death and torture and prison, whatever price it takes. Half the time these days when I'm talking separatism to guys who call themselves separatists they think I'm mad. Sacrifices, are you kidding, Gauthier? Torture, prison, where do you get that stuff, Gump? These guys don't even want to take a cut in living standards. What they want to do is have a vote, and then someone will hand us our country for free – I don't know who, the tooth fairy maybe. But we'll get our freedom for nothing, sure. Well, if our friend Pardiwala thinks politics is a game, Jack, he's more innocent than any barroom separatist I ever met, for sure. Sure politics is a game, like baseball at the Sky Dome is a game. Hockey is a game. Sure.'

'Thanks for the water, Gump. This is terrific pâté.'

'I told you. You gotta be careful how you order here. Try a little of the red cabbage salad if you're still around tomorrow, don't eat the white asparagus. Send it back if they put it on your tray. The espresso here you could use to rustproof your auto, that's my opinion, it's got your ideal mix of oil and phenols.... There's something else hard to understand about Pardiwala, on account of his polyp problem his coffee tasted funny he said. How does that work, eh, the god damn polyp isn't in his mouth, is it? What makes coffee taste different is if somebody puts something *in* the coffee, you know? That's what does it. Then the poor guy's sent here as a patient of a Dr Vic Ogliaruso – hard to figure what's happening there again, because I do know a Vic the Pick Ogliaruso, hangs around with this exact crowd, across the bridge mostly. Little skinny guy with a bad face, owns a used-car lot out by the Metcalfe cutoff, but he isn't any doctor. Somebody who sticks it in you they call a pick, right? Well, it's more like a scratch awl they'll use, it'll likely be a sharpened screwdriver, any cheap tool they can throw away. I guess they used picks in the olden days: the iceman delivered ice to your ice box and you had this spike with a handle to break up the blocks....'

Just then Nurse Koo swished past in the corridor and Mr Gauthier, who was leaning on his cane by Jack's side, favouring his unfractured knee, stood up straight, shoulders hunched alertly, as if facing a forward on a breakaway. His face, which was textured like a photo of the moon and shaped like a half-deflated football, became radiant. The raisin eyes brightened into black hardness and all the seams and fissures were overlaid with an adolescent youth's shyness. His flattened nose flared with desire and the outbreaths of hopelessness.

Said he hastily: 'I'll tell the doc you're awake now, okay? See you later, Jack.'

He had old-fashioned ideas of manliness, holding the cane casually when he stepped forward in a sprightly manner, like a character in a forties musical. The agony this produced turned his cheeks and neck as white as chalk. Beads of sweat popped out on his forehead and along his top lip. But he moved carelessly and gracefully. He showed no wound or defect to the female. He even managed a jaunty swing of the cane which caused Jack to shut his eyes tight in a sympathetic wince.

On short acquaintance Jack had recognized Mr Gauthier as one of those profuse inhabitants of reality, a character out of Stendhal. Gump Gauthier had no understanding whatsoever of Nurse Koo, nor would his ignorance be improved by a hundred years of study of her. He seemed to understand politics very well, however. But it would be his nature to prefer the most constrained access to the nurse, a few minutes of talk, say – while she looked puzzled or exasperated – to any political reward you might name, like president for life or a long reign as a monarch.

The sailor slept for an hour. He got back on the Wonder Food Mart loading dock again in his dream, eavesdropping on Tybalt of the magnificent uniform and many-pocketed Prynne.

Of a sudden, before he woke up, Jack understood who they were. Indeed he had seen both of them, separately, before. He had said good evening to each man more than once. Tybalt wasn't a nineteenth-century cavalryman out of old Germany, nor was Prynne a plain-dressed private of Oliver Cromwell's Model army. They were the doormen at the John Peel Lounge! Tybalt worked Tuesdays to Fridays, Prynne did the weekends. What foolishness not to remember that! Jack scolded himself. He was still asleep. I hope it comes back to me after I wake up. They are not time travellers. They are not phantasms, or symptoms of mental decline. They are doormen!

Dr Baumgardner awakened Jack soon afterward, arriving on the ward after he had made sure Mr Pardiwala had left it in pursuit of Mr Kjarsgaard. He was affable and garrulous, though somewhat tired after a long morning of surgery and drug-dealing, and shifty in manner because he was keeping one eye on the door, on the lookout for the bothersome Mr Pardiwala's return. He had Jack turn this way and that, lie on his stomach, raise his leg, make a fist, take a deep breath. He peered at Nurse Koo's records of temperature and blood pressure. Then he had a look at Jack's injured eye. He reported trauma to the cornea and a lesion and recommended a patch for the eye while it healed. Said he: 'I had some nice flesh-coloured patches earlier, but they're all gone. These black ones aren't bad, fifty-five dollars. Be sure to drink lots of the water, I'm talking medically, though it's true we're charging forty dollars a jug for post-op hydration these days. Well, I'll take it now, if you have it handy, this isn't covered on the main bill. Eighty if you're having another jug, plus the patch, one thirty-five. See me next week and I'll pop those staples out, two hundred and seventy. One good thing about our operation here,' said the doctor amiably, 'is that we don't charge sales taxes. You get full value for every penny you spend with us. The govenment takes nothing.'

The main bill hospital charges were coming off Jack's Mr O'Fit credit card, which was a platinum and fully paid up. He assumed that the Mafia folk who owned the Wasfi Tal wouldn't be less sensitive than a regular hospital front desk about getting paid, and he wasn't questioning any of the amounts either.

Dr Baumgardner talked about money, and doctors who shrank from touching it, while he went through Jack's billfold, abstracting twenties. There's a shyness about laying hands on the patient's cash during office hours, the doctor explained, lest the matter of motivation should come under scrutiny. But was there a doubt ever, in anybody's mind, about who got to spend the money? No, said Dr Baumgardner, peering with interest at the twenties that remained in the wallet. Hypocrisy. He asked if Jack needed painkillers and the sailor chose aspirin, receiving for three more twenties a small yellow tin box, with a price sticker that read Shopper's Drug Mart $2.75. Complained the doc: 'You'd think they'd take the trouble to peel these stickers off. That drugstore isn't two blocks from here. Well, drug price markups are a national disgrace anyway, aren't they. Somebody should do something about that problem, you know, and it can't happen too soon for me.'

The sixty-dollar aspirin must have been good medicine because Jack felt much more comfortable very soon and fell asleep. He remembered right away that Tybalt and Prynne were doormen, and hoped again he'd recall the fact after he woke up. Then he fished the Black River for an hour with Horsy Stacpole as a boy of ten, but he was too conscious of being in a dream to participate seriously. Toward the dream's end Horsy kept tumbling into the water and calling out for help, and finally Jack couldn't get a good grip on his collar and had to watch his old teacher slip deeper and deeper under water. The Black froze over soon afterward in grief, and Horsy was entombed beneath the ice. Jack found himself with a road-worker's axe, chopping at the river ice to get at the old man. This was futile toil and he wasn't sorry to wake up.

Down by the Freeze-Glide the helpful Mr Kjarsgaard was waving a flashlight in the doorway of Jack's dim hospital room, strobing the walls and ceiling. The yellowy beam flashes were to aid Doc Baumgardner and another man, who were transferring the body of Mr George Pardiwala lengthwise from a gurney into a freezer drawer. That seemed to Jack, for a moment, a normal activity – Mr Pardiwala had failed surgery and was now being frozen for economic shipment back to Calgary. However, hadn't Mr Pardiwala expected a transfer from the Wasfi Tal to Memorial for surgery? Then too when Mr Pardiwala's upper body came into the yellow light, just before it slid into the Freeze-Glide, Jack clearly saw something sticking out of the oil man's neck – the handle of a scratch awl, or a sharpened screwdriver it might have been.

The sailor had probably been awakened, he thought, by the sound of bags of ice clunking as they were heaved out of the freezer and stacked on the lower shelf of the gurney. Mr Pardiwala was more than halfway in head first when he jammed. Some swearing occurred. Mr Kjarsgaard put his flashlight down and bent to haul out more sacks of ice, assisted by the stranger. This third person in the ill-lit group would be Vic the Pick, guessed Jack. Sure enough the man just then plucked the pick out of Mr Pardiwala's neck and dropped it into a wastebasket. He looked to be short in height and skinny. When his face crossed through the strobe it could be seen to be ravaged by acne. He wore an auto-dealer's white coat over a blazer and Royal Robbin cotton slacks. Across the back of the white coat Jack could read OGIE'S USED GOOD ONES and a phone number.

They finally closed the freezer door on Mr Pardiwala's feet. Mr Kjarsgaard switched the flashlight off. Jack became conscious then of the three at a standstill in the twilight, listening, their heads turned in his direction. They'd probably like to hear a snore, thought the tar, and honked convincingly. They turned away then and left the ward, silently except for one squeaky wheel and the clink of the ice bags on the trolley.

He awoke in darkness, aching, and washed the last of the aspirin down with the last tumblerful of the forty-dollar water. He dressed, taking it easy, groaning and yelping as he went.

In the semi next door all three beds were empty. Mr Kjarsgaard was never in his bed but Jack had hoped to see Mr Pardiwala. Gump Gauthier stood out in the corridor keeping a watch beside a small window that commanded a view of some crumbling concrete steps. Nurse Koo sometimes used these steps in leaving the Wasfi Tal in her street clothes and Gump, after a vigil of a few hours or so, could on a lucky night get a glimpse of his beloved that lasted nearly a second. Little dots of blood glistened redly among the sweat drops on his brow.

The netminder shook the sailor's hand and they hit each other on the shoulder and wished each other well.

Jack didn't look in the Freeze-Glide although he could have – it wasn't locked. He'd also deliberately turned his head away when he passed the wastebasket near the door. He was, he thought, sick enough for the moment.

For now he was interested only in good news and pleasant discoveries.

This worked for him for an hour, which he spent sitting on a Wasfi Tal bar-stool. He consumed a medicinal brandy, and thought he would go call a cab to the Sutton when he had it down. The piano player started on an easy, melodious thirties set just then though and a middle-aged lady in a black dress with sequins began to sing pre-rock standards with easy control. He had two more brandies and a couple of beers and ate a bowl of peanuts. Then the piano player and the singer closed down and four dancers came on, which was the act the patrons of the Wasfi Tal had been waiting for. One of these dancers looked like Nurse Koo to Jack, in a clouded glimpse through the tobacco smoke veil.

Here too Jack wanted to know nothing for sure. He didn't look at the dancers again but paid his check and left. His nerves were unsteady, that was all. On a day that his nerves were steadier Jack wouldn't have hesitated to open up the Freeze-Glide to see if Mr Pardiwala's frozen body lay inside on the ice-cube rack. He would have searched the wastebasket for the pick that might have been plucked from the Calgarian's neck and he would have inspected the dancers of the night unflinchingly to check whether or not Nurse Koo moonlighted as a stripper floozy. That is the way of science. It is just that the way is on occasion much too rigorous for the sailor, especially when his body is taking unusual wear and tear.

Chapter 14

Blow the Man Down

MR WYSTAN MANDRAKE is a small stout undertaker in his late thirties with a wart or sty on his left eyelid that gives him a winking ruffianly appearance. A silken brown moustache, shaved clear of Mr Mandrake's nose, following his upper lip to the corners of his mouth, produces an offsetting expression of melancholy courtesy. In a black blazer and grey slacks he sat behind the desk in his principal consulting room, an office carpeted in soft blue lit by brass wall sconces. The barely audible music was a Cole Porter piano medley.

The man in the customer's chair on the other side of the desk is Cleveland Dan, looking irritated because he can't get a price on a coffin from Mr Mandrake who doesn't seem to know how to bargain. There's been no zip of offer and counter-offer in the consultation so far. The undertaker hasn't uttered a word about new features. He has shown no interest in offering a percentage off for cash, and just looks blank at the idea of a demonstrator discount. He doesn't appear to comprehend scratch and dent.

Moreover to Cleveland Dan's surprise Mandrake Funeral Services is carrying last year's models at full list price. Dan knows this because he always researches his purchases. While he tries to strike a spark from Mr Mandrake he has his own collection of catalogues and wholesalers' flyers on his knees, checking through them.

Mr Mandrake sees that he won't need to pass Kleenex to this customer during the consultation. The bereaved's not distressed and in fact he's wearing a pair of sporty sky-blue jeans and an unbleached cotton shirt with red buttons, as of a bachelor shopping around for a new two-seater. Mr Mandrake said: 'We can't make adjustments to our casket prices, unfortunately. Other services are included in those prices, sir, you understand.'

'That's what I mean,' said Dan, somewhat encouraged. 'I want to move us away from the package deal. Right now I'm interested in purchasing a coffin. I'm not in the market for a funeral to go with it just at the moment.

Those Kitcheners you showed me aren't bad looking. But I think I'd like lead-lined. The Canterbury is more what I'm looking for in brasswork but the buff isn't right. Do you carry Broadacres?'

'We can get a Broadacres casket for you, certainly, sir,' said Mr Wystan Mandrake. 'That will be possible.' He then put on a sympathetic face and drew a pad toward him, poising a pen over it. 'May I make a note of the details, sir? A family member, would it be?'

There are five ex-wives and a dozen or so ex-children in Cleveland Dan's past. However just at present he doesn't have a family. Mr Mandrake was off the subject again. Also, which annoyed Dan, he seemed to think he'd already closed the sale.

'I only asked about Broadacres. I didn't say I wanted one. Why don't we break my choice down to three or four models. Then we can talk prices. I can tell you now though, Wystan, your prices are a big problem for me. Those Allenworths in the showroom at twenty-seven go for twenty-four fifty anywhere west of Toronto. I could order the same model from the States, add on shipping and exchange and duty and all taxes and still come out under twenty-three hundred Canadian. Plus it's last year's coffin. This year's has a polymer shellac and six handles.'

Mr Mandrake thought he could account for this glib talk of brands and pricing, so unbecoming in a bereaved person. 'Are you from a consumer group?' he asked. 'I'm afraid we don't give interviews to the consumer press at Mandrake.'

The suggestion was a shocking one for Dan. 'I'm not anti-business, Wystan,' he said. 'I'm pro-business loyal and true. I take my hat off to business. I'm a barefoot boy from Cleveland who had to work for every penny he ever made.' In some ways this is true. The family's thoroughbred stables are near Cleveland and Dan had to do chores for his allowance when he spent summer breaks there. He often went barefoot in winter on the family beaches in the Bahamas. He said: 'So now I don't have any qualms about enjoying myself. If something takes my eye, well, I'll buy it. When I'm dead I'll need a coffin. We all will, Wystan. I just don't see why somebody else should get to make that purchase after I snuff out. It'll be for me. I should be the one who gets to do the buying. It'll be my coffin, right?'

Mr Mandrake said: 'Well, let me see if I understand – this'll be a prearrangement?'

'I'd like to take it home.'

'The casket, sir?'

'If I buy something I want it. What else should I do, pay for it and leave it here with you?'

Mr Mandrake searched in a drawer and found a cigar. He bit the end off and spat it into a waste basket. Normally he didn't do this when he was with a customer. The cigar in his mouth, tilted upward under the sty in his eye, gave Mr Mandrake the aspect of a tough, tubby gangster. 'Dan, is it?'

'You're spoilt rotten, Wystan.'

'Dan, we're in the Sutton here. I don't have to say anything about rents, and you wouldn't believe the overheads and extras. We have to charge a bit more.'

'Yes, but you're still miles out of line on these markups. Excuse me if I speak frankly. I don't know when it started but you aren't working for a living, are you? You're spoilt.'

'Jesus, Dan. Have a heart.'

'It's a fact. I haven't seen a speck of salesmanship since I came in here. I mean it's like selling liquor for the government. Big fat prices I'm supposed to shell out without dealing, two minutes in the showroom and you're ready to write the order. I prefer a businessman, Wystan, a guy with teeth and hunger. Someone who knows how to smile and shake my hand and size me up. A real salesman'd be bored out of his socks in your job.'

'Maybe we are getting a little lazy at that.' Mr Mandrake chewed on his cigar, thinking about himself, not exactly worried but self-conscious. He said with some diffidence: 'Sure I get bored but I can live with it. In the first place they're not spending their own money. Secondly they're in a hurry, being in here isn't the best part of their day.' He slipped into a mood of pensive melancholy then. 'There's nothing happening to keep me sharp, Dan. I haven't seen an eyebrow raised at a price in here in five years. That's not my fault. I used to,' Mr Mandrake said fondly, 'carry cookware on a truck through the Eastern Townships, selling in French and English. This was a good copper-bottom line, mind you, but two other companies worked the same route with a better product. And I made a fortune. I got repeat business, Dan, from penny squeezers. You should have seen me in those days.'

Cleveland Dan wasn't interested in undertaker reminiscences. 'Well, I'd hate to go outside the complex....'

'You'll be trading up next year, then, is that what you'd like to do?'

'Sure.' He added with a shrug and a smile: 'Unless something happens and I'm stuck with using the model I have at home.'

In Mr Mandrake's tubby body heroic thoughts had been kindled, the usual remembrances of youth and power. The sunburnt township faces in his mind's eye were looking again into the soul of a lean lad, Wystan himself, a magic salesman. He had conquered them in their own front yards and by their own frugal rules, bleeding them for dimes, haggling over nickels. A man mired in fat times lately but he knew he could be himself again any time he wanted to. He could be as good as he'd ever been.

'I have a classic downstairs, Dan.'

'What, a McCready Classic? No, thanks.'

'No no no. I mean a real classic. Dan, I have the best box ever made downstairs. I've been saving it for somebody who'll understand what he's getting. I believe I'd like you to have it.'

Cleveland Dan's low and faltering respect for Wystan Mandrake steadied and took an upward hop and steadied again. This was the kind of talk he liked to hear. This was reality. 'What have you got? Don't tell me you've got a Moorcomb in stock?'

Mr Mandrake took his cigar from his mouth, feeling youth in his blood. He blew cigar smoke through his teeth, sheesh, like a poker player pretending disappointment while looking at a super hand. He slouched down in his seat as if suffering through an uninteresting day, watching Cleveland Dan from under the lid of his styed eye, seeing the alertness and quickened desire which meant that the hook was in. 'Hold on, now. A lot of people don't want to pay the price for a Moorcomb, they think they're shelling out big bucks for the name.'

'Well, they are, if they're buying from that waterbed factory in Hamilton who bought out the plant when Moorcomb closed in Kitchener.'

'Okay. What I have downstairs is a Moorcomb Royal, out of Kitchener before Kitchener ever got on a map. This is a Berlin Moorcomb Royal, Dan. They never made anything better. Damn me for a fool, I should keep the beauty for myself. I know my wife wants it, and I'll be in big trouble at home when she hears I let it go. But all I'm saying to you is it's not a cheap box, Dan. If you don't like to spend a dollar on quality this isn't for you.'

'Matched grains?'

'All from one piece.'

'Lead-lined?'

'You bet.'

'Tea-chest?'

'No, sir, full quarter inch.'

Cleveland Dan now takes a handkerchief from the breast pocket of his cotton shirt, wiping his nose to hide his excited face. He'll have to look at it, of course. But he thinks he wants the Moorcomb Royal.

Mr Wystan Mandrake gets ready to be tough on the price but not immovable. The casket in question is an old asset from a mausoleum company that was taken over by property developers who owned Mandrake stock. It is something he would very much like to move out of the basement, heavier than a refrigerator tare weight, solid oak and massively grape-garlanded on top, with intaglios of trumpeting cherubs sunk in the side panels, an antique from the days when labour was free and death was surrounded by excessive emotion and ceremony. It's a product that Mr Mandrake himself wouldn't be seen dead in, so to speak. An expert in Berlin craftsmanship would hardly miss the replated hinge-sets. The satin upholstery has yellowed and gotten, regrettably, spotted. This asset has been below ground at least once since the Moorcomb cabinetmaker affixed his company's brass plate to it in the long ago.

'...and Dan, I can give it to you for seven thousand.'

Cleveland Dan put his handkerchief away and nodded, gathering his wits. 'Like I haven't figured out yet where I'll keep a coffin, and now with this one we're talking about two-inch solid oak and a quarter of a ton of lead, aren't we. I already have a space problem and if I go for the Moorcomb I'm also buying a weight problem. I'll have to move to a ground-floor apartment. I'd need the heavy-duty bier and trestles....' The undertaker wasn't reacting, so Cleveland Dan put on a judicious face – nobody likes a closed mind. 'On the other hand an old-wood job like the Moorcomb might solve the problem of explaining a coffin in my apartment to my friends. I could fit a sheet of glass on top....'

'Coffee table.'

'Well, maybe.... The main thing is you're just dreaming when you say seven thousand, Wystan. I suppose I'd consider paying thirty-five hundred just for the name. Like, I don't even *need* a coffin, I keep coming back to that, Wystan,' said Cleveland Dan with an innocent, intelligent stare at the undertaker. 'I don't need a coffin.'

Mr Mandrake isn't in a hurry to drop the price to forty-five hundred, which is what he thinks he can get from Cleveland Dan for the ugly old box.

He doesn't even care whether or not he makes the sale to this customer. He can sell it to someone else who doesn't need it. He feels like a boy again now and life is good.

Douglas T. Harder and his group made the trip downtown in a Tercel, a Civic, a Chevette and a Taurus wagon, the cars belonging to the parents of the Harder movement. General Schata was to be the guest of the government at a secret address for the talks, but directly on his arrival he had temporary quarters at the Lord Elgin Hotel for press conferences. Several streets away from the hotel the Harder cars had to go through a police barrier. A huge crowd mass on foot converged on the Lord Elgin with the cars, some in organized regiments, hundreds of placards waving in the rainy streets to a background hubbub of blaring horns, police sirens, and barbaric shouts and chants.

The mounted police who were riding herd on these pedestrians seemed to Douglas T. Harder few in number, timorous, and not doing much to contain the potential violence. It was a far larger turnout of duped people and liberal crybabies than he had expected, also, and unexpected in nature. He knew what liberals looked like, certainly. In his mind's eye he'd seen greying leftovers from the seventies, straggly beards and minds weakened by a lifetime of fuzzy thought and want of self-discipline, with feminists as mates, either too fat or too thin, and then a periphery of welfare-dependent immigrants and other parasites but – and this was the problem – he'd imagined only a couple of dozen or so in total, on an empty street outside the hotel. In the loom of reality as he sat in the back seat of the halted Taurus wagon the writer first saw a squad of giant booted men in plaid shirts tramping by, fifty or more of them, kicking the sawhorse barrier aside when they reached it and grinning at each other with savage faces. Their placard said SAVE THE OLD FORESTS. A multicultural serry tramped through next, of all non-white hues, having in common only largeness of size, and there seemed to be six or seven hundred of them. Crowds of seamen followed, a hundred or more, muscled and weatherbeaten, having come from the coasts wanting the cod stocks protected or replenished or armed, and he saw Amazon universal child-care advocates, and wetlands for wildfowlers, joggers and giant-thighed cycle pathists of both sexes, deep-chested non-smokers' righters shouting abuse at the shrinking police with their powerfully healthy lungs, same-sex benefits crusaders, remarkably heavy-thewed and

wide of shoulder, anti-pesticiders, recycler evangelists and composter mis-
sionaries all very large in size and plentiful in numbers, prompting Douglas
T. Harder to think that the demonstration outside the Lord Elgin might be
too undisciplined to learn anything from his own small and more or less literary group. One of the signs in the station wagon reading WELCOME GEN-
ERAL SCHATA! lay face up, and had already drawn a few rabid glances from
the passers-by, and now an Inuit man as tall as a basketballer though more
muscular – whose own sign said FORK SCHATA + HIS DOG + HIS CAT –
had pressed his face against the rear window and was grimacing horribly,
indicating that he'd like to talk to Harder and his group if they would
unlatch the doors.

Harder reached into the luggage space behind and turned the placard
face down. 'Get us out of here quickly like a good lad, Gregory,' the writing
man said to the driver. 'This is a self-righteous mob. You can't reason with a
mob.'

Mr Smith heard the firecrackers popping off below in the Nailer, then the
howl of the shriek alarm. Not so bad, thought Mr Smith, bangs and screams
and fearful dreams. The motorcycles moved across his sights from left to
right and he took up the slack on the trigger. One limousine passed and Mr
Smith tracked it, leading the limo's rear window. If I'd met her years ago it
wouldn't have meant anything, he told himself, making the swivel back to
the next limo. When we're in the meagre years we'll take the meagre rewards
and be glad to get them. Now is always the only time. The sandy-haired
head came like a blob into the cross-hairs and Mr Smith was conscious of
fractions of a second, saying to himself: now. That's always the only time we
get, for sure.

General Schata's limo was driven off the highway and, following procedure,
down the steep cut to the foot of the ditch. Here the big auto was protected
on both sides by the slope of ground. The escort surrounded it in two lines,
the outer one of about a dozen men, motorcycle provincials who faced the
highway and pointed automatic weapons. The inner line had about thirty
cops and soldiers in it, some also flourishing weapons but most just shouting into phones and radios. This was fine in its way. However, there was no
attack to meet. It had been an assassination. Now it was done.

One of the feds in plain clothes recorded the scene with a video camera.

Having taped the limo and the mess in the back seat he moved out through the frantic shouters, shot a few takes of them and of the perimeter guardians and then stood on the gravel shoulder recording the terrain with cameraman phlegm. He was looking at two broad fields of stubble and behind them a sweep of rain-flattened hay. Then marshland and pine scrub. Beyond the scrub was the Parthenon Tower of the Sutton, distant and with its penthouse lost in a cloud bank.

He saw three unprospering farmhouses to his left and four to his right on the highway, two of them far off and near the horizon. He recorded them. He taped the cloud-girted Tower. Police vehicles continued to arrive meanwhile, hard-braking, locking wheels and tracking rubber. The site began to look like a Tim Horton's parking lot. Army trucks and personnel carriers were now appearing also, including Sergeant Tunner Halsey, leader of a twenty-man strategic response unit, followed by waves of Mounties and Quebec and Ontario provincials in unmarked cars. As soon as they got parked they all started yelling into their cell phones, and roadblocks soon went up on every county road that touched the highway. Army squads directed by the escort commander, Major Lloyd Barkman, flowed in a steady stream across the ditches and into the hayfields, where they formed search lines.

Major Barkman of the Secretary of State's office stood two hundred centimetres tall with a narrow waist and wide shoulders. His head was square and his hair cropped. He had paratrooper tattoos on both arms and other places. He understood that the worst thing that could have happened had happened and that he'd be getting more than his fair share of blame for it. Now he needed to arrest somebody very soon. The major saw those seven farmhouses as his best bet – farmers nearly always had firearms. He'd command that operation himself, smashing down doors, rousting, arresting, interrogating. Then maybe later, if he got the breaks, standing in the bright lights like General Norman Schwarzkopf to explain everything with touches of humour and manly understatement. It was the kind of ghastly crime and emergency, the major understood, where all civil rights, which are such an essential part of a democracy, are suspended, to be restored later with the return of order, when they are rarely threatened.

Though tough as iron the major was an urban man. His was an Ottawa gym fitness. He was in country here, something he hadn't seen this close since tactical training days at Kingston. He would have preferred a town for this. Any town could be made to yield a few plausible terrorists. But he'd been handed a zero, what you looked down at sometimes from an aircraft or saw from the car window as your driver sped you through it from an airport, country, a dreary sight, colourless and boring. It was nothingness. It was a null, although he understood that food could be grown in it. He saw no food now, only a void of sky and empty land, and a severe vacancy of humanity, a place on land as blank as seascape except for those farmhouses, shining like jewels while he eyed them, harbouring the terrorist assassin.

Major Barkman had a knot of commanders in his face clamouring for orders to do this and that. Many wanted permission to bust the farmhouses, which was like asking General Schwarzkopf to delegate the TV briefings. He sent more squads into swamp and copse, hayfield and scrub, but paused when he reached Sergeant Tunner Halsey. It was a fact that helicopters with big-shots would be arriving shortly. The essence of big shot status is guaranteed parking. But here at the assassination scene there was no more parking. Hardly anything riles a big shot more than no parking. Sergeant Halsey had super-aggressively got his squad's four vehicles on to the choicest parking on the road, looking directly down at General Schata's busted limo.

The major stared with recognition into the sergeant's bony face and pale immobile eyes. Halsey's kind you could send with his men into the deepest swamp in the field of operations and they'd wade into slime shoulder-high and search it, and count every frog and beaver, and report back in clean uniforms with dry weapons in about an hour. He needed Sergeant Halsey much farther away, with much more to do. The major looked at the Parthenon Tower of the Sutton on the horizon rim. Everything said and done now would be replayed and studied at the inquiry, and whereas Major Barkman didn't believe that an assassin's bullet had come all the way from that misted tower, it was undeniable that a marksman with an up-to-date weapon and having a lucky day could have made the shot from the distance. That would be irrefutable. That was what freed up the parking.

Sergeant Tunner Halsey took the order and saluted and slammed his right heel down hard enough to turn the shoulder gravel to sand and swung away in unison with his men, down the ditch slope. The major had to bawl to bring him back. Not cross-country, said Major Barkman, still courteously, with the sound of the first big-shot helicopters in his ears already, by road, if you please, sergeant. Take your vehicles.

The anti-terrorist squad broke into the Sutton at a trot through the main entranceway with the big groundstanding letters that said THE SUTTON. The soldiers looked authentic to the shoppers and drew a few appreciative handclaps as they jogged toward the Tower elevators. At the same time a cheer went up from the audience at the Superstar platform outside the One-Stop Jock Shop. Sergeant Halsey was about two hundred metres back of the crowd fringe, trotting past, when Jean-Guy Pickett stepped forward to hold up the first prize in the day's contest, the sport store's best deer rifle. In fact Jean-Guy held the weapon above his head in both hands like some fatal peasant guerrilla of the hills, wearing a face of terrifying enthusiasm. The sergeant had a direct order about exactly this situation, so his squad hit the audience with a violent wedge from behind, making a path with elbows and rifle butts. They realized their error very soon, of course – Tunner Halsey himself was a Habs fan and knew Jean-Guy Pickett's cheerily scarred face as well as he knew his own. But the crowd had closed in behind the soldiers, who then needed to clear a way out again, to get to the Tower and search for the assassin. They fought their way free, that being their nature as men at arms in a combat situation. They'd received no training in saying 'Excuse me' and 'I beg your pardon' to civilians when they were on combat duty.

Now a Sutton crowd was always immoderately sensitive to jostles. They were jealous of their honour in those rich souks. Also, this was a particularly touchy market group, sporting guys. Hairy-chested body-contact fans were toppled like dominoes by the shoppers who stood next to them, and struggled to their feet in aggrieved rage. Shoving and shouting ensued, and knuckles came up. When the fist fights broke out the young lads clustered near the platform edge started helping themselves to the hockey sticks and baseball bats that had been autographed as giveaways by the Superstars. The handouts were random anyway, so why not? But the idea that stuff might be free to take could have got its start here.

One of these boys, Paul Trasker, had wandered down from the Tower, feeling ugly and outcast. Sue Ellen was at the airport to meet a visiting aunt. Ralph Jim should have returned from the studio long ago but had not. Considering his whole life, about three years that he could remember, Paul thought he wanted to die. He was gripped from behind in a tide of bodies, borne off his feet for some distance and then flung hard against the Tiffany Pastries window. The glass bent and then broke in long falling shards. The boy found himself sitting unhurt in the centre of the window display. For a footrest he had a heaped tray of cherry turnovers decorated with wax cherry bunches, and his back rested comfortably against a cardboard Eiffel Tower rising from a hillock of French crullers. Paul ate a doughnut, dazed and unhappy, then a marzipan square and a slice of strudel. He watched the staff fleeing from a store on the far side of the Concourse where violent sports fans had spilled through and were seizing leather jackets without trying them on or proffering credit cards.

A wiry little man of middle age wearing an old wool suit and carrying a Paul Bolitho bat on his shoulder stopped to look at the boy. He had on a Panama hat and his skin was all wrinkled and sunburnt. 'Did you break the window?' this man asked. 'Yes,' Paul admitted. 'But it wasn't my fault.' The man put the question again in a different form: 'Are we breaking windows now?' Paul chewed a mouthful of cream horn while the man waited, and mumbled finally: 'I guess so.' The man nodded his thanks and went away.

A minute later there was a whomping crash of plate glass from the next store along, Atlantis Stereo, and the wiry sunburnt man passed within Paul's view again, a compact disc player under his arm. A price tag was still attached, with the message YOUR CHOICE BLACK OR SILVER. He had chosen the black. The sound of glass breaking and falling could be heard then all along the Concourse, as if in response to a signal. Paul reached for an éclair with the thought that he would eat until he was sick enough to die, and then die.

You could call it a two-headed monster let loose in the Sutton, looting and mindless violence, which is nothing else except a metaphor for the wipeout of retailing in those days by those same human traits. Having escaped to the main door with the Superstars, Imogene abdicated as leader of the horde that had coalesced around her at the One-Stop Jock Shop. She shook a few hands that were within reach. The Superstars signed a last round of autographs. Then with the athletes and their entourages she departed from the Sutton. Imogene and the Superstars played no further part in the mellay, nor do they in this story, although detectives some days later questioned Jean-Guy Pickett at home in Montreal, having been told that the inciter of the worst wave of violence and destruction in the Sutton was a right winger.

Douglas T. Harder was allowed through the side door, with his followers who were down to three in number now, two of them Tower residents. 'The peasant fools,' said Douglas T. Harder. 'He was our last chance. Now we deserve everything that happens to us.' The writer pointed angrily at the message-board's bitter flash above the fountain. ... GOODYEAR — WEEKEND WARM SHOWERES — SCHATA ASSASSINATED, HUNT FOR TERRORISTS — WINTER RADIAL SPECIAL 30% OFF AT GOODYEAR.... 'He was our final hope so they killed him,' Harder said. 'By God, it's too much.'

He jumped up on the fountain rim, a fine haze around his head like a halo, settling on his clothes and matting his hair. No doubt some of the people closest to him could hear what the writer was saying. Most couldn't. He told them that our own country was at a crossroads – the ever-open tap of immigration continued to wreck our economy and dilute our integrity. Moreover, Western civilization was at a crossroads with the fall of the East, our will power had failed and our freedom was up for grabs. He spoke urgently but with no particular expectations. He'd delivered the same message often enough in columns and lectures. This time to his delight his meaning was immediately grasped. He had chanced upon an intelligent crowd. Fifteen hundred or more souls instantly understood the issues and the dangers. Every time he paused to take a breath the people roared and cheered.

As powerful as a great river the crowd broke back down the Concourse once more, yelling and howling. Stores that had escaped damage earlier because of their inconsequence – Lily's Buttons & Bows, which sells dressmaking supplies, and the Little Angel Poodle Parlour – were breached and looted. For those doing their peaceful shopping in the untouched outer malls of the Sutton, who heard the whoops and then saw the fronting wave of invaders, it must have been an experience of old terror, as peasants would have felt in ancient days looking up from their hoes and furrows to see savage armed men spread across the horizon. Soon the looting horde had split into divisions, slipping its lawless bands into all the far corners of the great Sutton complex.

Some of the rioters grabbed the Wake-Up Man. He had been annoying people for years, with his impractical injunctions and mannered dandyism. They marched him to the entranceway where the SUTTON letters stand beside the fountain. Their original idea was just to eject him from the Sutton. As he was being hustled along, though, his spindly legs flailing, the Wake-Up Man offered a dissertation on human curiosity, since he had been given the audience, however red-faced and violent. His main instruction was that though we are always ready to praise ourselves for our curiosity as Newtons and Galileos that kind of laudable inquisitiveness is in fact rare. Our deepest and fiercest and commonest curiosity is firstly about other people's sexual behaviour, and secondly about their adversities and pain, unsympathetically, as if we were all primitive tribesfolk still, having made no advance in intellect since prehistoric times.

'Wake up,' said the Wake-Up Man. 'The oceans are nearly empty of fish as I speak to you and struggle in your grasp, oh *homo sapiens.* The forests will very soon be bare of trees on the same basis, that we never stop doing harm until we've killed it all. We're just sleepwalking toward our own deaths, aren't we. Let's wake up before it's too late.'

That kind of talk by the Wake-Up Man was what always irritated his captors who felt that their status as civilized people was being challenged. This particular mob carried baseball bats and hockey sticks, putters and curling brooms, fishing rods and tennis rackets. Some spectators on the fringes cried 'Shame!' when the mob, hearing another lecture, started flailing at the old man.

He couldn't be swung at in the throng – all the sportsmen in front wanted to get in a lick at the same time and hampered each other. So the Wake-Up Man was pushed among the big letters and tied between the verticals of the U with fish-line and a skipping rope. In fact after he'd been trussed up there with his toes touching the bottom curve of the letter the old zealot was protected by the uprights of the U from most of the scything blows. A more imaginative rabble would have strung him up on the crosspiece of one of the Ts. Still, blood from the cuts in his scalp trickled down the Wake-Up Man's face where it ran together with the blood from his nose.

Above his head the messages scrolled right to left: ... QUALITY-TRIM RIBEYE AT WONDER FOOD MART $3.29 LB – WARM AND CLOUDY SHOWERS FRIDAY – SCHATA ASSASSINATED, FARMER HELD – FLORIDA ORANGE VALUES AT MIKE'S MARKET $1.79 DOZ –.... His knees buckled and he hung on the ropes. He showed no sign of life hanging there. The attackers shouted invective at the Wake-Up Man for a while and then moved off to seek other action.

He did raise his head some time later, with difficulty, blinking the blood from his eyes. His heart was failing. He saw a few other casualties of the pandemonium, trampled old folk and children mostly, lying unconscious on the shiny tiles of the Concourse or sitting up and calling out piteously for aid.

Files of looter and vandal undesirables were being roughly herded out of the Sutton through the middle ranks of the Concourse's doors by uniformed police who didn't hesitate to swing their batons at the laggards and the defiant. Other files of cops were toe to toe with rioting gangs, breaking them up and moving them out. About this time Sergeant Tunner Halsey's squad was on the fourth floor of the Tower and making excellent time. The sergeant himself had checked every room with an east-facing window in the Nailer, leading a four-man detail through the clinic at a trot and being careful not to collide with any of the fragile grandmas and grandpas who hastened to move out of the way. Mr Smith was in the front rank of patients the soldiers saw, invisible to the tough young sergeant because of his limbs like spider webs and his soft garb of velour and terry, imperfectly tied. Having pocketed his teeth again Mr Smith let his chin hang low and squinched his eyes half-shut, gaping in bewilderment and awe at the young soldiers as they passed him in their grace and youth.

Young Paul Trasker came and looked with distress at the Wake-Up Man, hanging on the U. He went away and brought back a shopping cart, which he turned on its side and stood upon, fumbling with his small hands at the cords that bound the old man. He said: 'My dad is coming soon. He'll help you.' The boy's fingers slipped hopelessly on the rock-hard knots in the exercise rope and the net of fish line. He kept trying though.

'Well, I've had enough time, lad,' the Wake-Up Man said, blood burbling up in his throat. 'I wouldn't know what to do with any more.' His eyes were filming over as he turned his head to stare along the Concourse. The stores were becoming just hollow squares, and smoke was billowing out from some of them. A gushing pastoral sound like mountain streams could be heard as water from the fire hoses ran down the Concourse parquet through the strewn garbage left by the ransackers. 'I always knew it was this fragile, lad, the great place. Beautiful, you know, but with no real strength to it, nothing you could rely on. Like the mighty kingdoms of the east, you see, built to our glory, on our corpses. We rot and the wind blows our dust away.' The Wake-Up Man swallowed the blood in his throat, taking a deep breath. His heart gave up on him then.

One of Jack's sternal ribs was broken and taped and Dr Baumgardner didn't offer much hope for the recovery of sight in his left eye. Jack's walk was a gimping one out in the Wasfi Tal parking lot, where he had to pay big bucks to reclaim his little Renault because the hourly rate applied day and night. His black eyepatch held a gauze square in place, and before Jack drove away rain had begun dripping from his hair down his forehead and into the eye. So he had to stop to wipe his face and then to tie his big red sailor's handkerchief around his head.

Coming back into the Sutton Jack was surprised to see smoke pouring from many doors on the ground floor and hundreds of cars burning in the parking lot. The burning cars were a result of secondary looting where valuables from the stores had been loaded into their autos by people who forthwith hurried back inside to get more stuff. Some of the smart marauders, as the pickings began to thin out inside, realized that much of the richness of loot was not actually gone but merely moved, and that the question of ownership could be regarded as still undecided. Hence the looting of cars. Burning the cars was also a continuation of what had been going on inside, with a small company of actual arsonists and pyrophiles active among the straight looters and pillagers too. The victims of the overthrow of rules were increased in number in this way, as was the misery of the afternoon.

Jack made his way past ranks of fire-trucks, senses dulled by the anaesthetic hangover and gaping in outrage at the scenes of destruction. Past busy firemen and gloomy victims he limped, to the main entrance.

First he saw the rampagers in small vicious gangs, whooping and prancing and hurling debris at the police lines which were trying to clear the Concourse. Directly behind a five-man cop line he was dismayed to see the Wake-Up Man, slumped unmoving between the uprights of the u. Standing on his overturned shopping-cart, Paul Trasker struggled still with the old man's bonds. He had gotten most of the thick rope off. A pool cue aimed at the youngster in the mindlessness of the affray, only because he stood above the throng, came sailing out of the mill and lodged itself in the shopping-cart's mesh.

Jack couldn't find a pulse in the thin neck. 'He's dead,' he said to the child. 'Get down. Stay behind me.' He kept his head up, fortunately, watching the police line. It flew apart of a sudden, violently attacked on the flank by four toughs swinging hockey sticks.

It was a gang with its blood high and its wits gone. Being defenceless didn't get you a pass. Jack was looking at old folk down and bloodied and children also, some of them younger than Paul. So Jack was not now in a temperate humour himself. His head ached and his sightless eye shed tears of pain. His busted rib sent agony up his spine each time he moved. He seized the cue and laid into the four toughs.

These sportsmen, when they broke the cop line, thought they would just hack down the guy and the kid and move on over them to other fun. But instead of an easy check they were met by a berserk patch-eyed pirate, hopping and spearing, an agile homicidal gimper swinging a thirty-two ounce Brunswick ash-shaft by the butt and seriously trying to take their heads off with the whippy end. He was out of control. While he lunged and slashed he let loose unnerving screams of pain, so they fell back. The police line then came together again in front of Jack.

He kept the cue for support, leaning on it as a staff, blowing hard and watching the hockey-stick sports retreating among the other rampagers. None of the four walked upright now, and they all had knots on their foreheads and split scalps and noses streaming blood. But, he noted with disappointment, they were all alive. The gentle old dandy was dead.

'My mom and dad aren't home yet. I came down to wait at their parking spots. I'm like an orphan.'

'All right. We can go outside. Just stick near me, would you. This is perilous.'

'Have you had an accident, Jack?'

'Yes.'

'Are you going to be okay?'

'I don't think so.'

'I'll show you where I wait.'

'Right. Stay close.'

What has the aging young man learnt that he can teach the child? Jack had learnt very little. The years had provided him only with an understanding of how temporary the folk were, how vain and shallow, violent and tribal. How like the monkeys in the trees.

Jack's real experiences had all been unlearning ones, not of gaining knowledge but of discarding it, beginning with Horsy Stacpole's links and bridges to and from the god and continuing into many revered books. He had to unlearn every brick of the edificed towers and Jacob's ladders that filled the old man's maps and charts, all linked out on the largest scale and footnoted down to the most precise detail. Nor did these castles burst like a bubble for Jack when they were brought under his scrutiny. It was a dying

LEO SIMPSON

experience for them, and all bad deaths, slow and unpleasant. Take an idle glance at a piece of filigree on a staircase and notice that it is unsupported, afloat in air. A mighty pillar can be seen one day to rise out of weak water. These kinds of unlearnings ate into Jack every moment of each day after Columbine died, when his body was in torment adrift in fever and scoured clean.

It might only have been a shedding of outgrown skin, and life goes on. But unfortunately Horsy had been the tether of Jack's life, and everything Horsy thought was connected to everything else in Horsy's system. So it was for Jack too, and continued to be after it started to rot and break. There was no boundary in what he'd learnt that protected him from the counter-march of the unlearning. Everything was monkey glory, the marble and paint, all the anthems and mighty accomplishments and the breathtaking courage, every scrap of beauty in word and stone. He did certainly, at one time, shuck off a rattly old dried-up skin but the rest of what happened was the departure of his soul, he thought. He didn't believe he'd get it back either.

But he could remember only good times with the ragged old preacher. He had suffered no deception. Revd Stacpole had practised no fraud. He remained a man of magic and awe still, a creator of a world. It didn't matter what Jack taught the child. His memory wasn't of packs of lies but of doors being opened and of gazing into vistas and secrets. His memories were of stories by the storyteller.

That's better, Jack decided with deep relief, we're beginning to see a clear horizon at last on this tack. He did always want to see the next horizon too, the old man who loved the Elzevir hills. The first door he opened for me was the door that kept me in my room, locked in a lonely cell as this child is. 'What do you say we ramble over the hill there? It seems to me a most interesting hill, on this side anyway. And for sure we must climb this side before we can see beyond ...' The importance of a childhood in memory isn't that the teaching should be always true but that the teacher spend winter evenings and summer days with the child and speak with confidence and affection. So what if the tale won't test true? The winter evenings tested true. Those good summer days with Horsy Stacpole never saw a twilight over the long years.

Outside the big doors Jack skirted the ranks of fire-trucks and police cars again, stepping over hoses and cables. Paul Trasker began coughing on the oily smoke rolling at them from the burning cars. 'Right by the far gate,' he said, pointing at the north end of the Tower lot.

'Okay.' Jack looked beyond the lot at the grass slope that rose upward into wild green countryside. 'What we should do is climb to the top of that hill,' he said, squinting through his bloodshot eye and leaning on his ash staff. 'We can watch from up there. Where we're safe from these mobs down here. Where we can breathe the better air.'

LEO SIMPSON is the author of three novels (*Arkwright*, *The Peacock Papers*, and *Kowalski's Last Chance*) and a collection of short stories (*The Lady & the Travelling Salesman and Other Short Stories*). Born in Limerick, Ireland, he now lives and writes at The Moodie Cottage in Belleville, Ontario.